"AN OUTSTANDING HISTORICAL DRAMA."
—Publishers Weekly

"This big novel is packed with practically everything the days of yore have to offer.... Still, the dominant sensibility throughout belongs to the late 20th century."

—The Boston Globe

"*Nicholas Cooke* is a stunning evocation of a golden age and some of its giants. I read it with deep admiration."

—Frederick Buechner

"Appealing ... Cowell's cast is rowdy, kindhearted and sanguine, as is her portrait of the London stage."

—The New York Times Book Review

"Nicholas Cooke is as charming a character as ever graced the pages of a novel. From the brilliant first lines to the compelling end, the reader is thoroughly engaged by Nicholas's story.... Brilliant, roguish, bawdy, and utterly delightful."

—Madeleine L'Engle

"An exquisitely drawn portrait of a robust age and a complex man at war with himself. Highly recommended."

—Library Journal

"Set in the seventeenth century, this is a remarkable novel about a contemporary of William Shakespeare and Christopher Marlowe. It is a poignant and powerful account of one man's spiritual journey."

—Isabelle Holland

"Notably well written ... This book shows remarkable historical imagination."

—A. L. Rowse

Nicholas Cooke

Actor,
Soldier,
Physician,
Priest

Nicholas Cooke

Actor, Soldier, Physician, Priest

A NOVEL

STEPHANIE COWELL

BALLANTINE BOOKS • NEW YORK

Copyright © 1993 by Stephanie Cowell

All rights reserved under International and Pan-American Copyright Conventions. Published in the United States by Ballantine Books, a division of Random House, Inc., New York, and distributed in Canada by Random House of Canada Limited, Toronto.

This edition published by arrangement with W. W. Norton & Company.

Latin translations from the *Aeneid* and Cicero from *Latin Made Simple* by R. Hendricks, reprinted by permission of Doubleday, a division of Bantam Doubleday Dell Publishing Group, Ltd. Lines from *The Diary of Baron Waldstein* by G. W. Groos, reprinted by permission of Thames and Hudson Ltd. Copyright 1981 by Thames and Hudson, Ltd.

Library of Congress Catalog Card Number: 94-94241

ISBN: 0-345-39016-4

Cover design by Barbara Leff
Cover illustration by Bryan Leister

Manufactured in the United States of America

First Ballantine Books Edition: October 1994

10 9 8 7 6 5 4 3 2 1

Dedicated with love
to my sons Jesse and James
and my beloved Bob,

and

The Saint Thomas Choir
of Men and Boys, New York

The order and power of light and darkness are not equal: light is diffused and penetrates to deepest darkness, but darkness does not reach to the purest regions of light. Thus light comprehends darkness, overcomes and conquers it throughout infinity.

—GIORDANO BRUNO,
De Immenso et Innumerabilibus, 1584

Nicholas Cooke's London

Office of the Revels

Fleet River

Oxford

Gray's Inn

HOLBORN

Bishop William Sydenham's House

Southampton's Drury House

COVENT GARDEN

Lincolns Inn

Newgate

STRAND

Margaret's House

FLEET ST.

CHARING CROSS

Essex House

Ludgate

Whitehall Palace

River

Black Friars

Paris Garden Stair

Palace Yard

Old Palace Yard

Lambeth Marsh

Cripplegate

Westminster Abbey

SILVER ST.

ADDLE LANE

St. Mary Aldermanbury

Aldersgate

Mitre Tavern

LOVE LANE

OAK L

Guild Hall

STAINING ST.

WOOD ST.

Heminges's House

LOTHBURY

CHEAPSIDE

CHAZAUD

The Theatre

BISHOPSGATE STREET

Cripplegate

Moorgate

Bishopsgate

dersgate

Guild Hall

Shagspere's Room

Morley's Room

Aldgate

WGATE

LOTHBURY

CHEAPSIDE

THREADNEEDLE ST.

CORNHILL

GRACIOUS ST.

LEADENHALL ST.

Paul's

Mermaid Tavern

WATLING ST.

LOMBARD ST.

Royal Exchange

FENCHURCH ST.

EASTCHEAP

Fish Street Hill

TOWER ST.

The Tower

THAMES ST.

Thames

LONDON BRIDGE

to Greenwich and Canterbury

BANKSIDE

Bear Garden (Later the Hope)

The Rose

Tom Pope's House

The Globe

SOUTHWARK

THE
FIRST
PART

ONE

Canterbury
1592

I WAS FIVE YEARS OLD WHEN I SAW MY FATHER HANGED FOR A THIEF IN front of Canterbury Cathedral with the priest reading Scripture and a crowd watching. My mother fainted, and, sinking down beside her on the cobblestones, I patted her face. For weeks I played outside the house, terrified of her wild crying. We had no money then, so she became a washerwoman.

I remembered him vaguely, a big man who loved me and carried me about on his large shoulders. I was named Nicholas after him, and when I was little I thought every stranger passing through our lives must be he, restored to us by the angels. He had been a sailor long before we fought the war against Spain, but after could get no steady work or any that he felt well suited him. "Now little man," he would say to me. "Dost think thy mother shall have common things? Why, she shall have a house with glass windows and a chair with a red cushion!" These hopes ended at the gallows, and our lives went on. At six years old I was taken to the clerk's school to learn my letters, and at ten they received me for my quick mind as a scholarship pupil at the King's School in the Cathedral precincts under the shadow of the bell tower, and so time passed until I was just thirteen years old, curious, wild, and generally hungry.

We had always lived in the medieval town of Canterbury between London and the Dover coast; it was here four hundred years ago they had murdered stubborn Thomas à Becket, and for generations after the pilgrims had clambered up the mounting stone steps for penance, kissing with rapturous lips the very stones whereon the martyr's blood had spilled. Then the Reformation had come, the old Roman Catholic religion forbidden, the monasteries shattered, and the King's men descended upon Canterbury to confiscate all ecclesiastical property for the crown and cart away the relics of bones and shrouds from a thousand crumbling saints. These things my grandfather had told me, for he could just remember them.

Pilgrims came no more, though sailors and merchants continued to travel our streets towards the coast. Then and anon I heard their heavy laughter in our house after midnight and my mother's silvery reply. "Have naught to do with them," I begged each morning when they had gone, and sometimes she would weep and lay her beautiful head against my small shoulder as though she were in my keeping, rather than I in hers, and whisper, "Yea, Nick, it shall be no more."

But it did not cease.

Days came when she did not rise from her bed but lay under the fleece, weeping. Then the foul clothing accumulated in heaps before our door, the dogs got into it, and the owners took it angrily away and swore to bring no more. I was a small boy, quick, thin, and angry, and the rough black gown the parish authorities gave me rubbed coarsely against my narrow chest and was for the first years of my schooling, too large and for the last, too small. I do not know how I got to school, or ofttimes what I ate. And yet I loved her terribly with a darkness of the heart I could not understand.

Above our house, whose rotting second room had long ago tumbled into the open sewage ditch that ran by the Roman city walls, rose the eternal towers of the Cathedral. Raised over centuries to the glory of God, its sacraments were judiciously given to those who deserved them by the cerebral, black-frocked, untouchable priests who fluttered through small Canterbury as if it belonged to them. I loved these men also in my childish way, for I felt they and they alone held heaven enclosed in their hands and might, if they opened their reluctant fingers, one day give it me.

They taught me many things and at the prayers that ended each long schoolday ofttimes read verses from the newly translated English Bible that affirmed the poor were blessed and would see the kingdom of heaven. Sometimes when I could not sleep for hunger I thought on it. As one of the foremost boys in examination, I would within the next few years be sent on scholarship to read divinity at Cambridge, and some years after this study be ordained priest. My mother should live with me then; she should have a hooded wool cloak of burgundy color with fur lining, a barrel of small beer to draw upon when she wished, and a pair of embroidered shoes. There should be bread in the bake oven and dried fish hanging above the hearth.

I wanted to be good, absolutely good, and I might have been but for my inquiring mind and for my anger. And thus it came together on the morning of September 1592 when I was thirteen and a half years old.

The five-o'clock bell from St. George's awakened me, and slowly following it, the greater one from the Cathedral. Already from the street rumbled cartwheels on the cobbles, and in the air was the rising smoke of fires. I tumbled from my mat, thrust my arms into the black scholar's gown that was now too short for me, drank water dusted with cinders from a half-full pail by the hearth, and turned to look at my mother.

It had happened yet once again.

Under the draping of the thin covering, hard and round, was the small mound of her belly. Weeks before, mayhap more, I thought to see the changing of her shape and roughly thrust the possibility away. Three little brothers had been born dead and buried in secrecy in the fields outside the city walls, she and I alone as midwife, priest, and mourner: that another should come was bitter indeed.

The bile rising in my throat, I ran to the door. A scrubby dog was sniffing the unclean wash, and with disdain lifted one leg and watered upon it. With a curse I hurled my book at him, running immediately with sorrow to retrieve it from the ditch, for it was my undermaster's own copy of Cicero, which he had lent me. On the shelf of our house I found dried meat and stood munching it, calming my fear. I would speak to her this evening when I returned from school: somehow I should manage it. When I became a man I'd take care of her altogether and her belly would swell no more.

The narrow river ran through Canterbury, under arched little bridges; the crooked houses stooped down in their wattle-and-daub way under the massive walls and ancient gates, and the high lacy stonework of the Cathedral tower rose to the white early-morning sky. My way to school was through the Cloisters, the stones yet damp with the night's rain. Our late benefactor, Archbishop Parker, had established scholarships there for fifty poor boys to study without fee: of this benefice I was a recipient, rubbing elbows each day with the sons of more prosperous families. We sang in the Cathedral choir, and from six in the morning until the winter darkness of five we sat in one room construing and comprehending the noble Latin authors (Plutarch, Cicero, Horace, Virgil, Terence), developing the gift of classic oratory and verse-making, and competing in declamation. These coming months I should likewise be introduced to the sweet intricacies of Greek, some writings of which I knew already in translation. Benches were arranged against the wall, and over this restless, ofttimes arrogant crowd of young boys ruled my beloved undermaster, Geoffrey Falkes, whose goodness I will never forget.

He was old even then: a stooped fellow with a full, drooping underlip and watery eyes and a way of shuffling belly-first. He seldom struck us, but he had a passion for the distinguished writers of the classical world, whom he affirmed were moral, reasonable men, not like the decadent fellows of today such as Francis Drake or Wat Raleigh. A narrow room he occupied above the school, and there he ofttimes took me, feeding me meat pie and wisdom, walking back and forth with the *Analytics* of Aristotle in his hand, which he translated aloud from the Greek for my elucidation. That I was one of his favorites was our secret. His cold room, full of books and cats and bruised apples, will never leave my memory as I live.

With my book in my arms that September morning, I gained the Cloisters, running across the wet stones towards the dark passage. Muted laughter rang from behind the pillars; mud fell against my gown with a heavy splat. I stiffened and looked about me in the grey wet light. From the shadows of the tunnel five or six boys came in their black scholar's gowns: Michael Toole, whose father dealt in Irish wools, Mark Collins, the horse breeder's lad, and some others whose names have now escaped me. On all sides they surrounded me.

" 'Tis near to six," said I. "Why tarry?"

"What's that to thee, skin and bones?"

"Sayst thou, pizzle? Hast pig's turds for brains."

"Throw the book down, Nick Tomkins."

"An I shall!" Hurling the book away, I put up my fists. "Only come one and then the next in fair fight, thou girl." Their dusky faces under the aged, stone tunnel confronted me, while above the slow solemn ringing of the Cathedral bell told that the hour of six had come. Still nothing mattered but the horsebreeder's son's thick, disdainful breath and my own concentrated dance about him. My fist met his cheek; the others groaned but in whispers, for six was striking and we were late.

I said, "Thy father breeds mares with his breeches down: he serveth as his own stallion."

"Thy mother spreads her legs for the whole city: only last night my father had her by the sewers. He turneth pale, boys! Who made her belly swell, by Christ she loved men well, dilly dally . . ."

We were on the Cloister stones, everyone shouting in excitement, and I thinking to kill him. The blood was so hot in my head I could do nothing but hit him without ceasing, the others trying to pull me off, and at last one hand I knew shaking me, turning me, and lifting me to my feet.

Geoffrey Falkes, my undermaster, shook me still, saying, "Nick! Nick! What dost? What hast done now, bully boy?" The shaking released the blood from my head mayhap, for I could see, though unsteadily, the Cloisters stones, the righteous, frightened scholars in their muddied black gowns, and my sobbing opponent, who whimpered on his knees, holding his head. Stroking my dirty hair as if to smooth it, my teacher said with some tenderness, "You must go to the headmaster."

"Don't send me!"

"Nay, he hath said it."

"Is he very angry, sir?"

"Thou art done for, boy."

I said nothing more but turned to the little door adjacent to the class and mounted the dusky steps by feel to the place where I was most reluctant to ever go again.

Our headmaster, Dr. Lawrence Judd, was remote to us, though he personally examined us weekly, hands clasped behind his back, accusative eyes sweeping our faces, waiting for us to stumble on Latin syntax or falter in recitation. Tall he was and slender, yet with a jaw as hard as the stone demon that perched before the doors of my parish church, its unforgiving eyes knowing my most secret thoughts. Though slender, he had a hand to grasp one's arm as tightly as the irons must hold a man in the condemned cell above the West Gate.

Knocking, I called out for permission to enter, and when there was no answer, slipped inside. Against the wall on the shelves dozens of precious books, many handwritten and centuries old, were stacked with brass clasps turned outward, among them Chaucer's *Canterbury Tales*, whose stories I knew well. On the desk stood a terrestrial globe, a quadrant for measuring the altitude of the stars, and a little lead armillary sphere, the rings representing the earth surrounded by the seven wandering planets, including the sun and moon. When he had first admitted me here he had let me touch it, but never since. Still under my palm I could feel the cool spheres. I put my hands behind my back and stared out of the small leaded windowpanes to the yard below.

He came from the closet, wiping his wet hands, and said cheerfully, "Ah, Nicholas, my young fighter! Come in." Black-frocked, a medal around his neck bearing his family coat of arms, he strolled about the desk towards me. He did not, however, strike me at once, but folded his arms (how neat-clipped were the nails!) and gazed at me as if he were considering purchasing me and not certain of my worth.

Badly I wanted to explain everything that had happened, but my lips dried with the words upon them before this revered man who had read divinity at the university and often dined with the Archbishop. My gown, which was too short for me and showed my strong wrists, and my tangled hair, thrust back into my collar, made me compare myself badly to his ecclesiastical elegance. He smiled slightly and my heart leapt. Aye, I thought, it may not be for the scramble he hath sent for me at all. It may be today he'll say my scholarship's granted and I shall go to Cambridge early this Michaelmas term where there's none to taunt me.

Without touching me, he said, "How old are you, my boy?"

"Thirteen since Ladyday, sir."

"You've had good teaching here. 'Tis a pity. You've not been chosen for Cambridge, nor can you remain here. Your days of study have come to an end."

At first I could only stand in silence, reading the titles of the books on his desk, and looking at the cold ring on his graceful long hand, certain that I had heard him incorrectly. "But I've placed above the others in competitive declamation, sir!" I murmured. "In syntax and logic, I've placed far above them."

"Nicholas," he said, still smiling a little, "we will speak with logic, you and I, since indeed you have excelled in it. It is common knowledge that the scholarships for Cambridge are for young men who wish to take holy orders. My poor lad! For you this is farfetched, impossible! You're more suited to any common trade than the priesthood. You fight, you curse, you get on poorly with your fellows and never for long. A young man who cannot control himself cannot be entrusted to speak God's word." Touching a speck of mud on my gown with the edge of his hand, he delicately dusted it away. "In addition, you have the arrogance to interpret Scripture in thy youth. Even the adulterous woman, you said in the disputation last week, shall not be condemned, when thou knowst she shall be cast into everlasting damnation."

I burst out, "But, sir, that can't be so! The woman taken in adultery was forgiven."

"If she sinned no more."

"And if she could not . . . if she perhaps had not the wisdom or the means . . . if circumstances . . ."

Dusting the mud from his hands, he answered flatly, "There would be no mercy. Your father repented, however, as I recall, kissed the Book and wept. You would not remember, being very young at that time."

"I remember."

"He had, it was said, a temper like thine."

I hung my head: what could I say? I was very young and this was a point where I was reduced to speechless grief, no wit, no logic, only the ache in my heart that never went away.

Abruptly Dr. Judd turned, putting his desk between us. "Let us make an end of this," he said, looking about for his seal. "Nicholas, you lack humility: you lack restraint. This school has no more to teach thee, and Cambridge would not suit thee better."

I knew him and that he never changed his mind, and that he had decided about me quite some time ago. It was the same when my father died: he had stolen and been strung up for it, and there was nothing we could do. Staring at the inlaid flowers of his desk, I muttered, "Shall I be cast aside? What's to become of me?"

"Come, come! What's this talk of casting aside, Nicholas! We'll find a good apprenticeship which shall make an honest man of thee and a credit to Canterbury township."

My voice rose. "Must I be a tradesman?"

"Come, come boy!" he said sharply. "We'll have no more. Thou hast not the means to discriminate. Shalt do as thou art told: a tradesman you'll be, for you're fit for nothing else. Is it thus you take my kindness?" Then he added, "We're sometimes not meant to have the things we think we'd like. Nicholas, know this and you'll be a wiser man. Kneel for my blessing: God knoweth I wish thee well." He raised his hand to place it on my head, but I cried out and struck it away, running down the worn stone steps and across the yard. Tripping, almost falling, I tore across the broad, uneven stones of the dark Cloister walk, the words of Virgil's *Aeneid,* Canto Six, pounding in my head.

> *Ibant obscuri, sola sub nocte, per umbram*
> *perche domos Ditis vacuas, et inania regna . . .*

(They walked obscured by darkness, in the lonely night, through the shadows
And through the vacant kingdoms of Pluto, and the empty homes . . .)

Close before me my schoolmates in a discreet undulation of black wool gowns were filing into the morning service. I flung myself behind the pillars, and somehow into the arms of my teacher Geoffrey Falkes. "Art done for, Nick?" he said in his scratchy voice, and as words would not come, I nodded.

Through the Cloister I could hear the boyish voices stumble with hesitant trebles in the first of the daily Psalms. For some time we remained together, my face against his linen hat and scant grey hair, my ribs wanting to break apart for their aching. He said, "Ah, the world's a bitter place! Who knoweth if education maketh a man closer to God? Know mercy and forgiveness and let them be stronger than any anger you may feel. God be with thee all thy life, dear child." His rough wet kiss on my cheek was long and sweet. And then he walked towards the Cathedral and I away from it and all that I had loved.

My mother was washing as I came through the yard, her thin shoulder blades stooped over the tub, the sloppy hem of her brown dress dragging in the mud. I wanted to go to her as a child might for consolation, only I knew in that moment that I had so seldom been the child and she so very infrequently the mother. She saw my face and understood at once that something had happened. "I've lost my scholarship," I said. "We must do the best that we can." I made my voice gruff because I wouldn't allow it to break and went inside. And that night when we knelt for prayers I compressed my lips and was silent.

"Oh Nicholas, wilt close thy heart to everyone now?" she said.

I would have liked to think that had my father had been alive, he should have chosen more suitable work to which I would serve seven years' apprenticeship, but as I'd neither father nor indenture fee, the parish bound me to a wheelwright. I lay awake until the morning bells my last night home, resolving to take my life as it had been sent until I could see a way to do better for myself. So I calculated the days until I should be old enough to shake the dust of this work from my heels and with pack on my shoulders, trudge off to read divinity at Cambridge and prepare myself to enter the priesthood. She and I would have a stone house with two rooms, and a chair with arms and a velvet cushion; she would never wash for strangers anymore, nor should I hear the dissonant laughter of strange men at their pleasure as I hid under my quilt and pretended I knew nothing.

At seven in the morning, I kissed her goodbye in the yard of the house beside the city walls and walked down the main street of the town to bind myself to a trade I despised. "God's wounds, could they send me no better than thee?" cried my new master when he came to the door. I saw at once that his wife and children were frightened of him, but I was a proud boy and I did not lower my head but gazed at him, I think, rather contemptuously. And in my head I calculated rapidly how many hours in each day, in each month, and in each year and in seven years. I knew the hours of my indenture and under my gritted teeth, I muttered, "One . . ."

My master was called Jack Michaelson the Bull, for that he so loved the baiting of the bull at the Butter Market stake that they said the death agonies of the shackled beast from the tearing jaws of the dogs was his deepest interest. He never missed, they also said, a hanging. An enormous man whose thick ears looked as if some creature had twisted and molded them, he had provided bad meat for the Queen's sailors before he turned to wheels. A man so muscular I have seldom seen, though he was far from young. His breath stank, for he despised the cleaning of his teeth. He despised books as well and said they made a boy useless and soft.

The kitchen girl pulled me aside and whispered, "Art come to be bound? Mind thee be most servile! The last lad was struck so hard about the head that he's never been right since, and must stay at home in his mother's kitchen not knowing his own name."

"Surely the Bull was called before the Guild for this!"

"Nay, for he said the boy had a fall, but I know what 'twas for I saw it myself. Do what thou art told, for thou art a fine lad." She kissed my cheek, her clothes fragrant with bacon and flour, and pushed me up towards my dinner.

There the family sat to an uncongenial meal in the kitchen parlour with its fine painted cloth hangings of Biblical scenes and its pewter plates and mugs. I could not bear to hear the way he chewed his meat or slapped the mug down on the table so his wife might fill it from the keg of ale, and I forced myself to eat though the sight of his unclean teeth nauseated me. After he took me to the front room, which was his shop, and well stacked with wheels and fragrant, aging lumber: ash for the body of the huge carts he made and elm for the wheels. That afternoon he bored a hole through a wide slice of elm and put it in a spindle, and while he chiseled, I turned for hours until my back ached and all the while I counted the hours and knew that only five had gone by from my seven years of indenture.

At night I was sent to sleep amongst the fragrant lumber on a board with a sleeping mat. Though I was warm enough with the coverings and well fed, I slept badly with fear for my mother's safety, wondering what strange men might come and, forgetting themselves, hurt her. I had pulled one off her before I was six, biting his neck, and had never forgotten it. Once when I was very young she had stayed away from the house for a day and a night, and I never let on in school, but ate what dry cheese or bread I could find, and washed my hands and face at the public fountain, wiping my teeth clean with a bit of rag. Then she came home running with something hidden in her thin shawl. "Come Nick, see!"

"Nay, I don't want it!" I had been tearful.

"Oh but it's good."

I was ashamed that I took the little meat tarts flavored with bay leaves and the orange, which I had never tasted before and found very sour. When I had been pacified enough to eat and wept over her absence and my impotence, she spilled from her hands lovely coins that we spread on the bed and counted between us, and I felt the stern hook-nosed profile of our Queen in the gold.

"A fine gentleman," she said, "gave them me and will give more. Oh Nick, don't be angry, my wag!"

I had thrown my arms about her, and we walked together to the stalls in the marketplace, where she spent the coins on new hose and soft red shoes for me, which I swore never to grow from, even if I had to walk with my toes curled under my feet. She bought for herself a blue shawl embroidered with thread of gold. In those moments we were exquisitely happy and talked about buying chickens and raising them for the eggs, but we never did. The coins melted away and she wept dejected and I tried to sing to comfort her. When we had no food again she took in more washing.

I had brought with my clothes to the wheelwright's two books that my teacher had given me; he found them and took them away to sell. "I'll not have thy time wasted," he said, and set me the task of shoveling away the muck pile heaped before his door. My disdain grew to hatred, and I knew not how to control the look on my face. I passed from counting hours to counting minutes and muttered what I had of Cicero's *In Catilinam Oratio Prima* under my breath until it became my incantation against ignorance.

*Ad mortem te, Catilina, duci iussu consulis iam
  pridem oportebat . . .*

(You, Catiline, should have been led to your death
  by the order of the consul long ago. . . .)

Early one afternoon while walking past the market bookstalls on an errand to the smith, I noticed a printed paper nailed to a post announcing the play to be given that afternoon in the innyard past the West Gate. Several pennies in a leather purse had been entrusted to me to buy nails, and from that errand I was to hurry back to complete the sweeping of the shop, the Bull being gone for the day. Yet by the post I remained, rereading the announcement of "the magnificent drama by Christopher Morley, as presented on the London Stage, with the Lord Henderson's Men." Though we had given Latin tragedy at school, I had never seen an acting troupe other than religious plays by the guilds; professional troupes came seldom to Canterbury, and my beloved teacher Geoffrey Falkes had said that players were vagabonds and wastrels and no good could come of playgoing.

I had seldom wanted anything more than I wanted to hear the drama. And when I had paid for the nails I kept back a penny in secret, and ran back to the inn.

They had just begun, and because the men in front of me blocked my view, I clambered up a pole and balanced against the overhanging second story of the courtyard. The drama was the bloody tragedy of the tyrant Tamburlaine, and as the actors spoke I forgot both who I was and where I belonged. Never had I heard such English verse in all my life:

Nature that framed us of four elements
Warring within our breasts for regiment
Doth teach us all to have aspiring minds.
Our souls whose faculties can comprehend
The wondrous architecture of the world

And measure every wandering planet's course
Still climbing after knowledge infinite. . . .

I knew nothing but their speaking, and the words went burning, burning into my very soul. "Nature that formed us of four elements . . ." And I said, yes, it's true. I am water, air, earth, and fire. I can understand and comprehend and there is nothing that I cannot do.

Six actors and two clumsy lads composed the troupe; the pink satin of Zenocrate, daughter of the Soldan of Egypt, was wrinkled, the enunciation of barbarous and bloody Tamburlaine himself unvaried in timbre, and they spoke fast as to have the play done before rains came. None of this mattered. Two hours later I left the inn hardly conscious of where I was going and no longer myself, for I was mighty Tamburlaine and the world applauded me.

Untroubled I was in my absence, for my master, the Bull, as I said was from home, delivering a wagonful of wheels some miles off, and his wife and children gone with him for company. If there were drying cakes about the pantry, or a few extra herring in the barrel, I might wrap them in the playbill which I took from the ground as souvenir and walk to my mother's house with the present. I might take too a wedge of sugar, and moreover a little flask of wine. I could do as I liked, for I was not myself, but the man I knew I could become, conquering and brilliant, and above all petty stipulation.

Thus whistling, I pushed open the door.

Our dog snarled at me: feeling the stiff hairs of his head, I sought to light the oil lamp, for the house was all but dark. The bad oil fluttered and sputtered, and in the shadows I took dry bread and hacked at the sugar, all the time muttering to the beast and feeding him scraps to quiet him. The wine barrel was gone from the parlor, though I felt along the back of the painted hangings and puzzled. I turned to the shop.

Shadows of boards and wheels greeted me: scarce room was there to move past the area of the door. Only when half across did I understand the congestion of the wood, for the shipment of wheels had not been taken. Someone had gone somewhere, for the house was still, but the wheels had not been delivered.

The dog snarled, then lay low and whimpered.

The Bull was standing in the door. My lamp lit him unevenly, but his eyes were malevolent the way the fettered beast himself is when he first sees the dogs and supposes himself the match for them. He stood there, barring my way, swaying slightly, and said, "Nicholas, for thee I waited, son of a whore."

The bread I dropped, but the dog was upon it, worrying the playbill with his teeth. And he said to me, "Son of a whore, come hither."

Were there window large enough to fling myself through though it had been ever so hard a fall I would have gone. Faintly I shook my head, and held to the table behind me. He said, "Where hast been?"

"Out walking by the river."

"You were seen at the play. What troubles the beast?"

"Fleas, mayhap, master."

"I watched thee from the stair. Open thy hands."

"Nay," I said.

"I'll teach thee to steal, son of a whore." We were facing each other over a pile of aging lumber, and with these words I saw him take up a heavy stick. "Come, thou thief," he said. "Mayhap I shall not break thy bones and mayhap I shall."

So clear to me was the fight in the play, the rapier held in the actor's right hand and the cloak cast over the left arm to ward off the opponent's blows and the dagger held for the kill. I threw my cloak over my arm and seized an awl from the shelf for my dagger.

My heart was beating so loud I could hear it.

"Wouldst stand against me?"

"Aye," I said.

He strode towards me and brought the stick across my ear, sending me staggering against the wall. An apprentice who fought his lawful master could be condemned: I could see myself hanged before the Cathedral and my mother weeping on her knees. He struck the side of my head again and my blood mounted with the pain of it, and I seized a thick shaved spoke of my own as rapier, for in my mind I was more with the play than in a wheelwright's shop, and more a hero than a bound boy with no rights of my own.

He would not bear his will thwarted, and a pride and anger rose in my own body that I had not known I possessed. "Well, come then," he hissed.

We circled each other, the pile of lumber between us. He struck suddenly at my shoulder, and the pain brought hot flashes down my arm. The threat of even the gallows was irrelevant to me then. I held out my cloak to entangle the stick as he struck again and it jerked from his hand. He shouted and leaped at me, his hands on my arm, forcing me to drop my improvised rapier. My left arm half tangled in my own cloak, I hesitated only a second and in my panic and rage plunged the awl into his shoulder. Smelling his sweat and blood, I flung myself at him, pushing him back to the ground, where his head struck the pile of boards next to my sleeping mat. The awl was still clutched in my hand and I needed only to strike again to his heart, but something held me. I don't know what.

A wet patch had formed on his sleeve, and his breath had thickened; his eyes rolled back. Absolutely still he lay. And as I knelt there, I knew I need not strike again for the blow to his head had not only stunned but killed him, and I should be hung for it.

I do not remember how I got to my feet and from the shop, but found myself running down the narrow winding lanes of Canterbury. Oh it was dark! Muddy, endless darkness, and from the eaves of houses and beside the waterways, the shadows of gargoyles, half demon and half human, seemed to turn their heads to watch me go, wishing me every evil on my way. Bells rang dully through the light rain, and the nightwatch came, his stick over his shoulder, his lantern swung before him. I hid behind the stone bakehouse and then, taking my work boots in my hands, ran over the cobbles around the side of the Cathedral.

The cat darted before me in our cottage as I ran to my mother's bed and touched her forehead. It was cold with sweat.

"What is it, beloved?" I said, stricken.

"Naught." Her back arched and she cried out in a hard, resentful voice. I understood it at once because I had seen it before, though I'd been much younger.

"I'll run for Granny."

"It's too late." She began to gasp and cry. "Pull the covers away, Nick, for the love of Jesus." I pulled and heard her harsh straining, though I could see nothing. There was only her screams and then silence and the baby wailing.

"Cut the cord," she whispered. "Take the knife from the chest."

It was a rusty knife, and I wiped it on my shirt before using it. I lifted the wet, bloody baby against my shirt and laid him at her breast. She was incoherent with fever, and I prayed over her, sprinkled her with spices and herbs, invoked demons and offered my soul. Just before dawn she died in my arms.

I packed some bread, the few things I had, and her blue shawl, and touched everything in the cottage once to say goodbye to it. In the light of early morning I wrapped my sickly, silent little brother in my own blanket and laid him in a basket before the Cathedral gates.

Then I ran.

TWO

St. Paul's, City of London

I**T WAS FOR MY LIFE THAT** I **FLED, INCOHERENT AND CHILDISH AND STUM**-bling over my feet, past the milestones on the Dover Road that told how far it was to London. One ran there never to be found again: so the ballads sang and so my father had once most wistfully speculated.

A few miles from Canterbury I threw myself down by a stream and bathed my face in the cool October waters, resting for as long as I dared with my school satchel hugged in my arms. Its contents were only her blue shawl, such clean clothes as I possessed, and my warm cloak, a present from yet another traveling merchant who had left unredeemed promises to her and some small amount of coin. Memories made me bow my head: my dented tin drinking cup with the smooth curved handle, the comfortable declivity of my straw mattress, the soft paws of our cat Nell as she leapt from the cupboard to the floor, the sound of my mother calling me, romantic and musical as if she'd been a lady calling from her balcony. Dear Nick! Dear love!

I wondered what Nell would do, and how long she'd wait in the deserted house before padding off to find another boy who'd feed her. Sweet Nell had slept in my arms, and I knew intimately the smell of her fur. With these thoughts I stumbled back upon the road, half hiding in the wild bushes and trees. Yet when I arrived at the next town, I allowed myself to linger in the marketplace amidst the people for the common comfort of it, my cap pulled well down over my eyebrows. No one noticed me at all. Their lives were ordinary: mine on the edge of extinction. How could they not sense it? Attracted after a time to a table of fine ivory combs, I stood staring at their carvings: every night before bed my mother had taken down her long, pale-red hair and combed it, drawing me to her then to comb mine. Sometimes I ran away so she could not find me. Now my hair hung tangled almost to my shoulders, and I thrust it impatiently from my face, all the time panting under my breath, "Oh mother, couldst not wait? Couldst not wait till I was older and able to provide for thee?"

I reached for the last of the hard bread she made from peas, but thinking of her tumbled into earth, hurled it from me and stood panting, not knowing which way to go. The housewives who had come to market began to look at me curiously, and the bookseller by whose stall I had been lingering folded his arms and said, "What lack thee, young master?" Startled to be spoken to, I ran, turning down an alley foul with muck heaps, under a line of wash someone had hung low, and felt a smock catch at me as if to apprehend me. And all the time as I ran I heard my hot breath and said scornfully, you run from smocks.

I knew not if there was one man or twenty or none behind me, yet I would not stop until I was past the town, and on a narrow road in the coming twilight. From the Cathedral I heard the tolling of the solemn bell for Evensong, and shivered as I recalled my schoolmates processing towards the service. Good Matthew! Would he remember me? And Benjamin? And might the little tailor's daughter wonder where I had gone?

The bell seemed closer than it had been before; in crossing a field, I must have circled back the way I had come.

Dusk had begun to drift down from behind the thick leaves of the early-autumn trees. I had been taught since before I was breeched that with the night came malevolent spirits in branches and brambles. I held these things to be but old wives' tales, yet now the branches seemed the tangled, bent head of some old woman: aye, one they'd burned for a witch though I hadn't been allowed to see it. Fear entangling my legs, I walked on more slowly, my hand on the knife from my mother's chest, following the deep ridges which heavy cartwheels had left in the roads until dusk had almost swallowed the branches.

Above me, I saw the jagged shape of a little church on a hill. An iron gate led to the path, which wound up through the graveyard: tombstones everywhere, some tilted and some fallen. Mounting to the top of the path, I touched the damp panel of the church door, which creaked open to perfect silence.

If this had once been a holy place, it was no more. Lighting the flint I carried in a pouch at my side, I saw that some of the old pews had been partially chopped away. Dozens of heavy burlap bags rested against the walls; I crossed myself before coming close to them, feeling their shapes. No bodies lay within, merely grain. It spilled, soft and ticklish, to my roughened palms. Undoubtedly wrecked by soldiers in the Reformation, this was church no longer but some miller's storage house, and against his coming, I dragged one of the broken pews before the door to barricade it.

Once some of the boys had dared me to go into a chapel such as this on All Hallows' Eve, and I had stoutly refused; now I felt some pride to be here and regretted they'd never know it. Triumphant I stood over those old fantasies, only to replace them by a more terrifying reality. Sooner or later they should come for me and end my life by hanging. I should be neither priest nor scholar: I should be carnage and dust.

Perhaps it was a boy's way to delight in tormenting himself, and I succeeded quite well: my fascination for the gruesome was here more satisfied than I could have wished, but it is one thing to have such fantasies while in one's own bed and another when one cannot know who may come up the path to take one away. The creation of a refuge became my most immediate need, and I pulled a few of the heavy empty bags to the chancel to make a bed. Where the altar had stood I would find some sanctuary; surely some compassionate angel looked down now and then, and might know that I sheltered there.

It was then that I remembered my satchel, which lay by the bookseller's stall where I had dropped it. How could I turn back? Surely every man in the south of England now knew that I had murdered my master; even now, surely, they sought me with the rope swinging in their hands.

Through the broken section of the roof I saw the moon move behind the clouds. Pulling one of the bags over my head, I listened. There was no sound but the high, drying grass against the tombstones. I sought for the familiar sounds about our house: shutters creaking, wild cries of the quarreling cats from the wall. When my thoughts became dreams I know not, only that I fancied the pew had moved, the door opened, and my wheelwright master stood powerful and spread-legged with his heavy stick in his hand.

I covered my hand with my mouth; I dared not let even my heart beat. "Nick," he said.

The grass blew about the stones and the dead rose from their graves, disintegrated and ashen. They came through the broken windows, and hovered about my shoulders, nudging the burlap, trying to reach even my feet or my fingers and to take me away with them. And all the time I knew the wheelwright waited, smiling slightly, and on the shoulder of his jerkin was a bloody wound that would never go away. "Nick," he said. "Come out and get what thou hast merited, lying whoreson boy." I had lived a hard enough life to know how to be clever. As long as I would not move from under the wheat bags by the desecrated altar, I was safe. Wrong I was. His hands were on me, he knelt above me and began slowly to pull the coverings away, and I struggled and yelled and cried out, leaping up.

Alone in the church, my cry echoed against the roof beams and died away. Exhausted, I lay down fully covered once more and waited for numbing sleep.

Someone sang to me. Something silken blue touched me, making me rise to my knees once more and gaze about. How astonishing it was! The church was now as tidy as it must have been in the days before the Reformation, the candles were lit for service, and in the middle stood the Virgin Mary herself, extending her gracious hand to me. I felt a rush of yearning and pure love. O Holy and Pure Mother, pray for thy child! The old prayers, secretly muttered by renegade priests, once echoed in the sacred undercroft of the Cathedral. *Holy Mary Mother of God.*

Yet as she stood there she proceeded to change, to look more ordinary and somewhat slyer until she had become the cripple's daughter who in her free ways had showed me the manner of men and women in the fields behind Canterbury, and laughed when I was too nervous to complete my part in it. Rising to my knees, I held out both my hands. She smirked, changed once more, and became my mother. "See what I have, darling," she said, taking apples and meat pies from her wicker basket.

I cried, "Where have you been, Mother? I was frighted thou had died!"

"Oh Nicholas, how couldst think it!"

"You always went away."

"And came back again, thou knowst!"

"Then cull me to thee." I held out my arms but she was moving away into the shadows, her voice a little crosser.

"What hast done with thy packet? Such a careless boy!"

"I've lost it."

"How couldst! We have nothing else."

"I'm very sorry, Mother! Art angry with me?"

"So many things hast thou torn and forgotten."

"Wilt forgive me?"

"Show me the blue shawl and I will."

I could not see her anymore and I cried out, "I was so frighted that I left it behind."

"Then I shall never more return to thee."

I woke sobbing, kneading the stones with my fingers. For days after my knuckles were bruised from it.

Dr. Judd had often said we were but sojourners in this sorry world, and his words returned to me time and again on the several days of my journey towards London. Falling into ruts of bad roads which led from village to town past fields and orchards, I passed more people than could be enclosed at night within the oval walls of my old city. The world was perpetually traveling.

Wryly I remembered Chaucer's tale of how the pilgrims had come with holy hearts to Canterbury seeking benediction: I, in my more unholy way, rushed in the other direction. It was three shillings to rent a horse from Canterbury to London, but I had not three pence, so I walked.

Tinkers and peddlers I passed, priests and travelers, the carriage of noblemen broken down upon the road, inns whose ostlers stared at me with hostility. Some miles from Canterbury I overtook the players' troupe trudging beside their cart. Tamburlaine himself, much older without his crimson-velvet breeches, stopped to piss against a tree. I was profoundly disillusioned. Still, one of the men gave me a bit of roast fowl and some dry bread. I do not think they recognized me. A wild black-haired beggar cursed me for his long-gone prodigal son. I hid behind a barn until he was gone.

At Gravesend, ferries waited to take passengers to London by water: gentleman returning from Calais stood with their trunks and serving men at the wharf. "Goest on thy master's business?" one asked me in a friendly way. "Dost seek employment?" I shook my head, making no answer. "He's dullwitted," said one, laughing.

The gifts of dry bread and a finger's worth of roast fowl could not sustain me. By the time I came to London I was a thief: pies taken hastily from market tables, a cotton shift from a washline, a purse cut with my bodkin from the waist of a woman who stood waiting for cream and which contained nothing but a farthing. Never leaving me was the certainty that sooner or later I should be caught, if not for the wheelwright's death, then for my thievery. So intense was the nightmare that I often cried out against it in my sleep in fields. Even as I rushed along, I did not cease to bargain with Our Lord. Sweet Christ, I have sinned but let me live! I knew that my hopes of becoming a priest were gone, for I had spilled the life of the man appointed to be my master on the very boards of his trade and my hands would never be clean enough again to consecrate the bread and wine.

And so I came to London.

Over the fields past villages and markets I went, thinking to have arrived when people assured me it was farther yet, sometimes seeing, as a haze beyond me, grey steeples rising to the sky. Stomping over marshes and wetlands, I at last came to the city walls and was swept through Aldgate with coach and wagon, peddler and drayman, into crooked streets where my feet slipped on the sewage and ever downward towards the river Thames.

That afternoon I climbed for the first time to London Bridge. High above the clear, crowded river on twenty stone arches it rose, and I stood between the houses and shops that were erected along its span to gaze down, almost numb with exhaustion, at the grey stone palaces and hundred church steeples of London and Westminster, glittering against the early autumn sky. Below me the Thames was a forest of ships and masts, ferries and barges. No one came to apprehend me or noticed me at all: it is peculiar that a boy may walk in anguish and be absolutely unnoticed by all who pass him. I crossed the bridge and stood for a time upon the south side, staring back at the majestic palaces that lined the bank. Crossing back again more slowly, I wandered into the heart of London, bewildered by the noise of iron wheels upon the cobbles and the stench from the gutters, sour, decaying, full of horse feces and rotten food. A crowded, dirty city it was of timber houses in narrow alleys and illustrious stone mansions on the riverbank before which the graceful swans swam. Thus I walked this way and that until Watling Street, perpendicular to the turning river, led me uphill to the walls and gates of St. Paul's Church, whose five-hundred-foot spire had been struck by lightning and burned away some years before. The churchyard contained not gravestones but bookstalls.

For the better part of an hour I wandered there, studying massive volumes, rich with plates of the heavenly constellations, and Fox's *Book of Martyrs*, its painful illustrations depicting the infinite variety of tortures by which the saints left this shoddy world. Several other stalls had put forth sixpenny playbooks, and others secondhand prayer tracts. The scent of paper and ink and the sound of pages turning were rapturous for me. I'd had no books of mine own since they'd been taken. Happily, I forgot the world and would have greedily finished the first scenes of *A Spanish Tragedy* had not the youthful bearded bookseller, who had been scratching under his arm and watching me for some time, barked, "What lack you, pisspot? Wilt rob me of my price by reading all without paying?"

"Nay, master!" I murmured, and stumbled into the Cathedral to escape his critical eyes.

Few shadowed, hushed, or private places were in St. Paul's Cathedral in those days, for the nave was more like a market than a church. Women with lapdogs embraced in their arms dallied with friends, and under the crumbling stone arches several men were shouting at each other concerning a lawsuit in Middle Temple. A coal carrier, his load on his back, taking a shortcut through the church, glanced at me: I lowered my eyes and moved into one of the little chapels between the many crowded monuments of the dead. The memorial plaques kept me but bitter company: all was cold without and under the immovable stone lids of sepulchers, colder within. I touched the engraved letters. Would the dead remain buried with much pomp, their souls enriched by bequests to the church, while I met (if not this day then surely in the days to come) my end?

See here the certaine end of every mortall one,
Beholde todaye alive, tomorrow dead and gone,
Lyve well, so endless lyfe by death ye shall obtayne,
Naught lose the good by deathe, sythe lyfe thereby they gayne.

Walking up and down the side chapel, I did not notice that I wept until I could not breathe for the congestion, and ceased only when I heard the sound of singing.

Evensong had just begun, the young choristers raggedly attempting the first Psalm of the service. They were a cheerful group in shoddy surplices who jostled each other, throwing bits of paper torn from the prayer book across the choir between verses when the elderly choirmaster was not looking. Yet nothing drew me like music, nothing outside of words, and I had a fine, commended voice when we sang at home. What of their music I knew I sang with them under my breath, until it was over. The boys trampled out, pushing each other happily, and the evening began to fall: dimmer grew the light through the majestic Rose Window, and one by one, in the churchyard, the booksellers were gathering in their wares. I began to sing softly to myself, the concentrated and pure Psalms set by Tallis to Archbishop Parker's hymnal.

> "E'en like the hunted hart the water brooks desire;
> E'vn thus my soul that fainting is, to Thee would fain aspire.
> My soul did thirst to God, to God of Life and Grace;
> It said e'en thus, When shall I come to see God's lively face?"

A stout woman waddled over to drop a halfpenny in my hand. Taken with this new possibility, I forgot my precautions and began to let my voice flow out. What did I sing? Anything I could remember. After the hymns came country love songs, a bawdy ballad: "When night came on to bed they went," etc. In the protecting shadows of the chapel to the emptying Cathedral, I sang as if it would be both my last and my beginning.

By one of the thick stone pillars, a young man had stopped to listen and pulled away from his companion. He began to walk towards where I stood, and my voice died away; then he put his hand on my arm. Terror filled me where there had been bliss: I fought him with both my fists. "Why, what is it with thee?" he said. "I only seek thy name."

I struck wildly, the only thought being they had come for me at last and I was going to die. He took me by the shoulders, shaking me as if I were a puppy and forcing me down. "Loose my arms," I cried, and then I shouted out at him every curse I had ever heard from beggarmen and whores whipped at the cart's tail, and bit his arm through his doublet. He gave a cry of pain: he may have struck me or I may have fainted. I knew nothing more for some time.

It was a common, small room in which I awoke with whitewashed walls and no cloth hangings, and dusk falling outside the tiny lead-paned windows. From the pallet where I lay, I could make out a single table, covered with papers and books, on which a rushwick dipped in rancid fat gave a dancing, uneven light. The young man I had bitten sat writing, his quill stabbing repeatedly in the ink and his full lips pressed angrily together. His brown hair had perhaps been hacked to chin length in a moment of impatience and his neck was bare, for he had thrown his ruffled collar to the floor. His boots lay to the side.

After a while, noticing me looking at him, he faced me with his hands on his knees. "Dost live?" he demanded. "I feared I'd knocked thy wits from thee, though thou deserved no better. One more offense against the law and it should go hard with me. So much for my temper, so much for thine. Dost always bite and curse when asked thy name, jackanapes?"

My voice was so faint that no sound came from me.

"Thy singing enchanted my ear, though thou art a common thief."

"No thief am I."

"Aye," he said scornfully, "and a liar as well."

I would have stumbled from the room, could I have risen, but as it was, only murmured, "Sir, what will you do with me?"

"Sell thee: thou wilt fetch a fair price."

"Why shouldst sell me?"

"For thy voice: 'tis one of the best I've heard."

"Then will you?"

"No: I lied. You're in the last of thy singing days."

"What is this place?"

"My room, or my half room, for I'm forced to share it. Enough questions: you grow tedious and I regret my kindness. I should pitch thee down the stair did I not think thee only a poor fool run off from a good home. You're not clever enough to steal for thy bread. Stay until you can stand and then go: I weary of thee."

I watched him with my head on my arm until I slept and he became part of my dream. It was full night when I looked about me again; only the rushwick lit his round, unshaven face. Such a vast intelligence was there that it seemed he could not help but grow fast impatient with this ordinary world. Whoever he was, he was not like other men.

The rest had done me good: I could almost find in myself the strength to rise and go away, but the night was ominous and I knew nowhere to go. "Master," I murmured politely, "what do you write?"

"Nothing that thou canst read."

"I can read fairly," I answered resentfully, propping myself on one elbow, "not only English but Latin. *Aeneid,* Canto Six: *Ibant obscuri, sola sub nocte, per umbram perche domos Ditis vacuas, et inania regna...*"

Leaning towards me with a frown, never taking his eyes from my face, he ordered, "Continue!"

"*...quale per incertam lunam sub luce maligna et iter in silvis, ubi caelum condidit umbra Iuppiter, et rebus nox abstulit atra colorem.*"

He gazed at me in silence for a few moments and then turned abruptly away. "Someone hath taught thee more than cutting a purse. Shouldst face hanging one day, only say thou canst mumble a verse of Psalm or six lines of Virgil and they'll but brand thee and send thee to steal again. This is the only merit in education. Too many men are educated these days and starve. Thieving pays better than writing, sir cutpurse, at least better than playwriting. Wilt go from me now?"

"Dost write plays?"

"Among other things."

"True plays such as are given in inns?"

"Yes, such as those. Whence came thy Virgil, boy? 'Tis not the common tongue of cozeners in this city. Where had thy schooling? Thou art run from somewhere or towards something and are half ill with fright. Art a schoolboy or an apprentice? Where's thy family and parish?"

I hesitated. His eyes were beautiful, very large and brown and soft but not to be trusted. They were like those of an animal which might bite when you put forth your hand. I looked once more about the shabby room with its plaster ceiling blackened by taper smoke, and nothing in sight to eat but a small fish on a wooden trencher. He said, "I grow weary and inclined once more to throw thee down the outer stair. Speak! Where art from and why here?"

"I can't say it."

"Will not, rather."

I struggled to sit up. "Give me your name first."

"I'll not do it. Wouldst only lie to me about thine." He folded his arms and looked at me: again I had the peculiar sensation that he was not quite like other men, that he would presently throw off his doublet and become a creature half wild. I knew not what but I remembered walking into the woods once at night and seeing golden brown eyes from between the leaves.

"Nay, come!" he said, sprinkling sand on the paper and standing abruptly. "We'll share a penny plate of beef for dinner and some bread that will pay for thy song. And then never let me see thee more, jackanapes: I've better things to concern me."

Walking to the tavern I turned once and again to look at him: shabby, unceremonious, unshaven above the small pointed beard, and of medium height. I doubted, however, he were the writer of anything but accounts, for Dr. Judd had assured me that solemnity and wealth were the marks of such a trade. Still, I was strangely drawn to him. "Jackanapes, thou art fair for a cutpurse," he said, cuffing my head. For a moment I wondered if he intended to lure me somewhere and injure me; even had I believed it, I think I would not have turned back.

We dined in a corner of the tavern. The beef and ale loosened my tongue and I told him many fanciful lies, swallowing the constriction of my throat, my hands nervously clutching the knife handle. Such stories I told of having been to sea, and my father's wealth lost from foolish investments, and relatives of great wealth from Flanders and beyond even now in search of me. He listened carefully, picking his teeth with a twig he pulled from his doublet; then pushing the meat trenchers aside, took me roughly by the hair. "Pretty as a woman," he said, "but stubborn like a man. Sings like an angel and swears like a devil. What will become of thee in the streets?"

I was silent, so he pulled my hair harder until I yelled. Shaking me, he said, "The truth now, thou young cutpurse."

Then I cried out, "My mother's dead and my father's hung and they turned me from school for fighting so I can't become a priest with a stone house for her. I've killed my master, who was a wheelwright. My name's Nicholas Tomkins, and if you tell them in Canterbury of me, I shall die." My voice trembled, and I was so ashamed of it that I tried to turn away my head, but he seized me by the shoulder and looked at me through and through. "God's blood," he said, laughing. "God's blood, you're more of a devil than ever I was, and it hath pleased me. I'm from Canterbury myself and like it no better than thee. It's a priest's town and they're as mean-spirited a bunch of bastards as ever one saw! How old art thou?"

"Thirteen years."

"And won't see fourteen! You'll be at the rope's end one day as I pass by, and my conscience will trouble me for it. I'd rather see thee a pretty singing boy. Drink up and we'll walk to Blackfriars and look to thy future."

I muttered, "Wilst sell me?"

"Nay: I've told thee, thou art near worthless."

"Canst keep me thyself?"

"Nay, come," he said sharply.

Thus we walked together down to the Thames and across to the old buildings by the water known as the Liberty of Blackfriars, a select neighborhood, he told me, for minor noblemen and wealthy merchants, to which he attested by indicating the sentry in his gatehouse. Passing that gate, we mounted the steps of a house that had once been luxurious, into a wainscoted and echoing hall with double galleries at one end, rows of benches, and iron candle brackets against the wall. From the floor above echoed the raucous sound of many boys. The door burst open, and a little man, whose fleshy hips swayed under green breeches, rushed across the room and jerked up my head to look at me. "Well met, Foster, thou slime," said my friend.

"The courtesy of Bedlam is greater than that thou ownest," answered Master Foster, dilating his nostrils. "Who's this boy? How old is he?"

"Thirteen he says, though he's been known to lie."

"Hast taken him to thy liking?"

"Nay, he knows naught."

"Thou sayst." Turning to me, he said, "Canst still sing?"

"Aye," I said.

"Then do so."

And so I stood between them, slightly dizzy still, and sang an English anthem from the Canterbury services. Smacking his lips, he said, " 'Tis a pretty voice but 'twill break before the spring comes and he'll be useless to us. Young Charles, however, who played the comic girls, hath pitifully died of the sweating sickness and we've no one for the high treble. Canst study quickly?"

I muttered, "Master, I can."

"Thy name."

I hesitated but my friend interjected, "Nicholas Cooke from Sussex, former tailor's apprentice. I knew his family. Take him before I offer him to your rival company."

And in this way I was apprenticed yet again. When my new friend had hurried down the steps, Foster said, "We sing services twice daily and give plays, here and in other eminent houses, two or three times each week. As for that one, he lives among thieves and blasphemes and will go to the Devil soon enough."

"Won't he return?"

"He hath forgotten thee already. To thy dinner and prayers."

I turned my head. Well go to the Devil as you will, whoever you were, I thought. May you be choked on your penny beef.

Once seated to a second supper of hot mutton, soft cheese, and warm beer, I looked about me, recognizing in the flickering rushwick light the faces of the boy choristers from St. Paul's. Twenty or so there were from the age of ten or eleven to about seventeen, and noisy companions they made at the refectory table with their shouting and banging of knife handles. One pale fellow kept wiping his nose on his sleeve, and someone said he'd been whipped for failure to learn his lines. As I memorized everything straight off, I thought him a deserving fool. Short time had we to become acquainted, for within the hour we were sent to bed in the damp upper rooms and I was trundled in with a boy my own age who asked me if I had come with the playwright Morley and if it were true that he communicated with dark spirits and had sold his soul.

"I know not Morley."

"Oh you country fool!" the boy laughed at me. "Who do you think 'twas that brought thee hither?"

At once several of the boys came from their beds to sit about mine and inform me that the man who had bought me beef and pulled my hair was the writer Christopher Morley, whom everyone called Kit. It was he who had written the bloody *Tamburlaine* whose lines still rang in my head from the performance at the Canterbury inn, as well as *Dr. Faustus,* where devils arose from below the stage and danced among the actors even as they played.

"Nay, 'tis all lies!" one boy whispered as he left us. "Kit's as kind a man as lives and fears the Lord as any!"

When morning came, the school matron having fitted me with a long woolen cassock and a heavily starched ruffled collar, we marched to sing in the Cathedral of St. Paul's over the raucous noises of peddlers crying their wares. Though we were chartered as a boys' school, our lessons were brief, for we had far too many rehearsals both for singing and playgiving, both of which were more profitable than education. Two of the lads had been abducted from country churches for their voices, and several of the older ones whose voices had broken were kept on to play gallants and villains, and would in time join one of the adult theater companies. Often during the day a playwright or two would come about to read the masters a new work, and share the gossip of both theater and court.

At night we cavorted in our nightshirts and carved our names with the year in the ceiling, into which we also threw our penknives for practice, or pummeled each other fiercely with the feather pillows. Someone caught a rat now and then and beat it to death in his hose, thrilling to the shrieks. I was as fascinated by blood and violence as any boy my age, and none of us would have admitted to each other that we didn't enjoy the sight of a good hanging. As we prepared for bed we could hear the carts carrying the dead rumbling across the cobbles.

The plague was heavy in the city and a thousand a week perished from it; they closed the large theaters, but we sometimes played to small audiences in candlelit rooms of wealthy houses. They gave me the girl's part, fitting me with a wire farthingale, padded sleeves, and a blood-red satin dress with copper lace. I read through the script thrice and knew my own lines and everyone else's. There were among the boys Tom Hawkes, and Wat d'Alessis, whose grandfather had been from Chartres: there were many but these I remember especially, for Wat talked incessantly of his mother's hot beef pudding and the dogs he had been breeding at home, and Tom could not keep his part in the madrigals and was sent back to Bath some months later when they found that punishment did not help intonation. John Humbert was the oldest fellow in the school, then seventeen, and had the leading male roles.

We rose each morning to prayers and went to bed with prayers, and dined and supped most heartily on fish, meats, and sweets. The first comedy I played, blinking a little from the smoke of the rushes and candles, was the charming if archaic *Endymion* (*The Man in the Moon*) by John Lyly. It was the sort of tripping and harmless fiction of Greeks, Egyptians, and mythology with much music between the acts, for which the boys' theaters were famous. I was cast as Cynthia, and as my youthful voice rang out with the words "Is the report true, that Endymion is stricken into such a dead sleep that nothing can either wake him or move him?" the echo returned to me from the hammer-beam ceiling. Ladies and not a few of the men gazed intently at my pale chest, exposed to the nipples in the low-cut gown.

I was in love with words.

We slept close like puppies to keep warm, tussling under the covers until the chaplain, Canon Burkes, rushed in to threaten us with the switch. We tickled each other and heard the death carts go by and the bells of the hundred churches of London ringing and the boots of the nightwatch on the cobbles below. "Say from whence thou came!" demanded my bedfellow, Thomas Hawkes. He had grown weary of talking about running off to sea, and wanted some diversion to his mind.

My answer was only, "No man shall know it."

Offended, he fell asleep with his back towards me. I waited for Kit Morley but he did not come.

THREE

Blackfriars

I DREAMT SOMETIMES OF HIM. THE LEAVES FELL FROM THE TREES IN THE gardens of Whitehall Palace and a cooler wind blew from the river Thames, bringing with it the fragrance of roasted nuts, of ships and the sea.

Twice daily at St. Paul's Cathedral our high voices rose in holy service above the men's deeper singing in the music of the new English Church. I was as solemn a boy in my carved choir stall before the altar as if the angels sang through me, almost as if my soul mounted straight to heaven clad in counterpoint and harmony, and walked there freely among the saints. No one could know that in those moments I recalled most piercingly what I had lost. But pain when one is thirteen can temporarily be lost in playfulness, and we tumbled out to piss in the cold air by the side of the church until it froze into a slide, on which we slipped and fell until one of the masters cuffed us and dragged us away. We were cloistered and pure: a swathe of heated, curious boys none older than seventeen, who tumbled over each other, and the world that we saw from our wainscoted cathedral stalls through the heavy choir screen dazzled and invited us.

Weeks passed and Kit Morley did not come. Then I said, I'll see him again if I suffer for it. On an early winter's night when the torches had been snuffed and my bedfellow, Tom Hawkes, had fallen asleep to his stories of navigation, I slipped down the steps, out the door. Though the judicious watchman at the Blackfriars gate had stepped away, I did not light my lantern wick until the chapel had been passed, the street twisted to an alley and the alley to still more obscure lanes. For over an hour I lost my way. Bells had rung ten of the night when I ran across Bishopsgate at last, and climbed the outer stair to his common lodging.

Though the door was unlatched, the room was empty and the cold night wind from the open shutters blew across the unpolished floorboards. Papers tumbled from the table, books lay heaped upon the chair, the trundle beds were piled with clothing, and from his own sleeping quilt feathers disengaged themselves and floated towards my feet like wayward spirits. Murky was his wooden bowl of washing water; I put my finger in it and, wandering to the table, took up his quill pen, pressing it against my thumb until it left its inky mark. Stairs creaked, and the companion I had first seen him with entered the room.

Wat d'Alessis had told me Morley lodged with Tom Kyd, author of the bloody drama *A Spanish Tragedy,* and that though they got on but moderately well, they were poor enough to afford no better. "What! Art here?" Kyd remarked when he saw me. "I thought we'd been well quit of thee! If it's Kit you seek, you'll find him in the tavern across the lane."

Barely thanking him, I ran down the steps and across the paved way, my shoes splashing in the puddles. Pointed down the steps by the tavern drawer, I descended into the dirt cellar, rich with the smell of bitter ale and salted pork. There, squatted in the middle of the room on the moist earth, were Kit and some other men, and as I came closer I noted they had drawn a circle in the dirt with a knife and placed a burning candle in the center.

Precipitately, I cried, "Jesus! What do ye?"

They had half leapt up at my footsteps, but Kit sighed and held out his hand. "Young nuisance! Art so soon weary of singing and acting? This boy won't tell tales; he loves the law no better than we. Come, Nick, put out thy light. We'll see if the darker spirits will be summoned up to us this night."

Clutching my lantern as if it were some holy thing, I hesitated. "Will they harm us if they come?"

"That shall be seen."

Extinguishing the flame, I dropped to my knees beside him before he could change his mind. His hands held out before him as if in prayer, he slowly let drift a scattering of fine grey ashes into the circle, some dusting the edges of my mended breeches, whispering, "Prithee, let there be no sound, good men, an we will see if he'll be summoned." My hand slipped into his; deep was our silence and our listening.

Above our heads in the tavern came the muffled bootsteps of men about more ordinary business, but here was the stillness of something beyond earth. I yearned for its mysticism, yet feared its evil. We were summoning the darker spirits of Hell, and drawing in my breath sharply, I thought, who can say what may come? And of what or of whom were made the ashes that fell so softly?

Yet I did not move, not bearing to pull my hand away from his fingers or to lose the touch of his lace cuff against my wrist. The warmth of my belly increased as if someone had lit a fire within me. For a moment I opened my eyes, as I sometimes did in church to gaze curiously at the faces in contemplative prayer. Morley's profile was soft. With a frown to push away the strangeness of my feelings, I began to study the candle itself until the yellow flame almost drew me within. And I thought, when shall I cease to be alone?

We should all come into joy on the day of Resurrection, as I had been taught. Yet mayhap on that day on which the trumpet should sound and the dead arise from the earth, I should be forgotten. Mayhap all others whom I had ever known would ascend into the security of eternal love, and I run shouting below to be taken as well.

Someone blew out the candle: I shut my eyes. Our hearts beat as one and our breaths were warm. I could sense the lines of the circle as if they burned with fire. Something was within it: something twisted, inhuman. It had happened. We had summoned the darker spirits indeed.

The thing was there and I dared not open my eyes, for it knew me. I sought to name it. Satan was too simple: it was far more subtle. Yes, the evil had come, recognized and awaited me. And I understood that if it escaped from the circle, as it even now strained to do (clawing at its sanctified edges), it would not touch these men. It would take me alone. It would drag me away, my mouth stuffed with ashes, my arms bound, tumbling to fire and endless pain. It had come for me and wouldn't leave without. Had I hidden from its insidious waiting in my boyish pledges to serve God all my life? And did it not, knowing me better than ever I could know myself, laugh and await me here?

My stomach revolted, my knees dug into the cold earth, my body ached as if I had the sweating sickness, and I wanted only to blurt out that someone must save me before it was too late. My breath rose faster and faster until it became a gasp for my portion of the smoky cellar air, and with a stifled cry I pulled away from the men and buried my face in my hands.

"Give us light," someone whispered.

A torch was lit and someone knelt, resting his hand on my shoulder, saying, "What troubles thee, boy?" When I raised my head I saw the face was thoughtful, the nose long and thin, and the linen the quality of a gentleman's. His ring brushed my cheek. "I was afraid," I whispered.

"Twas only a game."

"I felt the Devil rise, my master!"

"He rose in thy mind alone. Have ale to comfort thee. What dost here?"

Kit Morley only answered, "The lad sings with Paul's Boys, Hariot, and has a liking to follow me that this evening's cured him of. Light torches: we've had enough of this damned nonsense. More men believe in witches and devils than not. I've seen women burned for it. There're no devils but those which lie within men's hearts, and God knoweth those are plenteous enough."

Two more torches showed the low ceiling, and the platter of meat pies and cheeses as we gathered about the table. Kit speared a hunk of cheese with the point of his knife and held it out to me. Ashamed that I had cried out in my fear, I drank deeply of the bitter beer. But for Tom Hariot, the gentleman who had spoken kindly to me, the others were profoundly disinterested in my presence. One rubbed the circular marks out with his heel. "Aye, they burn more than witches," he muttered. "Even the Queen still burns Roman priests for heresy, or destroys them on the rack with pain."

Beyond the cheese on the table lay a wood cylinder; Tom Hariot pulled it closer and laid it courteously in my hand. "Hast ever watched the moon of a night, my lad?" he asked. "This perspective glass enlarges it. 'Tis a wondrous and mysterious thing, the moon, and with this I have seen its mountains and craters."

Turning the instrument, which was fitted in a case of tooled leather, I lifted it curiously to my eye and slowly moved my body to gaze at the wall beyond. Glittering and gossamer in the flames, a spider's web was of a sudden so near that had Mistress Spider and myself been so inclined, we could have kissed. Then I could not look enough at empty broken bottles, the splintering cellar steps, the dry rafters of the ceiling. All the time Tom Hariot leaned his arms upon the table's edge and gazed upon me. "Hast heard of Copernicus?"

"No, sir."

"Sometime I will tell thee of him. I live at Syon House with my lord the Earl of Northumberland and tutor his children. There I have several perspective glasses and attempt the measurement of the distance of the stars." By this time I had risen, too excited by the instrument to remain seated, and was studying every crack in the wall. In truth I was a little drunk. The rapidly consumed ale permeated my blood, and though they spoke of alchemy, the movements of the planets, and the uses of tobacco, I understood little and murmured unsteadily from time to time from whatever corner I found myself, "What meaneth it to rectify? What is the alchemists's stone? Can gold be made of common rock?" At last I settled behind Kit, poking his shoulder, dreamily swaying.

"What is this and what is that? Pretty fool!" cried Kit, springing about with his hands on his knees to study me. Taking from his jerkin a small circular brass nocturnal engraved with the constellations, he dangled it before my eyes. "Canst do naught but ask questions? Canst read the hour of night by the Great Bear?"

Joyfully I held out my hands. I thought he meant me to take it outside and find the time, in which case I should run up with the perspective glass as well and stand beneath the tavern sign, gazing at the very stars, which I so longed to do. Yet when I reached out he pulled it away. "The hour hath been read," he said flatly. "It's time thou wert abed: you weary me. Begone, Nicholas."

I lost my way twice before finding my way back to Blackfriars. Immersed in the events of the night, I did not hear one word of the chaplain's lecture. I had seen the face of evil and knew how sharply it contrasted with love and beauty; I had seen Kit Morley, and parted from him once more.

In addition to our services at the Cathedral at ten and four each day, we gave plays (such as the schoolmaster Udall's *Ralph Roister Doister* or Lyly's pastoral *Love's Metamorphosis*) in our theater or the halls of wealthy houses whenever we could; for a time we presented Preston's *A Lamentable Tragedy Mixed Full of Pleasant Mirth, Containing the Life of Cambises, King of Persia, from the Beginning of his Kingdom, unto his Death, His One Good Deed of Execution, After That Many Wicked Deeds and Tyrannous Murders,* etc., but there was not enough music in it and it was not popular. Sometimes we came home late on the river half ill with cold, and the masters had to pay extra for coal to warm us before we bedded. During the Psalm-singing at the Cathedral services, our eyes, supposedly on our choirmaster, wandered to search for young gallants who had worn their spurs into the nave: leaping down between verses, we would demand the small coins known as spur money from them. Pretty faces made our attention wander as well. I felt with a new appreciation the sensual, mysterious, languorous beauty of women. The plain wench who cooked our meals enchanted me by her sad, narrow mouth, and I tried to kiss her by the stove, pressing the glory of my hardened body against her smoky, splattered skirt; I wanted the dairymaid as well who sold whey at our door. And yet there was one person alone I longed for, and that was Kit Morley, who had sent me away.

What I could remember of his plays I recited under my breath before sleeping, feeling the shape of the words with my tongue. Yet he was not good, he was not placid, he was not any of the things I was taught I should be. He could also, I suspected, be cruel. Cruelty fascinated me. I both felt it in myself and saw it in the world about me. Once when spur money was dropped into my hand, I cried out in pain, for the gentleman who offered it to me smiling had first heated the coins. I bit his hand and they had to pull me from him. I had been taught to turn the other cheek, and got little for it: Morley had never turned cheek for any man. In the moments when our chaplain salved my blistering palm, I wondered if in spite of all I had been instructed, rebellion were not the better way.

Though we boys were cloistered, we knew very well the life of the city and a good deal of court gossip. The brilliant young Essex, Robert Devereux, was at the age of twenty-four the favorite of the old Queen, Elizabeth, now past her sixtieth year. We also whispered of Henry Wriothesley, the Earl of Southampton, who had just come down from Cambridge to occupy his London house and patronize young writers and who was the ward of the Queen's Chancellor. His curling lovelocks so intrigued me when he came to hear us at Blackfriars one night that I almost forgot my lines.

I bought a copy of *Tamburlaine* with the spur money I had won from a cavalier and read it with a stolen rushlight after hours.

> Nature that framed us of four elements
> Warring within our breasts for regiment,
> Doth teach us all to have aspiring minds . . .

Lanky Tom Hawkes crept across the shadows of our chamber to look over my shoulder. "What read ye? Ah, there's no finer poet in London than Morley, Nick, but he traffics with spirits and blasphemes Jesus."

"What doth say?" I muttered, biting my sour apple.

"That Jesus and the beloved John were sodomites, that the Bible is filthily writ."

Almost choking on the skin, I cried, "He cannot say such stuff!"

"That and worse," was the solemn answer. "He hath said Moses was but a juggler and the magician Tom Hariot of London can do a better trick than he."

Weeks passed. We talked between rehearsals and services of the Queen's beauties, her ladies-in-waiting, whom no man dared approach and who, cloistered under her aging eyes, embroidered linen smocks for her bony, brittle body. Walter Raleigh had married one of them without permission and been sent to the Tower for it. I thought of the immensity of this world and the fantasy of it: I regretted I had not seen the Indian that Raleigh had brought from the New World, but the poor creature had died, they say, of the London air and pining for home. I longed to see the shabby lion in the Tower zoo. I yearned to be a soldier even though the sight of life spilled sickened me, and I never thought of the Bull's head striking the aging elm boards without a feeling of terror. We went to see a hanging in Tyburn; when the victim jerked in agony and his friend ran forward to pull his feet and bring his quicker end, I threw up in the lead gutter and said it was naught but tainted dinner meat which caused it.

December came, and the slow-flowing Thames, impeded by the huge pillars of the bridge, partially froze. With the cold, the severity of the plague lifted. The death carts came more seldom, and in Shoreditch and in Southwark, the rival theaters raised their silk flags and announced that they would play again. Posted to the very doors of St. Paul's were fliers for the dramas, and as we rushed past with our cloaks about us, I saw that Morley's *Tamburlaine Part the Second* was to be given by Lord Strange's Men, who were favored by the Queen and noted for their performances at court. Under the protection of Ferdinando Stanley, Lord Strange, this talented London ensemble of men and boys had refurbished the aging Rose Theater the year before for an astonishing sum, and raised its new flag mast to announce it.

Signs of Christmastide hung in our halls. We lit white beeswax candles and climbed the galleries to tie green branches with hard red berries to them. There was carol-singing. We were always damp in our attic and some mornings found our washing water turned to ice. The Thames froze even under the bridge, and we made bone skates and skated across, though one of the boys fell through and almost died of the chill. We wore heavy undyed wool hose and warm wool cloaks as we set out one after-noon, shoving each other and shouting, over the bridge to the fields of Southwark, to pay our penny and stand in the uncovered yard of the Rose to hear the acclaimed actor Edward Alleyn play Tamburlaine. Ap-prentices and tradesmen crowded us about, and above us in the three galleries the gentlepeople rested on rented cushions, eating nuts and oranges, their feet on warm bricks that they'd carried from their homes. "Pennyknaves!" some called down to us. In the cold the actors' breaths were white, and the whole of the play was violent, emotional, and to me very real. From the little hut above the stage the stagekeeper's boy low-ered clouds, and the curtain of the back alcove swung open for the chariot to drive out with mighty Tamburlaine whipping on his captured kings. ("Ye pampered jades of Asia, can you draw but twenty miles a day?") " 'Tis Alleyn himself," said my friends, "the finest actor in London but for young Dick Burbage. Mark his copper-laced collar! Look how his brow's bent!"

I arched my neck to look about, and after the play was over and the gentlepeople hurried across the fields to reach their homes, we lingered and wandered around to the tiring room to stare at Alleyn when he came from changing his clothes. Cluttered it was with discarded costumes and several boxes of severed heads made from plaster and smeared with fresh sheep's blood, and the charcoal brazier burned with a sweet, stuffy smell. At the end of the room was Alleyn, and with him Kit Morley. Pulling away from Tom Hawkes's arm, I went forward as if in a dream.

Cautiously he whispered, "Don't go! It will be dusk soon and we'll be late for organ lessons. Come!"

They forced me into the murky field, but I shook them off and shouted at them, and ran back. He looked tired as if he'd just come from a long journey and not yet washed or changed his shirt, and though he didn't say he was glad to see me, at least he didn't turn himself away. "Why Nick," he said softly, "I thought I had frighted thee enough to stay from my company."

"I do not frighten," was my reply.

"Art bound towards St. Paul's? I'll walk along with thee."

Twilight was falling over the grey city, over chapel, palace, and brown field. Behind us soared the Rose Theater, its flagpole now empty of scarlet banner. Casually he said, "When in Canterbury I asked for thy old master, jackanapes and saw him at his work."

"At his *work*? Is he not dead?" My heart almost stopped in my breast.

"As I have said, it would take more than thee to send him to the Devil. You left him with naught but an aching skull, an unimpressive wound to the forearm, and no more kindliness than before."

"Truly doth he live?"

"Aye, and with small fondness for thy memory. Thank thy sweet stars, my friend, they've not the wit to search the London singing boys for thee. I've been to see the play, thou young beauty, and there's no prettier lady in London."

I had stopped by the stinking riverbank, no longer feeling the frozen ground through my boot, no longer hearing the sounds of hooves and wheels on the bridge. "Morley," I said, "if my old master be not killed, my hands are clean of his blood! And then I can go once more and study to be a priest!" With rapture I turned my face towards where the river flowed to Dover and the sea. I do not know why I did not spin about that moment and run towards Canterbury, down the nave of the Cathedral itself and to the very feet of priests and headmaster.

Morley was silent, and when after a time I turned my flushed face to his, I saw his soft full mouth had lifted in a slight sneer. "I thought better of thee than that, my friend," he said coldly. Pulling away, he adjusted his rapier hilt with an impatient gesture and began to mount the path to the bridge.

The sun was almost down and a chill crept over the back of my neck: my throat ached with tears. "Morley!" I cried, leaping up past an elderly woman, my heel catching the hem of her farthingale, then clattered to the bridge past horsemen and a hot pie shop, and caught him by his sleeve. "Kit," I pleaded.

He looked down at me, coldly and a little amused, the last of the setting sun catching the bristly, badly clipped hairs above his beard and his soft mouth. He had known the truth at once, and was impatient with my stupidity that I did not. I could no more return to Canterbury: how could I think for one moment that I would be sent off to my studies once more? If they did not conduct me to the condemned cell in the West Gate, I should be forcibly apprenticed again, and wheelwright, baker, brickmason, or butcher would I become. And I knew as we stood on the crowded bridge, I knew between the tears I fought and the desperate, rising need to be loved, that my headmaster had been right. I had been looked over by Our Lord and found wanting. And until He sent a sign that He had changed His Mind about me, it would remain so.

Morley smiled, showing his crooked, small teeth. "Well, priest's harlot?" he said softly.

"Don't call me that!"

His finger traced my cheek. "You'll grow from thy nonsense. Come, pretty scamp. Waiting for Heaven to call can't mend thy loneliness, and any fool can see how deep that lies, Nick Cooke." And he slipped his arm around me and kept me near him as we walked.

I said nothing more, struck as I was by the truth of his perception and my vague, disturbing arousal at his touch. Below us the Thames swirled in clumps of dirty, frozen ice, and before us to the west in the deepening twilight we could see the lights in the Whitehall windows and, majestic against the early evening sky, the towers and buttresses of Westminster Abbey. Yes, I stayed close to his soft, stained leather jerkin because I was thirteen years old and no one cared for me truly but this man in his odd, carnal, careless way. As we left the bridge I didn't turn west to the comfortable supper awaiting me at Blackfriars and the new anthem to be rehearsed at St. Paul's, but continued with him across Bishopsgate Road. He did not ask me to come up the outer stair which led to his room, but neither did he say I couldn't. The room was bitter cold and we could find no matches to light the fire.

"What shall we do for warmth?" he said.

He was all that I wanted in this world, and I threw my arms around him and rubbed his rough, unshaven cheek against my own. We undressed under the covers and my hands were shaking as I touched him all over and he touched me. His belly was warm as fire and I rubbed my face in it and kissed him and tasted him as if I were starving. Afterwards he kissed me once, rolled me over to my back, and looked down at me.

"Get thee home, Nicholas," he said.

"Keep me with thee."

"Nay, I've said it before: thou knowst little about my comings and goings, and I'm not the friend for thee. There's thy boots: my landlady will give thee light." And with this he sent me away once more.

I had become most valuable to Foster in those days: still I can see him coming at me, wide hips and little feet, with another lute song under his arm for me to study. The surly chaplain, Canon Burkes, of whom it was said he had never read divinity and was in his private life most perverted, was given special watch over my whereabouts. My predecessor dead of the sweating sickness and Wat's voice broken early, they could ill afford to let me slip away, as mayhap they sensed I was most eager to do. Six days had passed since I had seen Kit Morley and it seemed half a lifetime to me, impatient and lovesick as I was, and randy with wanting him.

We were to give *Endymion* once more, this time for the students of Middle Temple, one of the four schools of law for young gentlemen which lay between Londontown and Westminster. A large fee was involved, and Foster with customary practicality kept us from both lessons and sleep to prepare for it, adding several dances and three new madrigals between the scenes. I had by this time learned some simple music on the lute, though as tuning it tried my patience sorely, I happily played without until Wat d'Alessis ran from the room with his hands over his ears. Standing outside the wainscoted, hammer-beamed hall of Middle Temple in my pink gown, I waited for my entrance with the lute in my arms among my squabbling fellows, my attention nowhere but upon massive front doors from which a cold wind blew each time another gallant and his lady mounted the steps to hear the play.

Our chaplain guarded the hall's end.

We made our entrances and exits, tripping and pinching each other as we did, and each time I came from the stage he was there with his beady eyes upon me. Luck held me in her embrace, though, for no sooner had I made my third exit and put down the lute than quarreling in the hall broke out and he strode at once to settle the matter.

I did not hesitate then, but lifting my sweeping pink skirts and the heavy wire farthingale hoop beneath them, I ran as if for my life towards the door and the street, which was well blocked with carriages and yawning coachmen. A cloudy night it was, and the bitter winter rain had just begun to fall. Once I slipped, skinning my knee and tearing the fabric of my gown. Bishopsgate Street almost missed in the darkness, I found my way only by the candle above the sign of the Archer's Tavern and climbed the outer stairs, my finery heavy with rainwater and the once starched ruffs in a sodden mass about my neck.

"Who the devil may it be?" I heard him shout, pulling open the door; then taking but one look at the gown running in pink puddles to the floor, he burst into laughter. Humiliated enough was I to strike him, but he caught my hand. "Why Nick," he said, "no offense. Thou art the finest lady come to these humble chambers in many a day, only we know in truth what lies beneath your skirt is man enough! Is it not so, Nick?"

I understood that he welcomed me in his odd way, and I leaned against the door near him and laughed until my sides hurt. When I stopped, I stripped off the sodden dress and he had the devil of a time unpinning the farthingale, never having done so before. He didn't care for women, he told me later, and never had. The ruffs we cut away and likewise the pulpy cardboard that lay beneath it. Once wrapped in the quilt that spilled small feathers about the floor, he threw me a dirty shirt to dry my feet.

"I've come to live with thee," I told him.

"Oh art thou, nuisance?" he answered.

When I awoke the next morning he was already writing furiously at his desk, papers falling to his boots, the fire out, the room icy, and nothing to eat. I was shy with him and a good part of the day passed before I had the courage to mutter that I was hungry. He burst out with exasperation that there might be old bread above the shelf and I mustn't expect to be waited upon. I climbed up and found some so hardened that no hunger could allow me to bite into it: still, after I had soaked it in half a glass of wine dusty with cinders, I managed to get a little down.

"What wilt thou now, nuisance?" he snapped at me. "So it profiteth thee to run off from a good dinner and warm bed! And when they come for thee, dost think I'll stop them?" Tears filled my eyes, and seeing them, he cupped my face in his hands. "Nay, they'll fight me for thee! I like thee well enough." Then I made free of the room, sprawling upon the bed on my back to read his erotic translations of the poet Ovid, kicking my feet at verses of extreme passion and demanding he explain them. That done I looked through his heaped clothes, dirty shirts, unpublished playscripts, counted the spiderwebs in ceiling corners, and scribbled my name in the dust of the window. All this time he wrote, answering me uncharitably with grunts. Once he sent me below for a half pail of beer.

Evening had almost come when I heard Tom Kyd's footsteps on the stairs. Begrudgingly looking me over, raising his sharp nose as he did so, Kyd unwrapped cooked pigeons and a round loaf of wheat-flour bread, the crust burned black. We sat on the floorboards to eat and threw the bones in the corner.

"Wilt keep the boy here, Morley?" he muttered between bites.

"I fancy him."

"A lad of thirteen! You'll hang for less one day."

"I could not hang for better," said my friend. "They are fools that like not boys and tobacco." He rose and threw on his cloak.

I said, "Take me also!"

"Nay."

The rushlight expired, Tom Kyd rolled into his cloak on his trundle bed, and I sat up for a long time, gazing through the dirty window at the narrow street. About two in the morning by the bells of St. Helen's, Morley returned with unsteady steps across the floor. He threw his doublet across the chair and his boots under the table, laughing softly to himself. Then he came to me and rolled me in his arms; his breath was sour with wine and his unshaven face rough against mine as he rubbed it hard so I should feel it. "Thou art sweet," he murmured, "like sugared ginger."

Passion and anger rose together, and I tussled with him until Tom Kyd stirred resentfully in his sleep and Morley put his hand over my mouth. Then I knew nothing but his languorous body.

After he muttered, "Tonight I looked up at the stars. . . . God knoweth whence we come and whither we go. Give me thy charity and compassion, sweet Nicholas, and let thy anger rest. I am as I am, and that is not kind." He began to sing in my ear,

> "Come live with me and be my love
> And we will all the pleasures prove
> That hills and valleys, dale and stream
> And all the craggy mountains yield . . ."

Touching his cheek, I murmured, "Why art not kind?"

" 'Tis a boring, Christian thing to do, a priestly thing. Still thinkst to be a cursed mass-sayer? I'll kick thee from the bed, make thee sleep on the floorboards with the rats for bedfellows." He pulled my hair with no gentle hand. "Say, boy."

"I do not think on it."

"Swear on the Devil."

I was silent.

"Poor fool! Likst my song, Nick? The verses are mine."

I threw my arms about him, hoping he was not still angry. "Always sing me thy songs!"

"Mayhap."

"Teach me to write such things!"

"There's no teaching: it cometh or it cometh not."

"Speak to me then."

He wanted to sleep, and I shook him hard. "Of what should I speak, jackanapes? We live but an hour, we die, in betweenst we sleep. Of what should I speak?"

"Tell me how the stars are made. Tom Hariot said they're made of flame: why don't they shoot fire and burn us?"

"They're farther from the earth than man can tell."

"Cannot I get there?"

"Only in thy mind, sweet wag."

"Morley! Had I wings, I'd fly up in the night."

"Wouldst, my young Icarus? Fly so close that thy wings scorch and thee tumbled down to earth, thy pretty body all broken in St. Paul's churchyard? That would grieve me. Let me sleep."

"Nay: tell more!"

"Shake me not, nuisance! Lean close and I'll whisper it unto thee. Here is thine answer and it answers nothing: where the stars hang we'll never travel."

Hopefully I suggested, "Mayhap when we die."

"Mayhap."

"Where do the heavens end?"

"They neither begin nor end, and beyond these are many universes. Say that before the court of investigation, the Star Chamber, and you'll find yourself uncomfortably on the rack for heresy. We live in one universe and it all goes on forever."

"God hath made it."

"Thou sayst."

I sank into silence, pulling away from him, biting the side of my hand, alone in the depth of reflections I could not begin to put into words, and when he reached for me, I shook him off. Gruffly, he said, "Why must know these things?"

"Because I must." I felt in that moment that I would die if I couldn't know them.

"Must know them all this night?"

"Aye!"

He drew me down again with my head on his chest. "It strikes three. Stay close and keep warm: the night freezes."

He took me to taverns, and the houses of friends where he made me wait outside and then hustled me away again. One late afternoon, though, he took me by horseback to Syon House over the fields and through small villages some miles from the city, where lived Henry Percy, the Earl of Northumberland, and the tutor to his children, Thomas Hariot the mathematician. By early dusk we had arrived, and the Earl being from home, Hariot came himself to greet us. Cordially he took my cold hands in his and looked at me with some interest.

His own rooms were full of scratched and scrawled papers of which I understood nothing, for I had only briefly studied mathematics. Shelves were stuffed with star charts, perspective lenses, astrolabes, and nocturnals. One table was strewn with convex and concave lenses, bits of wood and metal and leather. I wandered about, looking back now and then at Morley and his friend. We ate a fine supper, and I went to sit on the small stair from which I could see, through a little window, the night.

Then he put his hand out to me and said, "Nicholas, come! You only saw spiderwebs through my lenses before. Now you must see the stars, and we shall find if they are to thy fancy." I half ran beside him then, following the soft white linen of his shirt and Morley's darker form through the vast kitchens of the country estate and out to the lawn.

Clear and cold was the evening, and every star that had been made since time began hung over the house and gardens. All the time I trotted close like a puppy, interjecting questions whenever they paused in their conversation. "Doth grind the lenses thyself, master? With what is it done? Might I see it? How do they fit together, the concave and convex, to make the perspective?" Each time he raised his hand, and stopped to thoughtfully answer me.

"How large might the stars be, sir?"

"Larger than the moon. They are of far greater distance: but looking up, alone, how can one know? You said you knew nothing of the revered teacher Copernicus, Nicholas. What I could say of him might last a year and more and tire most people, but mayhap it would not thee."

Shyly murmuring to the ground, and stroking the lens stand which he had allowed me to carry, I murmured, "I should never tire of it."

"Copernicus," he said, "conjectured that it is the sun and not the earth that lieth in the center of the universe. 'Tis contrary to biblical teaching, is it not? About this sun move the six planets. We move even now." He took two small apples from his pockets and slowly began to move the smaller one about the other, turning it gracefully with the slight movement of his long, ringed fingers. The cold wind lifted his fine hair and stirred the plain linen of his collar. "Why, it grieves me to my soul that I am allowed but a small span of years here to understand so much. Didst ever see white light pass through a prism and break into colors? Dost know refraction and optics? Hast measured the velocity of wind, wag?"

"Nay, master, none of these things."

"One day mayhap I shall show it thee."

The smaller of the perspective lenses he gave to me, and I wandered about, now lying on the cold earth to look up, now leaning against a tree until I felt my intellectual leanings turn sensual, and I became one with earth and sky. When I returned to them, my eyes aching and my mind now weary, they were seated on a garden bench talking softly of church superstition and the reality of the Trinity. Sleepily I followed them to the house, reluctantly surrendering the small perspective lens. Hariot brushed my long hair from my face. "The boys I teach have not minds as sharp, Morley. He should be gone up to Cambridge and scholars' commons."

"There's none to send him thither," said Kit, and he talked to me reflectively, as we rode all the way home, of Copernicus and the mysteries of the moon.

Portly Master Foster from the Blackfriars Theater came to fetch me the next day. Righteously up the ladder which led to our small dwelling he climbed, banging on the latched door. How he had found me I cannot say, and I think he would have taken me by force and dragged me off had not Morley stood between us with his fine, nervous fingers on the hilt of his dagger and his beautiful dark brown eyes sparkling. After Foster had stalked angrily down the ladder again and waddled off towards the river, I threw my arms around my poet whom some called the darling of the muses, and announced I would stay forever. "Ah," he said, thoughtfully. "Forever is a long time, jackanapes."

Those weeks were wild and free, though I was often hungry, having gone to bed feasting only on sour wine and half drunk with it and the poring over of astronomical charts borrowed from his friend. We had between us some differences. I had always liked to be clean, but he bathed seldom and I felt it a matter of honor to be as dirty as he was. Having no regular washerwoman, we seldom wore clean shirts, and that aside, I had none of my own, and wore only his, which hung slightly below my wrists. He would come home perfumed, washed, and clothed in embroidered orange velvet, strip it off, and hurl it around the room. He hurled a valuable gold ornament into the cracks in the floor once and we couldn't pry it up for a time. Sleep itself was erratic, because he either waked me to talk of poetry or science or to stroke me half the night, then rose at dawn, never seeming to mind that he had just come to bed. Once he went off to buy a round hard cheese and never came back for two days.

Bewildered with love and resentment, I said, "We never know, Morley, whether we eat or no. It's as it was with my mother at home."

"A pox on thee, nuisance, thinkst thou I'm like her?"

"Thou . . ."

"Hast compared me! Speak!"

"Hast mistook me," I stumbled, confused that I had spoken of it.

After that he said occasionally, "Come, I'm not thy dam, thou knowst," and I punched his shoulder harder than I ought and he only laughed at me and caught me in his arms and bruised my face with his unshaven cheeks. "Need a wetnurse still, little one," he said. "Shalt nurse from me, pretty fool?" When I interrupted him he cursed me with such names as I had never heard, not even from the whores being whipped at the cart's tail nor the madmen that beat on the iron window bars in Bedlam. I learned quickly and cursed him back, and soon he was playfully slapping me, we both rolling over on the floor, shouting and tickling.

The third week of my new life he woke early, threw my boots towards me, and said, "Up, slug! An actor I know is in his barber's stool this morning and we have business with him."

Sleepy (we had bedded at two), I made him stop by the cistern on the street's end so I could wash my face in the icy water. Over the skyline of the city rose St. Paul's. I glanced hungrily at the cooked pigeons and roasted larks offered for sale on the carts of Cheapside, seduced by the apprentice's bored cry, "Masters, what do ye lack?"

Without stopping, we made our way down the wide street past the two-wheeled carts, the men on horseback, and the ubiquitous water carriers with their heavy lead-rimmed containers, and found the barber-surgeon's down two crooked steps off Eastcheap some doors from the Bell Tavern. I was attracted at once to the tools for teeth-pulling and cutting the stone that hung on the wall beside razors and scissors. Then, from the cracked cup of rosemary sprigs on the dusty window seat, I looked to the round-bellied man seated under the barber's razor, his fat hands on the stretched, tearing wool of his breeches.

My friend said, "Tom Pope, a goodday."

"What, Morley? I thought ye'd left the city." His voice, rich and deep like goose fat, was fair loud enough to knock the bottles from the shelf. I remembered that he had played with Lord Strange's Men, roared to the galleries and tumbled with the clowns.

"How fares thy Shagspere, Tom?"

"Little good it maketh him. He lives badly as we all do, scribbling love poems to pay his lodging; if he hath a gold angel to send home to his family it hath surprised me. 'Tis no time for actors or playwriters with the theaters once again in danger of closing, Morley! Mark, they will by Candlemas Day. The very cockpits are shut down. We shall have to tour again if we're to eat. What brings thee hither?"

"I've come to rid myself of this young encumbrance who eats all in the house and grows daily out of his clothes and mine own. I've not the patience to keep a 'prentice, and what I teach him he does better not to know. Have him! He speaks well and is lately run from Blackfriars, where he made a pretty enough girl in the plays."

Tom Pope, standing up, handed his shaving cloth to the barber and put his hands on my shoulders. "Canst dance and sing, boy? I like his face, Morley: 'tis full-spirited and unbeaten. Canst tumble and leap?"

My hand on the door's edge, I nodded dumbly, too shocked to do otherwise.

"Then I shall tell thee: I have two 'prentice boys at my own table now, which is far more than a bachelor with only a housekeeper and four orphans should manage . . . but John Heminges and his wife, Rebecca, told me this very morning they were thinking of taking on a new lad."

"Then take this one," said Kit, "though he's the very devil."

In that way we turned west to the parish of St. Mary Aldermanbury in Cripplegate Ward and to the new timber-and-lime-plaster house of the actor John Heminges on Wood Street across from the Mitre Tavern. Behind the house stood a large walled garden, though now the apple tree was bare. The whole of the front floor was occupied by the kitchen with its long trestle table, a large hearth with a baking oven to the side, and one coffer-backed chair, a cupboard in its seat. On the floors were clean rushes and on the table two or three books and several sprigs of rosemary. The outer floors overhung each other, the second containing three small bedrooms with an inner stairway and a ladder mounted to the top where a garret room with a tiny window overlooked the garden. Two straw pallets on leather-strip frames were stacked against the wall, and the windowsill was set with drying fruit.

When we climbed down again, we found the master of the house, John Heminges, had just come in. He was a large, soft, broad-shouldered fellow, his good-natured face shaven clean. "The lad's old for an apprentice," he said when he had heard a mottled version of my history. "Canst sing to the lute? Canst read?" He opened a playscript and pushed it before me. "Say these lines for me."

I spoke the text, and he listened gravely. "You speak fairly," he said, "though I'll not be a fool enough to trust thee. A boy who runs from his master runs against God, and thou art run from two though you're not fourteen. When wast first 'prenticed?"

I muttered unhappily, "In the fall, sir."

"What trade?"

"Tailor."

"Why left this master?"

"We did not get on."

"In what county, pray, was this interrupted indenture?"

"Sussex," I muttered.

"Indeed? And then were 'prenticed again at Blackfriars with the St. Paul's Boys and ran off. Why?"

I could not tell him because I wanted to be with Morley, so I waited uncomfortably. Then his pretty young wife, who was standing by the door with her arms folded across her full breasts and a small child hiding behind her brown skirts, said, "Take him, John."

Heminges hesitated for a moment. "Very well," he said, "I'll try him, but I'll not trust him. We shall wait and see, Nick Cooke, how we fare together."

I looked at him closer and found that his bulk and serious manner made him seem older than he was indeed, and that I guessed him to be not yet forty with a broad, youthful face and only a few grey hairs. After a time his wife, Rebecca, who was big with child, began to pluck the birds for dinner. I looked about with some pleasure at the comfortable kitchen with its barrel of white herring in the corner and dozen little round cheeses ripening neatly in cloth upon a shelf.

My new master had gone into the garden with Tom Pope, so I slipped out to follow Kit Morley to the corner of Wood Street by the holding prison. "Shall I see thee?" I muttered sullenly, stubbing my boots against the tethering post.

"Not as like. They care little for me here. I've many enemies."

"Oh Morley! Only send word and I'll come to thee!"

"And what should we be to each other, jackanapes?"

I was silent. He said carelessly, "Divided thou art, sweet Nick, and shall always be." I hoped he might kiss me but he only cupped my face for a moment, and turned off down the lane. I stayed looking after him until my mistress called that pickled eels and roast fowls were served for dinner, and I went inside.

FOUR

Kit

THE PLAGUE RETURNED.

Dark and strange it came, seeping through the ancient timbers of houses on crowded city lanes, growing in the mildew of cellars. As strange as desire it came across the foreign lands whose names I could but pronounce: through the lapping waters under high curved bridges in Venice, whispering across the Germanic towns of Heidelberg and Hamburg, and in the university and slums of Paris across the sea. For years it waited, slumbering for generations, then seeping down roads once more towards the cities, past the swords of the guards at the city gates, past the prisoners slumbering in their fetters, into the cup and dish of the merchant and his wife. First came headache and chills to a man, then aches and fever and then the black, swollen spots upon the body. No cure was known; we heard the plague carts. Hundreds died, thousands. Samuel Pavey, who had played the old men in Blackfriars with me, was taken suddenly. He had been but eleven years old. Weekly were posted the listings by parish of those stricken, and on Candlemas Day the theaters closed once more.

Evening had fallen and I lay alone in my garret room in the house of my new master, John Heminges, indifferent to the rising voices below. Black it was outside the small glass panes of the window and already the night watchman had passed, calling: "Eight o'clock, good people! Mind your candles and your fires!" And then his harsh clanging bell, which brought to mind a scolding woman. I wondered what kept the actors in the kitchen so late when it was unwise to travel through the streets once night had come, even though they all lived not half an hour away.

Turning on the ungiving straw mat, I stared up at the rough beams of the ceiling. There was nothing in the garret but several iron-bound trunks with shabby costumes, and a pile of mildewed books next to the bags of onions and last fall's apples, and another low bed for my master's apprentice John Rice, who had just turned seventeen. I wanted to ignore the smell of hot spiced wine that rose from the kitchen below and the laughter of the men and of Heminges's two younger children, who undoubtedly bounced on his knee or played by his feet or under the trestles of the table.

Two weeks I had lived with this family, steadfastly maintaining my solitude. It was difficult, not because of John Heminges, whose thoughtful, stolid manner was not to my liking (I was an adventurer to my mind, and he the sort of hesitant man who thinks each step over for an hour or more), but because of his young wife, Rebecca. She had asked me after our first supper (during which I had said no word), "Are you sorry to find yourself once more amongst strangers, Nicholas?" Her voice, low and mellow, threatened to make me soft.

Coldly I replied, "It matters not to me, mistress."

"Such a lovely face you have! Full of private thoughts! Your mother must have treasured you so!"

How could I tell her that every kindness hurt me? At last I leapt up and walked about the garden with its narrow brick paths between the dead vegetable beds. She rubbed my long hair with bay oil against lice, handling me with the firm good nature of a woman ready to accept a recalcitrant, emotional boy. Loyalty forbade me to love her, and I resolved to like neither of them.

Worlds lay between myself and the actors who sat below on the hard bench, drinking spiced wine. "Join us, Nicholas," my master had said, but I shook my head, taking my rushlight upstairs, where all evening I had pored through the musty books, wrapped in my quilt against the cold. Among them were some dull plays written to the rules of classical tragedy, a prayer book, and a medical book, which disturbed me for no place in the human anatomy could I find the soul. From below Tom Pope's booming voice shouted, "What shall we do, John, but pack the wagons to tour with Ned Alleyn! God knoweth if the plague keeps longer in the city, we'll starve like the bastards that lie in Newgate cages."

I couldn't help but be drawn to this fat man Pope, though he rebuked me in greeting each time he met me, and thrust me rudely by the shoulders during my first fencing lesson. "Art obedient, bully wag?" he said, and never waited for the answer. Just under six feet he was, with shoulders and belly almost as broad, solidly unsanctimonious, pleasantly insulting; he played every fool and lecher in the repertoire and it was said he but played himself. The very boards of the unstable theater platforms which thrust into the audience creaked when he, three hundred fifty pound were he an ounce, tumbled with the clowns, balancing on his large thick feet. I had been briefly introduced to the other players of Lord Strange's Men as well, holding out my hand as it seemed was expected of me, though their names and faces hardly came together in my memory. There was, I thought, Henry Condell, far slighter and more methodical, a longtime friend of my new master and also of this parish, and handsome Augustine Phillips, who came one evening to play sackbutt and viol. Of Will Shagspere, who lived in lodgings on Bishopsgate Road, I knew nothing. Most of the men had houses in the theater district of Shoreditch, where they raised children and grew lettuces in their brick-enclosed garden beds. Listening to their voices, I was tempted to descend the ladder, my back warmed by the ashes of the fire and my stomach by their wine, but I muttered, "No." Morley had not come and I was unwilling to trust anyone else. There was folly to say that a man controlled his own destiny when he couldn't control the yearnings of his heart, and, remembering his black doublet with the missing buttons and soft, roughly cut hair, I shuddered. Loneliness overcame me, and to escape its aching, I threw off the quilt and descended the narrow steep steps.

Only my master and Will Shagspere remained in the warm kitchen by the fire. Sinking down with my back against the brick bake oven, I studied this actor curiously. I had read his playscripts of *Henry VI* stamped with the Master of the Revels' approval and next to Morley's work found them mediocre, though I had a grudging respect for any man who could put two lines of blank verse together. I fretted that, though I could memorize anything, I had little originality to write, and so I watched him, sensing the closeness between him and my master, and wondering how he made up the things he did and formed the thoughts into verse.

Some men called him handsome: I would not. About medium height and with the concentrated, inclined head and rounded shoulders of the scholar and hair already thinning, he seemed not city-born, but slightly trapped by the small niceties of civilization about him. His clothes were a little shabby; however, when he sat back, I noted his breastbone was high and beautiful like a deer's, and suddenly he shook his head and laughed and became another man. Then he glittered. His eyes were the small, steady ones of a man who calmly plans his life, but his lower lip showed he could be impulsive to his own cost.

John Heminges said, "There's no help for it, Will! Pack thy quills and foolscap, 'tis time to tour again."

"Aye, it needs be."

"We can't take all: nay, but six men and four boys. There's a few old plays I'd like to rework and cut for the doubling of parts. Canst do it?"

"As always."

What roles would they give to me? I couldn't imagine.

My master said boyishly, "It came to me tonight, marry! There's something solid about the lot of us. Christ's wounds, it seemeth only a short time since Pope returned from Denmark and we first played together. We pawned our rings to pay for the velvets, it rained and naught but twenty folk paid their pennies to hear us. 'Twas some months before thou camst to London, stubborn blessed innocents that we were. But we're coming into a company, methinks. Aye, we might do well if we can bring in enough coins. Condell talks of returning to the tailor's trade: it troubles me."

Shagspere stretched; his arms, as he moved them, had a quiet strength in them, although his cuffs were shabby. "The Lord knoweth," he sighed. "The Lord knoweth I can't fault him for it, John! 'Tis a devilish unreliable way to pay for a family's keep, this playgiving. I am eight and twenty years, and show no signs of fortune, as my wife hath so oft reminded me."

"Hast done with the new poem?"

"Nearly. I try to rush invention to sell it sooner."

"What subject hast chosen?"

"Venus: a pretty thing, where the man's unwilling. I remember my countryside when I write it."

"Men are seldom unwilling. A love poem, is it?"

"Of a sort."

"I warrant ye put no stock in love."

"Why, I'm as hopeful as the next man, John!"

"Who holds thy liking these days?"

"No one: I'm far too poor to be looked kindly upon. I'll ask the printer for as much money as he's willing to give. No, I'll ask him for more. God wot I need it badly."

"Needst thou a patron?"

"Every writer in London hopes for the same."

"Hast spoken aught to the young Earl of Southampton, the Lord Chancellor's ward?"

"Other poets seek his patronage, some far better than I. Thou knowst well of whom I speak."

Warmed by the fire, I closed my eyes for a second and listened to the sounds of the house. From the bedroom above came the creaking of a babe's cradle, and Rebecca Heminges's low voice singing a song I could not make out. I was half asleep; the men seemed to float before me, and the single gold earring which Shagspere wore glittered in the dull light of the fire. Had they meant Morley? Aye, it was certain to me, but I would not speak his name, so private was it to all my longing.

Passing the mug that had heated in the cinders between them, my master asked, "Hast regret that thou left Warwickshire behind?"

"Seldom and then only for . . . thou knowst."

"I know it well. How is it with thy wife?"

"My father hath writ the children are well."

"She sends no word herself?"

"Nay, she's too angry since I've come to London. I ought to walk home and see the children now we have so little work. I think on them a dozen times each day."

"Then go."

"I dread her angry tongue. You were fortunate in thy marriage, John. When you chose to leave the grocer's trade, she said aye and willingly." The thought seemed to bring the need to move, and as the watch cried nine o'clock, he carefully shook out his cloak and flung it around him. "Go with him, Nicholas," said my master, "and light his way. Take thy dagger and keep thy eye sharp for cutpurses."

We moved along the narrow streets, passing houses whose second and third stories overhung the cobbled streets so closely that they almost touched across the way. From Aldermanbury near the church came the splashing of the fountain. Then, passing the sinister shadow of the whipping post in the churchyard, I touched my dagger's hilt, almost hoping we would be set upon by robbers for the adventure of it. Shagspere limped slightly; it seemed odd that an actor should limp, but then I had heard he played nothing but loquacious old men, ghosts, and deposed kings. Now he looked at me carefully as if he had just noticed my existence and were turning me over in his mind. "Does it suit thee to be an actor, Nick?" he asked.

Above our heads swayed the signs of tavern and tailor, gently clanking against the houses. Looking down the shadows of Ironmongers' Lane, I muttered, "Rather I'd be a gentleman."

"That would I also, but fate hasn't made it so. Likst thou London?"

"I cannot tell."

"My son speaks constantly of it."

"Does he wait up for you at your lodgings, master?"

"Nay, he lives in Stratford; I see him seldom."

The conversation in the kitchen became clearer; I had been privy to some partially expressed sorrow, some complication which I could not quite understand. If my father had lived, he would not ever have been a hundred mile from home. I accompanied Will Shagspere as far as Bishopsgate as I'd been bid and lit his torch with my own, then stood watching him turn down the silent street, a quiet man of middling height whose balding forehead made him seem older than his twenty-eight years and who appeared more a scholar than a player. An actor, I conjectured, should be more gallant, and yet I was curiously drawn to him and wished we had had longer to speak. When I went home my mistress kissed my cheek and sent me up to bed.

Weeks passed, and as the Master of the Revels forbade the reopening of the public theaters because of the plague that yet ravaged and pillaged the crowded city, we prepared to tour the countryside with Ned Alleyn under the protection of Lord Strange. John Heminges had begun to train me at once. I was bound till the age of twenty-one, that being three years younger than in the other guilds, and until I left my apprentice days behind or grew to unreasonable size, I would be expected to portray a woman. We began lessons in movement, deportment, and dancing, and sometimes, in the early mornings, Tom Pope walked across the bridge and took me and two other apprentices to the deserted Rose to instruct us in fencing and tumbling on the platform in the middle of the courtyard. I climbed to the hut to see how the flying mechanism worked and found that mice had come to live in it and had nibbled one wool cloak.

We spread poison against them and listed the costuming we would need to take with us on the tour, and I pulled on white velvet doublets and gold-striped breeches and wished I had a reflecting glass.

My chambermate, the young actor John Rice, who was eighteen and known for his female roles, offered to coach me. "For when I'm taken on as sharer and play men's parts, thou shalt have mine." He explained patiently the economic structure of the company and how each man was responsible for expenses and in turn given his due portion of the profit. I made no answer. I did not expect to remain an actor, nor did I intend to stay.

Wood Street wound down to Lothbury and then to broad, noisy Cheapside, the central thoroughfare of the city, upon which passed processions of both royalty and condemned men. Here one could find more taverns than a man could get drunk in from Michaelmas to Trinity. Through our ward could be heard the same Bow Bells which bade the young runaway Dick Whittington centuries before to turn back, turn back and become thrice Lord Mayor of London; here also ran the sweetest water from two conduits collected by the carriers to sell throughout the city. Walking east towards Aldgate one came to Cornhill and the Royal Exchange.

This assortment of merchants was to my mind of all buildings in the city most fantastical. Its founder was Sir Thomas Gresham, a goldsmith and banker from Lombard Street. Behind the arched entrance, the tall Corinthian pillar topped by a golden grasshopper of immense proportions, stood an arched walk within a quadrangle containing hundreds of shops, and there had I been sent on some humble errand one March morning. Music filled the Exchange, for the city waits had set up their instruments of tenor and base viol, krumhorn, recorder, and lute and were sounding gigs and gavottes to the gathering crowd. So interested was that I almost failed to notice the man who hastened down the steps from the shoemaker's shop, and turned under the arched walk towards Cornhill.

Then almost tumbling into the band itself, I fled behind the flapping cloak I knew well, turning him, shouting with a full throat, "Kit! Comst thou!"

"Nick!" he murmured. "Thou young jackanapes! What are they making of thee? Ah, shalt be a tall and beautiful fellow one day if shalt live long, though that I doubt."

Throwing myself against him, my hand gathered what I could of his doublet, rubbing my face against the shoulder. "My cutpurse," he said, pushing me from him and cuffing me lightly. "Doth the actor's life suit thee?"

"Nothing suits me, Morley but to be with thee!"

"Thou comst at the odd hour, Nick Cooke," was his indifferent reply. " 'Tis almost midday and I wait upon my lord of Southampton. I must be gone."

Several women, finding we had blocked the milliner's door, nudged by us resentfully; he thrust his arm about my shoulder and pulled me some feet further before the confectioner's shop. "When wilt come for me again?" I murmured. "Then the world can be damned and I care not."

"Oh 'tis so?"

"Tis, Morley!"

He looked at me for a long time and then cried suddenly, "Then damn the world for I've missed thee sorely! Come thou with me. I go to Southampton's and thou shalt attend me."

Joyfully I answered, "Then I shall come, only I must first run home to ask permission."

He threw back his head. "Wouldst *ask*? God's wounds, they have ruined thee already! Thinkst I to go about with a lad who must run like a twittering girl to *ask* if he may and he might? Art not the free lad I thought thee. Those many weeks I mistook thee, Nick!"

We had already passed under the entrance arch, people rushing through, and horses, coaches, wagons, draymen, and sedan chairs from Threadneedle and Lombard Streets all about us. As he strode up Cheapside, I caught his sleeve and cried, "I'll come! I care not two pins for them, thou knowst!"

He turned to look into my panting face, reached out, and smoothed back my long hair. "Walk with me, Nicholas Cooke," he said, and taking my hand in his, kissed the edges of my rough-cut nails until I flushed close to tears in pleasure.

Down sidestreets and alleys we went, the two of us together, strangers stopping us now and then, for many people seemed to know him, and while he was drawn aside once under a feather merchant's sign, I pawed the ground with my boot in jealousy and love. Past the burnt spire of St. Paul's went we with more rapidity, beggars huddled by the gates of the churchyard, their ragged sleeves clasped over their heads, the air rotten about them. Coldly he glanced at them, for he was revolted by ugliness. It occurred that soon I should lose my charm and he might find me ugly as well. Seizing his hand as we rushed through the booksellers of the yard, I demanded, "Tell me, Kit, where you go!"

Glancing at a volume and hurling it down again, he answered, "On whatever I'm paid to do."

"But what are you paid for?"

"Nay, it concerns thee not."

"They say thou art a spy."

"So 'tis said, among other things."

"Have you writ more? Tell me!"

"I've an unfinished poem. Don't look for me where you found me last: Kyd and I have quarreled and parted."

"The men say you're quick-tempered."

"Yes, as much as thee."

"Where do ye bide now?"

"'Tis my private matter."

"Why wilt say naught when I love thee so!" I cried, stopping before Paternoster Lane, and twisting my cap in my hands. "Why art so to me?"

Gently he took my cap and put it back on my head. "Nay, my sweet young friend," he said, "I'm troubled lately, but why I don't know. And I shall tell thee the one thing thou wouldst hear above others: they found a boy drowned in the river by Canterbury and thought the body thine. None shall follow thee anymore."

"Ah then, Morley! *Fetch me to live with thee!*"

"Nay, I'd suit thee ill!" he replied with such sharpness that I dared say no more but continued in silence beside him up the Strand until at last we came to Drury House, the London home of the Southampton family, who within three or four generations had risen to preeminence and wealth. Giving our names to the sentry, we turned down the brick path to the mansion, whose mullioned windows and clean pinkish stone reflected the late-morning sun.

The hall opened into a large room, its dark wood ceiling carved in English flowers, a chimneypiece of stone likewise sculpted. Several soft chairs were upholstered in red, and a table was set with a pair of globes, wine decanters, and bowls of strange fruit. No women were present but half a dozen young men, diffident and beautiful. They were standing about a chessboard placed in the center of the table, one leaning to one side and others facing him. Feathers drooped on their broad-brimmed velvet hats and cast shadows on the smooth cheeks.

I recognized Southampton at once.

The most sweet-faced of all with his wheat-colored hair hanging past his shoulder, he appeared to be not more than twenty years old. He remained by the window when Morley and I came in, allowing his hand to be kissed, then dropping it once more to his side. Not once did he glance at me. "Morley's here: pour him wine," he said dully, and then turning his back, again began to study the paper in his hand. The young men gathered about Kit Morley; one stared at my apprentice cap, then looked indifferently away.

I kept as close to the door as I could. The glittering Venetian glass, silver plate, and silk seat cushions seemed to dare me to approach them as if my hands were yet rubbed with the chores of players' boy. How could Morley call me beautiful when all this was past beauty: wood, marble, velvet, and silk, and myself in contrast, a boy in somber browns with rough-cut nails, watching from the shadows, a most humble one whose father had died ignobly, whose mother had known no shame.

More wine was brought, heated and spiced by the fire by a serving man, and the fragrance of tarragon and thyme rose up in the room. The voices rose, amused, over Morley's movement of the Queen upon the board. Light and frivolous, they drifted to the ceiling as I stared at the space of room between them and the young lord, who remained by the window reading the papers he held, leaning against the green velvet hangings by the small, frosted panes. Then he cried, "There's no hope for it! I will never be permitted to follow Essex. Just as when he was at Rouen I was too young to join him, he will go against Spain and I shall be left behind once more. The Queen refuses me, and I lose my youth in waiting." Crossing to the chimneypiece, he hurled the papers into the flames and stood brooding there, lashes fluttering, his long delicate arms across his chest. "They all want to marry me, as well. What should I do as a husband?"

Morley turned with a pawn in his hand, throwing it in the air and capturing it once more between his fingers. The young men fell into the upholstered chairs, drinking wine and murmuring among themselves. Morley joined them, holding his hand seductively to the rare hound, a creature of Florentine breed, who came to sniff. "You must obey her wishes, my lord," said one young man.

"I must of course!"

"Spain dares not move against us once more."

"She will, and even then our Queen will not let me go. Essex hath spoken to her for me, but he must also do as she wishes. We must all do as this aging woman with her white painted face demands! I must go to the coast and watch the ships readied for war and be sent home like a boy to bed."

"Should war come, speak to my lord Essex to petition her once more on thy behalf, for she cares for no one but him these days."

Southampton flung himself down on the last chair, and the fickle dog came to his hand. He said broodingly, "She looked at no one else when he fought in the tournament at Whitehall this season past. Hast seen it?

They say that late at night she keeps him in her room alone at cards, but none may come near. The Lord knoweth what they do."

"Nay, my lord! She is aged, he young."

"Nevertheless . . ."

Their voices dropped to whispers until Morley stretched and exclaimed with some amusement, "My good lords, the puppy listens all too hard! Come, peaspod, drink of my cup and close thine ears lest thou come to grief."

Pale with excitement, I knelt in the rushes beside him, taking the warm goblet in my icy hands. The taste of burgundy and thyme met my tongue, his casual hand lay on my hair. Knowing they watched me, I reddened and began to scratch the ears of the dog. Southampton's fingers also moved to the soft, warm neck. Flushing, I thrust my own hands between my knees that my common touch might not taint him. Too near the fire, dizzy with the scent of drying flowers and the taste of warm thyme, I struggled to understand it all. Worlds lay between all I had known and this. All here was beyond my reach, even the man I had embraced on Cheapside not two hours before.

My throat ached with confusion, and it was for this reason that for some time I did not notice that my master's friend the actor Shagspere had come in. He stood hesitantly on the edge of the room with his hands before him in his plain brown doublet, the best I think he owned, in the way a man stands when he wishes to protect himself. No more noticed was he than the soft servants who came and went, and I thought suddenly, he stands on the edge of this world as I do myself, wanting it so badly because he's only a tolerated servant and not, as he is in John Heminges's kitchen, an honored friend.

Morley said, "Shall I read to you, my lord, from a new long poem of mine?"

"For whom 'tis writ?"

"My lord, who else but to you?" Then drawing the creased pages from within his doublet, he began to recite. He had said his poems to me in the deep night, pulling me to his will. That familiar low voice (the soft bass of it) murmured past me to the candlelit, paneled room. Most sensual were the verses. I glanced at Southampton, who was contemplative, frowning and chaste as a young priest, yet towards the end his lips parted and he smiled.

There was silence in the room when Morley finished. Shagspere had not moved. The young Earl stood up abruptly. "I soon tire of love," he said. " 'Tis a game and nothing more. Write of warriors. Thy *Tamburlaine* is more to my fancy! Take the lute, boy and give us a song."

"He knoweth naught but love songs and singeth them in endless repetition."

A lute of inlaid wood lay on the table; I took it up, feeling them look at me. The top string would not be brought to pitch, and my unsteady treble quivered to the room.

> "Fortune my foe, why dost thou frown on me,
> And wilt thy favors never greater be?
> Wilt thou I say forever cause me pain
> And wilt thou ne'er restore my joys again?"

Southampton's curious blue eyes were upon me. It was an angular face with no trace of beard as yet. I remembered someone had told me he had just come from Cambridge the year before and was now studying law at Gray's Inn. His mother, the Lady Southampton, was irked that he would not marry, and the Queen kept him from war. Between the two of them, he lingered before his life.

He said suddenly, "This boy sings worse than your last, Morley, though his eyes are beautiful. Where did you find him?"

"I needn't find him: he finds me."

"Then you don't keep him?"

"No: he's apprenticed to a respectable player who'll tame his wild ways soon enough. He shall be as dull as any merchant come this time next year. Sing, Nicholas! Why do you stop?"

My voice had died away to nothing, and I forced myself to begin once more, though my intonation was breathy and all seven courses of the lute had suddenly gone from tune.

> "Fortune has caused me grief and great annoy
> Fortune has cruelly stolen my love away.
> My love and joy whose love hath made me glad
> Some great misfortune never young man had!"

My voice broke, and the young Earl said sharply without turning, "You sing poorly, and the lute's in six keys at once. Give over, boy, and be silent."

I laid the instrument aside and would have gone back to the door, but Morley pulled me to him absently and stroked my hair. I tried to turn his palm to look at it, but the afternoon was drawing to a close and the room quite dim. They began to speak of poetry, of comets and planets and how one could read the will of the stars in a crystal glass. They spoke of the four humours of the body and the black biles which made one melancholic and brought unremitting sadness. For a long time they spoke of melancholy, and I felt as if they spoke to me and dared not show my face. Outside the mullioned windows I could see the pale lavender of early twilight and the glittery frost of February.

"Shagspere!" cried my lord suddenly, turning to face my master's friend. "How long hast stood there unattended? Did no one offer thee wine?" He had leapt up, extending his hand, apologetically.

Will Shagspere stepped simply, graciously, to meet him. "Dear my lord, I had no thirst."

"I saw you not."

"You sent for me."

"Thursday after dinner."

" 'Tis Thursday, and past dinner, my lord. Supper shall be called soon."

"Ah, the fault's mine!" Suddenly courteous, young and embarrassed, the Earl of Southampton looked about for an empty goblet to fill. "You must drink! What sayst thou? 'Tis almost supper and I'm expected elsewhere and we've no time to speak. Tell me briefly of thee. This cursed plague continues. Will your men tour the provinces once more?"

"Aye, we must."

" 'Tis a hard life."

Shagspere smiled slightly, and the young man demanded, "You'll send me more verses? I liked the last sonnets exceedingly."

"Your generosity overwhelms me."

"I shall miss thy company."

"Less, my lord, than I shall miss thine."

"Had I but seen thee I should not have let thee stand there unwelcomed."

"Your thoughtfulness honors me."

"It was thoughtfulness come lately!"

"Nay, it matters not, dear my lord."

Gratified and released, Southampton gave Shagspere his long, pale hand but motioned him up embarrassed when he would have kissed it. "It groweth late," he said. "Supper's come: my lady mother expects me. My steward will give you a torch to see your way."

Morley turned to me then, his eyes shining with wine. "Go thou with him, Nicholas," he said casually. Nor did he look at me again, though I turned to gaze at him once more before leaving the handsome room.

Shagspere and I descended the stairs and walked out past the gate: behind us the house shone faintly with candlelight, and music for supper had just begun. Torches held before us, we continued carefully past muck piles and through the fields. I sensed the vague depression of the man beside me, and it added to my own unhappiness. After a time he murmured, "Are you so very sad also, my young friend? Why should love cause such heartbreak? We're better without it, wag."

In the shadowy streets and under the overhang of the upper floors of the half-timbered houses as we walked towards the city gates, he took my hand in his. "Aye," he said in a soft and deep voice, chafing my cold fingers in the consoling way that a father might, "we're better with friendship alone, far better."

I was puzzled. "Why master, dost love?"

"Aye, to my cost." Suddenly he hurled down his torch in the mud, where it seeped into the wetness, and he stamped the flame and left me standing there with my pulse rushing, astonished. Then he remarked sadly, "This hath earned me naught. We must go by thy light alone, young one."

I nodded respectfully, and we walked on in silence. Then, we turned down Wood Street in Aldermanbury and beheld the faint glimmer of the single wick light that hung neatly in the horn lantern before our door, I hesitated.

"What is it, boy?"

I muttered, "Naught, only that my master will punish me for being away this day without his leave, and I can't bear it tonight, I can't."

"Nay," he said. We saw the firelight through the small lead-framed window of the front room, and we bent our heads to enter. "John!" he called. "What, hast supped? I borrowed the lad without thy leave. Don't fault him for it."

"Marry," cried John Heminges, "I have looked for him these many hours! Where didst take him?"

"My lord of Southampton's."

"Ah, Will! I have thought better of thy trafficking with him! He's more loyal to young Essex than the Queen, and it likes me not." Then, noticing that I listened, he told me I might go to my room, and I ran upstairs to shiver under my quilt, allowing hurtful tears of jealousy to wet the feather pillow. In between was the wonder at Shagspere's having told a lie for my sake, and I liked him the better for it even though I thought he was overrated as a poet and could no way compare to Morley.

I had never lived in a proper house before where food was set at just the expected hour, and clean shirts dried for me by the fire every Monday morning and my hose mended. Since my italic hand was fine, my master set me to recopying old scripts to save a scrivener's fee, and sometimes I sat for hours at the kitchen table, I writing and Rebecca Heminges kneading out dough for bread. I liked to watch her round, supple arms rolling out pie crusts, and in profile, her large belly. Once she laughed and said, "Feel how it kicks, Nicholas!" but I pulled my hand away as if she had burned it. Later I hurried to St. Paul's and spent my only penny on a long ballad for her to show her I was sorry. She said, "Wilt sing it, Nick?" and I fetched my master's lute and sang it, and after a while she made a pretty harmony with her soft alto voice.

"Oh why do you keep from us so?" she murmured.

In the late winter we made final arrangements to depart on the tour that was to take us to Cambridge and then down the towns of the coast, where there were guildhalls and inns fit to mount a play and a city council willing to have us perform before them. We were to take two wagons with the props and costumes thickly laid in ironbound trunks, a few extra horses, and two hired men plus the six actors and four 'prentice boys, including my master's well-trained John and me. I folded the heavy fur-trimmed robes of kings and archbishops in lavender leaves, the mitres, crowns, and severed heads in trunks and baskets, and the men sang as we worked:

> "Hey Robin, jolly Robin,
> Tell me how thy leman doth
> And thou shalt know of mine. . . ."

Still at night we could hear the carts over the cobbled streets and the awful cry "Bring out your dead." Then I shivered for my mother and the touch of Kit's warm belly and his arm flung over me in sleep. Though I looked often from my window to see the girl in the house across the way washing in her white smock, dreaming of her swelling breasts, I still longed for him. Still I could not bring myself to seek him out. He did not want me and it was something I could not bear to know, and so I bore my grief in silence.

We departed the city on a chill winter day in our carts and horses, the women and children blowing us kisses and pressing hot pies and potatoes into our hands to warm them. There being not enough rides to go around, Shagspere said he would walk, and I strolled gladly beside him and thus we passed through the wide portcullis of Cripplegate, the old people from the almshouse by the wall come out to wish us well. Seeing him deep in thought, I asked, "Do you think of poetry, sir?"

He smiled. "No, of my son."

We left the wide foul ditch outside the wall and the city of London itself behind us, grey and brown against the smoky white winter sky, and turned up the road towards Cambridge. Proceeding by foot and wagon, we were slowed for some hours by the front left wheel breaking off in a deep rut, to the mending of which I gave no advice, for fear of betraying my training. Fields just dusted with green above the brown earth reminded me of my childhood in the farms out of Canterbury when we strolled out to find fresh milk. With dulling frequency the lauded London Company of Lord Strange trod past uncountable numbers of sunken muddy villages, thatched roofs rotting, squat old churches with neither bell nor steeple, graveyards rift with broken stones whose names had worn away. Holding to the side of our cart, I beheld the poverty and ignorance through critical eyes and longed for cities and universities, for men who talked of science, who went not to bed but watched the stars. Carefully ushering the aging cart down muddy roads, across groaning bridges, and now and then over ancient stones which thirteen hundred years before the Romans had laid, I moved towards the city of Cambridge whose university was yet my dream.

Hertford we passed, and Stevenage. For one afternoon the sky blackened, and we trudged soaked to our skins, shivering, with Condell muttering that a tailor's humble shop must be better than this, boys. The first night we took our rest in an inn, where we tried to dry our clothing by small fires, but the second bedded down in the damp fields, quilting about us, so that our limbs ached when the pale cold sun came to greet us. Food we ate from packets provided by the women, and the smallest boy, Wat Herrick, who was Tom Pope's favorite, perched on the cart with his lute and sang to cheer us. We had made to play in the Bull and Bear, a fine inn on the Cambridge Road, but the town council had decided against us, so we left after some hot words. A poorer inn we found in which to spend the night, the bed so occupied with lice that I was unwilling to share it and rolled myself in a cloak on the floor. Several times we had to show by our papers that we were honest men from London, under the protection of Lord Strange. Masterless men were not looked kindly upon.

In Royston we played twice, then packed quickly to make the next town by bedtime. As we approached it two old men, hearing our heavy carts and slow weary steps, emerged from their cottage doors. "Be ye peddlers?"

"Nay, players," said John Heminges.

"Players!" said one. "I saw players once. *Abraham and Isaac* by the bakers' guild, with old Marty Squire hardly a tooth in his head playing the angel. Aye! That was rare theater. What play ye? *Judith's Revenge,* mayhap, a goodly play."

"Marry no," answered my master cordially. "We play *Harry Sixth* in three parts."

"A religious play be it?"

"Nay, one of true history."

"Hmm: who hath writ the same?"

"Why that goodman there who walks with the pack, gentle Shagspere our fellow."

"Him that limpeth? Never heard his name. *Abraham and Isaac* was a good play, master! My daughter wept mightily."

Twice we played next day to little profit, for someone said we might have brought the plague, and in the morn departed. In the cold wet light of an English dawn, we saw what had once been a black-clad priest hanging from the gallows. The light rain had weighed his clothes, and on his shoulder a crow perched: the creature turned his black eyes to watch us go. Young Wat slipped his delicate hand in that of his master.

"A poor bastard Catholic," muttered Tom Pope. "Strung him up on a charge of conspiracy. I saw the bill posted at the inn. Curse any man who thinks one fellow's conception of God is right and the other's wrong. Can finite comprehend infinite? Sons of pigs." He spat several times on the ground. "I'll tell you, boys," he said as we walked by the wagon. "There's those that say Our Lord blew His nose in a kerchief and others that say He used His sleeve like an honest tradesman, and from this comes all the division. A hundred men have their own way to worship, and each swears by his salvation that he's right. Now as for me I hold no truck with prejudice against any man's beliefs. The only pisspot fools I can't abide are the separatists. Why, some years ago when first I came to London they were for forbidding honest bearbaiting and pleasure gardens on a Sunday, but the Queen wouldn't sign. Why, they'd forbid playgoing in London at all, these Puritans, an they could!"

I cannot remember what else he said, for as we came to a clearing, the university city of Cambridge with its lacy stone towers of King's College Chapel rose before us, the golden sun descending behind them, and my heart beat with love.

At dawn we rose to put up our stage. In the innyard children sprawled about us, plucking the fur edging of a royal gown, darting between us to dig into the prop box and exclaim on what we had brought. Our host came out on his way to see to the horses. "What play bring you, masters?"

"*Harry Sixth.*"

"By sweet Lyly?"

"Nay, Will Shagspere of Warwickshire, a bully lad."

"Ah, all these young university wits think they can write plays!"

I wandered across the town, having gathered scant leafy branches for our forest scenes, peering into the gates of the college quadrangles over which young gowned scholars walked. Tiny windowpanes glittered in the sun, and the boys were meandering towards service. I climbed one of the church towers overlooking the valley, holding my branches and gazing out through the leaves, and then stood for a time in King's College

Chapel, whose beauty of architecture moved me very much.

We dined at eleven and played at two, my first role being that of a tree: rather to say I held my branches, concealing my humanity, and represented a battlefield near a forest. Talbot, Earl of Shrewsbury, had just come when from the audience came the cry of "Pickpocket, pickpocket!" Some scrawny fellow was being shoved and beaten and subsequently hurled from the yard. Phillip's eyes flickered, but he never ceased his noble speech, though some of the words were lost over the grunts and blows and whining of the miscreant, and the subsequent crash of body to the dirt yard beyond.

Talbot breathed his last with his dead son in his arms and the crowd wept: unashamedly they groaned, and I envied the actors and wished the part were mine to create such emotion. When I ran back for Evensong at King's College, it was already done, and the chapel shut up for the night.

They gave me the smallest parts to play, both boys and women. At night I slept by John Heminges's side, moving to the edge to avoid his touch, for no one had a bed to himself in an inn. One morning as we rose and packed, and I as usual not willing to look at him, he put his hand on my shoulder. "Condell was a fair tailor," he said, "and hath told me no boy stitches worse than thee, Nick Cooke. Could not have apprenticed two hours and do so badly!"

"I have forgot my trade."

"We have inquired of thy apprenticeship and found no papers."

I turned away my face, but he held me and said, "What's the truth, wag? Canst not trust me?"

The words stuck to my throat and I couldn't answer. He hesitated, his hand feeling my shoulder as if trying to understand me, and in that moment I knew he deliberated between keeping me and sending me off. Even then I felt his unbearable, burdenable kindness. He said, troubled, "We shall see, Nick, we shall see."

Later I found he had repaid the Blackfriars men for the dress that I had ruined in the rain, and still I withheld myself from him. We toured for some weeks, and I added soldiers and ladies to my repertoire. Heminges wrote home, asking me if I wished to enclose a letter of my own, but I said no. At one of the inns I was successful for the first time with a woman, but it was over in a few minutes and left me disappointed. I gave her the copper coins I had, and she cursed at me and said it was not enough. I did not want to tell anyone about it; I had spoken not more than a few words to a soul all the time, and when we returned it was full spring.

The air was fresh and the banks of the Thames green and full of flowers, and I picked the earliest daffodils and brought them back for Mistress Heminges. I was weary of the salted meat and fish of winter and hungry for fresh vegetables, which they said kept scurvy away and made a man's teeth strong: mine were white and I rubbed them with a toothcloth and honey every night. Though the plague carts had come and up to a thousand a week had died, we had washed our doors with fresh water each day and laid them with rosemary and had been spared. May Day came and the other apprentice boys took me to the forest at dawn to gather branches and flowers, the girls following to wash in the streams so that they would always be beautiful.

In the middle of May my master, sitting gravely among us at supper, related that the playwriter Thomas Kyd had been arrested on suspicion of heresy, that his chamber had been searched and blasphemous papers found, and that he had been put to the torture. I put down my knife and fell silent. My master said, "The papers they found were Morley's. They question the equal divinity of Jesus."

"What hath Kyd said of him?" asked my mistress.

"Much more than is needed to condemn. They've sent for Morley as well."

"Will they torture him?"

"Mayhap."

I jumped up to walk the narrow brick paths of the garden between the potted flowers and the knotted herbal bed. Unbearable was the thought that Kit Morley, whose body seemed an extension of my own and whose mind was valuable above all on earth to me, should suffer pain. Now I erased, in my loyalty, the things he had said to hurt me and remembered only how I was drawn to him, more than to any man on this earth. Not believing that God would help him, I invoked the Devil, using lard to make the circle as I remembered it on my floor in the middle of the night, and lighting the candle. Not knowing how to pray to demons, I ended up praying on my knees as devoutly as I prayed in church. I whispered, "Take my soul but don't let them hurt Kit Morley." Afterwards I rubbed the lard into the floor so that the circle wouldn't show and condemn me, and crawled into my icy bed, expecting the Devil to rise in the middle of the night and take me away. I awoke yelling in fear and knew the hand on my shoulder was my master's. "What means this?" he muttered. "Nick, thou wilt bring the watch."

On the morning Morley was to be questioned, I fenced so badly that I scratched my opponent and was sent to observe. We were still in the empty theater when one of the boys brought word that he had been released again untouched and had gone away from the city, the boy knew not where. My fear for him made my heart ache: I felt half sick with it and could neither eat nor talk civilly with anyone at the supper table. Though my fancy was full of women, I loved him still. I loved him past any carnal embrace, with a pure flame that seared me. "Mayhap his patron hath protected him," my master said, but I knew only one thing. He would no more come for me.

Early in June when I came home from an errand to the Master of the Revels, I found all of our men gathered in the garden. Tom Pope took me by the arm gently (he did not pinch me that day) and said, "My young friend, it grieves me to tell thee. Kit Morley's been killed in a tavern fight in Deptford, stabbed above the eye two days since. He died at once."

I turned and ran from the garden, ignoring my master's call. The boatman would not at first allow me on the ferry at Bridge Steps for Deptford, for I had no money, but for my collar I persuaded him. The tide was rugged and shook the pain from side to side of my belly.

They had buried my friend already in the churchyard, the earth loose on his grave. I knelt and rubbed my face in it as I had against his shoulder when he was warm and alive, and filled my hands with it because I couldn't fill them with his dirty brown hair. The long afternoon began to close with the changing of the sky above the new trees, and yet I would not go away. In doing so, I should lose him forever.

Towards twilight I heard footsteps up the path. They hesitated at the graveyard wall, and I turned my face to which the moist dirt still clung, hardly caring who had stopped there. My mistress, Rebecca Heminges, stood by the wall, her cloak covering her head. She said coaxingly, "Nicholas, come away."

I only shook my head.

"You mustn't grieve longer, for he's safe with God."

"No, he is part of the stars now," I cried fiercely, "for none of the heavens could ever hold him. . . . Not this city, nor these theaters, nor me could ever ever contain him! He mocked at God and yet he lived! God didn't want him any more than He's wanted me! We were the same, just the same! And all my life I'll never love anyone like him!"

She held her hands out to me. "Nicholas, why do you say such things? Where do these passions come from? Turn home with me, dear heart. We've come for you."

I could say no more. At last I rose and dusted my knees, but I would not sit beside her or her servant in the ferry, not bearing to be touched in any way. I only repeated silently again and again, whosoever hath done this, believe me shall pay and shall face my retribution as certain as I live. Oh, do not think I shall ever forget thee, Kit Morley.

FIVE

Newington Butts

I CAME TO KNOW THE STREETS OF OUR PARISH WELL, AND BESIDES THAT much of London, which drew me with fervid curiosity. I explored the alleys, stables, and buttery shops. There were one hundred and nine parishes in London then; ours was St. Mary Aldermanbury, but Shagspere lived not a mile away on Bishopsgate Road. Dick Burbage, who had played some of our protagonists since Ned Alleyn returned to the Lord Admiral's Men, lived slightly farther above us in the parish of St. Leonard's, where the stocks and whipping post in the pleasant garden reminded me of what retribution I might have faced had I remained a thief. Beyond were the fields and the theater: if you walked down Bishopsgate you eventually came to the Thames, and must either ferry for a penny to the south side where the Rose Theater and the brothel district lay, or jostle across the crowded, house-lined bridge to reach Southwark, where Tom Pope and his brood of happy children lived, tended by an elderly housekeeper. Excluding that, our side held all things that most compelled me: Drury and Essex House, the palace of Whitehall with its splendid tilting yard, and the medieval church of Westminster, where lay entombed the occasionally disreputable early kings. Sometimes I sat up in the hut above the stage amidst the machinery for operating lifts and lowering clouds, looked over London to the river, and felt it were all mine.

Though I had turned fourteen years in the spring, I remained small and my speaking voice light and clear. The men treated me with courtesy and teasing tenderness. Against my future, Tom Pope continued my lessons in fencing, for which I was eager, having never used a rapier and dagger, only sticks and rags in the manner of boys in the empty halls of Blackfriars and in the old cloisters of Canterbury. Between these lessons they taught me dancing, lute-playing, and tumbling. I memorized everything straightway if it pleased me and always leapt and danced when I could, and my singing voice was rich. To keep the thirteen gut strings of the lute tuned exasperated me, but the melancholy of the music suited my nature and I would take the lute to the kitchen corner and play softly to myself.

"All in a garden green, two lovers sat at ease . . ."

London was full of music: from every corner you heard it, from windows of merchants' wives to the processions on the Thames. The barber kept a lute and viol in his shop for the amusement of his customers. My master himself played several instruments.

I watched him when he did not know it. A burly, deep-voiced man, he preferred to walk slowly but could leap and jump on the stage when needed, resonant in his lines. He was a solid, reliable actor and additionally kept the books of the small troupe of six or eight men who remained under the protection of Lord Strange. I suspected he knew more of my inner thoughts than I wished, and resented it. Listening carefully to others rather than speaking a great deal himself, he considered me in silence.

So in the year I was fourteen I began to learn to be an actor. Sometimes I was six different characters altogether in one play, and brushed and cleaned costumes by smoking taperlight late in the same evening. We seldom played in London, for the plague was still about, but rode out frequently to the sweet green countryside. I liked riding in the carts with the men singing catches and rounds.

"Three merry men,
And three merry men
And three merry men are we ..."

They smiled at me the first time my singing voice broke, though I did not return the pleasantry. It was only Will Shagspere, with his quiet, reflective nature, who drew me. Sometimes he stayed late to speak with my master, and one night I awoke because the light of a taper from the kitchen shone faintly up my ladder. All was silent but for the mice under the floorboard, and when I crept down the steps to see who sat up this late hour, I was startled to find him writing at the trestle table. So rapidly and intensely he composed, not moving his eyes from the paper even to redip his pen, that he did not notice me standing there for a time. "What do you?" I said curiously.

"I stayed far too late to walk home safely, and my poems keep me from sleep."

"I would like to write, master!"

"Here are pen and foolscap."

I hesitated. "It cometh so poorly."

"Thou must work harder."

Because I could not express the impossibility of gathering my feelings into sentences, I slipped in silence into the large coffer chair in whose seat my mistress kept her sewing, and after a time my eyes closed. I must have slept for a time, for when I awoke the taper had been extinguished, though the room still smelled of warm, burning fat, and Shagspere was asleep uncovered on his side on the brick floor before the raked ashes of the hearth.

The early-fall night was damp. I tiptoed up the steps to fetch my quilt, and returning, dropped it over him as silently as I might. He never opened his eyes but muttered, "My thanks, Nicholas." When I awoke at five he had gone already about the business of his day and the ink had been corked and put away on the shelf.

My voice broke, and my body, which had been compact and graceful, was gangly: I hardly knew what to do with my legs, and though I was kissed in an alley by the ragman's wanton daughter, I lived between the excitement of my life and the pain I carried. How could I not remember Morley? We played his plays and I spoke his lines. I'd forget, and then walking down the street the anguish of it would strike me again and I'd stand not knowing where nor who I was, only that I missed him so. Cruelest was that the world went on in the same way: the rising in the morning to warm ale and toast, and at night the watchman calling, "Good people, bolt your doors and see to your candles and fires!" We kept a leather bucket and a large fishhook for pulling down houses in case of fire, always a danger in a city full of thatch and timber. The world went on. I grew a few inches and refused to cut my hair, binding it back with a bit of cloth when it caught in my way. "Nick shalt prove a tall fellow," said my mistress. And so I continued my playing of damsels, servants, elves, boys, and fools.

Besides the men there were five other indentured boys who were hired by the company at sixpence a day to play women, as were John Rice and myself. He was still small, though he was eighteen, four years older than I, and while I was given damsels, fools, and servants at the gate, he played the leading parts, and my master was paid by the company at a higher rate for his services than mine commanded.

I had to be first and best in those days, for it was my suspicion that I did not really belong with the players, and one day they should know it as well. I had come late to the profession (most boys were apprenticed by eleven) and lurked about the edge of my lack of confidence. That I should play the smaller parts and John Rice be given the very best speeches irked me past bearing, and there was no opportunity I did not take to shower my scorn and vindictiveness on him. Slow and unimaginative and of a monkish nature, he did not know how to respond and only muttered, turning his expressive, strong shoulders on me.

We were playing for a time at the Newington Butts Theater in the fall after Kit Morley had died, and hard pressed the eight men of the company were, for money was scarce, the competition keen, and we never knew how many weeks we'd be allowed to work at our craft before the plague warnings forbade public gatherings once more. The second play given was *Titus Andronicus,* a popular tragedy well packed with rape, murder, and severed limbs; it was Shagspere's perfunctory reworking of a much older tragedy that we brought out whenever we wished to draw a crowd. At the penultimate moment of the drama, Lavinia staggers before the audience, "her hands cut off, and her tongue cut out, and ravished," carrying between the stumps of her wrists a basin to receive the blood of the soon-to-be assassinated sons of the Gothic Queen. John Rice was Lavinia, Heminges her father, the noble Roman general Titus, and I a wide assembly of insignificant female attendants and soldiers with not five words between them.

I had dressed in my shabby brown frock, and in the long interval towards the end of the tragedy when we were not needed upon the stage, followed John to the field behind the theater, teasing and tormenting. He, in contrast, was adorned in peascod-green satin, two fine bloody stumps over his hands, and infuriating it was to know how the audience awaited his next entrance and how indifferent it was to mine. "They gave you the part because you're the older," I said, "but I'm the better actor and thou knowst it."

"Nicholas Cooke, leave off," he said patiently.

"Fight me an you're not a coward, pisspot."

"Nor will I," he said, and in fury I seized him by the newly starched neck ruffs, pulled off his curly and carefully combed wig, and threw it across the grass. Anger passed over his face, and removing one gory plaster stub from his hand, he plucked the wig from the wet ground and walked ahead of me without a word. I heard Tom Pope shouting and, raising my long skirts above the moist long grasses, marched into the tiring room. The ravished Lavinia was now making her most pathetic entrance upon the stage, the bowl between her stumps. Quietly I slipped down the ladder under the platform; above me came footsteps and clear voices. Light shone through the slats of the boards as I unloosed the hinge of the trapdoor and let it down.

John Rice stood not six inches from the opening. Reaching my hand stealthily up, I seized his ankle. He knew not at first what held him, nor could the audience see my hand under his long kirtle. "Come, come, Lavinia!" roared my master to the galleries. "Look, thy foes are bound . . ."

It was a long, affecting speech, mentioning in the middle the forthcoming grinding of the bones of the villains to dust and the making from their blood a paste. Next was to come the most affecting scene of all, where the disadvantaged yet not entirely defeated Titus brings in his daughter carrying the villains now baked into a pie, that nourishment to be fed to their mother, the Gothic Queen. Now, throats of villains cut and blood neatly poured into the basin (it was sheep's blood, as I recall, and we were warned not to let it splatter about), John Heminges raised his voice and dismissed his daughter to the necessary cookery.

John Rice did not go; he could not.

Once more the noble general dismissed his ravished daughter to her piemaking ("I'll play the cook and see them ready against their mother comes"), and I held on for my jealousy. My fellow apprentice, stupefied, looked down to see what held him. He caught his breath at my mocking face, but I shook my head and held fast to his ankle. His voice rising in breaking treble, he shouted, "Damn thee for a poxy fellow! What means this prank, Nick Cooke?" And wrenching away, he dropped the basin of sheep's blood, dosing his gown, my master, and myself, who awaited below.

I tore off my skirts to the laughter of the audience and took off across the field. I had no idea where to go, and might have run as far as Graves-end before I understood that I had no destination. There was only one place I belonged, and it was long dark before I had the courage to return there.

I knew my master's anger the moment I saw his face. He stood up at once and told me to go into the garden and remove my jerkin and shirt. My knees trembling, I obeyed him, waiting by the row of empty common clay pots behind the splintering, dry house that had come to be mine.

There was a little table by the garden shed on which were laid his gardening tools for sorting, and on it the sharp knives for digging out roots, and as I stood there, my untrussed shirt in my hand, my naked shoulders shivering, and my heart beginning to beat so fast that it hurt me, I reached out my fingers until I touched one. I whispered, he shan't beat me for I'll serve him as I did the wheelwright, and the Devil take the lot of them.

Then I heard his footsteps across the rushes of the parlour towards the garden door and, biting my lip, I pushed the knife from me and threw my shirt to the ground.

Though he whipped me very hard, I never moved to stop his hand. From the house, I heard the children crying until my own tears came. I begged him to forgive me, but he shouted, "I should have known better than ever to trust thee. Seek thy own way, Nicholas, for I'll have no more of thee." Shaking me off, he strode out of the garden and down the street, not pausing to take his hat.

Dazed with the pain of my cuts, I leaned against the side of the house until my mistress coaxed me inside. Seating me at the table, she bathed my back with rosewater and a salve, but burying my head in my arms, I only murmured, "Mistress, I must go."

"Where wilt thou? Night's come."

"I must, for he's said it."

"Oh, Nicholas!" she said, weeping. "What hast done?"

It took her a long time to get me up the ladder, and there I crawled under the covers of my low bed, knowing that my world had come to an end and the fault was mine alone. It was some hours later I heard him come in, walking about the crackly rushes on the brick kitchen floor as he did when agitated, and talking as much as ever I had heard him do. Their voices lowered and she said, "Go to the boy, John."

I heard him climb the ladder and cross the bare boards of the room, sitting on the small stool that stood beside my trundle bed. He said awkwardly, "Art greatly hurt, Nick? 'Twas not my intent to cut thee so."

"Must I go from you, master?"

"Nay, I spoke in anger: 'tis forgiven."

I sprang up and buried my swollen face in his broad shoulder, and he let me cry against him. He stayed with me a long time, telling me of the difficulties in keeping an acting company together. Lord Pembroke's Men had gone bankrupt in the summer on tour and had to sell their costumes and playscripts. We had nothing but our craftsmanship and our determination. "Thou wilt make a fine actor one day, Nick," he said. "Wilt learn thy trade from me?"

"Aye," I said, and wiped my face.

After he left me I thought differently of him: there was a security in his slow-spoken ways, and I remembered how he would sit an hour at table recounting the day's expenses to find where the odd penny had gone.

I fell into a fever and was ill for several days, and the men came to see me. Tom Pope told me salacious jokes and brought me a bag of nuts, and Shagspere loaned me Holinshed's *Chronicles* with their fantastic stories of kings and plots. Dick Burbage came also for a few minutes, only because he had business nearby, but I was never comfortable with him and glad when he descended the stairs again. He was but twenty-two years old, was well situated in his theatrical family and already a leading actor.

In those days a kind of healing came over me for everything that had happened in the past year. I mourned, looking out the small window over the apple tree, for the loss of my scholarship, the death of my mother, and the murder of my friend. I mourned for my own stupidity in my months of coldness to John Heminges and my relief that he had not turned me into the streets. I prayed for forgiveness: my spite and fury undermined me. Unless I mastered and humbled myself, I should never be sent a sign by God that such and such a way had been laid for me to serve Him at last. That thought was unbearable, and I waited impatiently as one does for a letter. The occasional times when couriers were sent to Wood Street on behalf of the players' business or litigation concerning some property belonging to my mistress, my heart always throbbed and I thought, perhaps it is for me.

My master's child from his first marriage, Susan, who was about eleven years old, sometimes climbed up to sit on my bed and told me stories about elves and fairies. Once she whispered, "There are elves in the garden. Nick, I know it!" And so we took a candle at twelve of the night to look for them under the lettuce leaves. Something ran across our hands and she gasped, "Oh there's one!"

I rather thought it had been a mouse, but I said, "It must be indeed."

We felt around the well-richened earth (for my master was a fine gardener) for more, and my fingers touched hers. "It's late," I said. "We must be abed." Tiptoeing inside, we slid the iron bolt together.

I tried to make up for my indiscretion to my master in those months in every way I could, prompting forgotten lines during performance, ripping open the mattress for my mistress to search for bugs, and spreading the goose feathers in the sun to air them, cleaning his broadsword that I coveted, and recopying the prop sheets. Though he was kind to me and wary for the loss of his temper, I knew he would not hesitate to beat me twice as hard if I failed him again, and I didn't fault him for it; their rules were strict and I knew that I was lucky to have been pardoned. I wanted to be a good actor, but I knew he felt me to be erratic, and that was my failing. And yet I loved our cleanly house with the sweet smell of drying herbs and the rushes spread new four times a year across the brick of the kitchen floor.

Sometimes as we walked to the theater with the other boys, he told me of his life: how he had been a grocer and a widower, and young Rebecca Heminges the widow of an actor slain in a quarrel. "Thy mistress," he said in referring to her, and I heard the awed, simple love in his voice and wondered at it. And I could imagine him counting and weighing cloves and bay leaves and medicines (for grocers still dealt in them) as he counted out pennies and gave them to his children.

In that season, Will Shagspere turned to me in the theater and said with a slight smile, "I have a new part that will suit thee well, my young rebel."

"What can it be, sir?"

"You'll know soon enough," he replied. And it was in that way that I came to play the difficult Katharina, attired in a green velvet dress and sparring with Burbage as Petruchio. It was the important part that had been entrusted to me. My master didn't think me ready for it, but when he had read the common copy he laughed heartily, and said that it belonged to no one else. I was to be the fiery shrewish maiden who would bow down to no one, and Petruchio the man come to civilize and wed me.

Our first performance came on a warm fall afternoon. First stepped upon the boards Henry Condell to blow the horns thrice, urging the audience of several hundreds who both hung from the galleries and gathered about the foot of our stage, to give us silence to play. Then came Augustine Phillips, his intelligent dark eyes sparkling, wearing a wreath of bay to ward against lightning and thunder, and carrying the board on which was painted the title of our play, *The Taming of the Shrew*, and a second bearing the location of the action, *Padua.*

My voice was not well heard at first, and the crying for the lad to speak up, as it came from the galleries, encouraged me to shout. Satisfied, the gentry leaned upon the railings to look down at the pearls in my headdress, and the pennyknaves raised their faces to look up at the swirling hem of my skirt.

At last entered Burbage in slit scarlet sleeves and velvet, grasping my hand and saying, "Hearing thy beauty praised in all the lands, myself am moved to woo thee for my wife."

And here I struck him away, replying, "Let him that moved you hither move you hence."

We fought, and he clasped me around the waist and cried, "Will you, nill you, I will marry you . . ."

"Ah bonny Kate!" shouted some goodwife in the first gallery, standing up to wave at us.

I spit out my defiant words: my eyes flashed.

"Wanton slut!" groaned an elderly clergyman. "Let us see a happy end, let there be a happy end. Will there not be dancing? Where be the recorders, masters? I have paid three pence and want the recorders sounded!"

And then several stout merchants, very red of face, stamped their boots on the creaking boards of the highest gallery, roaring, "Silence, whoreson caterpillar! Silence for brave Dick Burbage and the lad!"

By the time came Katharina's deferential concluding speech, my voice was little more than a forced croak, and it was somewhere in the lines that read "Such duty as the subject owes the prince, Even such a woman oweth to her husband" that there came indignant cries of "Pickpocket! That one in the red cap, goodmen! Take him!" and the howling and punching and cursing as the miscreant was dragged by his heels through the dirt of the yard, wheat hair rubbed in the dust, and above this the last of my voice bellowing, ". . . place your hand beneath your husband's foot . . ." Two gallants seated on three-legged stools leaned closer to me and whistled softly, offering me sixpence for what specific favors I could not ascertain for all the shrieking of the crowd. The musicians came on then and there was dancing.

My master was waiting for me when we returned to the tiring room, and clapping his large hands solemnly, he shouted, "Well done, Nicholas, well done!"

I reddened, muttered hoarsely, and turned my head, yet more than the applause and laughter, his voice hung in my heart. John Heminges and I had come to a truce, and I respected him and loved him in sudden, unreasonable boyish devotion that I couldn't contain, though still, I knew, when he would show me a particular cut of the broadsword, I would strive to perform it differently, and as like when he would demonstrate the proper movements for a woman, I would alter it again.

Sweaty and tired, we changed our clothes. "Belike someone hath already stolen my play to print by next Sabbath," said Will. "Methought I saw two scriveners crouched over their foolscap, scratching as we spoke. Half the words they'll have as I writ them, the other they'll make up, and not one penny shall I see for any of it."

Thus we all left the theater and found our way home, my master whistling all the way and my mind filled with how I should bring the news of my success to Rebecca Heminges, and how pleased she would be.

Mornings now and then when we did not rehearse, I would stand by the door watching her sew by the hearth. These were the moments in which I found my deepest peace and they filled my heart in ways I could not understand.

"Penny for thy thoughts, Nicholas!"

"Nay, mistress." I would say, kicking the floor rushes.

She would take the book I was reading from my hands. "What lieth here?"

"Cannot read it?"

"Nay, though I can make my name."

I proposed to teach her, and she would laugh and say she had no time, but in those mornings I sat beside her and poured out my fascination for astronomy and mathematics. She listened carefully, and when her youngest child ran in, took it under her arm and nodded for me to go on.

"Had I been a man I should have studied well," she said.

When did I begin to read to her? I can't remember. Our moments left me contented, and when others came in, I escaped to my inner world. In my bed by the window overlooking the apple tree I kept my several books that I bought with pennies. Once it rained too hard, the casement leaked, and the books were partially soaked when we returned from rehearsal. It was a while before I could control my misery enough to think how to manage it, but she spread them in the sunlight the next day and though the pages had curled and some of the ink run, they were not a total loss to me.

SIX

The Lord Chamberlain's Men

I TOLD HER MANY THINGS, BUT I NEVER SPOKE OF MORLEY.

Yet I had not forgotten him. In the taverns, where we sometimes went to listen to a new play read, or to stuff ourselves with brawn and beef between performances, I learned the three men who'd been with him when he died had been found innocent and released. Morley had attacked first in his anger over the tavern bill, and all the theater world knew he was a hotheaded, impulsive man, a man you couldn't reason with, tumbling towards his own destruction. Yet nothing could persuade me three men could not disarm him. I knew better: I was quite young and still had forced him down once or twice single-handed in play.

When most troubled or lonely I sat alone, thinking of ways in which I should settle with them. Frazier, I said. And Poley and Skeres. It was Frazier's dagger that had ended my friend, and his name was dizzy and bitter in my mind. At supper I sometimes ached for my apartness, understanding that I was not the sort of boy my fellow players supposed me to be and that they might cast me to the streets if they but knew the turbulence in my heart.

I never cared for them equally, of course. Tom Pope I adored from the start, and Condell and Phillips were good-natured and willing to lend me books, but Burbage always seemed to know my failings, and I knew he had not forgiven my prank and thought little of me. I disliked playing his wife and begrudged that he thrilled me in his mighty acting. The clown Will Kempe I liked the least, for there was a malicious cruelty about him. He had small teeth with little spaces between them, and always seemed to bite something when he smiled. He drank and smelled of it. One day as we waited in the tiring room for our entrances, I smelled the sack on him and moved prudishly away, and he said without looking at me, "See in the corner, boy."

Something black lay there; I moved it with my foot and when it fell limply against my boot, I saw that it was a dead rat. Disgusted, I said, "Was it friend to you?" for I disliked his cutting tongue and remembered how he had sneered at me when I returned to the company after my illness.

He said, "That's us when we die, boy. Do you hope for Resurrection? There'll be no more than that." Then he tumbled onstage to the laughter of the penny apprentices, who loved him. Years later before he died, still rather young, he had embraced the church once more and repented.

Still, most of the men being fond of me, I was not unhappy when we prepared to pack our props and costumes into heavy two-wheeled wagons to ride out towards Oxford to play. A boy in the theater has an unusual position of respect: half child and half man, he is depended upon as an equal colleague. I was flattered by it and liked it very much.

The end of fall had come as we jogged hard on the rutty road, and by the time we reached each evening's inn our clothes and hair were thick with dust, and our bodies sore. Shagspere often preferred to walk apart from us, blinking slightly and deep in thought. On the second day of our tour I took the courage to walk beside him, which he didn't seem to mind; indeed once or twice he turned to smile at me, the sun glinting on his single gold earring and on the shiny, high forehead. His teeth were fairly good but his skin had coarsened, and I wished for his sake he were more handsome.

After a while I said in a comradely way, "Do you write in your mind, master?"

"Aye."

"Will it be another history?"

"Nay, only a letter to my son."

We sang as we rode and walked:

> "Hey Robin, jolly Robin,
> Tell me how thy leman doth
> And thou shalt know of mine."

He fell silent with his thinking, excluding me.

The air was cool and clean, and as we continued along the northern roads, I remembered walking the first time to Blackfriars with Morley, and wondered how it was that a man could be alive and then molder in the earth. Shagspere took my hand in his and said, "Thinkst heavy thoughts of a sudden, dear lad?"

"That I could write of them, master! You write so easily and so did . . ."

"And so did . . ."

I fell into silence. He said, "Wilt speak his name?"

Fiercely I shook my head and kicked at the dirt to control my feelings. We walked a time, and I stopped to take a pebble from my soft shoe, yet as we passed farther along the early spring road I began to speak, occasionally finding a flower to pull apart, of my life with my mother and what I had lost. Of my fight with the wheelwright I said nothing: now that Morley was dead, no one knew of it at all.

Shagspere said wryly, "Why Nick, didst fancy to be a churchman? It seemeth an unlikely vocation with thy temper."

"Yes," I murmured, "that's what my masters said to me, and surely it must be true though it pains me awfully. I've no forgiveness in my heart.

When we come to those words in the Lord's Prayer about forgiving those who trespass against us that we might be pardoned our sins, I'm silent . . . I can't say it . . . nothing could make me!"

"And why's that?"

I threw down the remains of my flower. "Morley was murdered, and the day will come when I'll make them pay for it. And no prayers shall come in my way, this I swear." I kicked at the dusty earth and stared hard at the creaking cartwheels before us. "Aye," I said, "if I die for this!"

He lowered his voice so that the men riding before us should not hear. "Nick, put away these thoughts."

"Nay, I can't!"

"Put them away, wag. Hast certainty they murdered him? How canst know? And how canst think to throw thy life away in blindness of what you feel? What good can it bode to thee to seek revenge? It can't bring him back, and the law shall come down hard on thee."

I cried, "As his friend I must do it. Cannot you know? He surely would not quarrel over a tavern reckoning, for he'd gold enough when he wanted it and fine enough clothes in his chest when he bothered to wear them. I saw them. And they were low-bred men, scurvy-bred, that I heard him speak of! What he did with them I know not. He had finer friends."

"That he had: many men were glad to know him."

"They'll know him no more, master, for he's dead, he's dead and I loved him so!" The words burst from me. "How can he live no more! There are these flowers now and he doesn't see them and there's no one to whom I can speak of it, for my master and mistress didn't trust him. There's naught left of him but words in a play and it's like a fire inside of me!"

"You can speak of it with me, and write of it if you'd like, and show me what you've done."

It moved me so that I didn't know how to answer. All that I had held back for six months overtook me and I began to stammer, and could say nothing right nor could I bring myself to speak to him further. Instead I walked alone, avoiding him, making excuses to push him from me. I thought, I'll seek revenge if it pleases me. What unmanly advice would he give? And I treated him for the day as coldly as if he had offended me in the worst way.

On the third night I was assigned to the inn room which my master and Shagspere shared, for John Heminges did not trust me to refrain from tricks were I far from his sight. The sheets were almost clean and the floor rushes newly laid; yet, for much of the night I lay in wakefulness, aware of Shagspere's breathing. Turned on my side, I watched the shape of his small, narrow hand on the sheet and the leather boots that stood neatly by his cot: they were old boots but he was careful with them. He was meticulous in all matters: I was meticulous in nothing. Reaching over, I drew to me my own sloppy shoes that had been flung under my heaped clothes and arranged them neatly side by side.

My master was also a careful man, but not creative: nothing disturbing came from his mind to disrupt the plans he laid for the maintaining of his family and his life. Shagspere resonated with his thoughts, yet the production of them was as orderly as if he tended rosebeds and spinach patches. Both men had deep, steady plans in which they saw their way clearly; I could see nothing clearly of mine. I was astonished to find myself amidst these playing men, astonished that I had not been apprehended and hung, or stabbed to death by the side of Morley in the tavern.

Sleepless, I tiptoed down to the common room below, where for a penny I was given a rushlight, paper, and ink, and there sat down to write my first sonnets. Yet though my feelings were clear in my mind, they dissipated to naught on the foolscap. The dawn began to come and the baker's wench slipped in with bread in her shapely arms, and we spoke foolish things together, and I pressed her against the back door and kissed her before she grabbed at my breeches and ran away.

We played that afternoon in the innyard with the townspeople jammed together and hanging from the windows, and considerable difficulty we had in making our entrances and exits from a single door. My sleepless night of poetry had left me incoherent, and I stumbled about in the battle scene and scratched my arm by a careless parley in the duel.

Then, though we were weary, we poured into our carts again, pushing down the dusty road to reach the next inn before evening was long upon the countryside. So embarrassed was I by my poetry that I dared not try again, but carved a miniature wagon from wood while my master and Shagspere wrote on either side of the rickety table.

"Nicholas," said my master, "I send this letter to my wife tomorrow. Wouldst tell her news? She's fond of thee."

I flushed and muttered, "Tell her I'm well, I beg you."

He looked at me kindly and said, "Nicholas is well: it shall be writ."

Thus we proceeded until we came at last towards the market town of Stratford-on-Avon, even then a fair small city of two thousand people encircled by meadows in the handsome hills of middle England. Foot-weary were we and dirty with the road, glad to pull off our boots and wash our blistered feet in cold water. It was my turn in the morning to see that the horses had been groomed and fed, and as I came from the stables, blinking in the sun, I saw Shagspere crossing the yard. The light reflected off his high forehead and his step was rapid, and I knew how discourteous I had been and wondered if I could ever make it up to him. But he only said pleasantly, "The other boys have gone to shoot; dost not go with them?"

"No." How could he understand? Their lives had been ordinary, mine torn and uneven, and no communication could be possible between us. "I like them not."

"Come walk with me if you will. I go to see my children."

I finished my tasks and, having washed my hands in the bucket, fol-lowed him past our men, who were arranging the innyard for the play that afternoon, and towards Trinity Church across the water. "There was I baptized and my little ones also," Shagspere confided. "My father's a glover and once alderman of this town."

"Were you not brought up to his trade?"

"I was, but it liked me not. Dost see the boys there? I also swam in the chill spring and loved it upon my soul."

We crossed rugged stone Clopton Bridge over the river, and there he hesitated, gazing down Bridge Street towards Henley with a frown. "Nick," he said, "I've a favor to ask of thee, though it shames me I cannot manage these matters better. Since you've told me aught of thy life, I'll take courage to show thee this of mine. I'm hesitant to go down that street and knock upon the door, though it's my own house and I put all my pennies aside for it. My wife . . . we quarrel, and it hurts me to my stomach. It's a living reproach to see her. Go there and tell my children that I've come and wait for them by the riverbanks under the bridge. 'Tis at Henley, at the sign of the jeweled glove."

I would have done much more had he asked it, though to be reluctant to confront one's wife seemed a sorry thing. I found Henley Street to be lined with half-timbered houses and market stalls. When I came to the door above which hung a painting sign with a fantastical jeweled silk glove etched upon it now faded with weather, I looked back for assurance; he nodded, clasping his hands encouragingly together as if to cheer on football players of a Sabbath, and so I gained the courage to knock. An old man in slippers greeted me and left me to wait in the small, clean parlour: there lay a child's rag doll in a chair by the chimneypiece, and a schoolbook of Lily's Latin grammar on the table. I had not believed in his children until that moment: he always came and went alone, and it was difficult to think of him as a family man.

Presently a pinch-mouthed woman stomped down the stair, looking accusingly at my boots to make certain I had not dragged any street muck into the house. Warm to my ears, I remembered how Tom Pope had confided that Will had been forced to marry a girl he'd tumbled in the hay and then had fled ninety miles south to escape her. This one in my estimation was not worth the tumbling. The children, however, when she clapped her hands to call them, were sweetly disarming; they had their father's broad forehead and steady, warm eyes, especially the boy who was about nine years old. Strictly she said, "You may see no plays." Hanging their heads and studying me shyly, they let me take them towards the river. When they saw their father on the bridge they began to run, the boy leaping in his arms.

I turned back to the inn to help my master hang curtains across the back of the stage, and after the props were fetched, I was given leave to walk about the town for a few hours more before returning to tie on my farthingale and petticoats for the comedy. Finding it a dull place compared to London, I meandered to the graveyard under the heavy trees. Though Shagspere had been boy here, I could not quite imagine him dragging his feet to church among these stones. The rashness of boyhood did not suit him; I could not fancy him without his slightly receding hair and serious look, and I wondered if he had always been more clerk than fighter. Then I remembered the high chestbone like a deer's and the sudden laugh, the expansion into a self-willed and private freedom. I questioned if he were ever angry, and what it would be like to be bound to him instead of John Heminges. I wondered if he'd have me; I didn't think he would.

I could not imagine him as a glover.

Children's voices murmured from below the bridge, and I descended the bank and recognized my friend and his children. They were fishing with a large net, girls with skirts kilted to the knee, father and son without hose or shoes, and their soft conversation floated down the bank, amidst the sounds of birds chirping and the iron wagon wheels a distance down the bridge.

"Nay, Dad, thou hast let it free!" cried the dark-haired girl. "Canst fish in London, prithee?"

"Why, there are fair fishes there, lass!" he laughed, throwing back his head. "Why, fishes there art as large as galleons: one snaps the fingers and they come!"

And the girl, rubbing her face against his shoulder, murmured, "Nay, it cannot be! Still, an it were, I should like to see it."

Noticing that I leaned against the bridge stones, he called merrily out, "Nick, sweet fellow! We've nothing for our labor. Come hither and give us help for the country boy thou art."

I stripped off my hose to plunge into the shallow waters. The little girls had clambered to the bank and were wringing out the hems of their petticoats, whispering about what their mother would say. They perched prudently on a rock and wiped off their pale little feet before pulling on their hose and shoes, glancing at me every now and then. They were about nine and eleven years old and very charming: even girls that young could make my heart beat, and I knew that in their childish way they were estimating me, both as young man and as their father's friend. The net in my hand, I bade them be still until the muddy bottom settled and the fish came. I caught several small ones, and the younger girl wrapped them solemnly in her apron to take home.

"God's wounds!" cried Shagspere. "Look where the sun lieth in the heavens! Shall we be late for playing? Come merrily, my pretties!" The little girls clung to him as they climbed the bank and turned towards Bridge Street, the boy, whose name was Hamnet, following at my side, hesitatingly answering the questions I put to him in Latin: how fared his school? did he like the master? did he hunt hereby? "Shouldst like to be an actor, my little man?" I said playfully, and he frowned and grew silent.

"I shall be a glover, like my grandfather," he replied.

As we passed the high walls of an orchard, he slipped his hand into his father's. Coming to the corner of Henley Street, he turned and buried his face in Shagspere's stomach.

"Now my wag," my friend said clumsily, "what can this be, sweet boy? Canst think I'll not return to thee?"

The children receded from us down the street of carts and horses, glancing wistfully back over their shoulders, and as we turned towards the bridge once more, I said stoutly, "I like not thy lady wife, sir! She deserveth not a man like you."

He almost smiled. "I am much of the same mind, my young friend, though it's hardly gentlemanly towards the weaker sex to admit it."

Slowly we turned up the elm-lined road, hearing the cries of rooks in the eaves of aged thatched roofs behind the trees.

I said curiously, "How didst come to marry her?"

"Lust!" he answered practically. "Stay far from it, Nick. I was but nineteen years old and she waiting for me in the fields near her house. She was more than willing, and next her stomach swelled and they called the banns in a hurry. Between her father and mine own they made a husband of me, much to everyone's grief. 'Tis done. Yet it woundeth me deep to leave the children. Never never have I loved as I love them. Never did I think it could be!"

Respectfully I nodded until suddenly he murmured of the time, and racing we came to the inn, shoving ourselves into our costumes even as the Prologue had made his entrance. He was, I think, a rebellious duke that day and I a lady-in-waiting, a soldier, a stupid servant, and a page. After we had danced in the finale and were wiping off our faces in the room given to us to dress, he squeezed my shoulder and said, "Tomorrow's Sunday! If thou canst bear to miss church, rise before the light comes and let's off to the woods and steal a partridge. No bird's as tasty as one that's cozened. I was fair enough with the bow when I was thine age and set traps all over these parts . . . aye, and escaped many a whipping for poaching by the speed of my legs."

He shook me awake early and we walked across the yard with everyone still sleeping. Across fields we went with the mist rising from the harvested wheatfields and to the hills beyond, and the cry of rooks from the cottages. Passing a red brick mansion, with gabled roofs, we turned towards the lands. There he stopped to show me where he had carved his name and the name of his bride on a tree, and where he had lain with her in the leaves, a few months after dragging shamefaced to the altar to make good on his promise.

The white dawn just over the trees, whispering at the edge of the lake, he pointed to the drinking birds and cautioned me not to allow the leaves to crackle under my feet. Traps he had laid the night before, and one rabbit had been snared; he'd brought bow and arrow, though he meant to take no deer, "for what would we do with it on tour, Nick, and my wife will have none of it." Still, he said he'd show me how to draw the bow, which rubbed my palms sorely; he gave me his gloves and stood beside me, showing me how to pull taut. I splashed into the water to retrieve the fallen arrows, and above us the birds scattered, and rushed higher into the morning clouds.

He was stronger than I thought: an efficient bowman, he wasted not one arrow. I remembered years later the passages in his plays on poaching, and laughed over them. He spoke as little as possible, but taught me in those early-morning hours to be silent, watch and wait, to think carefully, draw securely, and let fly the arrows into the sky. We had birds that day with sling and stone, and the rabbits too; it being a Sunday we were not to play, and he said we might remain till church was out. A fire we made with dry sticks gathered, and sat about it. There he told me bawdy stories such as made me shout with laughter, and I told him about the kitchen girl and he told me about the use of a linen sheath to protect against unwanted fatherhood. We skinned and roasted bird and rabbit and ate heartily, licking the grease from our fingers. He sang me many songs he knew, and told me much concerning the history of the kings: he'd never gone to the university himself and envied Morley for it. He told me about John Heminges's wedding and how he had drunk so much that he fell down dancing.

He said were we men of fine estate we should hunt with falcons, and follow the royal deer. I said, "Marry, that I'd fancy!"

He said he hoped to be a gentleman one day, and when I asked him why, replied, "Why, there are two sorts of men in this world, my wag! One who'll live and die unknown, and the other who hath a coat of arms, therefore a heritage and the respect of his fellows!"

We walked until we found a stream, thirstily flinging ourselves on the bank to drink. His spring-wound watch told that morning service had ended, and he wanted to see his children once more. "Though God knoweth if the time's kept straight," he muttered. "Yet I shouldn't like to miss them for a quarter hour's time. What a poor estate I've made of family life, Nick! She won't forgive me my actor's life and my poverty, though one day I'll own both house and land here if I live."

Through the trees we could see the chimneys of the red brick mansion, and the walls of the gardens beyond. "Walk softly here!" he muttered. " 'Tis not our land we traverse."

"Why didst take to the stage? A glover payeth more, doth it not?"

"Aye, marry! But since my youth I've loved words far more than leather! At night I read whatever books I could find by rushlight until my eyes hurt me. I'm a bit short of sight these days, and it comes I think from that. My father expected I should become a glover and 'prenticed me; but I'd have no part of it, for I wanted to write poems and plays. I wrote in all my free moments, terrible plays, Nicholas! I blush to think of the foolscap I wasted. Naught did I care for but traveling players, though everyone said actors were thieves, vagabonds. London preachers still say it. One day while poaching I saw Anne and there was no peace anymore until I had her. They married me, I was lusty, and she conceived. Our oldest girl came, and twins followed shortly."

Running my hand along the cool stones of the kitchen garden walls as we passed them, I murmured, "What didst then?"

"Suffered for my pleasure for some years with her quarrels and accusations. An acting troupe passed by who needed a man, and I joined them. A foolish leap injured my knee, and I limp when I'm weary, which is well enough for the dignified old men I play. So I live in London in lodgings and yet hope to make my fortune." He added with sudden anger, "As ordinary a writer as I may prove, it suits me better than the tanning of fine deer skin for ladies' laced gloves."

After this he moved the subject carefully from himself. As we once again turned to the elm-lined road towards the inn and the town, I told him about Morley and he asked me if I loved men better than women, and mortified, I shook my head. At Clopton Bridge he left me, and I walked back to the inn alone. He came running back open-shirted just as we were making ready to leave, standing about the innyard with our carts and horses, packs strapped to our backs, turning at last back towards London. I would have liked to speak with him more, but he was silent and despondent. Tom Pope's apprentices asked me to walk with them, and soon we were chattering of muskets and archery and the ancient holy crusades. At the next inn I was allowed to stay with them, and no fighting was there save a battle with pillows and feathers about the room, and a tearing hurry to stuff them back once more.

Thus we returned to London to the first snow, our heavy cartwheels dragging through the white roads: there again were the towers of White-hall and Westminster Abbey grey against the sky, the smoke of a thou-sand brick chimneys burning the forbidden coal, and the feet of those with a license to beg bound in rags against the cold. As we rode into our parish, my mistress ran down the cobble streets in her hemp apron to greet us. Our kitchen smelled of wood fire and baking and there were dried rushes laid on the brick floor to help keep in the heat.

New playscripts must be heard, and the nervous, threadbare writers came of a morning to gather in the fragrant kitchen and read aloud, hoping we would buy. One was a man with a stubborn, quarrelsome face whose name was Jonson and who had been a bricklayer, and the unrest of my own nature understood his own, for position was important to him and everything to me. Will had completed *The Comedy of Errors,* and it was my task to copy every man's part with the lines leading up to his entrance as well as to compile the prop sheet. Comfortable in wool vest and leggings, I spent many an afternoon making fair copies at the trestle table, while the children picked over the goose feathers for new pillows and turned meat upon the spit. Sometimes I blew the feathers a little, and they shrieked and scrambled for them.

"Ah Nick, what dost?" said tender Rebecca Heminges, and in passing behind me, let her fingers linger on the back of my neck.

On St. Stephen's Day of the year 1593, we were engaged to play at Green-wich before the entire court and Her Glorious Majesty, the great and ordained by God, Queen of all England, Elizabeth Regina, a woman far past her youth before whose proclivities and prosperity the civilized world inclined its head. I had seen her on the Thames, reclined on her barge with her ladies about her, a bony figure heavily dressed, and the crowds stood along the bank, waving bits of silk. I had seen her on her way to St. Paul's, bowed low, and when looking up, found her gone through the doors to service.

Now for many an evening the men debated on which play to bring. At last we walked to the Office of the Revels one windy afternoon and played out Will's *Comedy:* the Revel Master's mouth quivering with the laughter he would not allow, he barked forth our fee and the time of our appearance, that being ten o'clock of the night after the most holy day on which Our Savior was born.

"We shall be in coals this winter, lads," whistled my master as we strode away from St. John's Wood to celebrate. "Seven pounds, by Christ's nails, and three more as gratuity from the Queen. 'Tis a fortune! Thou, Will, shall have an extra full quarten jug, bless thy dear bawdy wit!"

So they went down the streets, punching and embracing each other like boys: Heminges, and good Shagspere my friend, black-eyed Gus Phillips who liked women far too well, little Henry Condell, stout Pope panting behind, and we boys who hooted and sang and danced about them.

Then in our house and that of the other actors was the talk of nothing else. The Master of the Revels allotted us the spacious hall on his premises for our rehearsals, plenty of coals, fabric embroidered with gold thread, wood and paint and cloth for scenery, curled wigs to the shoulder, and soft painted shoes. The parts I had copied at the trestle table were distributed, and three days later we appeared for the first time in the hall. Sometimes the Lord Chamberlain came to see us rehearse. I asked John Heminges how we should fare if we pleased the Queen and he said we should have new boots and gloves for our playing, and I money to buy a new book that delighted me, though I was not sure I liked that he knew how much I needed to read.

We had seldom worked so hard.

On the eve of Christmas I fell asleep with my head on the trestle table and a pile of play posters, fresh from the printer at St. Paul's, under my hand, and the next morning awoke to the bells of St. Stephen's Day.

"Godspeed!" said Rebecca Heminges, pressing a small mince pie in my hand for luck and long life. We kissed her cheek to wish her the joy of the season, and with my master and John Rice I negotiated the twisting, narrow streets to the river with our draycart of props.

Tom Pope and his boys had already docked the Revels Office barge at our steps beyond the bridge and waved us to her, shouting to mind the ice. Weighed down to the Thames water, the vessel held trunks of costumes, painted scenery, and ironwork to support the torches that would light our play. In my haste I slipped knee-deep into the icy water. John Rice, who had long forgiven me my prank, hauled me out by the arm, and as the barge groaned softly over the white cold water towards Greenwich, he muttered that I should have a feverish ague before the morn.

Barges and merchant ships elbowed past as we floated away from the spacious medieval bridge, and I stood up to see the forbidding White Tower receding beyond the wide stretch of cold grey water and the waves of our boat. We all could recite the names of those incarcerated there over the centuries, many wrongfully: even our most blessed Queen had in her youth been shut away by her older sister, Bloody Mary. From its massive walls it was said there was no escape, though someone had once clambered down hand over hand on a rope: a Jesuit, I think.

Bitter cold was the hall at Greenwich in spite of large fires in both stone chimneypieces, but the men who had come before us had already, with the assistance of several Queen's footmen, erected the scaffold on which we were to play. We boys had to try our weight upon it, I somersaulting twice backward until Condell shouted that I was needed to climb the ladders and secure the iron torch brackets. The mince pie had been long squashed in my jerkin, but I ate it with slices of hot mutton and a mug of warm ale sent up from the kitchens. Not long could we stay. Twice I ferried back with John Rice and Augustine Phillips for the massive trunks stuffed with the remainder of our props, late being packed at the Revels Office. The wind blew my long hair as I stood near the prow of the barge, hands on my hips.

"Mind thyself!" grumbled my master's man Daniel, who on his several instruments played the fanfares and the galliards to which we danced.

"Forsooth, knave!" replied I grandly. "Speakest thou so to the Lady Abbess of Ephesus as this night shall find me?"

"Aye, pisspot!" was his fond reply.

The daylight hours passed, and we rushed about by scanty candles. Then came the torch lighters, clad in red, and the warm paneling of the hall dipped in the shadows of the flames. I retreated to the tiring room and began to pull on my abbess robes. "Hold still, wag," said my master with his mouth full of pins. The torch shone on the grey hairs by his ears. "Speak not too fast nor shout thyself into hoarseness, wilt? There, lad, look here at me!"

His broad fingers moved across my lips with the rouge.

Ten o'clock approached, and our chatter died away. Even Alexander, our smallest apprentice, who was only to dance, was motionless as Tom Pope adjusted the low-waisted dress over his flat shivering chest. From the hall we could hear the murmur of voices and the laughter; the voices hushed then, and Tom Pope put his thick finger to his lip, warning us with his eyes. There could be no more banter. The Queen had come into her hall.

My hands were cold. "Ah lad!" whispered Condell, slipping his arm about me. "Art afeared? Why, the Queen's but a woman like my wife!" And then he threw me aside, and rushed through the doors through which the lights glittered and the heat rose. Jocular rang out his voice in the Prologue. Music followed in the form of my master's man, the boys sang, and then the play began. Actors rushed into the tiring room, changed doublets, threw on hats, seized swords or bags, winked at me, and rushed out again as I stood by the coal brazier in my prioress's black robes, holy and reserved, speechless in my awe and with not one of my lines in my head.

The Lady Abbess does not enter upon the stage until the play is almost done, and after a time I grew restless, and creaked open the door to the corridor to look about. Not a soul walked the rushes, and softly I went with candle in my hand, hearing the laughter behind me, gaping curiously through this door and that. Through one I could see part of our audience, among them the ladies-in-waiting in white and silver. A stair of such width and carved magnificence as I had never seen opened before me, and, hardly breathing, I ascended. At the landing stood a suit of armor of such proportions as could have belonged only to bluff King Harry, him who had wedded in turn six wives. Corridors turned to corridors in the upper bedchambers, each furnished with statuary and pictures. In one was a bust of Attila, King of the Huns, and a circular table decorated in gold. In all the rooms hung painted hangings, and in many, portraits of the Queen when she had been young. I found a sundial in the form of an elephant and an organ made of mother-of-pearl.

One room led into still others: I passed a privy closet whose seat was embroidered velvet, and a couch woven in gold and silken thread, and through the last door, found myself in a bathing chamber whose water poured from oyster shells. I did not understand for some moments that I had come into the Queen's chamber at Greenwich.

The bedroom itself was hung with tapestries, and of the bed I can say I have never seen such a profundity of creamy white satin, of bolster and pillow and feather quilt. Pictures of the propitious Tudor kings hung high on the walls. A delicate pair of desks of Florentine design faced each other, upon which there were inkstand and pens and upon one of which lay an unfinished letter that began, "To Robert Devereux, Lord Essex. My honey lord, thy Queen implores thee . . ."

Jumping back with my breath high in my throat, I began my retreat, touching the walls as I went. Past rooms with silken-covered cabinets, past a cabinet of small boxes made of tortoiseshell, past a corridor hung with solemn portraits of English divines, hands on Bibles and lips pursed, then to yet another corridor hung with shields.

By my candle I read the verse upon one:

> Ut rota perpetuo raptans Ixiona motu
> Sic ego prepetuo raptus amore roter.

(Spinning round for evermore, Ixion to his wheel is bound,
I too upon the wheel of love am whirled incessantly around.)

From far below came the laughter of the play. My hand on the banister, I
flew down the steps towards the door of our tiring room. Six or seven
times I mistook it and was about to try the last when it flung open and I
beheld John Heminges's anxious face. "The Lady Prioress is come!" he
whispered. "Go, Nick!" I rushed through the door to the banqueting hall
and up the steps to the stage. The brilliance of the torches overwhelming
me, I looked into the audience.

At the end of the hall on a raised chair with steps mounted to it sat an
irritable old woman with a brilliant, curling red wig and a dress so
bejeweled that it hurt my eyes. I thought, oh this is she! And all I could
remember was the bed of creamy pillows and the unfinished letter that
read, "Robert Devereux. My honey lord, thy Queen implores thee . . ."

It so stunned me that when I opened my lips, no words came. Condell
spoke instead: inverting my sentences, he made them his own. From
behind me Shagspere took up the speech: the lines (theirs and mine) flew
about me like juggler's balls. I would not be outdone; my memory returned, and I burst into the remainder of my part with considerable
passion. We left the stage in a patter of applause, sweating from the heat
of the torches. Then, flinging themselves about on stools of the tiring
room, the men laughed until they almost fell to the floor.

I turned my face from them. " 'Tis a humorous thing, Nicholas," cried
Collins.

" 'Tisn't," I muttered, but Heminges pulled me to him and said, "Not
badly done, lad. It happened to me the first time I played before her. And
your voice rings out with the best." I squirmed away to find the pin that
had not ceased to prick me, and recall my steps for the final dance.

After the Epilogue we bowed deeply to the Queen and she left the
room with her dark sparkling dress sweeping in a circle about her, everyone bending the knee. Heminges stripped off the saffron satin doublet

that had to be returned to the Revels Office day after next. Under his arms, his shirt was damp with sweat. "To the boats, men: we shan't be abed much before dawn. Condell, shall we make free of thy house after dinner in the morrow? Canst host us? The last dance went but poorly and needeth an hour's more of work before the evening's play."

My black prioress robes lay in a heap in the rushes, the footmen soon come to clear away. "Come, lads," said Pope. He had gathered to him a small chest of leftover sweet tarts and pasties from the royal banquet that our households should divide in the boat before we made the steps of London Bridge. "A lord I know gave Rhenish wine. Shall ride back by the moon and drink of it." We hoped for the payment to come, but after waiting a long time, gathered our things and went without it.

Servants lit us from the palace to the dock, where we could make out the bobbing shape of several smaller boats awaiting us. Tom was carrying his apprentice, who had fallen asleep, against his shoulder. We were stepping into the ferry when my master cried, "Ah! I have forgot me the prompt book! God knoweth, they may use it for pie linings! Nick, run, boy, and fetch it. 'Tis on the small table by the door."

The corridors were far more silent than before, and the bored footman, hearing my errand, curtly motioned me on. Through the large and now empty playing hall, smelling of tallow and littered with orange peels and nutshells, I ran lightly in my soft shoes. The extinguished candles still smoked faintly to the high windows. Then, the prompt book under my arm once more, I started back down the corridor, not entirely sure of my way. To each side in the dim light morose pictures of the long dead hung high on the wall, and cabinets displayed dull white ivory figures. Before me a rat scurried in the rushes, stared for seconds at me with glittering, hateful eyes, and disappeared. Behind a closed door someone laughed.

In the dim light by one of the cabinets a man was standing with his arms across his doublet. I could not tell his age, and I do not know why he caught my attention; it was perhaps a stiffening of my back, an instantaneous distrust. Glancing at the rapier against his thigh, I took in the shabbiness of him. Then I understood as I knew my own breath that this was Ingram Frazier, who had stabbed Kit Morley. I had seen him but once when with Kit, and felt the same distrust move like a shiver within me. "Scum in every way," Kit had said. "My hand to my dagger when near him."

Scum in every way: yet Kit Morley had gone to dine with him and two others, and they had killed him and been released for it after a short time. My heart began to beat so loud I feared he would hear it, yet he remained slovenly leaning against the wall, and struck a flint to light his pipe.

I walked up to him. He looked down at me, and in that moment I knocked the pipe away with the back of my hand and slapped him across the face. It was instinctive, but ill judged; he took me as one might a puppy and threw me across the floor, came at me, and kicked me in the side. I rolled in the dirty rushes, crying out in pain and rage. He would have kicked me again but I had his leg and pulled him down, jumping him.

It was his dagger I wanted, and yet he was much the stronger. I felt his hot breath of beef, ale, and bad teeth. Though aware of the unevenness of the match, I would not give up. In those confused moments it seemed that all my losses centered in the thick body of this man, and that if I could kill him I would somehow have all cherished things back once more. My hand was on his dagger hilt, his large hand on my arm: we rolled in the dirty rushes in silence but for our breathing.

His hand captured mine. I pulled it loose with all my strength and sought his rapier. It was a slender, light thing and sharp, and he had not expected me to catch it. In a second I had it, and jumped up, holding it to his throat. Only his heavy breath and mine filled the long corridor, and still I hesitated. What did I consider? That if I stilled that heart it would never beat again? And in that second was the terrible knowledge, self-deprecating, that I could not kill.

Motionless with self-loathing, I hesitated.

He leapt and knocked me down, and the blood formed behind my lips. "I'd kill thee, thou pisspot, were it worth my trouble," he said. And he strode off and I heard laughter.

I lay in the rushes, the blood creeping down the side of my chin. He had not known me for the darkness, but he would not have known me anyway, for I had been all the evening a most holy abbess in shapeless black robes. Dizzy with the fight and despising myself, I stumbled out to the quay, where I could hear the water against the pilings and the gentle dip of our men's boat. By the lanterns their faces, tired from the performance, seemed strange. It seemed a year and then some since I had seen them.

"Wag, where's the book?" Heminges said, holding out his hand.

I had left it in the rushes.

"Never mind!" he said with a sigh, helping me into the boat. "We'll find it tomorrow when we fetch the prop trunks. 'Tis past two, and the night freezes."

We pulled away down the black water, the comforting bend in the river soon to come and the lantern lighting our way. My master looked closer at me. "God's wounds, art hurt?" he cried. "Didst fall, Nick?"

"Nay, master."

"Thou art bleeding from the mouth! Twas a quarrel?"

I would not answer: not if he had beaten me would I have replied. My body was shaken by my encounter and the knowledge of my ineptitude. I could not kill, I could not take revenge. What kind of man was I indeed? Neither of the cloth or successfully of the world but at both insufficient. I sat there with tears of self-disappointment in my eyes, my back to all of them.

London Bridge was before us, stark and huge. We slid between the pillars and to the bank. I could hardly walk the way to Aldermanbury in my weariness and fell into bed at once. I remember my master saying he wagered the Master of the Revels would take four months to pay us the seven pounds plus three in gratuity and we'd be a long time chasing after it.

The next evening we played again, this time at Gray's Inn before the law students and their guests. Stuffed with distilled herbs and essence of flowers against my coming fever, I accompanied my master to the hall, where he shook his head and advised me to keep my hooded robe covering as much as possible of my bruised, swollen face. Far too many people had squeezed into the hall, having heard the play was amusing, so that it became almost an impossibility to make our entrances and exits and we had to excuse ourselves each time. All the while the young law students laughed with each other, staring at us curiously as if they wondered what we did there: two or three I recognized from my afternoon at Southampton's house long ago. They may have heard our play that night, but there was so much shouting and laughter we had a difficult time in hearing each other. I was faint by the Epilogue, and Condell, feeling my head with his wrist, said my moon was in the wrong constellation and I must go to bed. All the men knew I had been in a fight, for I heard them speaking of it.

While I was still recovering from my fever and swollen face, a boy came to our house with a Christmas packet for me from Master Shagspere. In it were a paper astrolabe for taking the altitudes of stars, which he no longer had time to use, and two songs he had writ about poaching. I shouted with laughter and hid them between my books. What became of them? I know not.

So I lay in bed and dreamed of playing the hero's part before the Queen and distinguishing myself in the eyes of the men. Gossip resounded in our house: the noble actor Alleyn was now playing with the Lord Admiral's Men in his father-in-law Henslowe's prosperous theater, the Rose, and this brought to mind our own condition, for we had still no regular theater of our own. We had been for a time at Newington Butts, where I had met my disgrace, and for some Michaelmas performances at the Cross-Keyes Inn, and when I descended, coughing and sneezing, I found several of the men sitting in our kitchen, discussing the matter passionately. Lord Strange had died suddenly, and though we had been most fortunately taken under the patronage of Lord Hunsdon, the Lord Chamberlain, we were still gypsies in our borrowing of halls and innyards in which to play.

"By Christ's blood! We must have our own theater," Pope said.

Shagspere only came for a short while that day. There was a rumor that he had received a generous gift from the Earl of Southampton, to whom he still sent sonnets; there was also talk that he was in grief over love of a woman. Of this I knew nothing, and irked that he hadn't confided in me, resolved to give him my confidence no more. He sensed that there was some trouble between us, and sent me first the rough copy of part of a new play that I found to be fairly writ, and I began to think that he might one day make his mark upon the world and buy property in his birthtown after all. He addressed it to "Nick, my falcon," his private name for me. We leased the old Theater in Shoreditch and prepared to give serious competition to the Lord Admiral's Men.

"We grow from old dreams into new ones, falcon," said my friend when next we met. I thought much upon his words. I was become a little weary, a little discouraged in waiting for God's sign, for it was almost two years since I had left Canterbury. I did speak to Will about it that day, and he was very gentle, and said not to worry too much but that if it was meant to come, it would come indeed. I thought it a rather simple thing to say for a man so witty, but thanked him anyway.

And so I turned fifteen.

THE

SECOND

PART

ONE

Margaret

MOST OF LONDON WELCOMED THE ACTING TROUPES, THOUGH SOME religious dissidents, or Puritans as they were coming to be known, scathingly frowned upon us. They claimed playgoing was the cause of sin, and sin was the cause of plagues, and therefore if any pestilence should seep through the gates of the city, the blame must be laid upon the theaters. From various groaning pulpits they condemned the actors from Shoreditch to Southwark, demanding the doors of bear gardens and playhouses be shut, but the Queen would not acquiesce. As the last decade of the sixteenth century rushed to its close, we continued to prosper.

The playhouse we chose as home was called the Theater, and rested rank with leaks and mildew in the midst of Finsbury Fields in Shoreditch, directly across from the parish of St. Leonard's, to which the theatrical family of Dick Burbage and his father, James, belonged. In the summer the fields, abounding in wild flowers, were used as a military practice ground, and after sun had set one could, if alone, run into bad company. The structure, surrounded by a brick wall, had been constructed almost twenty years before by James Burbage, himself a member in his youth of Lord Leicester's Men. The rent on the land was moderate, allowing us enough coins to regularly buy new playscripts, with Dick Burbage often taking the principal role. We worked hard. Hardly had I memorized one part than I was given another, and when one of the extra actors fell ill for some days, they pinned me into his garments and I was rebels and ruffians at two hours' notice.

"Well done, Nick," said my master. I shrugged, for my fancy at this time of my youth was only to be a gentleman, to wear Spanish leather boots and dine in a house hung with arras cloths painted with mythical scenes of lascivious nymphs fleeing naked through English woods: a house to which I alone would have the private iron key.

By the fall of 1596 our props and costumes were stuffed into every corner of the dilapidated Theater, and the flags announcing our performance flew high and silky each afternoon from the prop-hut mast. Evenings now and then found us presenting our comedies in distinguished houses off the Strand. Excepting that I fell off the scaffolding at Gray's Inn during an intricate sword thrust and into the lap of a law student seated too close upon the stage, I was well commended. It satisfied me greatly when John Rice, playing a soldier for the first time, split his breeches to the waist in a battle scene and had to be covered over with a cloak and rushed offstage.

Once while coming down the stair of our house in Wood Street, I heard the voice of my master and Tom Pope from the garden. "Mark it," my master said, with a snip of his shears, "the boy's worth three ordinary apprentices. He could be the finest on the stage an he willed it, but he's more often foe than friend to himself. God knoweth, though, he's dear to me!"

My chest grew warm at these words, and I fled down Love Lane to Aldermanbury to be with my own thoughts and gaze at the girls who came to the cistern with the lion's-head spout for water.

Women held all my fancy. Sometimes I stood for an hour to observe the merchant's daughter across the garden washing herself at the window. I conceived she knew I watched her and had little peace from it. Every ballad monger sold songs about constant love for a penny, but no one woman held my devotion, and I held the very last one I saw to be the fairest. Seldom did the wanton girls of Bankside tempt me: my purse was empty, I feared the danger of sickness, and I wanted love. Neither could I sing at all and mourned it, being between man and boy and unsure of where I belonged. I wished for my treble voice again, and for the poignant songs I had caroled so easily. Oh break my heart my lady is cruel!

On an early fall day of 1596 sometime after we had first taken possession of the Theater, I accompanied my mistress to Cheapside market. The pigeons intended for our dinner squirmed against the wicker cage that swung from my hand, and between looking about at the new ballads for sale, I stumbled against a young woman, knocking her basket from her arms.

New little apples rolled to the gutter. Stammering my apologies, I dropped to my knees to retrieve them. Close by my groping hand were her petticoats: she wore pricked lavender shoes and white wool hose. When I had stood again with the bruised fruit, I was taken by her full, impudent mouth. Not more than sixteen could she have been, burnished wheat hair escaping from her white crimped cap, plump and slightly swaying.

Though I returned to the market many mornings to buy butter, cream, fowls, or fish, the fall passed and I did not see her again. Each day the memory of her full mouth and the way she had shrugged her shoulders as she walked and the white, white wool hose under the petticoat's lace pried their way deeper into my thoughts, until there was no escaping them. "What ails thee, lad?" said Heminges. "Naught," was my answer. She had worn a gold ring set with a stone. Jealously, I wondered if some prosperous city merchant had given it her in betrothal.

Mornings we rehearsed or heard new playscripts, or sometimes Tom's boys and I walked about the town posting playbills. Then we ran up the red silk flag that could be seen to the other side of the Thames and St. Paul's; and, having the self-control not to jostle each other overmuch, dressed alongside the men in the tiring rooms and played each day at two. I still struggled with my jealousy and temper, which brought me to shouting matches and blows with the other boys in the murky fields beyond the Theater, and my bursts of insolence were countered with a humble need to serve. I don't know why my master never whipped me: I think he understood me, and that in itself was irksome, for I did not wish to be known by him.

Then I forgot her: the image of her little feet in lavender slippers was replaced by the excitement of astrology. I was forever casting my horoscope from a book of the heavens, ever trying to predict what should become of me. Once I saw that I should be dead within the year, which depressed me greatly; yet another time my moon and planets revealed that I would come to magnificence and be revered.

Our household was still a struggling one, with only enough money for the week's white meats and breads, and it did not seem the life of an actor would bring the prosperity I craved. Thus, I begged my master to allow me to borrow a meager porcelain furnace and set it up in the small shed in our garden for experiments in alchemy. This he granted, and I bought a secondhand Latin instruction book on the transmutation of base metals into pure gold. The men heckled me, and I fell into offs with them and hid away in the shed, forcing the heat of the coals with my bellows so that I sweated profusely, and set about trying to create gold from a melted compendium of lead, mercury, and urine. The crucible cracked, the fumes choked me, I stank of sweat and lost myself in the hours.

"No one but a fool tries to make gold," said Tom when he came by with John Heminges, drawn by the smoke. " 'Tis forbidden! Thou shalt end in Newgate, wag, and we needs must pawn our swords to pay the fine."

Glancing briefly over the alembics and vials, my master shook his head good-naturedly. "Nay, Tom! I warrant ten men of this parish are now making gold in their kitchens while the watch knows nothing of the chimney smoke. They can't imprison half of Christian London. Let him have his games if he will."

"Games, master!" I cried. "How canst call it *games*? All matter is composed of one substance! I've only to break it down and add the components of gold to make great wealth."

Tom snorted. "So thou seekst thy future by pissing in the crucible! Many men have lost their fortunes and reasons in this work."

"I've no fortune to lose, and my reason's sound," I said resentfully. "And I'll find the substance though ye mock me."

I put all my hours to it for the next few weeks, shutting myself away directly after supper, yet though the smoke burned my eyes and my arms ached from working the bellows, mercury remained mercury and lead continued lead. Not in the least discouraged, I thought to turn my talents to the creation of a youth potion by rectifying seasalt and wine. Dazed with wine fumes and weariness, I dropped the crucible and burned my hands; then my master closed the door of the shed and ordered me desist.

"Do you seek the secret of eternal life?" he said. "Rather read the Bible, wag."

"I've read it many times, master."

"Dost find it dull, Nick?"

I was reduced to unwilling silence, for I recognized at this moment that I had not thought very much of my old dreams of late, though whether they had deserted me or I them I did not know.

Pulling my hair, he said kindly, "Nothing can turn into anything else other than what it is, lad, and no man can live longer than the years allotted him."

"I've one more plan for riches, master."

"Say it."

"Discolored pearls lose value."

"Sadly they do."

" 'Tis said they can be whitened again. Look here, where Trevisan of Padua hath writ it! One can whiten pearls with the urine of a pure youth."

"Canst still provide that thyself, wag?"

I flushed and muttered, "Mayhap."

"Young devil!" he roared. "Think on thy work!"

Still, John Heminges and I did not speak often. I thought, once he was a grocer and counted out nutmegs, and a grocer he is still, though he struts upon the stage and divides the profits between the men. He has little imagination and resents mine and will not let me seek my riches.

In October I forgot alchemy, for I saw her once again.

I was sixteen at that time, almost as tall as any man in the company though thin as a wheat shaft, my long hair bound back with an old cloth and still playing women. Trading bawdy stories with the coin gatherer at the Theater's doors, I saw her coming across Moorfields through the gate and fell to silence, knowing from the rapid beating of my heart that my indifference had been a sham, and I could trust nothing less than my emotions. As she reached for the coins in the purse at her belt, I stammered, "Do you remember me, my maid?"

With a smile to her friends she murmured, "Never have I seen you in my life."

All three were youthful, full of satin and flowers. Though it was four-pence to sit in the highest gallery under the thatched roof, I waved the gatherers aside so they should pay nothing and sprang up the steps before them, turning back covetously to watch them follow in a glimmer of pale satin slashed sleeves. Cushions I procured for them from the box, and yet they whispered behind their hands.

"He's half-witted, poor fellow!" one said. "It's plain by how he smiles and smiles."

Their laughter stung me like a switch, and I rushed away down the steps past ascending audience members, and weak-eyed John who sold nuts and oranges during the comedy. Though I had of late experienced a warm, peculiar pride in the growing reputation of our men, it dissipated this day: the play was but cloddish and dull, delicate Condell absurd in padded trunk hose, our lisping apprentice Robert Goffe stale, my own work degrading. I played a wanton bawd and had to sit on Tom Pope's knee, and never did I feel such a prideless fool, though the lutes and krumhorns sang very merrily from the musicians' gallery above the stage. By the time we came to the Epilogue dance, I was disgusted with the whole business of theater and women and wanted only to be off.

What did life hold? The call of the fish woman on Lothbury, the squalling of my mistress's new baby, the slender profits of our trade divided each Sunday night among the shareholders. I craved wealth, intellect, manly beauty, importance, and I was only Nicholas Cooke, players' boy, and if my master praised my skill I wouldn't believe him. Love made me wretched. "The boy's sick," said my mistress.

"Nay, he groweth faster than he can understand. It's the same with all lads," was my master's answer as he looked thoughtfully at me and felt the span of my back with his large hand while I squirmed. Sunday mornings we tramped to church on Aldermanbury, where he was appointed warden and I prayed for all that I did not have.

I had to speak my love.

It could not be to my master, for I seldom told him anything. I would have caught Shagspere by the arm, and standing with eyes cast down on the floor rushes, blurted it out as best I could, yet seldom did I see him alone. He worked with us daily, and was writing yet another play in which he had promised me some shining lines to speak, but he came not at all to our kitchen. I missed him sorely. Someone said that he was much troubled by love, and that necessity forced him to take the baths against the French disease. Once I met him by the civet perfumer's shop in the Exchange. He was wearing a fashionable gold-embroidered doublet to his thigh which must have cost him many a precious shilling, and said he was sorry that he could not stop to speak with me. He wore that garment only one time that I know of; these were his early flirtations with vanity, which his slightly parsimonious nature soon set aside.

Therefore it was to Tom Pope's house I went.

Most fond I was of him, and though he could be brusque, I knew he favored me. I liked to help when he buckled into his padding to play men even more corpulent than himself: after we would sometimes walk across the bridge to buy the bitter beer he craved, and in his ringing voice he would relate lewd tales which must have carried on easterly winds the full four miles to Greenwich. His farts were prodigious: when they burst from him during scenes in the tiring room the boys would scramble to climb through the open window to the field. In his younger days he had been an athlete and a fool, dancing and leaping, but each year he grew heavier and cared not who laughed at him. He ate enthusiastically, cared naught for fine clothing, yet he had saved money from other trades and investments and had accumulated two houses in Southwark. One he rented and the other burst with several adopted children whose mothers were nowhere about and whose fathers one might guess at. His apprentices adored him, including pale little Robert Goffe, who had been our first Juliet, shy and beautiful when he stepped out to the musician's gallery in pink satin at eight shillings the yard.

They said that Tom's housekeeper also warmed his bed, and so I knew it was naught but camaraderie when he felt my breeches and shouted, "You're a fine big fellow, by my faith! How many women hast had this week, Nick?" I did not want to disappoint him, so I answered, "Four." "What, only that!"

We were none of us shy, but Tom Pope went us one step further. When he played the Nurse I almost wet my breeches holding in the laughter as he adjusted his belly under his gown and squeaked, "Now by my maidenhead at twelve years old!"

And so it was to this friend that I went in my lovelorn restlessness, though it was a while before I could confess the problem. He listened seriously with his big hands on his knees as I had seen him the first time in the barber shop. I told him that I had encountered her but twice, and that she must be mine or I'd never have peace again.

He said, "Art tall and well formed! Needst only a single gold earring and she'll not resist thee." Then he sat me down on a stool before a pile of unfolded wash to pierce my left ear. "Dead center!" he said. "And if it weren't there'd be no help for it!" We found his jewel box at last in the wood settee amongst the children's broken rackets; discovering a single gold earring, he fitted it to me and fetched his looking glass. "Now thou'lt have every woman in Shoreditch to thy bed," he said. "For 'tis a fool who confines himself to one when London hath so many!"

My ear festered, I outgrew the only good clothing I owned, and I did not see her again. November found me morose and reading Machiavelli or Erasmus half the night until John Heminges mounted the ladder and sternly ordered me to sleep. Lying in the dusky, soft velvet darkness after he had gone, aroused both in body and mind, my room and bed and the house itself seeming too small, I fretted for the time when I should be my own master at last, with no one to tell me how I must conduct my life.

Morning came with its cluttered activity: my master's young sons rushing through the house searching for their shoes, already a playwriter at the door and the seamstress come to discuss the making of six new black velvet doublets that would withstand the tumbling and swordplay of an actor. I lay in bed staring through the window at the chimneys and dry thatching of the roof across our garden, sick near tears with wanting the young woman whose name I did not yet know. And rolling on my stomach, my head buried in my arms, I understood the impotence of my circumstance. Even if I had known in what ward of the city she lived, I could not send her presents to persuade her to my liking, for I owned nothing worth sending. I had to my possession several unbound and worn books, Chaucer's works in seedy velvet covers with broken clasps, my hose, and my doublets. One doesn't send a woman one's mended hose, and there was nothing else, for the coins I had been given had been diverted to metals and crucibles. I was sixteen and a half years, near penniless, and as Shagspere said in a sonnet I saw lying on his table in his lodgings once, "desiring this man's art and that man's scope, with what I most enjoy contented least."

Christmastide followed Advent, and we played before the old Queen, who greeted us, leaving a whiff of unwashed perspiration, cloves, and roses. On the bodice of her blue velvet gown were scattered fragments of white lead face powder; her teeth were blackened. I found her a fierce, unholy-looking old woman, and made the sign of the Cross on my thigh so that she should not have the power to read my mind. That I had been in her bed chamber and stared at her pillows was a thing I prayed most fervently she should never know of me.

We walked to our church of St. Mary Aldermanbury twice each Sunday down Love Lane, under the hanging washing, past the French cabinetmaker's shop. We were too small a parish to have singing boys or organist; only the congregation feebly intoned the daily Psalms, yet even there on the narthex wall hung a plaque to the well-being of the Queen:

> Spain's rod, Rome's ruin, Netherlands' relief,
> Heaven's gem, Earth's joy, World's wonder, Nature's chief,
> Britain's blessing, England's splendour,
> Religion's nurse and Faith's Defender.

For all the bad poetry praising Gloriana, or the Virgin Queen as they called her (and how odd I thought it that she had never bedded a man, yet perhaps being a queen she was not constructed in quite the same manner, and in faith, what proper man should wish it at her advanced and crooked age?), yea for all the madrigal books imprinted with six-part songs in her honour, I found her tiresome.

It was her favorite, handsome Robert Devereux, Earl of Essex, who absorbed me. The youth of the city from the apprentices to the neophyte law students at the Inns of Court discussed him with the greatest interest. He had succeeded his stepfather, Robert Dudley, Earl of Leicester, as the Queen's favorite and come to court at the age of twenty. He had been with Drake on the expedition to Portugal, and in Dieppe with forces to bravely assist the French King. Tall and muscular, red-haired with a small beard, he had tilted last year at Whitehall yard and since then had not left my memory. Thus I found a hero without knowing I sought one. I sometimes envisioned falling on my knees before him, blurting, "I wish to give my life to your service, my lord."

In the tiring room of our theater as we pulled off our costumes one day, I said, "Tom, if one must die, it should be bravely."

Wiping the sweat from his underarm, he muttered, "Talk of dying, wag! The best death's none at all."

But still I thought that I might die a hero's death one day, be mourned in ballads sold in the London streets and eulogized in one of the pamphlets hastily printed at a stationer's in St. Paul's. Then she, whom I never expected to see again, would hear them sung and weep for me. One night, I hacked off my long hair so that it lay roughly just below my chin and wrote bad sonnets to her, which I burned in the morning. Then when we played at Lincoln's Inn for a private audience, I saw her once more.

Augustine Phillips, who depicted our dashing young lovers, had sickened of tainted fish, and the role with its curled wig and red velvet doublet fell to me. On the first level of benches close enough to touch sat the sweet girl, plump hands folded in her lap. Hardly had we finished the concluding dance and bows when I rushed past my fellows into the hall. Very willing she was to speak with me, her glance straying to the silk hose that rose to my thigh. "Good legs shall not do thee wrong, nor shall gorgeous rags to cover them!" Phillips had assured from his sickbed that morning. Earnestly this young woman and I discussed the literary merits of the comedy as the hall emptied: we discussed many other things, all banal and silently interspersed with her new estimation of my worth and the greater pride it gave me. Hearing my master's voice shouting my name, I whispered, "When may I see thee more?"

She murmured, "When wouldst care for that to be, sir player?"

"This very night and evermore."

"Nay, for my father the alderman awaits me." Then, turning her pretty mouth to my ear, she whispered that she would receive me the following morning just at seven when her mother would be at market and her father gone early to the court, and that I must whistle and she would open the window and look out. So astonished did this leave me that I could only repeat the address she had given with trembling lips, and stand to the side as her friends gathered once more about her.

I rose at four in the morn to bathe in the river.

Bitter cold and dark it was, the bank lit only by the beggars' fires, but I stripped and washed my lanky body and my short soldier's hair, watching the slow early boats down the river and the massive grey stones of the houses on the south side. I would have heated water for bathing in the wood tub at home, but they would have been curious why I wished to bathe, having done so just the week before. My apprentice cap over my wet hair and my wool jerkin not enough to warm me, I lingered by one of the fires, watching the cold grey dawn rise over the houses on the bridge. Then as I had no penny for the boat I ran back to the Strand and the fields beyond towards Charing Cross, where she lived in a street of fair houses before the park, not a hundred feet from a tiltyard. There had been in the neighborhood a house for madmen, but their ranting so disturbed one king some many years before that he had them all sent to Bedlam. There had also been a hospital and hermitage, now likewise vacant of former occupants and turned to tenements. The Cross, an old one of stone, was built by Edward, first of that name, in memory of Eleanor his Queen.

Naught but a ragman with his wheelbarrow walked upon her street, and I strolled by several times and whistled, at first faintly and then with more pluck. The house had a sign of two doves upon it, which meant naught, for with much movement about the city one ofttimes found a butcher working under a painted board of needle and thread. When I was sick with discouragement and thinking she had meant but to tease and trouble me, the shutters opened on the third story and she looked out. "Go round the back," she whispered, "and clamber up the beams."

I was used to swinging up and down the balcony of our theater, so I climbed to my love, who opened her small window, allowing me to half tumble to the floor at her feet. She looked at me crossly as if annoyed I had come late, seized my fingers, and led me to a garret that was full of antiquated dresses, children's playthings, and a baby-minder; there amidst her childhood dolls and private world, she turned to me with her small mouth parted. Behind the clothes press she threw her arms about me, kissing me, biting my lips, and pulling me down to her: this with the heavy garments hung on clothes rods and pegs all but falling atop us and half suffocating our intentions. I was knees and elbows trying to be closer, aware of the heat of her round high breasts under the stiffened bodice. I had not thought she'd kiss me at all: I had not thought to be allowed to touch her. Yet she was passionate as the most wanton girl in the shabby streets near Bankside, where Tom said they were wild with wanting men.

I was all over her in minutes, and I don't know what further favors I might have been granted had not a door closed far below. With that she sprang up, pushing me away with the tendrils of her hair about her cheeks, and whispered furiously as if the fault were all mine, "Thou must go now . . . at once!"

And before I could protest I was dragged down the steps and from the second story half pushed from the window, landing in the alley on my feet by the good graces of my training. Yet I heard her whisper and she called down sweetly, "Boy, boy, it's no one at all."

"Let me up once more."

"Nay: Mother returns anon. What name hast thou?"

"Nicholas."

"Come again tomorrow."

"Aye, madam."

"But be not so shabby! I like it not. You were not so shabby when you played at Lincoln's Inn."

"I shall be what you wish, all that you wish!"

"Then you may return often. Nicholas."

"Aye, madam!"

"Your legs please me; in truth, none hath pleased me so much." Then she closed the red curtains and I saw the good dame her mother waddling down the street followed by a boy with packages from market.

Leaping with astonished joy, I ran across the tiltyard, gained the

Strand, hurled myself through the churchyard booksellers of St. Paul's, and so on to St. Mary Aldermanbury and home. That very afternoon after our performance, I plundered our wardrobe to unearth a white velvet doublet and a white beaver hat with a creamy plume. It was not until the morning that I could return, climb through the window, possess the costuming, and thus run west towards Charing Cross.

She did not give me the satisfaction to comment on my creamy plume, but she was more receptive to me, very much so. I have never been so happily suffocated as below those brocaded gowns and fur-lined cloaks that the moths had nibbled, myself nibbling her as much as I dared and wondering how far up her warm thigh I might slide my hand before her mother returned from the market.

Margaret may have been beautiful, or she may not have been so: I cannot remember. I only know in those early mornings I wanted nothing more than her. The pale freckles above the low neck of her green gown darkened as we touched each other, her eyelashes fluttered, and in the moment of passion, for it was passion I gave her, she moaned and bit with little sharp teeth into my naked shoulder. These marks I gazed at each evening by candlelight in my looking glass, until John Rice yawned and muttered if I were searching for plague blemishes he would take his bedding and seek a healthier place. "Nay, I love," was my brief response, and he whistled and treated me thereafter with a fair respect.

Three or four times weekly when her mother went to market, there walked I, giving every excuse to my master and the men that came to my mind. I think I claimed I went to pray, though I doubt in those days he believed me. Yet though my hand had achieved its place between her warm thighs, and she tossed from side to side on the garments that we had laid on the garret floor, I never knew subsequently how she would treat me. Sometimes when her passion was done she nestled close, tasting my ear: others she turned in silence to stare out the small window. One morning she sat up, pulling her bodice high (for she had not yet totally untrussed it) and frowning at the rumpled cloaks beneath us, and muttered, "Why were you 'prenticed to actors? They're shiftless and penni-less!"

Shrugging, I murmured, "They're not all that."

"They are! If you wish to say I lie, go from me!"

"Have I done aught to anger you, Margaret?" I said anxiously, bringing my hand up tentatively to stroke her hair. Aching in my groin as I did (for she would not allow me so much as to untruss my breeches, much less find the same release which I gave her), I could not see how I had offended. Amidst the furry and shabby garments, she reduced me to shabbiness as well. I believed so much in her and so little in myself that I was certain I had done something and hadn't the wit to remember it. Not daring to protest, I brought my fingers, rich with the half-bitter fragrance of her, to my lips.

Coldly she said, "You've done a wicked thing."

"What may it be?"

"You've told me false, Nicholas! You've no fine parentage! You've neither rings nor pins nor jewelry, and all that you bring to me are common sweets from the apothecary. Thou liest, Nicholas, and you may come here no more!"

I muttered that I would never deceive her.

"Bring me no more common things," she said sternly.

"No, madam."

And I knew I must have fine things for her, though I must become a thief again to get them.

At week's end the men came to our kitchen, the expenses reviewed, poorly received plays discarded, outlays for new costumes and hired actors charted, and profits divided. Late at night when the house slept, I heard my master descend to the garden and dig about there, and that is how I came to know that it was by the foot of the apple tree that he secreted his coins. When I had learned that, I had no more peace, and the coins in the cold dirt of midwinter called to me all the night long. I made reasons why I should have them: I worked as well as he, was paid only the occasional penny and my keep. And so I went to the garden one night when he was away and felt about the wet dirt under the apple tree until something hard came into my fingers: rubbing it clean with a leaf, I took it upstairs to look at it by candlelight. The features of our Queen in gold lay in my palm.

With a stifled cry I started down the steps to replace it, yet I met him as he ascended, his boots in hand so as not to wake the household. "A good night, Nicholas," he said absently.

I lay in my bed with the coin icy in my hand, unable to risk descending to the garden and having the watch cry "Thief!" I vowed to return it at dawn, but the next morning I delayed, until finally I gave in to my need. I spent the coin on a pair of perfumed white kid gloves with silver lace cuffs, and they burned as I tucked them into my belt. Margaret was pleased when she saw the gift, and took me to our place between the clothespress and the hanging cloaks, but my heart was heavy and I could summon little interest. She burrowed into me then as if she would slip past all my hesitations and whispered, "Dost love me no longer? Art not my lover as they are in the plays? Wilt not say the things to me they say at the Theater? I cannot remember the speeches, but surely you'll recall them!"

Because I had no words to answer her (plays were plays and life was another matter, to my mind, and I began to understand she didn't perceive the difference), she said practically, "Cannot we continue as we began? For all that we do here is but a fancy! I shall be married to a rich man, and should I grant thee better favors, thou shouldst spoil me!" In that moment I hated her, and yet my need for her did not diminish.

Sometimes we met in the park.

Towards me on the path that ran by the tennis courts and cockpits she came, her golden hair flying out behind her, biting her full lip in concentration, seizing my hand. Then on we went past dairymaids offering fresh cream. Sometimes when her mother stayed at home, we would wander to the Whitehall gardens, though the winter was yet upon us and the flower beds were bare. Fantastical stories she told me of the offers she had had for marriage, glancing at me to see how I would take them. I had known her some months by this time, and thought as we walked together, so this is what love is, and what a bittersweet thing it's come to be! But it must be so, for every ballad I ever sang to lute or viol described it just this way.

I sold my books and my gold earring, and when the coins were spent, I dug up another from under the tree, sick between the guilt of it and the wanting of her. It is wonderful how things withheld become the more precious, and in the empty striped-blue-and-gold tents of the deserted tiltyard she let me press her to the table where the jousters rest shields and gloves, and sighed when she felt my hand "where comfort is," as the ballad says. Yet as I rubbed my swollen breeches stealthily against her skirts and petticoats, I found to my astonishment that she was weeping. Then I drew her up, kissing her face. "Oh Nicholas," she burst out, "I'm wretched and there's none to help me."

Salty were her tears and her nose snuffly. "No, don't weep, Meg! What makes thee to weep so? Why art wretched?"

"I'm to be married in the spring."

"Married!"

"Why sayst it so! Nick, you know it must be."

I flung away from her to stare, arms folded, at the rows of wood stands wherein the jousters rested their lances; gold ribbon from one lay in the dirt, and moodily I kicked it. "Then why art wretched?" I said practically. "I'm the one indeed who's made a knave of, thou knowst!"

"He's old, very old . . . fifty! To lie with such . . . a creature!"

"Meg!"

"He's naught but bones, nor can he keep up his hose but with tight gartering."

I whirled about, shouting, "Nay, my love! It shan't be. Come away with me forever."

She ceased her absorbed weeping and stood still, and presently a slight smile formed just in the corner of her small mouth. "Thou? . . . but thou art . . . thou hast . . . naught Nick, 'tis madness to think on it." And shuddering, she glanced towards the tent flap which rattled against the ropes in the wind. "You must take me home now, Nicholas."

Despising myself, I muttered, "Say when I may come again."

Sweet and deliberate was her answer. "Tomorrow morning just at seven. Whistle and I'll open the window to thee."

As if some wickedness drew me, I could not keep my feet from Charing Cross and the street below the tiltyard. I lied, cheated, and once did not arrive for the rehearsal at all and had to think of a pocketful of excuses to escape the fine for absence that ranged from sixpence to two shillings. Beyond my will she drew me yet and again to the garret of her house. There we played until she was fair breathless and I so conflicted with anger and desire that I felt I no longer knew who I was and flung myself upon her. Pushing me away, she slapped me hard. "What, wouldst spoil me? I should never be married then."

"God-a-mercy, Margaret!"

"No, no! It will be my ruin. Cannot contain thyself?"

"Will you let me untruss your bodice, then?"

"Not today."

"Then when shall it be?"

"When I have the fancy to it."

"If I were a city alderman as is your father, wouldst let me?"

"Why yes, for then we should be betrothed."

"Then I'm undone," I said, "for I'll never prosper! Actors earn hardly six shillings the week, and the playwriters are paid but six pounds for a tragedy. I've nothing but my love for thee, and thou knowst it."

As I ran towards Charing Cross, I saw her mother, a somber and matronly lady with her baskets of salted meats such as we had to comfort ourselves with in winter. The bells rang and I knew I would be late for rehearsal and I rushed, arriving sweaty and breathless at the theater doors.

"From what battle hast thou come, young Cooke?" said Will dryly. We had to try the French campaigns several times that morning. Only Tom Pope's sharp reprimand brought me to my sense of duty, and I took out the passions in the War of the Roses that I had not been allowed in Margaret's bed. Then I rushed John Rice, who was playing a Frenchman, and killed him mercilessly, placing my foot on his chest. The next weeks were difficult for me, for I could borrow no more costumes, one of the men having found me out. And Margaret tired of our game and commanded me to come no more.

In the end I told everything to Tom, and he said I must go and confess to my master. He also said that he hoped I'd be whipped till my blood came, and he would be glad to do it himself.

I was very angry when I left him.

It was still early on a Sunday morning when I came home and found our little family setting out for matins and communion down Love Lane to Aldermanbury Church, under the washing hung hastily in the unseasonably warm midwinter day. I fell in behind them, unable to look John Heminges in the face, grunting when he spoke to me. Passing the churchyard under the winter trees, we sat down as was our custom in two pews, master, mistress, and myself, John Rice and Susan and the three small children, one of whom was yet nursing from my mistress's breast.

The sermon was incomprehensible: the dead from beneath their stones accused me. I knew I could never tell him, that I would die before I told him. My breath came shorter and my heart beat uncontrollably, and I walked as quietly as I could into the graveyard and, flinging myself down on the wall, buried my face in my hands. After a while I looked up and saw my mistress hurrying from the church, wrapping her shawl carefully about her baby. "Art ill, Nicholas?" she said. "You ran away so quickly. The babe frets: wilt walk home with me?"

I swung up from the wall, and as we walked across Love Lane past the cabinetmaker, she said, "Thou hast missed the bread and wine! Turn back."

"Nay, there can't be bread and wine for me today."

"Wilt say why?"

I shook my head furiously, and we walked on with no further words.

When we came to the house she sat down by the kitchen hearth and, opening her dress discreetly, began to nurse the child. Peculiar feelings suffused me; my knees trembled. Alarmed, suffocated, desperate, lonely, and near tears, I understood. In the quiet house smelling of ripening cheese, of raked ashes and drying herbs, I felt that I had come home at last, and that it could only be to her.

Yes, she was loveliness, and I had tried not to see it from the moment I had come to the house almost three years before. Oh, she was all loveliness, and more, she was peace. Wanting to run across the fresh rushes on the floor and bury my head in the plain brown linen of her gown, wanting to have her touch my hair and console me for my lies, my ingratitude, I clung to my stool with both hands and could only stammer when I tried to speak.

She said, "What troubles thee, Nicholas?"

Then I jumped up and began to pace about, kicking the rushes, turning the cheeses that dried on the shelf. "It's that I must go," I said gruffly at last.

"Why must thee?"

"I'm dishonest and a thief."

"Can it be?" she said gently. She turned, laid the baby in the low cradle by the cold hearth, and then held out her hand to me. I needed no further invitation and, falling to my knees beside her, buried my head in her lap and let her stroke the nape of my neck. I could hardly get the words out. I knew that her hand had left my head before I had finished, and the rejection of her fingers was unbearable. For I felt such love for her! Never had I felt love like that for anyone. It punctured me and wounded me to my heart, and I wanted only to touch the softness under her bodice, sulky and demanding and helpless for her love. It is the people you can open your heart to that you love the best in the end.

"This is a grave matter, Nicholas! Why hast done it?"

"I don't know, mistress! I don't know why I do the things I do, but I repent it so!"

Then she put her arms about me and let me bury my face in her lap again, and for a long time she did not speak, merely stroking my hair as some women do half-mindedly, giving comfort as easily as life. "You must let me manage it," she said at last. "I've a ring from my first husband; we'll sell it and replace the coins."

I muttered, "I cannot take thy ring!"

"You must give me something in exchange."

I looked up at her, half ashamed to let her see my face. "What can I give to thee, sweet mistress?" I said. I had never used this endearment, only it seemed there was no other way to call her for the wholeness between us then.

"You must promise never to betray John Heminges or the men and to stand by them always. They've much love for you, Nicholas. Will you promise?"

I nodded and kissed her palm several times, and after I had washed my face in the Aldermanbury pump and calmed myself with an incomplete and half-remembered act of contrition, I saw my master and the children returning from the church. Then I knew that I could not entirely keep my promise not to betray him, because I loved his wife. At night after the children were abed, he and I put up the shutters, checked the fires and tapers, and mounted to bed. Then they stood, master and wife, at the door of their sleeping chamber, his heavy arm casually about her small shoulders. "A good night, Nicholas," they said courteously.

Then their door was shut to me. I wrote sonnets, but they were not to Margaret anymore.

TWO

Rebecca

EVEN AS SHE HAD CONSOLED ME, SHE HAD BEEN PREGNANT ONCE MORE. Compact, round, and invasive, it lay under her heart; soft lines of exhaustion formed along her eyes. By late winter she had come to the end of her fifth month, and the sight of her descending wearily down the steps each morning was a misery to me. Though she had given birth a few months after I had arrived, I had at first been indifferent to her incessant childbearing. Now, loving her as I did, my hours were tossed with anxiety. Moreover, the nursing of young Peter by the kitchen hearth brought such a confusion of longing that I was often forced to rush from the room.

To forget her, I coaxed my incipient beard by shaving what was not yet there and fell into careless promiscuity. Though my horoscope, or one of the many at least, had predicted that I should become a man of some renown, I couldn't imagine how it would come to be. As soft as I had been during my days of longing for the pristine Margaret, I now courted roughness. I desired to put the boy I'd been behind me and achieve manhood and respect. My curiosity for all things, let free, drove me. Whilst reading one book I was irked that a second lay untasted; whilst with a wench I thought of another and walked about the city looking at gentlewomen with embroidered caps and wood-clogged market girls. John Rice and I had set aside our differences, and went wenching and drinking together wherein he was ill of it, and I felt myself the better man. Still he couldn't admit himself beaten, and we descended into a tavern down crooked stone steps, redolent with earth, ale, unwashed shirts. Someone shouted, "Lay down your rapier!"

My rapier was new and at my side, and my body was possessive of it.

The bargirl passed us in white apron and brown thick skirt, and with teasing, ruddy lips murmured, "Come, young gallants." There was shouting and drinking of ale and hot chicken roasted, and later the girl and I descended to the lower cellar where were kept the kegs of ale. Half drunk, I felt I must have her, but she slapped me lightly, which meant I might come again, and it was a matter of honor not to leave this thing undone. She whispered, "Are you seventeen?"

"Yes."

She put her hand to my crotch, shrieked, and ran away, leaving me in the damp cellar with the slow drip of water on the ale barrels, and the deep sound of many ages. I shivered. How long had I been alive? How long to live? With the plague come? Will God strike me before anything is achieved?

Laughter called me and I went back to them, desiring company.

Oh London was fine then, it was fine! Stunning earls draped themselves in embroidered, slash-sleeved doublets that would cost a laborer five years wages and more, and wool-capped apprentices roamed the streets, gaudy and insolent with their youth. My friends and I wandered to the Tower to see the severed heads of traitors rotting there and the black ravens fluttering about them, our hands guarding our purses. Behind every jostle and smile was a cutpurse.

Oh the women: I wanted them all. Life was bitterly short.

Food cooked on hot coals in every street: potatoes and meat pies, hot sliced brawn of the shops, warm tarts covered by cloth in the baker woman's stand. We ate bitter oranges at sunset and rambled to the water's edge to see the unwieldy coal barges creak downriver between the slender French sailing ships and the maneuvering, cursing London watermen.

Behind the palace walls, the Queen's women embroidered for a year to make her a chemise, little pearls in their fingers, and on the streets near Paternoster Row the ancient beggar with stumps for legs whined and pleaded, have mercy. The plague, however, had melted away as it had come, and all of the city frequented the theater to hear the plays.

On a stone signpost towards Windsor a boy sat with a broken-stringed lute and sang of death.

Oh come not to me. Let us go.

I quickly came to understand that my master was not innocent of the ways in which I spent my free time, for he took the opportunity of our walk across the fields to the Theater to lecture me on the depleting nature of sin. I remained silent, in no way able to explain my concern that all of life would somehow be used up before I could have my chance at it, leaving neither glory nor fortune for me. I was certain he'd never known these things and despised him for it.

He could not fault me on my work, for we brought in new plays twice a month, and the men could depend on me to play anything. As I was too tall to portray women and had as well lost whatever feminine grace I possessed, they assigned me to more reckless, masculine characters; if an actor was needed to leap in battle from the musician's gallery twelve feet to the hard stage below with drawn sword in hand, that actor was I.

My pennies gone and having nothing much to pawn to pay for women, I thought over my sins at home, morose and chastened, and, deciding to do something worthwhile to win my mistress's praise, began once more to put pen to paper and compose a five-act tragedy. It was a thick plot drawn from several old plays, principally *Ferrex and Porrex,* with much intrigue and a guilty relationship between a married woman and a young gallant. I was up until all hours covering page after page of foolscap with my blank verse, and, word blowing about of my composition, the men began to tease me as to when they would hear it. At last we gathered at the Mermaid Tavern one morning, where I read blushingly through the first two acts. The men looked silently at each other, smiling slightly, and Shagspere said it wasn't bad for a beginning piece.

"It's a fair plot but too many murders for one act," said Condell, his thin head nodding seriously.

"The verse sticks a bit," added Phillips. "You want experience in love, I think, my lad."

I threw the pages into my chest under the garret window. I had failed at writing, alchemy had brought me neither the elixir of youth nor gold, and the renown which my horoscope had foretold seemed a mere boy's fantasy. Life at seventeen held nothing for me which was achievable without riches or court influence, neither of which seemed to come with any speed towards my way.

The city was full of the news of the intended invasion of the Spanish port of Cádiz. Spies had informed the Queen that the Spanish were planning to attack in retribution for the Armada, the shame of which they had never fully swallowed, and it was the better part of wisdom for us to take them first. Essex was to have the command to sail from Plymouth in the southeast, and it was said the young Earl of Southampton, whose house I had visited on that winter's afternoon long ago, wanted to accompany him.

I saw Southampton in the fall when he returned from progress with the Queen, angry as a child who must follow the skirts of his tiresome mother. I looked at him as long as I dared. Though he was only a few years older than I, the world between us was a chasm as deep as that at the earth's end, and no cleverness on my part could ever bridge it. There had been some incident between himself and Will and a woman which the men joked of, but of which they told me nothing. It ended with Will taking the cure at Bath for the pox that comes from too careless loving, and a coldness between Southampton House and the poet in Bishopsgate Road. Nevertheless we were certain he had given Shagspere money, for our impecunious poet had secretly bought the best property in Stratford. He had also submitted application for a gentlemen's crest though it seemed to me a player could not be that, no matter what paper he held. My thoughts, however, were not of prosperity but of adventure: Essex and the young Henry Wriothesley, Earl of Southampton, who followed him devotedly, were never far from my mind.

On a spring morning in 1596, my friend Jack Lord from Dorset knocked upon our window on Wood Street and whispered from the side of his mouth that he'd news of the Cádiz venture, what captains would be sent, and who would have command of which fleet. Little interested me more, so I slipped from the door to join him in a back booth of the Mitre Tavern down the street. Jack had been apprenticed to a mercer, over whose counters we had met, but he was now out before his time at his master's wishes, and earning his bread we did not know how. He was a tall, willowy boy with a bad complexion who looked one but briefly in the eye. John Heminges did not like him.

Sliding the booth door closed, I cried eagerly, "Brave Jack, what news? Say quickly before I'm sought, by master grim-and-somber. Thou knowst."

His mouth grinned to one side, and then to the other. "Thou recallst Calais when 'twas nearly invaded, and the men mustered at St. Paul's under Essex? Last year 'twas, and I stood up the brave fellow to enlist when mine own master as was then, may he rot, dragged me away home. She called back brave Essex even as he sailed before the wind, and the supplies rotted. She can never make up her mind."

"Well?" I said, pushing his mug towards him. Ofttimes he bored me, for he liked to keep me with him buying ale, and for that time drew out his story.

"Now he's set for Cádiz."

"I thought she'd changed her mind again."

"Nay, he barked at her, 'Mistress! mistress! let me have my will with thee!' " His voice rose in a feminine shriek, then bending from the waist he shook with laughter, knocking his head repeatedly on the nicked boards of the table booth. "So news is my old master's called, for he led the drill in Finsbury these ten years. Four squadrons under Essex, Lord Admiral Lord Thomas Howard and Sir Wat Raleigh: he'll have the Lord Admiral. Dutch are with us. I'm going, Cooke: I've taken the shilling at the roll of the drum. What say you? What say you?"

His small eyes glittered, and he rubbed his pimply chin and banged the mug upon the board. "For the only man who's worth his weight in England!" he whispered. "R.D. . . . Robert Devereux. I'm sailing out of Plymouth, Nick! Thou art bored to weeping here, come with me!"

"Cannot."

"Sayst why."

Unhappily I scratched at the name of a girl which someone had carved, and hastily drank the bitter brew. Leaning closer with his small eyes sparkling, he threw his voice to a hollow place and accused me, "Dost not fancy war, fellow!"

"In my mind marry I do, but in truth I can't tell it," was my confused answer; then, knowing he despised me, I drank deeply. For some time we remained there talking until I was unsteady in thought and it not yet nine of the morning.

He shook his long finger at me. "Very well!" he said sternly. "Mark it: I shall be captain one day and thou still a bound boy mincing about in padded breeches for six shillings a week."

I lingered by the holding prison with my fingers thrust in my sword belt, watching him saunter towards Cripplegate to his life which I would not follow. War was but a game to me: I was the best swordsman of the younger men, and had died a hundred times upon the stage. God knows I would have liked to go, and how it ached my heart!

My mistress and her sleeping baby were alone in the house when I returned. Cowslips bloomed in the window box, and the sun that came through the small leaded windows touched the rich brown strands of her hair which escaped from beneath her cap. Her foot on the cradle and the curved mound of her belly just visible below the apron strings, she was mending by the hearth. "Oh Nick, art come?" she called, and patted the place on the bench that I might sit beside her. I flung myself casually down. I wanted to tell her how I had failed, but no words came.

I wanted to tell her how I loved her.

Pulling the sheet she was mending over her knees, she said, "John's from home! Hast the morning to thyself with all of London to see and the day so fair?"

"Wilt come and walk with me?"

"Nay: I've this sheet to finish before dinner." Sensing my disappointment, she bit the thread and added wistfully, "I thought just this moment how once you would read to me! Hast grown weary of my company that thou comst no more?"

Defensively I answered, " 'Tis you who have no time to listen!"

Sticking her needle in her bodice, she turned to look at me, and I flushed under the gaze of her grey eyes and round, serious, almost Dutch face. No sound came but the creak of the cradle, from which she had removed her foot. It was a small foot, and the hose beneath the skirt grey worsted. "Why what's this, Nick!" she said. "Nay, turn not thy face away! You reek of sack as a tinker on holiday! You know John forbids this, dear heart!"

Her scolding both thrilled and challenged me, and taking her hand, I kissed the slightly coarse fingers. Laughing, she caressed my cheek and reached once more for her needle. I gazed about the kitchen from the barrels of salt herring, the bacon drying from the rafters, to the large iron pot which hung motionless over the few warm ashes of the hearth, ever aware of her skirt which lay quietly against my leg.

How strange, dear, and provocative was our play to which this very room so often bore witness! Sometimes I would come behind her as she laid the trenchers for dinner and catch her about the waist, covering her eyes with my free hand so that she had to guess who it might be. She always knew. Or I would hide her knitting, her wooden spoons, or sometimes lift her in her arms, and she cried always, "Who can it be? 'Tis my Master Condell or Master Phillips . . . nay, young master Rice . . ." And then when I released her, looking up at me laughing because I still had her imprisoned in my arms, would say, "It can't be Nick! Why art grown so great a fellow as never I thought it should come to be!"

And from the corner, looking up from his accounting book, my master would murmur, "Leave her to her work, thou great lout! Wilt fetch the ale? Becky, when shall we dine?" The fool knew nothing.

For a time I stood, idly swaying the black pot back and forth, until she said reprovingly, "Shalt spill the water for boiling and needst fetch more?" I flung myself down on the bench again, felt the edge of the sheet, allowing my fingers to wander to hers; then taking the hand, needle and all, kissed her palm with more devotion and absorption than ever I knelt for the bread and wine. "Now, my wag!" she said, her voice quite low. "What dost? I've these ragged edges to turn before the hour of ten."

"Come walk with me."

Settling to sew once more, she answered, "Thou seest my work."

"Then I will sit here with thee!"

"Ah! Shalt read?"

"Nay. Tell me something of thyself. Wilt tell me aught?"

Shaking her head, she glanced over at the sleeping child. "Of me? Why, what can be said of me? I hurry from buttery to the mending to the making of pies: 'tis a simple life and no different today from all the days past."

"Nay, tell me of thy days before you came here."

"I can scarce remember them."

"How didst come to marry?"

Once more drawing the edges of the sheet together, she pursed her lips and said practically, "Why, all girls must marry or become spinsters and be made a pity of! An actor spoke for me when I was very young and we were betrothed. I meant to live all my days with him, but he was killed in a fight. And then John Heminges was grocer to our family, and came to know me and brought me spices and was kind. He spoke to my father, excusing that he was far older than me, and that is all of it, dear heart."

I thought it was a shoddy romance, and not worth a play, and that she deserved better. My lips were hungry to kiss that hand again, sweet and rough as it was, and small enough to be well hidden within mine. John Heminges, bookkeeper and grocer, had not the imagination to dream of the pale wrist beneath the stiff linen cuff. Then, mayhap, as respectfully as he spoke of her, as carefully as he stood above her (with as great care as he replaced in his pocket the keys to the parish strongbox and our house), he loved that hand too. With this, I hated him, and I pushed forward in our conversation with less naivety than she could ever imagine possible of me.

"Mistress."

"Aye, Nicholas."

"Art so fair, so beautiful! Aye, as any maid of sixteen!"

"Oh thou flatterer! Thou knowst I am eight and twenty, far past youth."

Playing with the folds of her skirts, I murmured, "What sort of maiden were you?"

"Disobedient! They tell me I was willful."

"Didst wear thy hair long?"

"Aye, past my waist."

" 'Tis as long still?"

"Oh aye! Thou knowst! I've never cut it."

"I should like to see loose."

"Only maidens wear it so."

"Didst anger thy parents being willful?"

Laughing, she cried, "Aye! and they made shift to marry me young. The young men hung about our windows like young dogs, my father said, and he knew I stood behind the curtains and listened to them call up."

Her placid grey eyes met mine, her sweet full mouth and the Dutch face round. My mouth dry and with the skirt's folds yet within my fingers, I murmured, "Didst answer them?"

"Nay!"

"Not ever?"

She laughed once more, shaking her head. "Nay!"

"I should have liked to be among them."

"You were but a child."

"But had I come to man's estate then and stood about your window, wouldst have answered me?"

"Mayhap! I would have opened the curtains for just one minute and thrown thee down my handkerchief to keep, but quickly, quickly, so that no one should see me!"

"Wouldst thou?"

"Oh aye, Nicholas!"

"The other men needn't come near. I'd beat them."

"Yes, thou would do it."

My head was so close to her that I could almost nuzzle her cap with my forehead. "But . . . wherefore?"

"Wherefore what?"

"Wherefore wouldst throw thy handkerchief to me and not to them?"

"For thy sweet young man's face and thy curious mind!" Our eyes met and then slowly she turned away, and began to rock the cradle, the sheet slipping to the floor. After a time she pushed back the few strands of hair from under her cap.

"Mistress," I said unsteadily.

"Well then?"

"Wilt wear thy hair loose once?"

"Mayhap one evening when the shutters are put up."

"Mistress."

"Aye, Nick."

"Likst thou me?"

"I like thee well," she said and took my face in her hands tenderly before releasing me, and fetching the sheet once more to her lap. Thus she consoled, efficiently and easily. She was always consoling one young person or another, and nothing was more natural. Yet I needed more than that, and God knows what prevented me from rashly, rapidly turning and kissing her sweet mouth. "Tell me," I croaked, "how thou camst to be married . . . about you and . . . master."

She said practically, "Oh, John! Why, he's always taken good care of me! Now that I'm with child again he sometimes makes me stay abed until five of the morning when I want to be up and about. Such a good man, Nick! Canst not see it?"

I did not answer. Her gentle mind was full of ordinary things: cookery concerns, the pox coming to a neighbor's house, drying shoes by the hearth when we had come in from the rain. "Tell me what troubles thee, Nicholas!" she said. "Canst speak to me?"

Her mouth was so very close to mine. Muttering, "Take down thy hair!" I reached up to pull out the first ivory pin that held her braids, but she laughed and caught my hand reprovingly with her small fingers. Then I flushed until I was breathless. What folly! For I knew I was no more to her than yet another young person to be coddled with plant juices in the winter against scurvy. Her life was predictable. Everything was at just one time and not another. In all things, she could be counted on, and most certainly she could be counted on to refuse me.

I ran past her up the steps, flinging myself on my bed, and made up my mind to go off. I saw the ships sailing down the Thames to the sea and felt myself nothing of a man because I wasn't with them. Oh there was life and I only a counterfeit of it! It was bitter to my soul to know that I played at noble deeds in a wooden theater when other men lived them. Oh God, might I have been at Agincourt with Henry! I saw myself returning from battle, wounded and weakened, and she regretful she had sent me off unloved.

Most uncomfortable, stringent, and wearing were the next three days within our house: most silent I was at meals, sometimes gorging myself, at other times toying with my knife with my ears ringing from the stupid high chatter of the children, and her admonishments to them to take only a fingerful of meat at once, and his admonishments to myself and the new small apprentice, Peter Hardy, to sit up straight, lads, one cannot walk a cripple upon the stage.

"Peppers gone up the penny a pound," said my beautiful mistress.

"Must we use so much?" was his answer. "Nick, what silence's this? Hast the bellyache and needeth a purge, lad?"

"Nay!" I cried suddenly with my voice ringing even up the steps to my garret ladder, and so that all the others fell silent. "Nay, master. Only I can no longer stay here but must sail with Lord Essex to Cádiz as soldier."

John Heminges leaned back, hands on his stomach, gazing at me benevolently. "What sayst thou, wag!" he said, smiling. "What new madness is this, prithee? You've your trade here."

"I'm past seventeen," I answered stubbornly. "And man enough to fight by the side of him who'll one day rule this land."

He played with the edge of his knife, his round, good-natured face growing stern. "What gossip's this? Elizabeth our Queen, praise her judgment, knows him for his erratic nature and would never have him successor. 'Tis bad enough she gives him command at all. Christ protect us should Essex be King. What gossip's this, what treason, Nick?"

"She should have given him better command before," I said. "Aye, long ago. 'Tis not fit that she still rules England, for she's grown too elderly to think! Old women shouldn't be masters of men."

Placing his broad hands on the table, he said, "Nick, be silent."

All the children were staring anxiously at us, and John Rice had twice kicked me secretly, but I could not have held peace for my life. " 'Tis because he won't love her," I said. "I've heard it said in taverns."

John Heminges stood up so suddenly that his mug spilled, and the ale went running along the table cracks. "Hold thy rash and untutored tongue!" he shouted. "We don't speak treason against the Queen in this house."

Rising as well, I cried half imploringly, "Master!"

"Nicholas, do you disobey me?"

"This means I mayn't speak of it."

"Neither may you."

"Nor of anything else . . . that you feel is . . . disloyal." My legs were trembling with my anger. "Not to feel or say what displeases you and to answer to you always. The most noble hero is undefended, while we scrape to the Queen for her patronage."

More reasonably he spoke. "Whence comes this madness? He'll prove a paper hero, Nick. And as for answering to me, why, we all answer to someone."

"And you?"

"To my fellows and to Christ."

"But this passes bearing!" I cried. "And I must endure it until I'm twenty-one and out of my time. Rather to be anywhere else than to endure this from you!" I pushed back my stool furiously and ran up the steps, where most mercifully he did not follow me.

We spent a silent evening together cleaning and mending costumes, Condell directing my stitches and telling gossip of rival companies. Late that night, I slipped out the door with a lantern and down the street towards Lothbury, almost feverish with my anger, all the time repeating in my head arguments to the man who would not hear them.

I was not free; I could not go to war. I was an apprenticed player, but when my time was up, I would find something more dignified and prosperous and they would see me no more. Thus I continued in my head as I walked to the bridge path, hearing the call of the river watchmen. Still and yet again, I was not legally bound to Heminges . . . this grocer! this small-minded merchant! . . . for only informal papers had ever been drawn. Stultified I was with the acting and reacting of other men's monumental deeds. I was cut out for an adventurer and not a stay-at-home. I did not wish to tread the boards each afternoon and coax the lettuces from the compost in the garden each twilight. They had mistaken me if they thought me to be that sort of man.

The gold grasshopper of the Royal Exchange glistened before the shops in the moonlight, the guard nodding suspiciously at me as I passed.

Then I walked east to cross the bridge by lanternlight and made for the brothels of Southwark. Winchester geese they called the women there, after the name of Liberty in which they lived. Many was the man who had to take the painful mercury treatment and be endlessly purged and bled from the wanton sickness they spread, yet in my youthful strength I felt me immune to these things which troubled weaker men. There was a house called the Cardinal's Hat which proclaimed itself for single women, but any boy in the city knew how they paid for their bread and cheese. They smelled tawdry, like stale beer, and of last week's chemises and other men's desires. A man came under compulsion and left in disgust, lice in the folds of his shirt and the Lord knoweth what else and where. It was sour-sweet and degrading, but I felt myself a degraded man already living without achievement, without respect.

A woman was there who reminded me in her broad, calm look of my mistress, and her I took, and tore away her cap and put my face in her hair. Yet all the while I was angry that life was so cheap. I had pawned the pendant round my neck, which had been Condell's gift of the New Year, to pay for it, and woke sickened with the wine to the harsh spring morning sun, knowing that for staying away without my master's permission I should have to face his anger. I had some vague plans of going off at once to join the men off to Cádiz: even Southampton was determined to go, they said, though the Queen had forbidden it. Yet I hesitated, feeling I should not see my mistress again and it was to John Heminges's blame.

"Oh sweetheart!" the girls of the brothel chattered as they showed me the door when morning came. "Come again quickly, for thou art a mighty fellow!" And because I could not bear to go from the city or summon the courage to return to all I knew, I wandered idly to the Bear Gardens. Bearbaiting had always sickened me and the ghosts of the persecuted, aging, and blinded animals and the fierce dogs who baited them coarsened the neighborhood, but paying my last penny, I forced myself to watch them to forget my troubles and come to one mind on what course of action I must follow.

Then I fell into conversation with a man who said he had been to the

Americas, and would tell me more if I'd take dinner with him. Honest Mark Freeman, he heartily announced himself, and a true West Riding man. I had read Tom Hariot's splendidly descriptive book about life in the Americas among the savages and considered that a chance of happiness might be to sail to America myself and begin my life anew and that providence had led me to this new friend who would show me how to do it. I told him that I'd been a players' boy but had no more money, and he said he would be glad to pay for my dinner for the pleasure of my company. Flattered, I went with him at once arm in arm to the Falcon Tavern, where they kept horses during the plays and which lay under the shadow of the Bear Garden; there, my tongue quickly loosened with sugared wine, I opened my heart and told him of my unhappiness as a players' 'prentice, and my love for my mistress and many other drunken things I would now give very much to never have spoken. I almost wept in my confidence of him, but when the reckoning came he gave a cry and said I had robbed him of his purse.

Quite drunk and with only the immediate need to preserve my good name (they knew me there for I sometimes came with Tom, whose parish lay quite near), and in panic for the things I had told him which he had suddenly began to shout out at me, I laid hands on him. He shoved me over and called me a lying boy. "Actors are naught but thieves," he said. "Vagabonds the lot of you. Show me the whore who you love and I'll have her for the price of a dozen farthingale pins."

He took his life into his hands to say it, and I leapt across the table as he tried to walk away. We began to fight, and the host threw us both from the door into the wet, marshy spring grass that grew all over Southwark from the Bear Garden through Bankside. By this time my acquaintance plainly saw he'd thought me weaker and younger than I was, and wanted to make an end of it and get away, but I was doubly enraged, for I'd opened my heart to him in that hour of dinner and he'd betrayed me. I leapt at him with a cry and held him with my arm across his throat.

Though he was broader than I, he couldn't throw me off, and he cursed me for a devil's spawn and kicked back between my legs. "Thou whore's son, I'll make a eunuch of thee!" he cried. Then we fell in the thick, soft grass, and I heard his breath in my ear.

Still I shouted, "Come on, come on," and had my dagger out. I had never used it but to cut my meat, but I leapt at him with all my strength, raising my arm to stab him. He rolled me over and we tussled in the long grass. I could hear people shouting and running and I knew I'd have to have his blood or it would be too late. Crying out in rage, I slashed his arm. Red blood seeped to the brown sleeve, and I knelt above him, gazing in horror and unable to move. We were friends but half an hour before; now I'd wounded him and should be branded for it. The thought of the disgrace and the red-hot iron sizzling into my flesh made me gasp for what I had done.

Someone yanked me to my feet and spun me around; Tom Pope held me, panting and sweating. He shouted, "Come then! Dost wish to see the inside of the Fleet? You fool!" He half dragged and half pushed me, and I stumbled and fought him and cursed him. He seized me by the hair and in that way made me come home with him, where he threw me across the rushes of his kitchen floor.

"We've had hard shift to do without thee this morning at rehearsal," he yelled. "And I find thee in thy cups in midafternoon preparing thyself for the hangman's noose!"

I could only gasp, "Let me go off."

"John Heminges has searched the city for thee."

"To what purpose? To keep me as a player? If I could go off and fight with Essex I would at least feel as if I were worth the very air I breathe."

He pushed me from him, took me by the shoulders, and shook me hard. "Thou art the best young actor we have, damned pretty fool," he shouted, "and with thy wild and wanton nature thou'll end dead in a tavern fight like Morley. What, art so eager to ship to Cádiz and die bleeding in a foreign land, trampled under the hoofs of warhorses?"

"Better to die at once there than slowly here!" My stomach rebelled and I began to vomit: he fetched a pan for it and held my head, and afterwards washed my face and gave me water to drink. Footsteps through the rushes aroused me and I leapt up, thinking it was Heminges come to fetch me, but found instead my friend Shagspere. I had not seen him very much of late with his fascination for property and crests and clothes of superior quality.

"If a man cannot live with himself, 'tis a serious matter, Nick," he said when he had heard the whole of it. "A man's in a pretty state if he cannot be content with his own body and soul."

"He quarrels with John over small matters and thinks it time he were on his own in the world, though he doesn't know enough not to open his heart to a blackmailer in a tavern." With a soft cuff, Tom released me, and I sat there with my grief expended, sick and exhausted.

They folded their arms to study me until Shagspere said, "Take him to one of thy women, Tom."

"He does more than well enough for himself."

"Think you? Methinks he's half swollen with sperm."

I shouted, "A pox on you both! Must make me speak of what brings me to misery and have a game of it . . . aye . . ." I hardly knew what I said: words tumbled from me. "I live without purpose, without honor, unnecessary in every way, and if I die who'll remember me? So much to do in the world and I fail at all of it."

Shagspere said, "At what have you failed? Dear wag!"

"I live without purpose: I live without love."

"Hast some woman told thee nay?"

Shocked, I was silent.

"Never mind such things: why Nick, we love thee. Canst not make it do for this time?"

"I'm unfit for this world and always have been! Whatever I do I make a muddle and a muck! I want a sign from heaven and it never comes, Will, never."

"The boy cannot leave off star charting," said Tom, feeling the roundness of his belly under the hefty jerkin newly enlarged with leather strips on the side.

"Thinkst I talk of stars!" I cried aghast.

"He talks of divinity," said Will, without taking his hand from my arm or his eyes from my face. "He wants a word from God."

"A muck he talks when soaked to his skin in wine and newly come from driving his dagger into some poor bitch's son's arm in the blessed Southwark mud. Signs! He's so swollen with lust it's gone to his brain, and I cannot wonder what man's wife he dreams of."

"Hold thy tongue!" I cried, leaping up with my hand to my side where my dagger had been. Tom's eyes grew round, and grabbing my shirt he cuffed my head with his free hand. "Wouldst draw on me? Christ's wounds, I'd take a switch to thee had I one! Art grown too exalted for that, thinkst?"

"I have only wanted to hide in God. He sent me here but for a while to wait His word and now abandons me forever."

"Then abandon thyself and draw up the winding sheets over thy face!"

"I should have been a priest."

"Be one to thy madness! Thou art as holy as a pig's snout, damn thee, boy."

"For God's love, be still, old friend Pope," murmured Will wearily, sitting beside me. Full of regret, I flung my arms about him, fighting my tears. He said, "Nick, my falcon," and held me against him, rubbing my back thoughtfully with one hand. And when I shamefully pulled away, not knowing where to look, I felt his tender golden-brown eyes upon me for a long time.

"Yes," I heard Tom Pope say angrily, "sin and repentance come as easily to this pisspot as the 'mayhap I will' and 'mayhap I won't' of a simpering virgin girl."

He said more, but I knew little. I slept. The last thing I heard was that they had gone to pay off my brawling friend; the wound was slight and the tavern keeper would vouch that I fought in self-defense were the matter come to the ears of the law.

Hours later I awakened, a foul taste in my mouth, an aching head and heart, and Tom's housekeeper looming above me, her enormous breasts straining against the hasty lacing of her blouse. "Looking for signs!" she muttered. "Expecting word from heaven and in the same breath offering to murder a ton of honest manhood in his own kitchen."

Aye, it was done. Word of my hasty outburst would soon be talked of by the children in the gutters and the apprentices in the tiring room, as well as the women at the pump and my own sweet Rebecca. I pulled myself up, shamefully asked for some water, and sick to heart, crept to the door and down the street.

It was come to the later part of an April afternoon when the world appeared so washed and cleanly hung to dry that it is indeed a time to begin again and put away one's own muddiness: the world seemed to hang like a white petticoat upon a line above a cluster of daffodils sprung from between the cracks of the bridge footpath. Even my shame lifted slightly to see it, and walking round-shouldered and penitently away from the painful scene of both my quarrels, I turned south towards Thieves' Lane and St. Thomas Hospital. It had once been a monastery; now the buildings were arranged in two large quadrangles, with a burial ground opposite. I poked about the windows until the red-frocked warden emerged, commenting that if I was neither leper nor patron I should be on my way.

Slightly further down the road I found the White Hart Inn with its accommodations for one hundred travelers, and clustered together beyond on St. Margaret's Hill, the publishers. There I went, seeking consolation for though my world was turned upside down, books remained. Shyly I first contented myself with studying the few volumes displayed outside and then wandering inside like a fellow craftsman to run my fingers through the boxes of loose type, taking pleasure in the ink that brushed my flesh, feeling comfort in the heavy-handed sound of the press being cranked by the printer and his boy. And all the time I muttered as I drifted from the piles of unsewn printing to the cakes of lead ink, what have I done now and where on earth am I to go?

The printer in his inky apron recognized me. He left his presses, and before you know had offered me on trust a copy of Ovid's love poems. " 'Twas just this morning sewn together," he said fondly. "And the ink smeared on two of the block prints: 'tisn't worth more than eightpence for that. But thou art like unto a clock run an hour slow, Nick! Thou must keep better time with thy master."

"Marry! Why should I keep better time with him?" I murmured, my face growing warm at the mention of his name.

"There's an hour's difference between you, for he was here about that much before, inquiring if we'd seen thee. Is it not so, Ned? We were just setting the title page for *The Merry Devil of Edmonton* when honest John Heminges looked in the door."

Sweet Jesus's wounds, I murmured to myself, and tucked the book inside my jerkin, suddenly warm indeed to be gone from this pleasant place. Walking rapidly away, I was saluted by one of the ostlers coming from the White Hart; he had worked a time in the mews near Aldermanbury and knew my people well. "Why, Nick Cooke!" he said cheerfully. "Thy master's been looking about for thee, hast heard? News of thy quarrel's about the inn from the middle chamber to the coal hole. What addlebrained moment made thee to sup with the man? Thy goodman Pope hath routed him with a kick to his breeches. Turn home, man: thou are wanted."

"I'll tarry yet," I muttered, squeezed his arm, and hurried away down the side of the hospital and Thieves' Lane. Its path wound around the high walls of the old monastery, though hardly quickly enough for me, and opened up into the fields. There were daffodils there, aye thousands of them: so bright and as far as one could see, and as I waded through they clung to me and wantonly embraced my boots and all the field spoke of sensuality and the spring. Troubles and responsibilities fell away as I frolicked alone among the daffodils, kneeling and gathering them into my arms. I cannot remember when I had felt such childish, simple joy. Aye,

mayhap in Canterbury when we played out the French and English Wars
in the ruins of Augustine's Abbey and I was Henry the Fifth leaping from
the fallen stones. There were daffodils then and nothing that I could not
be. And I walked on and on with flowers stuck behind my ears, and my
book in my jerkin.

Crooked planked bridges forded small streams; beyond were neat
patches of farmland and orchards and apple and cherry trees. Fields led
into other fields, and past small groupings of cottages hardly large enough
for a village, and there was the ringing of church bells. The sun had just
begun its descent to the west. I could no longer make out the spires of
London and Westminster: no master would look for me here.

From a narrow accumulation of cottages came the smell of fowls
roasting: hunger stirred. I sat down by a wayside Cross and began to read,
looking up now and then when I heard bells ringing or to watch a pretty
girl with skirts kirtled up, bringing home her cows. It fancied me to
follow her, and I did, not very discreetly; from time to time she looked
back, her bare legs speckled with mud and her small feet black from it.
How much had happened since I longed for Margaret, and how stupid I
had been! It lacked wisdom to long for anyone when it brought sadness,
but I had never known love to be otherwise.

The girl had disappeared into a tangle of thatched, sunken cottages,
and I followed, now more hungry than before and very much alone. The
road's end opened to another field and in the middle of that the remains
of a monastery. It lay there like something long expecting me, and there
was no sound but of the high grasses bending under my boots as I trudged
towards it.

No roof, of course: when bluff Henry in his pride had torn his church
away from Rome, his soldiers had made haste to tear the lead from abbey
roofs to make cannonballs and bullets. Fascinated, I continued to push
my way through the daffodils and grass until I came to where the doors
had hung. Faceless saints stared out across the wild field. Years since
when the monasteries had been dissolved some careless soldier had

smashed away their patient eyes, leaving them sightless and silent to overlook the fields and forests.

I thought, had I been born an hundred years before I should have come to such a place! Monk and priest I would have been, mayhap within these very walls, and safe from all my feelings and bad impulses, safe from myself. A deep peace settled on me like a shiver, and the air was wonderfully still. London and all my life there lay a hundred years in the future: I was here, the year fifteen hundred not yet turned. I was here when men could still put away their own desires and learn holiness.

Gently I fell to my knees amidst the flowers.

What wouldst thou, dear son? a voice seemed to say. (Ah, it was real, so real!) And I whispered, I have come to escape from the world and myself, my father! Wrap me deeply in a cowl, cut off my tangled hair, cut off my vagrant desires, enclose me, inhibit me, make me safe at last.

How strange! I did not raise my eyes, yet on the stone beside me I seemed to feel a shape in a heavy hood, quiet hands on a lap, and a listening presence. Now I shivered indeed, and a lump rose in my throat. You see, father, I've come back since I cannot manage in these bad times. I cannot manage myself.

Let not thy heart be troubled, he said, neither let it be afraid.

I was stunned into breathlessness, and after a long time my mind spoke alone, and said, what is this place?

Thou knowst.

How far have we come from London, father?

Very far. Let not thy heart be troubled, neither let it be afraid. Peace I leave with thee, my peace I give to thee: not as the world gives it do I give it to thee.

That is it exactly! I cried. Not as the world gives . . . but the world can give me nothing! The world has always been a place where I've stumbled and fallen. For instance, today . . .

Nicholas. Is it thy desire to part from the world?

Stunned, I nodded.

To leave thy house and friends. Say it.

Father, I do.

Then cast off mortal longing and put on the garments of holiness.

I rose clumsily, not daring to turn for the awful fear that the voice I heard came from nothing at all: if I did not turn, I could still feel this peculiar, gentle presence and not lose it. Carefully, I untrussed my jerkin and laid aside my book of poetry. Closing my eyes as if in the holiest of rites, I lifted my arms to draw about me the imaginary rough brown robe; with trembling fingers I drew up the hood. Coarse-spun it was, and inside it I was hidden as I had never been before. A deep sigh of satisfaction passed through my chest, and a sob of grateful loss. Nicholas Cooke is no more! I whispered. I have cast him aside like the works of darkness! All his impudent fancies, all his sins. I have cast him aside and am herewithin hidden. Lead me.

Go into the chapel and pray, said the voice.

I looked about me in the brilliant light of that late-spring afternoon: yes, all the air was sagging with the smell of flowers, fruits, the living and eternal English earth. Chapel? I could not find it. I am one hundred years late in coming, father! I whispered, but he said, never mind, never mind, find your chapel where you would have it be.

I bent my head to go past a low door. There was nothing remaining but one crumbling wall, and then all beyond fields and woods. There I knelt and clasped my hands. Say what you wish, said my voice.

To stay here forever. I will find myself different within these ruins.

Then to my astonishment I began to cry, and I wept there for a long time with my hands over my face. I only longed to return to the time when I was in Canterbury in my wool gown, dedicating myself to God, knowing that He held me in His hands and my life would be safe and simple: I would serve Him. Yet with the grief came joy from a place I couldn't understand. I felt God as plainly as I felt the sun on the back of my neck, the damp earth beneath my humble knees. I cried with a sense of joy somehow intermingled, as if at last I had found someone to whom I could say everything. Ah, where have you been! I cried. Do you know how long I have been waiting? And why today, and why in this place? I am no longer alone. Let me stay here, let me stay here forever.

Is that thy whole desire?

Aye, father! (And I waited with my knees pressed into the moist earth and my hands wet with my tears.)

There was a weighty silence. Then be it so, was the answer, you are here forever. Aldermanbury is but a memory, the past is finished and gone. This quiet world away from all the living is thy only reality, and here thou art safe. This world is narrow, forgotten, there is no room for stumbling or desire. What thou hast wanted always will be given: the loss of self. Rise up, my friend.

Still not recovered from my grief, I stumbled to my feet and shyly began to walk about this place that was now my own. Come to supper, said the voice. Your brothers are waiting.

On a stone I sat and looked about me. The other stones and flowers became my fellow monks as I bent my head over my soup bowl. I could see their faces, all placid and almost worn away like the stone saint's. After a time, I made the sign of the Cross in thanks for the meal. Richly I felt I had dined.

Wandering about for some moments, I found my cell. It was time for prayer. I fell to my knees and prayed for a long and sensuous time, then lay down and perhaps fell asleep. When I awoke I knew not if centuries or minutes had passed, but the sun was hardly lower and the grass tickled my nose. I am old, I thought. I have grown old here. I am no longer a young monk but abbot of this place. Many come to me for spiritual consolation and absolution: my fame is known throughout the land.

Slowly I rose and wiped the leaves off a stone to seat myself, again closing my eyes. Come, I said to the young monks about me, let us put aside our sins, both of the body and of the mind. Let us put aside all earthly desires and knowledge. Knowledge brings pain: desires leave one hollow. Human love disappoints, and the world is full of death.

They were looking at me, these ghosts of monks made from leaves and stones, from spring flowers and the field mice that startled the grass. I drew my hooded robe closer and closer, I shut my eyes to them. No, I must look only inside! I must not love others, any others. Peace I give to thee, not as the world gives . . .

With a gasp I opened my eyes again. They were gone. Ah, they were gone absolutely and there was nothing where they had been but stones, and the dirt pressed into my hose and my face streaked with tears. How could they leave me! Tears began again, and fury. I seized my jerkin and hurled it against the ground. Then I listened.

Someone was calling: it seemed at first to come from across the fields, and I raised my head. Now time had passed indeed. The sun was slowly descending to the west, and the stones of the monastery had a damp, shadowy quality about them. I listened anxiously for the call to come again. A woman spoke languorously as if leaning from a window on soft arms: Nick . . . dear love!

Nick, it's time to come for supper! Bring your book and read something to me of the Romans. Did they once walk the streets of Canterbury? Tell me these things, Nick! Oh Nick, why did you leave me? The baby will come and I will surely die.

No words came from me. I played with the thick Cross that seemed to hang about my neck and said, Mother! Wait but a little longer . . .

I cannot wait. There's no more time.

I covered my face with my hands. The voice changed. Oh Nick, come quickly! I've need of thee!

Leaping to my feet, my voice rang out against the broken stones: "Rebecca, 'tis thou?" The sky was moving: grey clouds rolled from the north and night was coming. I turned and walked rapidly away with my heart beating so fast my knees struggled to give under. My book and jerkin lay in the grass behind me, but I would not turn back. A few drops of water brushed my face like unwanted kisses; I shook them off and began to run across the flowers; not bothering to divert for the plank bridge, I splashed across the stream, soaking my boots. I ran until my legs cried for mercy.

Nick, fool, I thought . . . don't go back. You'll be whipped.

Let him, I answered. It's not him I care for.

Thy pride . . .

I've done with that! Does that matter?

Halfway across the fields to London the dark skies opened and cold rain poured down my neck and face, almost obscuring my way. Foggy and insignificant were the occasional lights of the outlying houses, and as I splashed across Southwark, even the flares inside the innyard of the White Hart seemed to urge me faster home. Then as I ran towards the bridge path, I heard cries and shouting. A few men ran past me, knocking me to the side, and I took to my heels to follow them towards the sound of the river until we came to the bridge itself.

The Thames had swollen, the grey water rushed against the arches, slammed upon the ancient stones, and thrust itself through. Barely in the violent rain could I see a few boatmen struggling towards the shore and hear the roar and subsequent fall of the water of several feet from under the third arch of the bridge, where sunken masonry from ancient times impeded the flood. Rocking to and fro like drunkards in the storm were the masts of larger boats at dock. With this sudden darkness and violent rain an impatient passenger who insisted his boat shoot the waters of the bridge could not much care for his life.

Another man pushed by me hard, and following him, I seized the end of the uncoiling rope he held. "Men drowned, men drowned," was the cry, and I thought, sweet Jesus! Then they did try to shoot the waters! Had the boatman a family? Was some fool so hasty that he had to ride to Greenwich in this storm?

Now there were more people running past us and the screaming of a woman. "Jesus have mercy!" she cried.

A man tossed me down a second rope and a boating hook; without thinking and with a shout, I had begun to rush down the obscure, slippery steps to the water when a small hand pulled my sleeve. Impatiently I turned to see our youngest apprentice shaking my arm, the water running down his face. "Someone's fallen in," I shouted. "They'll be smashed against the force pumps or the docks! Peter, damn thee, loose me!"

"Nay, Nick!" he shouted above the water. "Wilt come? John Heminges's from home and mistress's time's come early."

Even if he had been there I would have returned, hearing this news, and pushing past the men, ran up the bridge path, dropping my rope as I went. The cries were below us over the rushing of the water, and there was torchlight on the bank. The boy and I stopped for only a second in the narrow part of the bridge, which allowed us to see below; a woman stood, her hands over her eyes, sobbing amidst the sideturned boats, and many people were crying aloud. How the water pounded in my ears and their voices pierced my heart as we turned up Bishopsgate Road! My stomach cramped with my run by the time I entered our house.

The children had been sent off to stay with Condell's wife, and above I heard the slap of the midwife's slippers and the murmur of women. Rebecca's pain was written in her flushed, moist face. She lay in her cambric shift, having thrown the covers to the floor, the elderly midwife muttering as if to excuse her incompetence, "It'll neither be born nor stay. Sideways, 'tis, the worst way."

Though my clothes were sopping, I did not hesitate to run to my mistress, murmuring, "I've come to thee . . . all shall be well!" Grasping her icy hand, I chafed it and drew a small footstool to her bedside. Her back arched, the pains came, and she squeezed my hands until I thought my bones would crack. Pain receded, and once more I chafed the hand. Cometh the child sideways, I thought . . . how can a babe come sideways? Oh Lord, let her pain enter into me, for I'm strong, and let her go free, for she is all goodness and I am full of sin: I am angry, I have drawn a man's blood yet once again, I have disobeyed and blasphemed, I have never known humility.

The sheets on which she lay were soiled, having hastily been borrowed from another woman's lying-in. I remembered the rusty knife and my mother. Then her hand began to clutch mine the harder and the old woman pushed me aside. "The boy should not be here," she snarled. With that all the women murmured indignantly. They seemed to gather about me and push me from the door, and I cried as I went, "But cannot the child be moved about mayhap, to come head or feet first?"

"Tsh! boy!" they cried in a chorus, slamming the door.

My face burning, I tumbled down the steps and outside the darkened house. But cometh sideways, does one manipulate the belly or reach inside? It was too complicated, too intimate, too impossible. And I cried out in my heart to the wet street and swinging shop signs, Lord, I cannot know these things! Only give her safety so that she shall always be there by the hearth at night when I come home, and I will make a vow of celibacy and keep it, upon my life.

So shocked was I that I had promised such a thing that suddenly I seemed not to know on which street I stood. A soft silence was all about me; an inordinate peace filled my heart, and I felt as if I had been born again and new unto myself. So strange was all the world and my body to me that I do not know how long I stood there.

At last one of the women came down the steps with something in rags and said the baby had been born dead and that my mistress asked for me and I might go to her, and I ran up the steps.

Wisps of hair hung about her face; she held out one of her hands faintly, and I ran to her and gathered her fingers in mine once more. "Nick!" she whispered hoarsely. "Women suffer so!"

Huskily I asked, "Art sorry it died, mistress?"

"Aye. I love them all." And she stroked my cheek with the edge of her cold hand. "You are good to thy soul, dear Nicholas, to comfort me!"

I was too ashamed to answer: she knew me but halfway and would not know ever (sweet Christ prevent it) that I had boasted of her over drinks in a tavern and almost killed in my shame of it. Keeping her fingers in mine, she sighed at last and fell asleep. I found clean sheets folded in lavender in the clothespress and asked the women if they would lay them on the bed when she woke. Then I went down by the fire to await my master.

He had heard the news already when he came in and climbed up to his wife at once, and when he descended all I could see was love and grief on his face. Wearily he sank down by the hearth and at last put his hand on my knee. "A sad night! Three men drowned under the bridge," he muttered. "One her cousin, I dare not mention it now. But thou hast been of help to her, Nick. Well done, well done."

And I blurted, "Master, I was no help! We know nothing of these things, sir! The old woman knew nothing and the physicians hardly more. It was thus, you know . . . my mother died."

His deep brown eyes looked at me. "I didn't know."

"I should like to understand the body."

"How, wag?"

I was struck into silence.

He said gently, "Well, and one day thou might. Learn to control thy tempers, to consider and to think, Nicholas, and many things may come to thee."

Then to hide my face I kissed his broad hand and asked his blessing. He seemed surprised, for blessings were given at the beginning and closing of day and before a journey and most often shirked by me, but he placed his hand simply on my hair and said, "Jesus my Master, keep your child Nicholas in thy hands all his days and guide his troubled mind." Then in my pain and gratitude, I raised my eyes to his and smiled.

Yet the good intentions of a boy of seventeen are not always easily kept: my desire to heal became lost in other fancies. If I could not have the honor of war, I could at least strive for riches, and after our new apprentice lad, Peter Hardy, slept, weary of dragging about in his farthingales and singing to the lute, I listed the possibilities for my fortune on the back of one of my worthless sonnets, and rejected them one by one. And as I blew out my taper I fancied Rebecca Heminges as a widow, turning to me for consolation. My vision of Our Lord had been left in the field outside Southwark with my jerkin and book of poems, for something else had been dearer. And my prayers, sometimes fervent and sometimes perfunctory, were tinged with my aching love.

Each night my master and I put up the shutters, locked the house door, and checked the fires; they stood at their door smiling at me and said, "Nicholas, a good night."

Oh I was so alone, but I kept my vow.

THREE

The Globe

THE SUMMER PASSED INTO THE DAYS OF LATE FALL, AND STILL I RE-mained both chaste and chastened. Desire, though it came hot and disrupted all I was, was merciful and did not last. I plunged into the cold river waters, shaking her memory, and when I had mastered it once more there came to me my first and deepest lust, which was to comprehend. Then I climbed to the muddy banks of the great city to watch the copper sun sink down behind the stone palaces and glittering steeples and contemplate my world.

Standing there, my shirt half trussed, I listened in awe to the ringing of the church bells. How short was the time allotted to any man to walk the earth before crumbling into dust to await the Resurrection and the benev-olence of God! Kit had only twenty-nine years when his pen was silenced, and lost to me forever was his uncommon company. Had he lived I would have stayed with him, yet not to share his bed: women held all my desire. It was his mind and his unfettered spirit that had encaptured me and held me still, and this lust would never be satisfied. Other lusts had possessed me and, once gratified, left me to my deepest one.

I stood half dressed on the bank in my youthful strength, greedy for the last sights of the beautiful palace of Lambeth and the church of St. Mary Overy as they sank into the evening shadows. Above it in grave chastity rose the silent full moon. Then came to me one of those brief moments of pure understanding and happiness in which the soul almost leaves the body for absolute joy. Of all the spheres above and those undreamed of, I was part. Torn from a womb in poverty and with no certain world to receive me, still I was water, earth, fire, and air. In that moment I knew immortality.

Darkness came and hunger. I went home.

"Master, why has man been sent to earth?"

"By God's will, Nicholas."

"But what can be His will for me?"

He said patiently, "Could it be clearer, wag? He sent you to me to make an actor, and a splendid one thou art come to be. 'Tis done and plainly done. Why must question it?"

His answers never completely satisfied me, and wishing I had not opened my heart to him, I retreated to the privacy of my mind. Still regretting my lost university years, I nevertheless wished to understand everything about me. Of natural philosophy and mathematics I knew little. I was familiar with Aristotle, his *Ethics* and *Physics,* and from him I had learned those four elements of which all accessible things are made: the solid earth on which we stood, the fathomless waters, the air, and above all fire that nurtured and destroyed. About us moved the five planets, and beyond lay the fixed stars, the eternal heavens, and the realms of God, all of which were created from the fifth element, quintessence, the most mysterious and divine. These comprised all of which my mind could conceive. And this earth, so torn with disputation and gorgeous with the seasons, had been created five thousand years ago by an eternal hand. It had waited all this time for me, yet for what specific purpose had I come?

Though some of these things came to my knowledge, it was myself ultimately I could not understand: my vacillating desires, my wordless longings, the sudden angers and the joys that made me choke with tears. Though one day I defined myself clearly, the next day I stood no longer in the same relationship to the things about me. What bored me at Michaelmas enchanted me at Epiphany. I was as shifting as the wind in the trees, and in the quiet moments of early morning lying upon my cot in the garret, which now held two more young apprentices, I was certain that if I could somehow understand exactly how we are made and to what great purpose, my troubled mind would be at rest.

Then I remembered the graceful movement of Tom Hariot's hands as he portrayed for me with two withering apples the journey of the earth about the sun, and the glitter of the embossed brass nocturnal which Morley had held before me that night in the tavern so long ago. Kneeling upon the cot to gaze to the garden below where my master's small children had left their toys between the empty herbal beds, I recalled my mystical encounter in the fields outside London with some embarrassment. These ecstasies had left me: I had become once more practical, reliable Nicholas who read too much and played his parts fiercely and with delight. Defender of the half-timbered house on Wood Street I was: thieves had come some nights before while we slept, and my master and I, hearing the sound below, rushed them with our cudgels. I warrant their heads and shoulders ached for many an hour after that. They left the aprons of our little girls about the hearth where they had dropped them in terror of us.

"Well done, Nick!" he said.

Though I longed for the romance of God, the earth tugged at me, pulling me back to my more ordinary life. I resented God for the scantiness of His ecstasy: I did not belong to Him, but to myself. Though made in His image, I was far from compliant clay. Loneliness returned, restlessness and a lust of adventure.

When on tour early after Michaelmas with our men to Dover and along the southwestern coast, I found time between rehearsals to run down to the port of Plymouth, cloak wrapped about me and face stung by the November wind. Through the cry of gulls upon the rock, I gazed out at the galleons and men-of-war anchored far from the shore. Ours was a water-bound country, protected by cliff and sea from the invasion of Spain. Even so, every Englishman had known for years how Philip the Wily had watched us from his Spanish throne, licking his thin aristocratic lips, biding his time. The new King, his son, shared these goals. He would if he could drag our church shamefaced back to bow before what he regarded as true faith, pope, saints' bones, and all: he would have us recant our own beliefs, become his vassals, lick his boots. One armada they had sent to rout us: they would spring yet again, paws bearing down upon city, wood, and fen.

From across the water, in the very winds of the sea, we felt him, yet he should never prevail. Robert Devereux, Lord Essex, would stand for us: when the wearisome old woman who sat upon our throne had trotted off to bed, he would remain to defend us and preserve England to prosper unto all the world. I was more firm in these beliefs than the year before when Jack Lord had taunted me for not joining the fleet to Cádiz. What had happened to my tall, pimpled, and ofttimes tiresome friend, I could not say. I had not heard from him again.

The ships lay motionless, returned from the island of Azores. Tales of the storming of Cádiz I had heard: how these very transports, victuallers, and men-of-war had sailed under Essex's command with fastidious, touchy Wat Raleigh and the Lord Admiral, how the tall, red-haired, and sparely built hero had taken the walled city, sword in hand, and later all but burned it to the ground. Last spring it was he had sailed out again, this time to the Spanish islands of the Azores, there to intercept treasure ships bound home with silver from Peru. He had not done so: the bastards had escaped his vigilance. Now he was at court once more, made both Master of the Ordnance, all royal munitions under his control, and Earl Marshal of England as well. The day would come when she would give him command again and he would prove full worth. Not for naught had our poet Spenser called him "great England's glory and the world's wide wonder."

Then gazing at the galleons so still upon the cold, silvery waters and hearing the murmur of sailing men about me, I wanted only to fall for glory on a battlefield and have them sell penny ballads in my memory near the bookstalls outside St. Paul's. It was bitterly far from me. In spite of Heminges's kindness, I was still naught but a bound boy in a trade I never would have chosen. I wondered if Jack Lord had died and if even in those last moments he had been glad he had gone for a soldier.

November ended, and we returned to the city, I being yet eighteen years old.

Winter came. Ice crystals hung outside my window and broke in my hands. All the Thames was ice. We left our beds reluctantly each morning.

Ice crystals hanging from the garden potting house, ice on our windows, on the streets where the dreary horses carrying water spilled it. How grey the palaces and abbey and how white the sky! In that indifferent sphere was our hope of eternity: how much more pleasurable to trudge along here as we went.

Beggars in the church porch of Aldermanbury, their feet wrapped in old cloth. The ragman trudges down our street with his half-dead horse. Under the dross and shredding cast-off browns and greys of his merchandise lies something scarlet. Long after I wonder what it might be.

Nothing dies: the rats hardly stir. In this respite everything freezes and the church bells do not toll as much for death. Well enough, said our sexton, for the ground's too hard to break for burying. Vagabonds creep down Lothbury: harvest bad, grain bins empty, children starving, have mercy gentlefolk for Christ's sake.

The leaves of fall frozen at the water's edge. Things unutterable that have floated downstream tangle in the pilings of the bridge and impale there in the dirty ice. The lips of the corpses' heads stuck high on pikes above the bridge freeze.

Black crows against the white sky, perched.

God did not speak to me again. I was the grey of the river, and as for my youth, it was quite gone. There could be no glory for me.

Of that long winter of 1598 one memory returns whose hurt has never left me. We had assembled as we did most mornings for rehearsal by the coal brazier of the large room in the Bear and Bull, whose tables had been pushed against the wall: ice clung to the small windowpanes, and two of the boys had coughs. It had passed eight of the morning and Shagspere had not come, nor had he sent anyone to tell us. "Go and find if he be ill," said my master, and I leapt out down the winding alleys to Holywell Street. No answer came to my impatient knocking so I pushed open the unlocked door.

He was lying on his side in the narrow bed, face to the wall; he had not removed his boots, and the fire was out. I whispered, "God's wounds, what trouble's this?"

"My son's dead, Nicholas: a fever took him."

How did I, being so young, begin to console a man for something this tragic? What could I say? I only pulled a stool to sit beside him and bent my head so that it touched his shoulder. Each breath he took I felt. How did one begin to make this better?

After a time he murmured, "There's nothing I would not have done for him. God's taken him; there's no more to be said. He was a darling wag, just eleven, Nick! And when I went home he'd thrown his arms around my neck as if he'd never have enough of me."

That afternoon he returned to Stratford. We had hired an actor for a shilling a day to take his parts, but the man was a stranger among us. One week later when, as promised, Shagspere walked into the rehearsal hall to join us again, something in the dark brown eyes told me he'd changed and would never be quite the same. Only one time did I hear him speak of his loss: he came to visit Heminges and stayed past midnight, and he drank a great deal and wept. He was a temperate man, and never had I heard him cry. He did not want me to light him home, but roughly seizing a torch, I followed him.

"You spoke to my master, but not to me."

"My dear friend," he said, "can you fault me for that? I walk down these streets not knowing my own body, I turn down strange alleys and wonder where I've gone. If I've forgotten thee, forgive me."

I said clumsily, "Will you tell me how he died?"

"A fever in the bowels. He'd been playing in the rain, and yet we've been soaked, he and I together, and never was he ill. Whence come these things, Nick? Mayhap within the very dust of the air."

I thought, yes . . . and I looked at the black night lit barely by our torch and the faint fatty candles burning in the lanterns above doors down the street. Yes, but where?

He said, "My thanks for your kindness to me. Nicholas, as always."

He did not want comfort; it seemed he wanted to hoard the grief, to recreate within himself a time when the boy was yet alive and they walked hand in hand up Henley Street together. After some weeks he began to direct his energies into the building of his fortune and the improvement of our troupe, all in a compulsive, silent way. He had in Stratford's New Place, I heard, a large accumulation of malt and wheat and had bought stone left from the Avon bridge repair to build a granary. I was eighteen and he was thirty-three and yet there was something between us so deep that there were no words for it. His loss hurt me more than was reasonable: I didn't know what to think of it. And there was nothing I could do.

The year passed quickly. It was a good and difficult time for me, for I kept the vow of chastity I made though the aching of my body was nearly insufferable, and yet I was not granted the ecstasy of God. I gave no trouble to anyone; it was one of the few times of my life of which I can honestly speak those words. We added new plays every few weeks, and Shagspere wrote steadily. Every six months we had another from his pen. We always knew when he was writing, because he fell into silences when with us, and preferred to walk out alone. Then one morning he would come with the rough copy and read it aloud. I tried to write myself, but nothing came out as well as it did for him, and again I was disappointed.

My beard had begun to grow in and I was occasionally given splendid parts to play in alternating casts: Mercutio in *Romeo and Juliet* and the prodigal Prince Hal in *Henry IV,* though most often I served in far smaller roles. In addition I was a fair musician, singing alto and playing both lute and tenor viol, and had become the most athletic swordsman. My master treated me with more respect than I ofttimes warranted.

Once a comely woman came up to me as I was throwing away bad water at the tiring-room door and asked if I knew "sweet Mr. Shagspere."

"Aye, that I do," said I, surprised.

"Then will you give him this letter?"

When he had read it later over our common supper, he laughed. "Had I time and youth for such opportunities, Nicholas!" Yet I noticed he did not throw it away but put it inside his jerkin. Still he had time at last to read the five-act tragedy I had rewritten from the famous old bloody play *Gorboduc.* "'Tis neither bad nor good but somewhere in between," he said considerately. "The truth being that you want concentration, dear falcon, but time will bring thee that."

Then he looked at me and said, "You endure my endearing names with good grace. The boy is fast becoming a man." I didn't know if it pleased him or he regretted it, nor did I give it much thought, being offended that the men would not produce my play.

I read greatly in those days: both medicine, alchemy, and the *De Revolutionibus* of Copernicus, but when I asked my master if he thought indeed that the planets revolved in perfect unchanging circles about a motionless sun, and if the stars might be inhabitable by people such as ourselves, he said offhandedly that he didn't know, that he had other things to think of. He was concerned that Rebecca had not conceived again, and I hid that it was to my great relief. Her lyings-in and churchings had worried me very much, and I had bought her a garnet to hang around her neck against sickness. Sometimes she mounted up the ladder to speak to me at night before I slept, bringing me warm ale, but my room was full of bouncing, curious apprentice boys and we had no privacy. I kept things of hers because she was not mine: a feather from a bird she'd plucked, a bit of bodice lacing, and an ivory hairpin which I found beneath the stair. I did little more; I dared no longer play the games with her that once we'd played so freely.

I was nineteen years old.

All the summer the talk had been of Ireland.

From the twelfth century the kings of England had vowed to hold the green, boggy country across the west channel in their royal hand. Near the east coast of the country for some distance surrounding the city of Dublin, we had established us a province. Sullenly, sometimes complaisantly, the chieftains obeyed our rules, but in the early summer the most powerful of these, Hugh O'Neill, Lord of Tyrone, had rebelled. A wily little man trained up to manners in our own country, he had betrayed his uncivil blood by drawing the rebel chieftains of Ulster about him and defying our rule.

These rude clusters of skinclad, barefoot nomads with their odd Gaelic tongue which no Christian man could understand: savage, murderous men who ate peatbog for dinner, and drank milk mixed with blood. The story had come about London how when one rebel was quartered, his own stepmother sipped his blood, saying the earth was not worthy to receive it. We would take to them a switch the sting of which they should not readily rub away.

From Ulster through the ancient town of Kells to the southern sea, we should have them. Could there be talk of anything else in the city that summer? In August Sir Henry Bagenal, Marshal of the English army, had marched with thirty-five hundred infantry and five hundred cavalry out of Armagh to relieve the small English garrison holding the fort at Blackwater against Tyrone. The dirty barefoot rebels had waited for them over Yellow Ford at Callan River. More than half our soldiers with Bagenal and thirty officers lay dead by the day's end, and the province of Ulster was reclaimed by the rebels. The burning and killing extended to the Pale around Dublin: our poet Spenser had fled back to Westminster, where he had died of exhaustion and the horror of what he had seen.

Would the Queen give Essex command? Some said he wanted it; some said it horrified him, for his own father had been defeated and destroyed in the futile attempt to subdue the Irish. By November, however, it had been settled that he would depart in the spring against the wild Tyrone.

The men talked much of this, and then let it pass from their conversation, for we had problems to solve on which would rest the future of our company. We stood, in that winter of 1598, to lose our Theater.

Giles Allen, who owned the land on which it was built, had demanded a substantial increase in rent upon the expiration of the lease. The winter had been bitter, the Thames froze, and our audiences, bundled in their fur-lined capes and carrying warm bricks for their chilled feet, came more reluctantly over the fields. Our profits were down, and we were unwilling to pay our landlord more of our hard-earned shillings; these problems brought the men to our kitchen at night, the children peeking down the stairs at them when they ought to have been in bed. "I'll be cuckolded and racked before he takes our Theater," said Tom. "The land's his but the Theater's ours. What way out of this can there be?"

About the fire we sat, cracking nuts and throwing the shells into the fire. Shouting, arguing (Condell got up twice to go and thought better of it), they worked through the problem, for there was little time to do it. The Theater must be dismantled board by board and moved across the water to Southwark, where the Burbages owned a sizable piece of land, though in a marshy area often made foul by the overflowing Thames. It lay between the Bishop's Palace and the Bear Garden, but the Rose already did a profitable business there and people would come, especially if Shagspere gave us another play, which he said he would. Excitedly they planned for reconstruction while the Burbage brothers, Cuthbert and Dick, argued for points about money needed for the foundation. It was to be a new theater, a cooperative with each actor owning shares, the Burbages to have half and five other actors (Shagspere, Heminges, Phillips, Kempe, and Pope) to have the rest between them.

Landlord Giles Allen was to leave the city, and it was arranged that the carpenter who had constructed the Theater should take it down again. Dick Burbage and his father, James, announced, "Every man bring tools and dress warmly. We'll take what's ours and leave what's his. We'll build a new theater in Southwark with the lumber of the old one and leave him his cursed land. And we'll ferry the wood across the river, or if it freezes, go by cart."

No one needed to call me in the morning. Before the six-o'clock churchbells we walked across the fields towards our beloved, splintering old Theater, its boards stained by dirt and weather. I had come now to the fullness of my physical power and was eager to prove it by pulling down the old structure board by board with such alacrity as if it must be stacked and shipped across the river by noon. Thus I climbed up the ladders past the musician's gallery to the prop hut and knocking and jerking with my hammer, saw the first board pull away from its mate, the thick iron nail gaping nakedly betwixt. A chill, white London winter day it was, and from my place I could look over the fields, across the city wall, past the steeples and winding streets, to the river.

Augustine Phillips worked by my side, and involved me in a serious discussion against the French disease from loving too freely. "Live somberly, my lad," he said. Considering he had spent some weeks sleeping before our hearth when his wife had ejected him for infidelity, I had to smile at the handsome features now brought low by repentance.

Together we lowered boards into Tom Pope's thick hands. "Gently, by Our Lady!" cried Condell, his thin face long and anxious. "Wood costs, wood costs, my bully lad!" Far beneath me on the platform, Shagspere stripped off his thick jerkin to more easily load the boards into the cart. The arms under the plain linen shirt were muscular: he glanced up at me, smiled, and began an earthy song about a tinker, a lady, and the pleasures they found.

Tom Pope and two of our new men now climbed near us to break apart the boards of the hut, beginning to rope the precious iron wheels and cranks that lowered clouds and moved chariots across the stage. He shouted, "Look across at the Thames, lads . . . it's half frozen already. Tonight we'll see the finest frost in many a year."

I thrust back my long hair under my cap; the river was freezing indeed, a few runty craft stuck in the white ice. Already several ferrymen had moored their boats on the banks and pilings. Ice and mud were everywhere. "Thinkst it will freeze altogether?"

"Aye: the pilings under the bridge stop the flow. There'll be a winter carnival and belike fireworks. Then we'll cart the wood across the ice."

Joyfully I climbed down to warm my frozen hands by the fire of splintered boards; hours later, night having long come and aching from our work, we made our way to our homes. The temperature continued to fall, and though we lit the little iron braziers in our sleeping closets, the windows frosted and our feet and hands burned with the cold.

At five in the morning the boys and I walked out to look at the river, which had frozen across by the bridge. Carefully we walked out on the ice, I cuffing the little ones when they ventured to where it thinned, and slid about in the first white light of the winter's day, near the grey bridge and tower and the huge church of St. Paul's, its blackened stones and burnt spire grim against the sky. We ran up Gracious Street through Bishopsgate then, to behold our broken Theater: as if some demon had snapped the boards wastefully, the iron exposed like bones, the trunks of props and costumes roped and ready to move, the benches of the galleries upended against one of the round remaining walls. Neatly piled on dray-carts was much of the lumber I myself had disengaged, and upon it, as a sort of jest, our silken flag, which would mayhap be made into children's dresses, or pillow coverings. We would have a new one across the water.

Henry Condell welcomed us irritably; his bones ached, he said, for he had slept all night by an open fire with his sons to guard against thieves. Hurling more of the broken wood upon the fire, we warmed our hands and heated bread and sausages on staves. The planks burned, one from the top gallery with a fragment of impulsive carving: the name of a seaman and that of the girl he loved, the heart symbolizing their unity made deep and jagged with his knife. Bits of cowslip-yellow fabric clung to another board: torn upon a splinter, it may have come from some lady's drooping sleeve.

We found farthings embedded in the gallery floors, chicken bones, bits of dried bread. In the dry thatch of the roof we discovered the empty nests of birds, and in the closet room where the costumes hung, heavy with old sweat and firesmoke, I located in the upper corner of the room, in my own carving, the words *Sweet Margaret*. With these heavy garments I staggered to the draycarts, all to the banging above me which never ceased.

"A piss on the landlord!" said Phillips, pinching my arm as he passed me wearing a bishop's mitre, a fabric rose between his teeth. "To our new fortunes, men!"

Jagged and broken, like the trunk of a lightning-struck tree by Cripplegate, rose what was left of the Theater. The pale white sun hovered in the smoky sky. We sang as we worked, loading the lumber onto two-wheeled wagons and leading the panting, smoky-breathed team of four horses towards the ice to cross the Thames to Southwark. " 'Twill hold," said my master. Above us to the east the houses and chapels of London Bridge were deep brown against the sky: on the south side the ancient church of St. Mary Overy, where I had sometimes prayed, waited for us. We worked until far after darkness with torches, then stumbled home.

At dawn the 'prentices shook me awake again, and we descended to voices in the kitchen. "Wilt not come home, John?" said my mistress.

He sat at the table, his back to her. "Godspeed," she said, and raised her eyes to me; I saw they were dark and strangely tragic. I was not meant to see that look, and flushing, turned my face. She said, "Wilt not have warm ale to thee, boys?" and oh that she had spoke to me alone, that ever she would do that again as she had one day in the kitchen when I had almost been drunk enough to speak of my love. Still there remained that glance between us, my parted lips speaking in silence the words, what troubles thee, heart's love? Ah, sweet Rebecca! What is in thy heart I do not know?

I was boy to her: I knew naught and should never know more.

Late evening whilst holding a saw, I cut my hand. I had worked too hard to prove myself, and the blood which spilled upon the earth where our platform had once stood left me with a sudden sense of exhaustion. Pope spat on the wound to clean it, bandaged me with part of a stained costume petticoat, and scolded me for carelessness. "Send the pisspot home," he said gruffly, "before he takes off our heads as well in his eagerness. 'Tis a character which knoweth no moderation."

My master examined my hand and face. "Thou art come a fever, lad," he murmured. "Take thee back for a good sleep and tell my wife I shall not come this night."

And so I began my walk across the dark fields by torchlight and through the city gate of our parish. Below my feet the muddy ice shone between the cobbles, and above the light reflected off the small windows of the half-timbered houses down Bishopsgate, and from the icicles which hung from the second stories protruding over my head. Stumbling around corners, I was startled by a dog who snarled at me from an alley. My own familiar walk which I had so often made these years seemed strange and frightening as things in my youth had seemed when I was ill. The December wind buffeted me against post and gate: scarce could I fit my key to the lock.

Rebecca Heminges was standing inside the door.

So dark it was, for I had extinguished my light, that I could only see the whiteness of her gown. Throwing herself against me, her small hands grasping at my jerkin, she cried, "John, oh John!"

In shock to feel her close, I could only blurt hoarsely, "Nay, mistress, art mistook! 'Tis Nicholas." She came away from me unsteadily then like a drunken woman, and fumbled for the flint to light the candle. It glinted on her loose, long brown hair, which tumbled to her waist, and without turning she murmured, "What dost here? Hast come alone?"

"Aye: he sent me."

"Wherefore?"

"I have cut my hand and the fever's upon me."

"He should be here himself, for he promised me. Come here!" Bewildered as I was by the outburst, and the strange, dark emotions in that placid face, I obeyed her, allowing her small, plump hand upon my forehead. "Thou must abed," she said flatly as to a recalcitrant child. "Nick, go up."

Lowering my voice, I whispered, "May I not bide with thee?"

" 'Tis struck twelve."

"But gladly would I bide!" Slightly faint as I have ever been in moments of great emotion, I caught the fingers which had left my face. "I have seen your hair loose this night," I said, "and it is more beautiful than anything I have ever beheld. Most rich in fortune is my master to have won thee to him." My heart was very full with the work of the three days, the closeness to the men, my own slight fever, and the darkness of the hour.

She had turned her back to me. "Mistress," I whispered then, "may I touch your hair? This one time only, prithee?" With deliberate gentleness, I brought my palm to rest upon the loose curls that fell to the shoulder of her gown. My knees trembled.

For a moment she allowed me, then said, "It is enough. Nick, a good night. I shall to my bed and thee to thine. Obey me, sweet boy." Turning, she ascended the stairs, pale and white in the shadows, and disappeared into her chamber. The bed creaked once, and then twice.

Clasping my arms about my shivering body, I gazed up at the swaying bunches of rosemary and sage, at the cups upon the shelf, not daring to breathe lest I miss her movement against quilting or pillow or the sound of her plump arm stretching or her sigh before sleep or a whisper, calling my name. My face burned: so intense was the need to hear that whisper that a drone rose between my ears, until it seemed to form into the syllables by which I had since my birth been called. Oh Nick, dear! Frowning and enclasping my chest, I stared at the dim shadows of the hearth ashes and the black kettle, which moved at the urging of my hip. Across the rushes of the floor came our cat, rubbing herself against my leg. Silence once more, and my listening.

Rebecca Heminges needed me.

I flattered myself mayhap in thinking so, yet once again creating the sound of her voice calling my name, now demanding as when she chided me for dirty hose left on the floor, now coercing to bring me to my duty, now all gentle and goodness, and caring of me in a way no one had been before. Nick, it seemed to say. Sweet boy.

My face flushed: my groin warmed.

Then came to me how I read to her and she had listened, and how delicate she had been in her attention to me, far more consoling than ever I merited. My love for her spilled over until it covered all else in both of our lives, and I wanted only to have her in my arms, to be caught safe in hers, and to never leave her as long as I lived.

She was but up the steps.

Up the steps, her room on the left behind a door on which dried flowers hung, a gift of her children. She was but up the steps. With the peculiar hum yet in my ears, both feverish, frightened, and willful, I took off my boots and began to mount up. Each creak seemed loud enough to call the watch, each rustle of my breeches or gentle swinging of my shirt trussing, which lay down my chest.

Thus I came to the landing.

Her door was slightly ajar: a little light came through the small window, allowing me to see the hangings of the bed. A strange, evocative, troublesome bed it was: once I had brought my master a hot drink there in his illness, and she had come in and sat down upon it and patted his knee. He should come himself, for he promised me, she had said.

What had he promised? And in what way had he failed? And what was I doing here outside her door with my hand on the frame, and my groin warm, and all the yearning of my heart within the bed where now she lay? Even as I stood there, I heard the creak as she turned and the first murmur. Then softly, as if heard from another world, came the gentle sound of her weeping.

Shivers crossed my neck: my lips parted. How long she wept or how long I remained motionless I cannot say, only that after a time I pushed open the door and walked through the dry rushes towards the shadows.

She did not hear me until I was almost upon her, and then I slipped to the bed's edge. "Oh my darling!" I whispered. "Oh mistress, oh Rebecca, what dost? What dost, beloved?"

She had become quite still.

I laid my hand on her back. "Ah Nick!" she murmured with her face in her arms. "Get thee to thy sleep . . . 'tis nothing, sweet boy. I am not the way I should be, nor the wife he should have. Go now."

But I did not go: I half reclined beside her, gently turning her against me to my shoulder. With a sigh, she wrapped her arms about me and held me close, moving slightly in a rocking motion. For a moment I shut my eyes. I thought of my master and his kindness in sending me home, and that it was his vest that warmed me, his old jerkin that kept in my body's heat, and of all that he had done to nurture me from his simple goodness. I had never asked for his kindness: I had never wanted it. I had never wanted him at all.

Pulling her closer still I kissed her cheek, feeling her stiffen at the slight bristle of my small beard. Then, taking her face in my hands, I kissed her mouth, tentatively at first: her lips were very warm and sweet. God help me that I dared! Yet no resistance did she give. The bed creaked: her linen nightdress smelled of lavender. There was no indication that I must go, but the faint murmured words "Dear child—what dost?"

"Rebecca!"

O sweet Lord, did I dream? for such dreams had come before with no fruition until it seemed obscene to dream it yet once and again. We lay together as if we had become one and heard the lonely footsteps of the watch over the icy cobbles and his tedious drone, "Twelve's struck, good people! Mind thy fires! Mind thy chimneys! Christ keep ye this night."

"Poor man," she whispered to my hair as I lay within her arms not daring to move, "he must wish he were abed. 'Tis bitter cold."

And I said, "Then let me bide this moment more with thee!"

She never said yes, but neither did she tell me nay, and when I tried to loosen the lacing of her nightdress bodice, it tangled in my chapped fingers. I had not dreamed that love like that could be. Audacious, impossible and yet it happened. With great simplicity, she opened her arms and gave herself to me. If I had thought or planned it, it could not have been. The bed creaked yet again as I entered her body. I like to think I entered her soul: to this day I believe that I did. I know she entered mine.

She never turned away; she did not know how. Mayhap she gave herself to the man she knew I could be, for she withheld nothing. Sweet thrusting agreement, and she mine own at last. All was forgotten: nothing more primitive, more sweet. Seeking my comfort, stifling my cries in her shoulder, in the pillow, in her long loose hair that I never dreamt to see in such entanglement, she sighing in her own pleasure. Entangled there, unable to move, panting, startled. Who was I? Where was I? Had I lived before and would I live again? Then passion fading with its last small throbs and leaving us there together in the house on Wood Street.

In the dark we lay, myself still half covering her, her warm thigh under my hand. And even as I lay there, I could feel her move and whispered, "Rebecca."

"Ah, Nick!" Turning her back on me, she began to weep with her long hair upon the pillow. "Ah, sweet Christ!" she murmured through her tears. "Don't speak! What have I done, what have I done this night?"

"Naught but that must be good!"

"Canst say it, Nick!" Turning, she looked up at me. "You cannot know me," she said. "I am not as I should be."

Kissing her cheeks, I whispered, "What sayst thou? What sayst, Rebecca? 'Twas it this time only, this time with me?"

"How canst ask such a thing!" With her arms covering her breasts, she sat up to feel for her nightdress.

Ashamed, I whispered, "Dost love me?"

"Yes, always, sweet boy."

"Cull me in thy arms." I threw myself against her with my head against her breasts; cuddling me close, she rocked dreamily, her hair touching my forehead. Above me her face was round, placid, slightly frowning, staring at something within the folds of the bed hangings. She loved me; she had said it. There could never be, it seemed, anything to part us. And even as I thought this I saw by the door my master's best hat upon a peg, his dress clothes neatly hung beside. "Mistress," I whispered.

"Aye, Nick," she answered, as lovingly as to any child.

"Dost love my master?"

"Yes, with all my heart."

It shocked me. And as she turned (her eyes shining in almost perfect darkness), I understood that the woman who had opened her body so simply to me was turning slowly once again into the goodwife who dried my soft shoes by the fire and rubbed oil of bay in my hair. If I could have had both passionate lover and goodwife I would have been joyful, but as goodwife she belonged to the house and to John Heminges. What claim could I have on her? She would pray about this night in her distracted, child-filled moments in church, and I should be in her mind only a sin to be repented of. I felt her changing even now as if the fairies had taken her away.

Nuzzling against her, I pleaded, "Rebecca!" Oh do not turn, my darling, and leave me in the solitude in which I have been all my life! Oh my darling, do not turn.

She shifted the weight of my head. "Ah," she said, "the little one's waked in the room next. She's dreamt some frightening thing." Delicately disentangling herself from me, she began to rise from the bed, pulling her clothing ever tighter around her. Leaping up then, I fell to my knees before her, burying my face in her half-laced bodice. A misery of jealousy had encased me, and she knew it, for she stroked my hair as she had the very morning she had consoled me about the stealing of the coins.

She said, "Nicholas, we've done grave wrong here."

"Thou sayst it."

"Thou knowst it, dear heart."

I cried, "I know not, it matters not, mistress . . . Rebecca! Only say what I am to thee, what I shall ever be to thee. Say it, my love."

"Go down by the fire and wait for me lest the child come to the door and see us. Go down and I'll come shortly. Nick, be ruled by me in this."

I dressed slowly, for my hand had begun to throb once more from the cut. Descending to the kitchen, I saw the faint grey light of morning through the frosty windowpane. Shortly thereafter came footsteps on the stair, and the housewife Rebecca Heminges approached me, pinning on her cap. "The boys must rise in one hour for school," she said. "How didst leave our men? Will they take the lumber over the ice today, thinkst thee?"

"Aye, mistress."

"I should like to see it but I mayn't. 'Tis baking day."

Aching, I pulled on a woolen vest before lacing my jerkin. She brought me ale and bread without a word, her wrapper loose about her, and I kissed her cheek, angry, sorrowful and boyish, and went back through the grey ordinary streets to my master's work.

Had I really had her? And was it worse than the wanting?

"Did thou sleep, my wag?" said my master. In the early light I saw his exhaustion, the lines by his mouth, the grey in his hair. For one moment he brought his hand up to my face and muttered, "Thou art grown a great fellow, Nick."

I shook myself with as much grace as possible from his fatherly caress and mounted the boards to continue my work, cursing myself, saying, this is madness. I must forget her.

At nightfall we went home and she greeted us as she always did, kissing our cheeks quite alike, her husband, her children, the other 'prentice boys and myself. How bitter it was for me! Within a week we had dismantled the Theater, ironwork and all, and carted it away, and when Giles Allen returned he found nothing but icy muddy land and the remains of our campfires. We heard his curses clearly across the river, as clearly as he heard our laughter. The river was yet frozen, brilliantly colored tents with hot cook shops erected on the ice, bonfires made, and pigs and sides of oxen roasted. City apprentices to butcher and baker tied on bone skates, the metal ones not yet having come from the Netherlands, and slid and skated. Their girls held close, skirts pulled about over the nicked ice, sometimes falling with a flurry of petticoat and worsted hose.

The one I loved stayed at home lining pastry shells with layers of beef and leek, making jellies of eels. Her profile against the brick bake oven was serene but for the occasional biting of her lip. From her cap escaped strands of curly brown hair. John Rice, who now slept on the third story with the servingman who played instruments, took his lady love on his arm to the celebration. "Comst not, fellow?" he called to me.

The children were about my mistress's feet, marching small wood horses under the table trestles. Standing above her, I whispered, "Come skate with me."

Placidly she answered, she said, "Nay, Nicholas."

One week had passed and no words had been spoken between us of all that had occurred behind the hangings of her bed. Moodily mounting the steps, nursing my hand, which had begun to throb in my agitation, I found young Susan descending as quickly with onions in her apron. "Wouldst skate?" I muttered, and her eyes opening wide, she cried, "Oh Nick, wilst take me truly!" "Aye, why not?" was my cold answer. "Art not a pleasing lass?"

She knew nothing, and so she departed with me, her wool cloak wrapped about her, her arm thrust through mine. We turned towards Lothbury, and as we came to the Thames to the sound of krumhorns and trumpets which rose over the frosty, smoky, white winter air, I tried to put from me the memory of my mistress in bed with her dark hair loose over her breasts and her arms open to receive me.

Susan Heminges, child of her father's first marriage, was sixteen years old. From the beginning I had thought of her (when I thought of her at all) as a pleasant, soft little girl. Smaller even than her stepmother, her long wheat-blond hair braided intricately with ribbons, she was but one of the children who came and went about the house. This day as she ran by my side to keep up with me, I noticed that her eyes were almost violet.

In my agitation, I held her fingers too tightly. "Ah, Nick!" she said reproachfully as we descended the slippery steps to the water. Indifferent I was: I hardly knew she was with me, so wretched was I with jealousy. We bought slices of hot brawn and little bitter oranges that we sucked, and threw stale bread to the birds. Making her sit upon the dock edge, I tied on the bone skates with the indifference of a brother, adjusted mine own, and thrust us both out into the congeries of citizens who skated between bonfires and tents. She cried, "Why do you go so fast? Nicholas!"

"Let thyself slide with me."

"Nay, Nick!" she said, but I pulled her this way and that, not letting her stop but winding her narrowly about scarlet tents. Still faster we went until we fell. I pulled her below the massive stones that held the bridge and there in the cold shadows I kissed her roughly.

She allowed me. I pressed her soft little body against the ancient masonry, drinking greedily of her, yet after a time I pulled away, ashamed. Yet was this kiss given so visible on my face, when the great love I had for Rebecca remained hidden in my heart? For when Susan and I came home late, chilled and laughing, my master raised his eyes from his accounting book and looked at us for a long time. I had not blushed so since we played at court last and made the Epilogue speech after which the Queen took my hand in her brittle old one, weighted with rings, and I found later a gold piece in my palm. To kiss Susan had been a substitution: was its faint taste of oranges and roast pork, the pressing of her breasts against my chest, to bring other questions to our house?

Morning next when I came downstairs, John Heminges announced, "I'm abroad for errands, wag: come with me and we'll find our breakfast as we go." I had no excuse to give him, and he threw his arm about my shoulder in such a warm, friendly way that I knew not what to think. He walked that way sometimes with Shagspere or his young sons; in this way he chose to walk with me. The hearty good nature of him, heavy-bellied with too much food and as interested and passionate about his life had he been twenty rather than forty-five years made me like him, and that was difficult indeed.

We crossed the hard frozen ground down Lothbury and turned towards Threadneedle Street, where we bargained for lavender taffeta and velvets, then walking on to deliver a cloth bag of limp, dirty neck ruffs to the woman who starched and ironed them for us. Breakfast of chops and herrings we had, and difficult it was for me to swallow, for each time I raised my eyes I saw he had not ceased to study me. One time my heart sank. Rebecca! . . . can he know? There was nothing, however, but affection in his smile. "Eat, boy! Host, another cheese. The boy grows, the boy grows."

Almost sick was I at his credulity, and as we turned up Eastcheap I moved as close to the shops as possible to be apart from him. He would not leave me to myself, but thrust his arm about my shoulders once again. "Have you a mind to marry when your time's out?" he said. "It's best to have a girl bred up in the theater. Susan likes you well! When I was still a grocer and my wife died, she left me with the girl. A little quiet she is, but good, very good, and wag, she likes you well. What sayst thou, sweet lout?"

I stuffed my face down in the collar of my short, thick cloak, to hide my expression. What had I done?

"Aye, I've been up since before the light thinking on it. Susan shall have a small portion of my shares in the company as dowry, which will come to thee when thou art twenty-one and out of thy time. Thou only wantest settling, Nick, and you know my love to thee."

I wanted to cry out . . . settle? into what? No, he was incapable of understanding me and had always been. I did not expect to remain a player: it was temporary for me. I expected still to be something much different, though I did not know how and I never had. To be only a player and a player's son-in-law and close up my shutters like a good citizen each night, become the junior warden and bow to my betters, was bitter to me, yet to leave these men hurt hardly the less. They loved me and took great care of me. I had never been hungry, only lonely through my own stubbornness, never abused, and struck far less than ever I had deserved.

"And Nicholas," he said, "thou knowst my house is thine, but scarcely big enough for a new wed man and his wife. I shall make a purchase of the house akin to ours and we'll break through the walls to make them one. Aye, you're a sturdy fellow with a hammer, I've seen it. There's a fair sleeping room with a poster bed for thee and her and thy children to come."

I looked at my master's honest, broad, and sober face and knew I could never be what he wanted of me. I muttered, "Thank you, sir, I had not expected such great kindness," and saw from his disappointed expression that he knew I could not do it and he would never understand why. It was beyond where he lay with his good husbandry in which the very quills of the goose were used, ashes raked, worn costumes remade into new ones. He was like sturdily spun cloth that outlasts several generations and as endurable. What he said he would do indeed: there was no man finer, and I felt myself inadequate and cheap next to him. And I had sinned against him and could not wholly repent of it.

As we turned down our street I seized and kissed the rough, blistered palm of his broad hand. He said, "Why Nick! Do you cry, boy?"

Oh the gulls and red kites above the river and the Tower, and I to my perdition and too old to be stopped and yet unable to stop myself. I broke from him and wept in the fields for a long time, and then I went home where the children were playing at marbles under the stair.

A week passed until I could find my mistress alone, and that was with the youngest in her arms. Then I said under my breath. "You must know what my master's asked of me."

"Aye, Nicholas."

"How canst bear the thought?"

"Why Nick, 'twoud suit thee well! You'd find contentment, I know it."

Did she think me so changeable and shallow? "I'll find that with none but thee."

She had put down the little girl into the baby-minder, and held out both her hands to me. "Oh Nick! Why dost love me so? 'Tis past reason! What we have in a moment's passion is often apart from the whole of our lives. Thou knowst this, dear heart. And then the rest of our lives go on."

"Then it shall be no more with us?"

"Didst think it would be ever again?"

I tried to control the trembling of my lip. She was more than sweetheart to me: she was my very home on earth and my hope of Heaven, and she would never be mine. What else could I imagine? I could bear it no longer and, taking her by the arms, began to kiss her forehead, crying, "All my life I shall love none but thee."

"There shall be others."

"Dost say I lie?"

"Oh Nick." Taking the sewing knife, she cut off some of her hair. "Keep it by you," she said, and closed my fingers upon it.

Staring at the floor I murmured huskily, "Then it's that you love . . . him?"

"Yes, with all that I am."

"It kills me to hear it!"

"Dear heart! Much of this comes in that thou art nineteen. We'll laugh over this in years to come when I am quite grey and you a householder with six children at thy knee. And you'll not remember what you've done with my hair." Thus she pushed me from her, tidying her life until it was quite ordinary again, the way she set the trenchers neatly on the shelf after supper and swept the hearth. Tidy lives are formed by such minute acts, but I was neither dinnerware nor ashes: I was a mercurial, solitary boy who loved her with all that was in me, and I blurted, "If I offended you, madam, pray forgive it."

She shook her round face solemnly. "Why how you speak! And with such hurt! Nay, my young friend, this is the way of life. Confess thyself to God, and ask Him for peace."

"I want as little as possible to do with God," I answered, the table between us. "This life He hath sent me only leaves me wretched." I could see from her face that my answer had disturbed her, which satisfied me: oh, I would have sprung upon her the full force of cold logic and reason I had not forgot from my schooldays. Declamation was cut short, though, for I heard my master coming from the garden to fetch me to work. Fleeing from them both, I wandered disconsolately to the river, where the ice had begun to thaw, and a few weary merchants were pulling down the last of the silken, scarlet tents.

She was sick in the morning, and I knew her to be with child once more. I wondered if it were mine.

Thus the winter passed. The new theater was to be called the Globe. I missed Will sorely, for he had moved across the water to be near the new theater, residing there with a French family and working hard on a new play to celebrate the English hero. It was on the life of Harry of England, and one of our new apprentices was to be Kate. I was planned for the wastrel Bardolph, as well as conspirators and ambassadors. Burbage was to be Harry.

I could bear it no longer: I resolved to join my lord Essex's expedition to win Ireland back from the rebel Tyrone and prove my merit in the world, not only as a player of great deeds but as a participant in them. I left quietly one evening, informing the watch that I thought the door of Master Heminges's house had inadvertently been left unlocked. Then as he returned to make matters right, I walked away to join the soldiers in the Earl of Southampton's platoon by the west coast. We made ready to sail to Ireland.

FOUR

The Irish Wars

WE WAITED AT CHESTER FOR THE FERRY TO CROSS THE IRISH CHANnel, the cold, pure white air of the sea filling my lungs. I think in those moments I would have died for Robert Devereux, Lord Essex. Standing overlooking the grey waters that separated our country from the rebel dominion, I murmured . . . yes, to give him all my life! I would have then done something worthwhile.

Properly I had enlisted, coming forth at the sound of the drum which resounded over the Charing Cross tiltyard where once I had found shabby romance. The recruiting captain, Ned Taylor of Westminster, who was the owner of a secondhand clothing shop in Petticoat Lane, had since his youth drilled a small volunteer militia weekly in Finsbury Fields. He was a stout, fierce, ruddy-faced man, commissioned by the Privy Council to raise a hundred men to fight across the western channel. Turning to the apprentices who loitered near the tennis courts, he shouted, "Art men? Will ye not confront the savage bastards which have killed our honey-sweet poet Spenser, brave Sir Henry Bagenal, and two thousand honest Englishmen?" His flashing black eyes swept the irresolute gathering of men who kicked their shoes into the tiltyard dust. "Two thousand of thy brothers have fed the soil of Ulster with their blood, and wilt do naught?"

Slapping his chest and throwing back his head, he shouted, "For sweet Lord Essex, men, and for Good Queen Bess! Who'll take the shilling? Who'll come forth at the drum?" And I was propelled forth with several others, throats swollen with emotion, to sign and to swear. I alone could write my name. They spirited us through the city gates with all possible speed, should any mothers, wives, or betrayed masters follow. I slipped home for my things and joined them.

Essex had left the week before, riding down the Strand to the howling of the crowd. We were at war again. They took us by cart and foot from the city, turning northwest towards the Cotswolds. The drum preceded us: half drunk with expectation and my new freedom, I followed. A hundred of us were to muster at the town of Chester with arms. All the way from London through the Cotswolds and North Wales valleys Ned Taylor sang his tunes of loyalty, exclaiming against any man who was not an Englishman. By the time we came to Chester we had all sworn we would not rest until the dirty Irishmen were disciplined, and the whole of their land restored to the Queen.

What had been a port town and fishing village was now an army mustering camp. Crude stone storehouses groaned with grain, and in one small room of a former abbey sat a man selling stout boots, packets of food, papers of gunpowder, and rusty muskets. So many lads had gone over the channel that supplies were low. Captain Taylor had mustered a hundred, though when he gathered us to order in the early-spring sea-wind but seventy and two appeared. Quickly were found in the back streets and taverns men willing to stand for the rest. These departed, and the rest of us went to Ireland on a ferry which took three days crossing:

hardly was there room for so many with the bales and crates of motley coats, muskets, dried beef, and lye soap, but some of the objects provided for the war to recapture the land.

Most of us were boys from London and Kent, though a few had joined us along the way: these were men who could not get work or whose farms could not support so many sons. Wheat from a land-poor farm went only so far. The Queen, however, had endless wheat. She had wheat, dried fish and meat, withered apples, rusty muskets, wet gunpowder, and absolute benevolence for those who served her. Since we were now hers, we were heirs to such things to the amount of eightpence a day per man. I felt her sharp profile stamped upon one of my pennies, and new loyalty filled my heart.

No more muskets were to be had for the taking, and I could not afford my own. "Pikeman!" said my captain affectionately. " 'Tis the job for big fellows as thee!" I had seen such men drill in Long Acre with their fifteen-foot ash pikes, and it did not seem bad. I had in addition my short sword and dagger, and would soon change my jerkin for a motley coat. Greedily we ate biscuits, cheese, peas, and beer from the profiteers as the sails took wind towards Ireland. I was fired and hot to fight: I wanted only to begin.

"Where are you from, lad?" asked a small, hungry-looking musketeer who I fancy had seen better times.

"Rather would not say."

"Ah, suit thyself then!" he muttered. "We are all here together, you know: it won't injure thee to be friendly."

One is as one conceives oneself to be, and I was not so much one of the soldiers as myself alone. There was a burning, peculiar, almost hysterical sensation in my belly when the name of Robert Devereux was spoken; the next moment it was terribly calmed as happens when one has attained love. I felt a religious, solemn mission. I did not quite understand it, but it was a compendium of all I had ever been in my life. I wanted to be near should he have need of me, to raise him should he fall. I conceived of myself somehow as his friend, and so intense were these realities to me that the actualities of my situation hardly entered my mind. So I fled from the woman who had told me no, and all that had meant anything to me in my life.

No one knew my thoughts: I came into close conversation with no man even as the three days' rough crossing had ended and we saw the rocky coast of the land we were to conquer and restore to our Queen. There we diverted: Lord Essex conferred in Dublin Castle, but all we were to see of that was the Norman tower as we marched past, ending some many hours later in fields to the south of the city where the rest of the men awaited us to a total of fifteen thousand foot and three thousand horse. It was fair sweet weather, and I thought me never to have seen such a beautiful land as we had passed, with streams and tumbled Crosses, and high towers of rough stone rising against the sky.

Securing my pack in the corner of the tent to which I had been assigned, I climbed to the highest hill near the camp overlooking the small walled city of Dublin and the harbor. About me was early spring. The English-colonized section of Ireland, called the Pale, lay a semicircle not more than sixty miles about Dublin, and a small area around Cork, Wexford, and Waterford. Beyond that the land was wild, uneven, mountainous, soft, watery, woody, and open to winds and floods of rains. God alone knew the nature of the men who inhabited fen and bog under the loose reign of the Irish chieftains: they had ravished and mutilated our gentlewomen and cut down our finest forces. Some said they were but half human in their shawls and bangles. I stayed overlooking the countryside until called for muster and drill: darkness came and we bedded.

A week passed. Essex did not come. I stood on the precipice of that exciting place where death and life meet and was unable to move either way. In those days I did not think of her: I felt nothing but a desperate need for honor and how he alone was wound about in it for me. It was as if I had not existed before this time, and would at the end of this time mayhap exist no longer.

Morning began with men pissing in the near dark, then chapel and drill. "Advance your pikes! . . . Shoulder your pikes!" came the harsh cry of the sergeant. The musketmen, small and limber, made as if to fire and retreated to the rear to reload. It was but a tricky business. Made to carry the firearm on the left shoulder, they also bore gunpowder and touchpowder at the waist, a canvas bag for bullets, three or four yards of slow match, paper for wadding, and flint and steel to rekindle the matches.

The metal tips of the long pipes glittered faintly in the sun which struggled through the clouds. All this to the drum and the fife. My palms reddened and began to callous; I breakfasted. Piles of fry pans greasy on the ground, the smell of burning bread. After I slipped off to ask a question of our captain as he coaxed and petted his new mare, Bright Nellie, which he had bought when landed. "Sir, when do we march to Ulster?"

He answered, "Ah, Cooke, the same you asked me yesterday! When my lord says we march, we march. He meets even as we speak with the Irish Council. He shall then tell his High Marshal, his Provost Marshal, and so on until it cometh to thy humble ears, young Cooke!"

The ensign-bearer on the hill, the colors of the Queen fluttering, the cannoneer asleep, the chaplain summoning us to morning prayer with official words from London to bless our forces: "Let thine holy angels pitch their tents round about to guard them, and give them victory against all such as rise up to withstand them." Some of the men listened, some yawned. A group of thieves who had been sent to fight sneered. About us the morning rose shivering over the hundreds of tents, fires, tethering posts, bake ovens, water troughs, and beyond them all the empty gold-and-tangerine tent which awaited the Lord Lieutenant, Robert Devereux.

The field on which we camped was hilly and full of flowers, some clinging to my hair when I awoke in the morning. Down the valley were clusters of thatched houses pebbled about with sheep; at night we heard the new lambs. Still we did not move towards Ulster, nor was there sign of Lord Essex. No person could I find among my comrades to speak my thoughts: neither the boys who went whoring at the camp's edge, the pikemen in my line, nor the former thief with a branded hand who had served in the wars here before. "They scorched the earth then, boy," he growled. "They burned the crops and maimed the cattle and scorched the earth. Starved them, we did: they came crawling from the forests like ghosts."

I turned to my books, reading while the light lasted under the comfort of a tree. I had brought with me a few interesting medical treatises and my Copernicus.

Serving among our ranks were several Irish boys. It was the light, sweet complexity of their language which drew me to linger as a few of us went to wash in the river on the ninth day on which we awaited the pleasure of Lord Essex. While we splashed and tried to catch the salmon with our hands, one courteous brown-bearded fellow began to explain in broken English that though of Irish blood, he and his friends were loyal to England and had enlisted to fight against the rebels at our side. Before we supped he offered to show me a holy well that was hidden within the woods nearby. I followed him, not absolutely trusting, our feet breaking the twigs. The air was sweet and wet with early spring. A most ancient well it was, the carvings of saints and Christ all but eradicated around its walls, the bucket echoing as the rope creaked to lower it. When the water was drawn, cool and silver in the dying light, he bade me bathe my eyes and lips in it, for then, he said, I should always see and speak the truth. He had but poor English, and it being an effort to find words, he fell silent. We climbed the hill and stood looking over the countryside. Below us lay a small river and on one of the hilltops a tower. He said, "When Arthur was king in your country, this was here." I asked him whether there were monasteries nearby, and he beckoned me and led to what was left of one, pillaged as it had been for contents and stone. There was in the corner of one room an illuminated book of hours writ in Gaelic, but the rain had leaked for years upon it and when I picked it up from the floor to study it, I found it to be mildewed and spoiled. We found our way back to camp, passing many tall Crosses whose worn stories of the life of Christ were carved upon them. An owl called. He grasped my hand and said, "Friend," and I squeezed in return. God knows I needed one.

Again the chaplain prayed for our success, afterwards drawing me aside. "Don't speak to the Gaelic lads," he said in a brotherly way. "They'd as soon put a knife in our backs. I wouldn't have them in my company if I had the choice."

I woke to the screams of the Irish horseboys riding into camp with plunder from the neighborhood, and my depression over a dream in which I had quarreled with John Heminges, and Rebecca his wife would not open her shutters to wave me goodbye as I went away.

Then some thousands of us marched or rode out to County Kildare and waited there for Lord Essex. Everywhere we looked, sometimes fallen, sometimes broken, and often erect in ground or on church, were the same carved, thick stone Crosses, everywhere patches of thick woods and wet earth. Forested areas we came to, rich with willow, birch, pine, and ash: branches cracked, we turned startled, and heard the running of a deer. Fallen logs stopped our carts for half a day while we moved them. Before us came the sound of drum and fife. "Sir," I said to my captain, who was leading his mare, "are we not going westward towards Munster?"

"Aye," he said.

"But the rebel chief Tyrone is north in Ulster."

He spat upon the ground. "The rivers that way are swollen with rain and unpassable and we haven't the transport. There's provinces to secure in the west as well. Come summer we shall take O'Neill, Lord Tyrone, in Ulster and smash the ancient stone in the field on which he was crowned."

Robert Devereux, Lord Essex, had come.

In orange velvet embroidered with gold, he rode through the camp with his marshals and highborn captains, his private guard, wagons following far behind with what I could make out to be silver dining plates, rugs for his table, globes for his sideboard, hangings for his bed. His small blue eyes glanced at us as we stood at muster, pikes held high to the heavens, coats newly brushed. Even our horses reined still.

Lanky he was and graceful, sparse of build though muscular: auburn beard, long pale hands. Several times when our men played at court he was there beside his Queen, his melodic, slightly Welsh voice ringing out in laughter. Then in the dance he swept her to him, ruffling her, kissing her cheek, she flushing like a girl of sixteen, and hanging upon his doublet. He alone of all men in England could do this.

The delicate legs of his horse stepped over grass and flowers. By his side rode my lord of Southampton, his long lovelocks fluttering over his shoulder, the narrow face coming almost to a point at the chin, the pinched sweet mouth almost feminine. Followed by the marshals and guard of honor, they rode towards their silky tents and were gone.

The war would begin at last.

Word came halfway through the next afternoon that we should take the castle at Athy, which was held by rebel forces. I leapt to my feet, my stomach trembling as I threw my few things into my sack and buckled on sword and dagger. The fifteen-foot ash pike glistened in the sun. I took it to me as a lover. Even from the camp we marched in formation as joyously as did any of the troops in Moorfields upon the most beautiful English spring day to the sound of fife and drum.

"Hast family?" my fellow asked me.

"None."

"I've a wife and four babes." He made the sign of the Cross, and spit to the earth for good fortune. "Them or us, my friend," he said.

We were to approach the road in ranks of ten, eight abreast, four pikemen in center flanked by the slighter musketeers up the road, and turn to the drawbridge when lowered. In the twilight the ancient stone mass of Athy rose before us against the rapidly moving, grey-black clouds. Dimly could I make out the rigid profile of our captain. Our ensign-bearer walked between the second and third ranks of pikes. "Advance your pikes!" came a call from the company before us.

Silently we moved into formation.

Torchlight came from behind dense window slits, and the clouds shifted. The first drum was between third and fourth ranks behind the captain, our lieutenant and corporals following them. A burst of musket-fire came from above, blinding me: someone cried out and a murmur stirred like a wind in the ranks. "Make ready . . . present . . . give fire for charging . . ." The blisters of my palm closed more tightly on my pike: the silver top glittered in the twilight. We ran up the road with the first rank of shot firing, then dashed about to the back to load. The drums beat as in my heart. With it marched our fifer, a little boy out of Charing Cross with big ears.

I was six rows back and almost to the gates when the cry came from above, "Cease fire! Lower pikes!" With a great murmur, crowding together, we stared into the shadows. Dark figures began to emerge from the archway of the castle.

"It's over," came the cry from the company above, echoed back by the men. "We've taken Athy."

A sense of peculiar disappointment filled me, and I muttered, "How can be over? 'Tis not yet begun."

"A man of rare humour, are you not, young Cooke!" answered my captain.

Below us I beheld burning fields. The air was hung with smoke: there were three wounded from the front rank of the first company, one badly it was said. Stumbling by us, bound and prodded, came the captured rebels, long dark hair, thick beards, shawls rippling over their breeches. Someone spit upon them. "O'Neill has organized every chieftain to call out his men," one of our men whispered. "I heard one of our sergeants say as much. We shall have a fine war, darst not worry, lads!"

Birds called at dawn: the soft steps of a deer through the camp awakened me. After drill and prayers at dawn, I passed the victual line for beer and bread, and hurried to the tent of the barber-surgeon assigned to two companies. Bottles and bandages were thrown about in open boxes upon the floor; he nodded at me curtly and told me if I was well enough to walk I would have to wait. A short, gruff, black-bearded man was he, a pipe of weed from the Americas stuck between his teeth and his fingernails embedded with dirt. Several of our men lay about the ground low with fever, he preparing to bleed and purge them. "Why dost linger?" he snapped with the enema bag in his hand.

"I fancy healing," was my shy reply.

"That's more than I can say for myself!" he answered. "Give me that sharp knife there, boy, if you've a mind to help! Though why you're called to linger shows your want of sense."

I knelt as he opened the vein of one of the slumped men, and the bright blood poured into the chipped bowl. "Sir," I said eagerly, "may I speak with you?"

"Who can prevent thee?" was his gruff reply.

"Where had thy training?"

"Never had a bit of it."

"Thy name?"

"Jack Huntsman: don't tell me thine. I forget everything that's not worth remembering."

"Hast not let blood enough, Master Huntsman?"

"Mine to say."

I watched as he bound up the arm, then murmured convivially, "What think you of the Greek physician Galen, sir? Didn't Paracelsus burn his books in refutation of his inaccuracies? Methinks it was a telling act: what sayst?"

"Paracelsus was a black sorcerer, damn his soul."

"I think not."

"Thinkst a great deal for a boy who grows a beard but barely."

I fell silent for one moment only before curiosity made me speak again. In my months of longing to be at war, I had read besides Paracelsus a few of the books of the great French doctor Ambroise Paré, who had seen many battles and treated the sick. He had died but twenty years before, and I had suffered through his books, written in his native French, with a dictionary and our laundress, who spoke the language well. Most fascinating was his treatise on gunshot wounds, and his prohibition of the standard treatment of cauterizing them with boiling oil. On and on I spoke about his work until Surgeon Huntsman shook his head.

"Training!" he repeated, emptying the bowl of blood outside the tent and wiping his nose with the back of his hand. "Nay, I've no time nor inclination for training! The man who had this job ran off in Chester and 'twas given me. I castrated enough lambs as a boy to be handy with a knife. Books are a waste of time. Take that half-dead lad over there, guts hanging. You can see plain enough what should be inside and what should be outside a man. What's come out of a man I stuff back and cauterize quick, what's dead I bury. Boiling oil's best for wounds! I'd not let any Frenchman teach me my work. See if that one there's dead."

I wandered over to see if the wounded man lacked water. Bending over him, I recognized the Irish boy who had showed me the holy well. I went out then and vomited behind the tent. All I could think to comfort myself was that it would only be a matter of time. Essex should make it right and we'd all be home again.

Moving ever southward we went, to the fife and drum playing French and Spanish marches, and then and anon the English tune "Mr. Byrd's Battle," with variations. Our dipping silk standard borne before us, we negotiated the wet bog, shoes sinking down, the cannon sinking, and ten brave men to pull it out. We revictualed at Blackford, and made camp once more.

Others snored. I could not.

Overlooking the camp from the hill, I imagined I stood the standard flying in the darkness, and the men murmuring by fires before the woods and trees. The tent of my lord Essex called me as I gazed down upon it. I sometimes fancied being invited there to dine, advising him, and he walking up and down listening respectfully to me, saying, "What think ye of this, Cooke! What think ye of that?" in his deep, melodic Welsh voice. Now I stood without and he within, the tent glittering as if God had blessed it. Of tangerine and embroidered gold cloth it was, and inside music and rugs, silver and candlelight, intelligent conversation.

Reflectively I made my way back among our own tents, the glitter of candlelight as it must fall there on the maps remaining fixed in my mind, the rich carpeting across the table, the wine decanters. A thousand stars hung above me.

At the pass at Cashel we left our pikes to go with sword alone: twenty of us swordsmen, and forty musketeers. We were to find the rebels amid the rough, thick, endless woods. "Powder's damp," whispered one of the men.

With a flash of fire came the rebel muskets. We rushed against them, leaping over the fallen branches. Behind us came the captains horsed; the branches caught at their plumed hats. My arm was scraped bloody where I had fallen, and two of our men died screaming from their wounds, their blood pouring into the earth. Three others from our company did not return. "Deserted!" sneered our captain.

At dawn they had us from our beds to drill our marches in rank and file three hours before breakfast. Lord Essex, it was whispered, was very angry. The close-fitting steel hats which we called morions had arrived at last, but there were not enough cuirasses to go around.

The drum rang out for our drill with little Andy Birch on fife, he stopping now and then to wipe his nose. Rammers and priming irons clanked at the girdles of the slender, small musketeers. I carved Rebecca's name in trees, and once scratched it into the stones of a tower wall.

By the middle of May the weather was warmer, and we left the pass of Ballyragget with many wounded men. I stood in the woods and heard the sound of the owl and farther away, the drum. To the south we went until we came to the town of Kilkenny, where the streets were lined with people cheering for us. Further towards Munster we marched to the sound of the drum and fife, the banner glittering above the trees. We were fifty and six at this time, and our captain taking pay for the hundred, for that is what was spoken among those who knew. I would not believe it. On the march to Clonmel we could not pass for some time for the caravan of gypsies speaking their strange tongue which took all the road. They stared at us defiantly: one black-haired girl opened her red dress and showed us her breasts. It took my breath away and left me for days wretched with desire.

On the city walls of Waterford hung the remains of drawn and quartered rebels: like bits of old leather and metal they seemed, like part of a hull of a burned ship. I shivered. Below us from the valley the rising smoke blew our way, making us cough. Someone was burning a cornfield.

Rain commenced: a slow, unhurried drizzle which wet the leaves of the woods through which we walked, which fell upon the streams we forded. Our men hacked incessantly against their sleeves and complained of aching bones. Our breeches shrank crossing the cold water: we fell into deeper pockets, were soaked, and marched on ten miles a day. Through the steady splatter of rain on the trees we heard the drums, but not the fife. Young Andy Birch, who had been with us since Charing Cross, had disappeared. Someone said the Irish had captured and roasted him.

Behind every tree they seemed to wait, around the turn of every hill, and still the rain fell steadily. My fellows could not protect their dampened gunpowder; they cursed the luck, for they had to buy their own. So heavy were my legs that they more wanted to drag me down to the earth than uphold me as we moved now west towards Limerick. My bowels ran water.

Day and night the rain fell: I could not see the stars nor moon. Slightly feverish I was, and having to conceal it from our barber-surgeon for fear he would treat me. My Paracelsus book was stolen in those days by another soldier, though I could not prove it, likewise my extra hose and shirt. New muskets had not yet arrived for the men who had sold theirs for drink in Kilkenny. We saw the swift shadows of rebels running across a valley in the twilight, the fringes of their shawls overhanging their swords.

Sadness comes most succinctly to me when I am ill, and ill I was in the crowded tent with the rain scratching at the canvas, and the ground swollen with damp. There I lay until the faintest light of dawn shone through the tent flaps, and then with mantle wrapped about me I walked outside to gaze down across puddles of the fields to the orange-and-gold tent of the man I served, as I did each day. The rain had stopped.

With sadness came the memory of Rebecca yet again. I could no longer feel the dimensions of my love, but only the longing for all she represented and, in the cold of the morning, for what I had left behind. It became, in my slight fever, a matter of urgency to communicate with those who had been all to me, though the question I would most ask, of the child she carried within her body, I did not dare.

I crouched on the wet earth with a book on my knee, placed my ink on the rock, and bit the end of my quill pen. Suddenly I laughed aloud. Christ's wounds, how could I write to her? for she couldn't read but her name. And I leaned against a tree laughing with a mixture of bitterness and amusement that was new to me. At last I bit my lip and began to scribble faster to the only one I dared:

The Lord keep thee my dear friend Tom Pope.

This letter finds me alive and I prithee have no hate for me in thy heart for I love thee well.

Wilt do one kindness, my friend? Only tell Mistress Rebecca Heminges that I am well, and kiss her hand. Only do this for me and heaven bless thee alway.

thy Nick

Entrusting my words to my lord Essex's courier, who was riding out towards Dublin that morning, I walked back, and as I did so, I heard the sound of music.

Through the opened flap of one of the tents I saw a large, fair-haired fellow seated on his mantle playing a small viol which he held on his knee, eyes closed. So beautiful were the sounds that came from his bow that I stood unwilling to speak. Then he opened his eyes and smiled at me in a wide and gracious way. "Likst thou this piece? Come in."

My heart had always spilled open to music, and I had not heard the viol since we left London. "It's Gibbons that you play," I said. And rushing inside, I threw myself down beside him to sing the sacred words from the Gospel of John which are set to that tune.

"Ah! Thou singst fairly!" he muttered with appreciation. "Knowst this as well?" He played for a time longer, lovely dance melodies by Taverner and Holbourne and then some Dowland melodies, which I sang as well. Far away outside we could hear the droning of morning prayer service and from the cookery ovens we smelled fresh bread. Faster he played, the pavanes and country music that the bands in the city play on holiday, until with a snap the top string broke, and fell limply over his hand. "Where shall I get another?" he said sadly, lifting it. "I've no more with me."

Examining the string to see if it could be mended, I exclaimed, "What a fancy to bring the viol to war!"

"My younger brothers might have sold it. I carry this and five books that are heavy enough, except the smaller ones aren't bound. Hast any books about thee? I have read mine own to shreds these past months."

"What have you? We can exchange."

"*A Treatise on Melancholy:* hast read it?"

"I've enough of those humours not to have to read on them."

"What, dost long for home?"

"Marry!" I said, and stopped myself, unwilling to speak the sudden homesickness that filled my heart. "What canst play on five strings? I long to hear something else."

He was willing; though the instrument went frequently from tune, he remembered perfectly almost all the melodies I requested, adding in the end a Gaelic tune which he said he had heard from one of the girls who followed the camp. Finally he laid the bow across his knees and said, "Thou shalt have my books! I have Mr. Spenser's *Fairie Queene*. Tell me how art here! Wert pressed and made to come?"

"Nay, I'm here for love of Essex."

"Some love him and some don't."

"And thee?" I demanded.

He hesitated, the big fingers soundlessly moving up and down the instrument strings. Though larger and bulkier than myself, his mouth was as soft as if mother's milk lay yet upon it. "Doth it matter one groatsworth?" he said at last with a sigh. "I'm here and make the best of it. They were recruiting by York Minster where I'd walked home: friends joined and I with them. All the men who came with me have run off or sickened. My company was attached to that of Sir Harrington. We were for a time at Wicklow, which was a bad fight: half of our men panicked and ran. Now I'm here."

"Didst run?"

He regarded me thoughtfully. "Nay, friend," he said after a time. The drum was sounding for drill: he wiped his hand on his breeches and gave it to me. I hesitated before taking it. Again they shouted for us, and he packed away his viol with a soft cloth over it. He reminded me very much of an actor I knew once who was big, childish, and eager. There was a dreaminess about his large, soft body as if he'd just awakened and found himself here. Even so I decided to seek his company no more; he had opened for a moment my loneliness, and that I could not allow.

The rebel garrison was hidden in Cahir Castle on the island midstream in the river Suir. We ferried over towards the stone towers which rose to the midsummer twilight sky. As we hid among the orchard walls the skies opened: lightning slashed down, illuminating the ramparts. "It's a bad sign," whispered one of the boys, but we cut down the fleeing rebels in the darkness. All the time we slipped in the mud. My sword fell heavily into flesh, but I saw no one. Hours later I could not cease to shiver. Had I wounded one of our own men I would not have known it. We heard the sound of some fellow weeping in pain under the heavily leafed pear trees of the orchard but could not find him.

The rain diminished, stopped, began again. Our hose were wrung with water, our bones ached. Days passed: my shoes were almost too heavy to lift. I thought the viol player had gone to another company, or mayhap been left dead between the orchard walls.

The clouds blew west to the sea: we made camp, drilled, and broke it to march again. For days only the second drum sounded, the first man being ill of dysentery. The paymaster deducted money from our wages for the expense of the chaplain and new russet coats, our old ones having shrunk in fording streams. My morion was stolen, and my copy of Ambroise Paré. The men refused to fire their muskets at practice for fear of wasting the gunpowder which they themselves had to pay for, and still we moved onward and nowhere near the north where waited the chief rebel, Hugh O'Neill, Lord Tyrone.

The wind blew away the clouds, the stars returned. I lay outside one night to gaze at them, and there the musician found me, drawing his knees up to sit beside me, clasping them with his arms and murmuring, "What dost?"

Moving my cupped hands, I answered, "Attempting to measure the altitude of the north star. I have a paper astrolabe at home: I wish I'd brought it. A playwriter friend gave it me."

"Is he a good one?"

"Aye, he's fair."

"I have the Spenser poem in my jerkin: wilt have it? Or have I angered thee?"

"Nay," I said, turning to him.

"Tell thy name."

"Nick Cooke. And thine?"

"Tobias Mildmay, born in York of a shoemaker and my sweet mother, never the banns called between them. What trade dost follow?"

"None: I've run from it."

"Then what trade formerly 'prenticed to?"

"The actors of London under the Lord Chamberlain."

"Sayst thou! I saw them in Cambridge three years ago in a history of the War of the Roses." He clasped his thick knees with his large, pale hands: there was something pleasant in the softness of him. I was reminded of a large dog of our parish who came to my whistle, and rubbed himself against my leg. Cheerfully he remarked, "The night's clear."

"Aye! Canst see the markings on the moon? Someone gave to me a drawing of them and said they were but craters and mountains. Hast read Copernicus? I can loan it thee." For a time I spoke of the writings of the great astronomer, such as I remembered them, and he listened gravely, gathering long grasses and braiding them together. Then I said, "What think you of this war, Tobias?"

He frowned and then burst out, "Prithee, of what war speakst thou? If there's one about I have not seen it. The Earl can't make his mind to approach Tyrone in Ulster and must march us around the south of Ireland until desertion and sickness dissolve the best of his men. He'll wear out the Queen's patience and our lives in the bargain." Flinging himself on his stomach, he began to draw in a bare place in the dirt beneath the ash tree with his knife's edge, and I lit my candle stub to illuminate the scratches. "We go round about and never come to the point. I'm no strategist to know it, but 'tis like a girl who will and then she won't."

I shook my head. "Thou sayst, boy! Yet I'd lay down my life for Essex to aid him. I'd lay down my life."

"Dost speak in truth, Nick?"

"All men must die: to do it nobly is best."

"You esteem him so greatly?"

"Aye, with all that I am. Dost not thou?"

"Nay. By Our Lady, Nick, look how the moon's traveled since we lay here! If it's sizable enough, how big do you make the stars?"

"The stars are larger still. I've friends in London who grind lenses to magnify the sky: we measure it together. Yet though there are counted to be two thousand stars, methinks they're more. Knowst this matter, quintessence, of which they're composed? What metal can it be? Knowst alchemy?"

I glanced at him. Lying on his side with his head resting on his arm, he was listening intensely. With a shy smile, he said, "I wrote a poem of stars once."

"What did with it?"

"Sent it to a lady."

"What did she?"

"Sent it back again. Fortune did not smile on me."

"Women are like that," I said, stretching out beside him. Turning to me as he lay on his stomach, he gently laid the twisted grasses between us. "She had long braided hair like this . . . with a ribbon twined between the strands, knowst how? She married an ironmonger with two houses. I've told no one here of myself, for they already think me far too soft. I like not soldiering, my friend, but no profession but music suiteth me well, and from that I make but pennies. What a muck I've made of this my life in all my twenty years! Canst read the stars, Nick, and tell me what shall become of me?"

"Nay, I've not the books."

"Canst otherwise tell?"

I hesitated. "They say a man's future lieth within his nature."

"Go to! How can such things be?"

"I know not. Mine kept me from what I most wanted. I would have been a priest but my nature forbid it."

"How so?"

"My temper, my irreverence, the wrongs of which . . ." I was sorry I had told him and wanted to turn the conversation once more from myself. "Hast ever loved, Tobias?" I said.

"Many times. And thou?"

And I said, "I am in love."

"Tell me her name."

"No, that I can't do. Love hurts as the ballads say: aye, it's well enough to sing of love. Friendship's better! A friend of mine once told me that and I believe him, yet how quick we are to leave friendship for love."

"It seemeth so," he said.

"Moon's gone."

"Aye," he said, "and rain will come."

"Thinkst we'll move tomorrow?"

"I want to move one place, and that's towards England! Nick, God forgive my foolishness that ever I came here!"

Then as the moon moved across the sky behind the clouds, and the smell of the wet wind and weedy earth became part of our conversation, we began to speak of ourselves in the darkness beneath the ash tree, with the tents spread across the field below us. He recited me his poetry in such bits as he could remember, which was mostly about being young and poor and loving unattainable women. I spoke of myself: I told him not of my early life (I never spoke of that) but of the men of our company and my love of a lady of my parish who favored another over me. My words were short and hesitant, and I tore up the grass about us as I spoke. An owl called, was silent, and called again.

"I've no friend here," he said.

"Nor I, boy."

For a long time we lay beneath the stars, and then went back to sleep. Next day he signed to my company under Captain Ned Taylor, repeated his soldier's oath once more, and slept at night beside me, in tent or under stars. Broadly his large chest moved with his snoring. My lord Essex had turned us back towards Dublin: the rebels, being too wise to let us wedge them against the western sea, slipped around. We had skirmishes in bogs and woods, and saw one castle burned. The fires were dull against the white sky: my low fever had returned. Our company was now two and fifty and the first drum losing his rhythm in the conclusion of his sickness. Tobias and I slipped from the camp to walk about the countryside.

We watched the peatbog cutters, and explored chapels and once the spacious low log dwelling of a deserted chieftain. One warm midsummer's day we found ourselves above a sunken cottage with a scanty wheatfield behind it. From a wood bar hung a bell of folded sheet iron which, when we touched it, reverberated clearly. " 'Tis for calling the cows," he said. "Mayhap there's milk and we shall ask for some."

A girl of not more than fourteen years came running to the door, a shawl down to her skirt and barefoot. She had been weeping, for every now and then her small chest rose and fell. Throwing my voice low, I demanded gently, "Who are you? We won't hurt you."

She understood nothing, but wrapped her arms about herself. Blood had run down her leg and congealed about her ankle and the bottom of her foot. I glanced at Tobias, who was staring at the sod floor, biting his lower lip. Looking at each of us, she backed away from us into the corner where the broom stood, then flung herself on her knees and covering her head with her arms, rocked back and forth. The long warm brown hair dusted the bare floor. I muttered, "What's the matter with her?"

He whispered, "Someone's hurt her. Mayhap . . ."

We glanced at each other: the blood told that she had been cut or worse. Neither of us could speak the words, but tears came to his eyes as he trudged across to take her hand. "Don't cry! Nick, hast some sugar about thee? Give it her, an thou wilt. I have threepence: hast more?"

I had wandered to the second room, which was the stable, but it was empty: all up the hill I looked and shook my head. "There's no cow here: it's been driven off. We'll have no milk." There was neither hay in the byre, but something else dark lay there. Moving slowly around the barrels, I found the body of an old man. So startled was I that I cried aloud, and my friend came running hand to his dagger and stood beside me.

"He's cold!" murmured Toby when he had knelt to turn the body. "Marry, Nick, canst see wounds? Mayhap his heart gave out. 'Twas her grandfather, thinkst thou? There's no Cross, no burial . . ."

In the kitchen the girl had sat by the cold hearth, brushing back her thick brown hair, her face swollen with tears and the bottom of the small foot caked with blood. We ran up the hill to look, but there was no sign of anyone about. Tobias found a shovel and within an hour had dug the grave. Together we carried the curled, shrunken body and laid it within. Too awed to say prayers aloud, we covered the earth and stood with bowed heads. The girl stood next to us, sobbing now and then. Then most strangely in a small voice she began to sing. For a long time the verses continued, and then the song died away as softly as it had begun. When we made to leave the cottage, she dropped to her knees and kissed our hands.

Tears filled the eyes of my friend once more as we walked away. "You know what happened to her as well as I," he muttered. "And it wasn't the English at all who did it, Nick! It was the Irish horseboys out foraging for us, for I heard them talking this morning of some girl they surprised. I want her, Nick. When the war's done I'll come back for her."

"What, to live here?"

"Why should I return to York? My mother has many others, and my father won't call me his own. How much I love women, Nick, but I can't think one will ever want me. What do I know but music? And when I'm with them I have no words."

We walked arm in arm up the hills, he wiping his cheeks with the back of his sleeve. We turned to gaze back at the sod cottages, the gardens and orchards, the rough stone winding walls down the valley. After a time he began to hum the melody of her song.

Our captain barely glanced from the portable table in his tent when we passed. "Where hast been, boy?" He was counting out our pay and a large pile of coins he swept into his own purse.

"Dead pay," whispered my friend. "He's paid for one hundred and has but forty: the rest he pockets himself. War is lucrative, Nick."

Tobias and I lay awake hours speculating on how much cash he had accumulated. It stunned me. Unable to sleep that night, I walked out and climbed a tree from which I could see the tent of my lord Essex, the lanterns glittering through the folds, the sounds of laughter murmuring across the field. Tobias was sleepless as well, angry as he was for the ravished girl, and when I saw him moving across the grass I whistled so he should find me.

With arms folded across his broad chest, he said stoutly, "I've heard Essex wants to get home as fast as possible, that he doesn't favor this command. The first drum's gone as well: I just have heard it. We stay, fools that we are."

Leaping down, I faced him in the dark, my fists clenched. "One word further against his honor and thou'll fight me as I live."

"Ah! You deserve the whip and dark house as madmen do!" was his answer. When I returned to my tent he had taken away his things. Days passed and I saw him no more.

We returned to the fields outside Dublin, having lost through illness, desertion, and death more than three thousand men. Scathing letters came from the Queen to her deputy, who seethed, and exploded on an old injury. During the battle of Wicklow in the spring many of the men had panicked and run. As a warning to others, my captain told me, Lord Essex had assumed his right to shoot one in ten of them to be chosen by lots by the river that night.

Tobias, whom I had not seen in days, had been at Wicklow.

It was on the night of the St. John's bonfires, and far beyond on the hills the lights flickered, and people danced. I tried to approach the water where it was to be done, but was sent back. Five times I tried, repulsed once and again, until my stomach heaved. With my hands over my ears, I ran until I came to the holy well and flung myself beside it, beating my hands upon the stone. In the darkness under the gathering of trees, someone moved. I cried out. In an exhausted voice, he said, "What dost thou, Nick?"

My musician friend sat with his back to a tree, a darkened lantern by his side. Flinging myself close to him, I said huskily, "Christ's wounds, boy! I feared for thee."

"I never said I ran. Didst think I'd do it?" he replied in his blunt, childish way.

"Suppose they confuse the ones who ran with those who stayed?"

"They have: doth it matter to thee?" Then, stunned by the shouting and weeping in the distance and the first sound of the heavy muskets and the awful cries, he muttered, "Oh this is death, this is death! Dost judge them also, Nick? What man hath not thought to run?"

Then he cried, "What think ye now of your Lord Essex?"

I clenched my jaw and said, "Well enough."

"Well enough still, dost thou?"

I shoved him from me, and he jumped me, knocking me to the earth: for a while we wrestled and rolled there, our breaths against each other. I muttered, "They murder there and here we fight. Leave me my heroes, Tobias! God-a-mercy, do not take them from me."

He shouted, "Thou'rt a fool to have them."

And I cried, "I can't live without."

We loosened each other in the dark, springing apart at the bitter cries and then shocked at the loss of each other's touch, I drew his fingers against my heart and held them there. "Christ, I'm frightened," he murmured. "Nick, Nick it might have been thee as well! Pray for them."

My arm about his chest, we closed our eyes: I listened to his prayers, moving my lips to follow. Once more the muskets sounded and there came the agonized cry as another soldier died. He muttered, "It is madness, madness. The whole world is mad! They say it is more than four thousand years since we left the garden of Eden for our sins, and still we murder, starve. The brutality of it, Nick! Ah Christ, had it been us! Lord Essex! Can't you find a better hero? He doesn't even want to be here, Nick . . . should we be here? What think you?"

I could not trust my voice to answer. More softly then he said, "People who give themselves so much to another do it because they can't love themselves. Can you not, Nick?"

Hanging my head, I said, "No."

"Canst not say why?"

I bit my lip: too complicated it was, too long in developing to ever begin to unwind. Such a tangle it was: I only wished to forget it.

He said, "Tell to me."

I was sorry I had come away to war. Any independence I had so doggedly obtained had been wiped out by my own foolishness. Never did any man fall so quickly from the love of war as did I that wet St. John's Evening, though I could not say it for my pride. Under my arm which lay across his chest, his heart beat steadily and powerfully. At last the weeping died away and we sat there together, above us the delicate sound of rain beginning on the leaves. It fell on our hair and our hands, and yet we did not move, unwilling to release one another.

He said, "God willing the Queen will call us home soon! When we return, shalt take me to meet thy lady? I'll speak no word to anyone of it, not if I were racked and torn."

"My master would not have me in the door."

"I'll play my viol at their windows till they relent."

I smiled. "The watch will apprehend thee."

"Nay, thou shalt be home again."

"Whatever home I find it shall be thine. What I have shall be thine."

"Art my friend."

"Aye," I said. The tenderness between us being unbearable, he began to cuff me and then we wrestled in the dirty wet leaves, twigs, and stones. Within the sound of our laughter, they buried the executed soldiers, and the torches burned late in the captain's tents.

I remember the speeches of welcome in the small walled city of Dublin, and the drunkenness of our men, and that when we called muster, one corporal and three more soldiers did not appear. Dublin was an English town: our ships lay in the harbor, and there was no place we did not dare to go. Tobias was sick and moody, for there was talk we should turn west once more. No word had come from his mother, though he asked several times for letters, and so we parted ways for the day.

I went to knock upon the doors of the old monastery which was now a school for boys and lay just outside the city wall. One of our corporals who liked to read had told me of the rare and ancient manuscripts still kept within its library by Dr. Wilson, an aged and great scholar, whose translations of Aristotle from the Greek were respected throughout our country and who had settled in Dublin upon marrying an Irish wife. I left my donkey, which I had borrowed, tethered by the broken gates, and walked up the path, whose stones were interspersed with weeds. The main section of the monastery had been damaged, and the little glass windows were replaced with boards. The door being open, I walked inside and began to wander about up stairs and down halls. Heavy double doors opened to me, and I found myself in a scantily lit room of large proportions; down the hall were standing shelved books, thousands of them.

I had never seen such a thing in my life.

In the front sections were the classics which I had learned to love in school, but towards the rear were secreted the ancient religious books, many of them written and illuminated by hand, the date of one being the same year as William came to conquer England. One prayer book contained an angel drawn with such exquisite drooping wings that I lost myself in the hours looking at her, sensuality and mysticism winding within me, aware of her feminine beauty in both heart and loins. The language, though, I could not make out at all.

Something made me sharply raise my head.

A tall woman well past her youth, wearing a Celtic cross around her neck and a dark, plain dress, was standing before me. Never have I seen such beauty, but it was not touchable. It was like the sort of light which hovered as the day slipped behind the hills. Of such a beauty you can remember only the edges, and the feeling it gave your stomach: never the specifics, never the exact quality of light.

And yet she was not young at all: she was not young, but something made my heart stop. It is that feeling of breathlessness, of absolute awe, which has remained of her standing with the corridor of books behind her and the keys at her belt.

A question was put to me, but I could not understand it. Then in perfect Latin, she asked coldly, "English soldier, why are you here?"

Feeling for the words which had slipped away from long disuse, I answered, "I had hoped to see the library."

"Have you not enough libraries in England that you must come after ours? My sons have run away to fight against your armies with the rebels: my husband, who is headmaster here, is ill. Why do you come with your English prerogatives? Your sovereigns give gifts of our land to those they favor. What right had they to do it? Who can give a gift which is not of their giving? What do you here, boy, away from your camp?"

Embarrassed before her, I would have gone, but looked longingly down the hall. With difficulty I understood this educated woman, and wished I could somehow have the words to apologize. "I have only come to see the books," I muttered.

"With gunpowder in your pouch?"

"Nay, I have none."

"Why do you want us? You cannot understand us, we have nothing you could value."

"I do value it."

"Is it truly so? You think us savages. What knowledge do you have of our ways? How dare you superimpose yours upon us? For what can you wish to read if you do not know this, boy? Your Queen is a foolish woman who cannot make up her mind, and the worst of it to send a commander to this island who is even less decisive than she! We will die, you will die, but you will come away with nothing."

Murmuring, "Forgive me, madam!" I retreated down the hall, running across the monastery yard, its stones cracking with weeds and wildflowers, my face burning with shame.

We moved west: before us burned the cornfields of an Irishman loyal to our Queen. I remembered the scorched-earth policy of years before when we had starved the counties into submission. I stood above the smoking fields with darkness in my heart.

Captain Ned Taylor shook his head. "This is a bad war!" he muttered.

" 'Tis not the sort of war it should be." He left one morning without so much as saying goodbye, sullenly bent over his horse to Dublin. There were but eight and twenty of us remaining. We continued west. Some of the Irish boys told us it was Lughnasa, the festival which began the harvest. Everywhere we found Crosses, some with the Last Judgment worn away by rain, yet still visible in the scratched stone, and the children along the way asked us if we had food or coins to give them. Beside me, slumped and sometimes deeply saddened and ofttimes noting Gaelic words in a little book he carried, walked Tobias, the friend of my heart.

Then it must be that I must carry his pack for him and he mine, and that we must exchange swords, and he must tear off the edging of his shirt and give it to me to wear near my heart and I must cut my finger and he his and we press it together so that our blood intermingled, and all these signs herewith that we should never part the more. Then it needs must be that he could not begin a thought but that I guessed it, or that I could think of taking his hand but he must reach out for mine. And I said then when I returned I should earn my living by writing and reading horoscopes, and he should sing and we should presently buy a comfortable house and live there when we married. Our wives would be sisters: and we wondered where we could find two sisters who would love us, for we had neither money nor prospects. He was a musician who earned almost nothing and I a 'prentice boy who had run away.

Still I had come to fight and win, and that was what I would do.

Our troop was two and twenty, with but six pikemen, among which were myself and my friend. On a hot day of early August we entered the Curlew Hills. We were meant to go in square formation, pikes center, musketeers flanking left and right, but our captain had abandoned us and the sergeant gave us the call to march before we could properly assemble. Before us rose the towers of the castle which we were to liberate from the rebels who besieged it. They came too quickly upon us: someone panicked, broke ranks, and ran. The company who had marched before us also turned back: thrown off our feet we were by the fleeing English. Tobias's pike was knocked from his hands as the rebels gained us.

We had a handful of horse, he with my sword and I with his. I thought he was behind me, but then I saw him fall in the blinding hurry of men pushing past. I stood not knowing which way to turn. Someone shouted my name, and I was thrown to my knees by the rushing of a horse and the harsh splattering of mud from his frantic flight. I shouted the name of my friend and managed to reach him.

Tobias was bleeding through the back of his muddy breeches: I tried to gather him to me but failed to enclose him. Someone seized my arm, and I turned to face the Irishman. His eyes were very blue, and a scar ran down his cheek. I had no thought at all but to kill him; I struck him down and plunged my sword clear through his heart, and he died with his face in the puddles and his flesh spasmodically catching at the last of life and air. Tobias lifted to my shoulders, I stumbled over the bodies of horses, was lost some time in the woods, and at last returned to camp.

Even as I carried my friend from the field, he gasped, "Ah Nick, what of our plans? 'Twill be a sorry wedding if one of us is dead: my bride a widow before we've even met!"

I whispered, "Be still, fool boy!" I wouldn't let them take him alone to the tent of the wounded, but followed nagging, holding his hand, trying to remember between my grief the logical things I had read of healing. Galen . . . Paré . . . Paracelsus, what would he have done? Was there a bullet? I felt gently and he cried out, but I had located it: they seldom extracted these things but let them lie there.

I disagreed.

The hissing of hot oil over the flame brought my attention, and I saw Surgeon Huntsman coming towards us with the oil in a metal pot, and half leapt to my knees. "Thou'll not," I shouted.

"Move aside, pisspot boy."

"Thou'll not," I said and faced him on my feet. I was by a few inches the taller and in my strength, shaking and blood- and mud-stained as I was. Yet I kept my caution: the boiling oil was in his hand, and if we scuffled it should splash, perhaps upon my friend.

He thrust me aside, and seeing the right side of the tent was empty of wounded, I struck his arm so that it spilled out that way on the ground, staining the rough blankets, hissing and stinking, for it was unpure stuff. I would have hit him, but he put up his hands. "Let thy friend die in thy idiocy," he shouted. "Bury him thyself and have it on thy soul. When my work is done, thou shalt be in chains for this, my boy."

Tobias had fainted.

I remembered the army doctor Paré had turned away from using hot oils to cauterize, for the shocking pain they caused the wounded man brought death nearer, and had employed instead a compound of eggs, oil of roses, and turpentine. Once more getting Tobias to my shoulder, for no heavier a man have I ever carried, I stumbled with him to a small stone granary we had passed, and laid him there on the empty bags. Then I went in search of turpentine, roses, and eggs. There are easier things to find in a camp of wounded men, terrified with having retreated.

Turpentine I located at the other end of the camp in the supplies of the Master of the Ordnance. He demanded my written directive to receive it, then shaking his head, spent long minutes looking for his accounting book that I might sign on my own recognizance. Wild white roses grew outside the cottage. Eggs could not be found for love or money until I had walked three or four miles, come upon a chicken coop, and brought a few speckled from the hay.

The roses I pressed with my metal spoon in my cup: I had nothing else. The eggs were yet warm. It had been a close shot which my friend took, the outer skin of his thigh burned ragged with the powder: I was at first wary to touch him, but then a curious interest overcame me. I had no instrument but my knife with which to remove the bullet, and I first put the blade into the fire so that all impurities should be burned away. There was no one to help me if he thrashed: I could only give him my sword belt to bite upon and beg him to be still. Then I washed my hands in the ashes and water, and prayed; they were the most fervent prayers that I had said since long before I went to war.

The bullet seemed to be lodged in a thick place, and as I slid my fingers inside I felt his pulse. That stopped me: his lifeblood flowed there. "Be still, my friend," I said, and I took it from him. I gently salved the whole wound with my rose-and-turpentine compound, which burned him, and tore my clean shirt to bandage the wound. After I fell into a weary sleep with my arm about him, so that the angel of death should not come and take him from me.

In the following days I wandered around the woodland camp area gathering such herbs as I'd recognized from the garden at home, grinding them with my knife handle, and making hot drinks of them. At first he vomited everything: chills and fever coming, I redressed the wound while he cursed the pain. Sometimes I watched him as he slept, greedily, posses-sively: there was a fragility in his childish, heavy body, a deference to defeat, an easy loss of strength. Not wanting to leave him, I slept with him on the bags: we rolled together under one blanket. I knew nothing of illness: every fever panicked me. I could not tell minor symptoms from major ones; I knew nothing of living bodies, only books. And so absorbed with him was I that only dimly came the memory of the man falling dead before me and the knowledge that I had killed.

"When we come back to London," I whispered, "we'll lodge together, thou and I, and there we'll bring the girls to marry. Sisters. One fair, the other red-haired."

"I like the red-haired one."

"Fool, thou hast not yet seen her! The other will have a fuller bosom."

He smiled. "Oh that likes me very much, Nick. Is love once found forever, thinkst thou? I like to fancy it so."

"Oh aye, if a man findeth the proper maid!"

In the small stone granary we hid with the camp breaking up about us, and two musketeers in my confidence supplying us with bread, meat, and watercress salads. Tobias had dysentery and fever as well, stumbling out to crap behind the house, crawling weakly back. In those hours he confided that though he was full twenty years old he had never had a woman, which astonished me very much, and again I was pleased to tell him of my own experiences, such as they were. I held him to draw his fever into me: I wanted to pour my life into him and mend him. "Oh I long to be married, Nick!" he whispered.

We slept at last; near dawn I awoke and found Tobias standing alone by the door. "Thou fool, what dost?" For he was pale and could hardly keep upon his legs.

He whispered, "I'm going off. Sick or no, I'm going off, for I'll die here. Nick, come with me."

"We are turning towards the north this month to meet Tyrone!" I argued. "What of the glory? And in truth, thou canst not walk fifty yards, boy. Wilt crawl over the hills to the channel? They'll catch thee and shoot thee for deserting."

His large soft mouth was stubborn. "Nay! I'll see thee in London. Where dost lodge?"

"Nowhere."

"Thy former master's house. Where is it?"

"Wood Street in Cripplegate Ward," I muttered.

He threw his arms about my neck. "Thou knave, I've lived by my wits for twenty years and shall do so for another hundred. Remember me in thy prayers every night, and no evil shall come to me."

"My prayers have no particular value."

"Nay: when I come anon to Wood Street shall find thee chalice in one hand, crucible in another. Mark me, Nick." His unshaven cheek against mine, and then he limped away, turning back to look at me, and was seen no more.

The last of my desire to be at war left with him, yet the remembrance of his good-natured hug did not leave. Of his material things I had his sword, his poems, and his viol. These I wrapped carefully with my own pack and went on because there was nothing else that I could do. Each time I heard a musket shot I feared they had found him and shot him for desertion. I woke in the middle of the night crying out against it. If I did not come from my wits in those weeks, I know not why.

Depleted and exhausted, the army crawled north to meet Tyrone. Elizabeth our Queen had sent her command that Robert Devereux, Lord Essex, might not return until he had met the enemy. He was ordered to march and garrison on Loch Foyle.

Not one fifth of infantry or horse was left of those who had come so boldly the year before from Chester in motley or russet uniforms. Of my company were left four pikeman, six musketeers, our chaplain, and one corporal. There was no drum. No reinforcements could be sent from England for the rumour of a Spanish invasion, and militia mustering on every village green in preparation for what might come. By early September we had reached Ardee in Louth, where the rebel armies lay in healthy, eager thousands, out of the range of our shot. At night my lord Essex's orange-and-gold tent was dimmed, the voices within but murmurs. Sometimes I forgot to watch it, or repeat the vows with silent lips each night to give my life to the man who sat within.

Of an evening our company chaplain would recite the prayer office by a bonfire; to this a few men came for want of better diversion, and on the outer side of the circle I hung, my arms across my chest, between scoffing and longing, unwilling to come closer than to catch the mere drone of his voice. This chaplain, Mr. Stoneman, took this opportunity to treat me with a sort of fatherly interest, questioning the state of my soul. As for myself I felt almost as if that part of me were worn through like an old bone knife, dulled, useless, not worth the discussion.

When he made to leave me (which he was glad to do, for I gave him nothing and one cannot converse profitably alone), I said casually, "Should ever it pass my fancy to follow in your profession, Mr. Stoneman, how shall I begin upon it?"

He stopped in the heavy mist of that early evening, with the flames reflecting the heavy branches of the trees behind him. "Thou, Nick Cooke!" he said. (I knew him to keep in close company with Surgeon

Huntsman, who thought so well of me; I knew one night they had both in turn had their way with a young virgin and suspected they shared one opinion of me much as they shared one delight in the girl.)

Yet I flung out the words, "Nay, sir, tell me!" Half turned from him I was so that he should not see my face.

"Thou must first humbly confess thyself to a goodly priest and receive absolution of thine offenses."

"What offenses must I confess?"

"All those hidden in thy heart."

"Surely not all!" I muttered. My mouth dried. "I'd be a long time doing that, Mr. Stoneman. 'Twas a fancy, nothing more! Say naught on it."

Then he said more gently, "Hast some offense worse than others upon thy soul?"

None that I shall ever speak aloud to any man, I thought as I left him, least of all you! I imagined later that he laughed on my account with Huntsman, for that man himself passed me the next morning and said, "If thou hast the call of conscience at last, boy, at least say the prayers for the dead. With thy crazed ideas, thy friend lies rotting not twenty miles from here." I turned away before I could knock him to the mud; yet suddenly afraid that he was right, I threw away my medical books that evening. I could not bear to look at them anymore.

We found ourselves on the banks of the river Lagan, where Essex was to meet at last with Tyrone. The men were ill with disease and deeply discouraged, their strength squandered in the months of waiting. What they spoke of I was not privy to: I was naught but a common soldier, useful only to fight and die, and I cursed myself for where I had chosen to place my golden life.

We waited in camp while he negotiated an inglorious treaty. The captain who had taken us under his authority told his friend that they had spoken about what should happen when Elizabeth died, and who would have the throne.

That night our corporal woke me in the darkness and said I must make haste, for Essex was taking a small body of men home with him. "Two men are needed as guard," he shouted. At first I thought they would not want me, but someone said I knew something of medicine and had spoken always with fidelity and love of my lord, and so I was given horse, and allowed to accompany them.

Thus he abandoned his army about Dublin, and I went with them half in a dream, my heart indifferent to whatever my fate should be.

FIVE

Southwark

Thus I returned to London at the end of September 1599 as a man to my fate, and as we rode full of mud down the south bank of the Thames, the old joy of the city filled me once again in spite of my sadness. O London! . . . grey and dirty and brimful with science and poetry and all that had ever held my heart! More, for it held the comfortable and orderly religion that spoke to me from the steeples of one hundred parish churches and the ancient cathedral stones.

Through the North Wales valleys we had ridden, my lord Essex, the Earl of Southampton, half a dozen military men and knights, and three ordinary soldiers as guard. Across the northern Cotswolds we flew, their voices rising and dying away in murmurs and apologetic laughter. "When Scottish James is King . . ." "Can't last much longer at her age . . ." "Hang him up soon as trust to him!" He was feverish with brilliance, at night in inns singing war ballads, talking too much, pacing long hours in his room. To face the Queen under his disgrace was what he must do: to pull from his failure and depletion some of the charm of the days when he tilted victorious in the yard at Whitehall, and every man in London freely gave him his heart. I knew these things and yet I adored him still; yea, stubbornly and to my cost, I would not thrust him from my heart.

What had our army accomplished in Ireland? More had died from disease, more lost from desertion, than from battle. An inglorious treaty which he should not live down: the rebels were to retain all lands within their present possession, the English would establish no new garrisons or forts. As we made towards Whitehall, someone said the Queen was yet in Nonsuch. He dismissed me and the other soldiers indifferently, bit his lip, and rode away while we stood looking after him, afterwards shaking hands and wishing each other Godspeed. Later I heard that he had surprised the Queen, muddy and still in his spurs, throwing himself before her while she was yet dressing, her hair about her shoulders, and that he had been put under arrest at York House to wait her angry pleasure.

The last soldier, after our handshake, had led away the horses to ferry them to Essex House, and I was left alone on the banks of the Thames. So had my soldiering adventures ended. Begrimed from the journey of six days, I hailed one of the public ferries, and as we rowed down the Thames past the palaces and churches, the new Globe Theater rose before me on the south bank, dark wood galleries, thatched roof, round, comfortable, and prosperous. Little more than bricks, boards, and iron framing had it been when I had run off to the wars.

"Hast not seen it before, my bully soldier?" demanded the ferryman, noticing how I leaned to stare. " 'Tis talked of as far as France, I'm told! Why, it seats three thousand folk! 'Tis built on cursed muddy ground, you know, but that keeps no one away."

"I know not these things: I'm home just from the wars."

"With sweet Lord Essex! Didst bury the Irish scum?"

"Nay."

"Ha! A pitiful lot of soldiers have we if they can't rout a bunch of savages! Hast a mind to see the play? 'Tis just two o'clock by the sun! For a penny you'll find standing room. Playing's better than war, in faith. Dost not hear the trumpets call the clowns?"

We drew aside Paris Garden Steps, where I mounted thoughtfully, the new playhouse coming before me not a hundred yards from the dock. I shaded my eyes to look. I could never have expected anything so splendid. A magnificent polygonal structure of wood over iron, the ground made solid with stout pilings in the muddy earth, it stood by Maid Lane. Boys paid to mind horses lingered about near the door, and from the upper hut flapped the gold-and-green banner against the sun. Our men had done it: bravely and gloriously had they reerected timber and wardrobe rack, gallery and prop hut. Bravely had they done it, and all without me.

God only knew how much I wanted to rush inside, yet I did not dare. Every man, from the coin gatherer at the door to the lame fellow who sold apples and nuts, would recognize me. Wearily I wandered about towards the rear entrance, shifting my bundle upon my shoulders. From the tiring-room door I heard the laughter and shouting which announced the clowns had left the stage. Not bearing to listen further, I walked more slowly over the timber path, past the Falcon Tavern, where I had fought, past the parish church and laundry lines, turning a few times to gaze at the Globe's banner against the windy sky. For more than two hours I leaned against a tree near Pepper Alley, my arms folded across my chest, not knowing what next to do.

The late-September sun was slowly moving behind the palace of Whitehall across the river when the play ended and the public began to leave the Globe, stepping carefully across the planks that forded the muddy grounds towards the river and ferries. Telling myself roughly I had no business here, I turned into the churchyard of St. Mary Overy, wool cap over my eyes, but when I looked up, for a bird had fluttered to my feet, I saw Will Shagspere strolling towards the gate, his single gold earring glittering against his brown hair. My heart beat with joy, and rushing forward before I could lose courage, I climbed over the stone wall and cried, "For Christ's sake! Give alms to a poor soldier!"

The beard made me a stranger: he knew me not. Courteously he loosened his purse strings to give me something, and so much did I love the sight of him that my heart seemed like to burst within me. "Nay, Master Shagspere, but look at me!" I cried. " 'Tis thy Nick come home from the wars."

Bewildered, he seemed not to understand. Then his face broke into a rapturous, silly smile, and without thinking, he pulled me to him and kissed both my cheeks. "God's wounds," he muttered after a time, "an thou wert dead, Nick! By our sweet Lady of Heaven."

"I wrote Tom that I was well."

"Nothing was received."

"Must have known I was in health!"

"Must have known?" he repeated dryly. "We are not sorcerers here but plain theater men, Nick, God knoweth." He touched my arms and shoulders carefully, having to know himself that I had come to no hurt, contemplating me. Then he stood back and slapped me hard across the face.

So shocked was I that tears filled my eyes. "For thy careless, hurtful . . . aye, very hurtful leaving of us," he remarked coldly. "Thou knowst how I feel on this matter: I've made it plain to thee."

I could only nod. The blow had startled him as well: he seldom lost his temper, and never raised his hand in anger. Barely hiding his agitation, he retied his purse strings and said, "You're well: of this at least I'm glad."

"Essex's returned disgraced."

"I could have seen it."

Indifferent did he appear to shoddy playwrights and unreliable actors; indifferent did he appear to me outside the graveyard of St. Mary Overy in the Liberty of Southwark. "What brings thee hither?" he said.

Did he understand nothing? "I couldn't stay away! How fare my master and my mistress?"

"They prosper. John was very angry: you left without a word."

"Was Mistress Rebecca angry as well?"

"She wept herself sick: the babe she carried was lost."

"Ah!" I murmured. " 'Twas lost?"

"It can be small matter to thee, Nicholas. What do you here? What mean you to do next?"

Throwing wide my arms, I cried, "What mean I to do? Why could I want aught else? Speak to master and make him take me on again. On Our Lord's blood, I'll do whatever you want of me if you'll take me on again."

"Nicholas, what would my lord Essex have done had you deserted him? Hung thee for a traitor?"

"Aye, so he did to such in Ireland."

"Then what wouldst thou expect of John Heminges? In what have you repaid his kindness? In what way have you treated us all?"

It hurt too much to answer, and turning my face, I swung my pack to my shoulders and began to walk towards Pepper Alley. I could not see my way and stumbled; within ten paces I felt his arms, and he pulled me back, embracing me so tightly that I was powerless against my feelings for him. Hoarsely I whispered, "Only know that I love thee all, more than my fault." In the warmth of his chest against my arm was the beloved and never quite accessible person that was my Shagspere. And he caressed my hair fiercely as only he could do, as brother and friend and something more. I felt in my throat his own emotion.

His voice was unsteady also. "What would you of me, Nick?"

"Only don't desert me and I'll never on my life desert thee again, not on my life! I'll serve thee unto death."

"Then come with me and we'll see what can be done." And he wiped my eyes with his handkerchief, and swung the viol case from the ground. "Marry, art come to play me a song? Shall it be 'The Brave Soldier Returned to the Wars Once More'?"

"Anything but that, prithee."

"What, likst not that tune?" And as we turned towards the bridge he added, "I fancy thou art hungry! I've a fine pork pie in my cupboard, and we shall send my landlord's boy for bread and ale. I ofttimes dine alone, but you know I've my solitary moments. Thou knowst me, wag."

He told me that his younger brother Edmund had come to London, was a shilling-a-day actor, rewrote old dramas as a hack for Henslowe's company, and lived not far away. Then we climbed the steps of his lodgings with a family from France. I asked him how he liked living close to the new theater, but across the river from most of his friends, and he said again he liked his solitude. When it was between friendship and time spent in work, he chose work, and I gathered that both his shares in the theater and his property in Stratford were prospering. I remembered the impecunious player with the hesitant stoop whose obvious idealization of the young Southampton was incomprehensible to all of us; I recalled the money he had come by suddenly three years back and his purchase of the best house in Stratford, and so I mentioned how well the Earl had conducted himself in the war. He frowned. "Nay," he said, "Henry Wriothesley's rash devotion to Essex will bring him grief. He serves the wrong sovereign: this time Robert Devereux hath gone too far."

Not wishing to provoke him, I turned the subject. "How fares the new theater?"

"More work than one could ever have believed; each week it appears to double, though no one could be a better manager than John Heminges. As for myself, I rise at dawn and fall into my bed many hours after dark. There by the window I write my plays."

"When have you time?"

"When witches ride and all sober men sleep."

"And your family?"

"Ah, the girls, such beauties! Nick, shalt see them when we ride to Stratford together! I can scarce believe they're mine own."

I would have asked him if he had a woman he cared for, but knew his privacy on these matters, though his ease with women had been much joked of among our men. Now I watched him quickly descend the steps; he moved purposefully, wasting no energy, and there was a brisk freshness about his linen that told me he no longer had to worry to pay his tailor or his laundress.

So I was left to my thoughts. After a time the wife of the family mounted the steps; she talked pleasantly of her four children and the lacework which she made and sold so well on Threadneedle. A man's worth was judged by the quantity of lace he wore, she said with a smile. When she had taken my clothes away to delouse and scrub them, I washed and thoroughly combed my hair. It was past dark when I heard Will returning, and speaking with him was a hearty voice I knew quite well. Tom Pope burst into the chamber, his embrace almost crushing me. Slightly breathless he was and much heavier than he had been six months before; I fancied he still ate but meats and breads, despising lettuces and all green things as fit for animals, not man.

"My pretty young jackanapes grown into a damned English soldier!" he cried. "There's not a more ragged beard in all London. What have they done with thee! So you've a mind to return to us. Well and good! Dost think life's been merry without thee, peaspod? We've taken up the matter in conference over a good meal, and it stands as thus: Will would have thee as I, Dick Burbage doubts it, but Cuthbert's willing. Aye, they're all of a mind to try thee again, only Heminges must have thee back, as thou art yet bound to him."

"But will he?"

"Aye, there's the rub! We were with him more than an hour until he grew angry and walked out. He's dead against having you set foot in the Globe, Nick, even to sweep the floor. He says thou betrayed him and art his boy no longer."

"Then it'll not be!" I cried, and would have gone out of doors and away I knew not where, for I had no thought at the moment of what I should become and where I should house myself.

But Tom wrapped his massive arms about my shoulders and said, "Come, Nick, we'll turn him, only stay a while. House with me, wag."

I would have pulled away, but his playful cuffs and embraces won me over, and by the time we had walked east down the river to his house, I was able to unburden my heart and blurt out some of the events of my Irish sojourn. He was full of his work, his children, and the merry times he enjoyed with three or four women on his horsehair mattress; he demanded to know how many damsels I'd tumbled in the greenfields, and I said too many to remember. My stories pleased him, and he said I had lived up to his expectations and would be a proper rake almost as much as himself.

When I unpacked my few things, he saw the book of Tobias's poetry and his sword, and asked me questions touching them. "If he were fevered and ran off, the damp got him," he said after the story had been briefly told. "Pray for his soul." We spoke of other things, and he seemed impatient as I brought the conversation back time and again to the health of my mistress. Had she forgiven me? Had she truly? He answered that he was certain she had so many children to think of, 'prentice boys, serving maids, pies, bleaching, ale brewing, and baby knitting, that she gave me few thoughts if any. "Nay!" he growled. "I'd rather speak of the wars: a proper thing for a young man to go to war, no matter what thy master saith. Don't be soft on women, Nick: it'll take the strength from thee."

Then he added heartily, "Be of good cheer! It shall all wash clean! John Heminges hath more fondness to thee than he himself knoweth."

Weary from my trip, I fell asleep during his stories of new plays and the dowry for the daughter of a friend which he had provided and was shaken awake two or three times to hear the end of it. Then he took pity on me and sent me up to sleep, where I could share the bed of his apprentice Robert Goffe, who had grown taller and thinner in my absence. He asked boyishly if I'd been wounded and was deeply disappointed that I had not.

"Dost still play women?" I asked.

"Nay, I've graduated. Show me thy sword, Nick!" I let him look at it, and as I fell asleep he was still examining my tattered leather jerkin for powder burns or bullet holes by the light of the rushwick.

I slept well and deeply in the house of my old friend until he pulled me from my bed, felt my arms and back, and said by Christ's wounds he was glad to have me in London again. After he strode off to rehearsal I walked about the city, as hungry to look at the old streets as if I had been away a hundred years. So passed three days, and at the end of the third, when we heard Tom coming down the lane and the children ran to the door for his haphazard blessing, I saw through the small lead-paned window of the second story that my master had come with him.

I had meant to greet him humbly for all the grief I had caused. I had meant indeed to kneel for his blessing, but when I saw him standing by the front-room window hung with drying herbs and felt his kind, critical, and compassionate eyes upon me, I thought, he shall know that I'm a boy no longer.

"So hast been a soldier, Nick," he said.

"Aye," I answered roughly.

"And killed a man or two, I warrant."

"Only one: I had wished it were more." Though why I ever said such a thing I know not. We stood facing each other; I had grown still more while in Ireland and now stood slightly taller than he and must have made an arrogant sight, bearded and my hair long and shaggy, and the swaggering manner on me that I had despised among other common foot soldiers in the wars.

In that moment he closed his heart to me. "I think thee no longer suited for our company, which you would find tedious," he said. "You may consider thyself released from thy indentures to follow whatever trade pleases thee. And I wish thee greater fortune than thou hast had as a players' boy." And he walked from the room, his boots thrusting aside the floor rushes.

Tom whispered, "Nick, thou fool! 'Tis only how much he cared for thee and how badly thou behaved. Run after him and ask his blessing and he'll take thee to his heart."

I hesitated only a moment before rushing into the street to follow John Heminges's bulky figure as he turned towards the bridge crossing. Leaping down side streets, I came to the bridge path before him and waited, panting and ashamed, for his approach. And I blurted, "For my foolish words . . . your pardon! Only take me back and I'll never again betray you."

"Ah, Nick!" he said, and he could not disguise his pleasure.

And so we returned to the house on Wood Street in time for dinner. Comforted I was by the scent of meats cooked with bay leaves, firesmoke and bread and the children crowding about to see me . . . comforted and more shaken than I allowed him to see. Rebecca rushed up from the buttery and I caught her in my arms, all fragrant with flour and linen as she was, and there was no lust in it, only a boy's homecoming. The whole afternoon they gathered about me as I sat with a child on each knee, telling my adventures. I only missed Susan, whom I later found hiding in the garden and who wouldn't speak to me. I had thought over these matters very quickly: I was but twenty years old and not yet out of my time, yet if allowed to marry, I'd be released from my apprenticeship. If I married her I would seal my life with the family and the theater.

Well then! I thought. I'll ask her and have it be done!

But I couldn't bring myself to do it yet.

The men acquainted me rapidly with all the things which had passed in the city and in our business while I'd been away. *Henry V* had been a glorious success, and in addition there were many new plays by Ben Jonson, Dekker, and Beaumont and Fletcher. Little Nat Field, who had been at Blackfriars, had joined us, and handsome he was in his single earring; my master's new boy was a sweet lad who was also impressed that I'd been to war. There were several theaters working: the Rose and the Swan and sometimes the old Curtain. The Admiral's Company couldn't rival ours, but we did face competition from the Bear Garden and expected, as the cold winter came on, some fierce rivalry from the comfortable boys' theaters which played indoors by candlelight. They were charming performers with their piping voices and sang better than we. Cloaks were short, neck ruffs six yards long and starched, there were three new 'prentices and another sharer in the theater, which was passing profitable. In the taverns one could hear of the science of magnetism and the new cult among the sophisticated youth of the city: sexual purity. To long without gratification, rather a medieval sort of love, had returned to our cultivated age, and I liked the idea. I thought, yes! I shall be chaste and pure.

We played constantly: much in demand were we, not only for our afternoons at the Globe but several evenings a month in private houses and inns. I sold my soldier's leather jerkin, buying sugared nuts and honeyed sweets for the children and Rebecca, and books for myself. Hours I spent looking over the newly published editions in St. Paul's Churchyard, coveting them all. Then I showed Tobias's poetry to Shagspere's publisher, and he agreed to print; I brought the small paper-covered quarto to a book binder, who tooled the words in gold for me: *Ex Libris Nicholas Cooke, 1599.* It was not the name I had been born to, but the one Morley had given me, and so long mine it seemed that I could nevermore divide myself from it. Thus with this book I conceived the day when, as the owner of a house of my own, I should have a whole shelf of books with my name tooled into the covers. Tom Pope had applied for gentleman's arms, and I wondered if such would ever come to pass for me.

John Heminges had done what he had intended: he had bought the house next to ours to serve his growing family, and when he showed the rooms to me, I discovered there was indeed a sizable chamber on the second story which faced the street and contained a large four-poster bed which yet wanted hangings. He said nothing, but he knew I remembered our conversation.

There wanted only Susan to be spoken to, yet still I couldn't bring myself to do it. A hot, uncomfortable buzzing in my head accompanied the thought, the appalling feeling I had experienced as a boy when I knew I was to be punished. My reluctance astonished me, for she was a lovely girl, and I had always liked her. I could not speak words properly in her presence and in the presence of the family, all of whom, I knew, awaited this. I said, it must be done, as I am a man. And I was a man indeed, being twenty years of age and having seen war.

Thus Epiphany passed into Lent and I served with my master on parish business, collecting the fee for Communion and for the maintenance of the poor, counting it solemnly into the ironbound chest. In those days I took the Eucharist at the altar rail frequently, wanting to be good, wanting God to understand that I had returned and we might perhaps begin our relationship anew. He had not called me as priest: it was indeed time to put away such idle dreams. John Heminges had said once years before that providence had made me an actor, and an actor I would remain all my life under the kindliness of this man who would now be both master and father-in-law. I sighed, bowed my head, and drank from the chalice; indeed, the benign priest had never seen me so often. He said, "Hath the war changed thee, Nicholas Cooke!"

The solemnities of Lent passed us with the vigil in the darkened church to mourn the Crucifixion of Our Lord, joyous Easter came, and still I felt almost faint with apprehension at speaking the words of commitment to Susan. Then my master's speech became shorter with me, and a sort of panic overtook me. It was the loss of my position which reduced me to childish fear. I was in love, but not with her. I loved the men, the theater work, and coming home at night down our street. I loved the tiring room, the prop sheets, the book stalls and church bells. What manner of man was I to feel these things?

While I had been away in the wars, Susan had turned seventeen and come into her bloom. Altogether round do I remember her in the days of my return: a round face the lines of whose chin were soft, round-bosomed and soft of thigh. This I knew from coming upon the startled girl in her bath before the fire one afternoon, amused by the mixture of shame and flirtatiousness in her eyes as she folded her arms across her breasts and murmured me away. Brown eyes, thick brows, ravishingly thick hair, prodigious in sweetness, a lazy tendency to uncuriosity, a peacemaker whose preference it was to avoid disturbing thought or conversation. There are some women who you can tell would be off to war had they the chance, but Susan would not care for battles. Sewing in little stitches, smoothing the corners of beds, silently retrieving my worn hose from garret corners and returning them mended, washed, lavender-scented, folded. Such was her covenant to do for me, and such I needed.

My manhood was hot within me: I remembered the water dripping from the outer thighs to the cracked wood tub as she held her arms protectively before her, I bowing gravely as I backed away from kitchen to the garden. I wondered years later if I had been meant to find her there. Sometimes a tone in her voice to her young siblings reminded me of her father's righteous admonishments, or in profile the slightly arched bone of her nose brought to mind a far more delicate version of his. They placed her next me at the dinner table so that, my thigh touching her skirts, I could not coherently answer any question put to me.

And still I did not speak.

I cannot think but that she suffered as well, for one Sunday evening she stood up from the table and ran into the garden; everyone turning to me in quiet expectation, I made to follow her. What else could I do? These things must be done. Finding her absorbed in the study of the leaves of the apple tree, I came close and murmured, "Wilt have me?"

Her mouth was critical, womanly. "Oh you do not want me, Nicholas."

"Nay, I want thee very much."

"Then why didst run to the wars?"

"I knew not my mind or heart." And I thought, here we are saying together what I must say . . . oh what now? I bent to kiss her, but she turned her head and I kissed her nose instead; I pushed her gently against the half-timber house and stroked her cheek imploringly, until at last I sensed she would allow the kiss. Then I pulled a very small gold coin from my pocket and we broke it and she took half and I the other as a mark of our betrothal and we went in to tell the family what they knew quite well already. The next day I borrowed money from Tom to buy the three-hooped wedding ring: one for betrothal, one for each of us at marriage.

Tom gave me the coins at once, but he frowned and said, "Wilt marry, Nick? Thou art a free-thinking man and not one to come home to the same woman at the same time each evening."

I dared not tell him that I was marrying a company and not a woman, that the woman (as pretty as she was and fairly built, and another fellow of the parish irked because she had waited for me) was quite secondary, that I was not anxious for children, feeling hardly more than a boy myself. He muttered, "Ah, but a wife. This is serious work, Nicholas!"

Then he pinched my cheeks and told me that he would always stand by me. I said, "But what's the trouble with marriage, Tom?"

"No trouble for most men, wag."

The months of my betrothal passed rapidly, for I wanted only to work and reestablish myself in the good graces of John Heminges and our colleagues. Susan was mine. At night I began to teach her to read by lantern in the kitchen; we got as far as the first few sentences of the Old Testament, but it was slow work, and I sometimes tired of it and made excuses, going off to throw myself into whatever new book I had managed to buy on credit or to borrow from the men.

Sometimes I reflected if I loved her. The answer was that I did not; however, I did not suppose love a necessary ingredient in marriage. My passions had always come with much loss of dignity and sorrow, and I no longer wished to make them integral to my life. I no longer trusted my ability to direct myself and, deciding to model myself upon John Heminges, began to pour my prodigious energy into creating myself the man he knew I could be. I should be sober, industrious, reliable, and my wife should uphold our house and bless us with children. I saw myself as forty years old, heavy of paunch and shrunken of leg, counting out the theater takings with a judicious hand. Perhaps I should then seek public office: warden of the parish, alderman, mayor, respected by all. Men should doff their hats to me. These fancies made me flush for their very audacity: I became covetous, silent at times, unwilling to leave the image of myself as I should one day be. Once I wrote the words "Nicholas Cooke, gentleman," and another time, "Nicholas Cooke, Lord Mayor," and carried it around inside my jerkin for days before consigning it to the kitchen fire, lest anyone see it and smile at my ambitions.

I had cast our horoscope for the best wedding day, which fell in the month of June. As the time approached, Susan caught me in the corner beneath the stair to modestly inquire why I had not approached her to take what was rightfully mine. Our banns had been thrice called in the parish, and our prenuptial contract allowed me at will to break her virgin knot. Lustiness, so long restrained, cried out in my body. In the perplexity of both longing for and avoiding her, I rushed instead to the Winchester stews with Tom, whence we came home with lice in our hair and a growing panic in my heart. It was early one evening when I ran up the stairs and found my mistress coming from her bedroom with her bodice just laced from nursing that I realized how much had changed and that the boy who ran away to the wars in the middle of the night was long gone from me. Obscene to think of desire for this woman. I flushed as I stood there. How much I needed her position in respect to me to be ordinary again.

I don't know how much she understood of my thoughts, but she said, "Much joy, dear Nick!" standing on her toes to kiss both my cheeks. How greatly it relieved me!

And I blurted suddenly, "Last night I had a dream which troubled me, mistress, and now I cannot recall it. Thou hadst a comprehension of such things when we spoke of them in years past. I cannot remember it! Yet I woke startled, feeling there was a place I must go."

"What sayst thou, Nick?" she replied, puzzled. She stood with her hands, still lovely though worn from much laundering, on the waist of her apron. "What mean these words, dear heart?"

I knew she could not understand what I did not understand myself, and was ashamed of my tugging reluctance. "Naught . . . bachelor fears, mayhap. Good night, sweet mistress." Then I climbed upstairs and found the sonnets I had written to her since first I had loved her, and I burned them, intending, if God so stood behind me, to be a faithful husband, a useful, good son-in-law, and to go no unlawful ways.

Then came the day of our wedding in the parish church of St. Mary Aldermanbury, where my master was yet senior warden. Susan was dressed in blue, her hem embroidered with flowers; entwined in her braided and ribboned hair were forget-me-nots. Her flowers were for purity, and I carried rosemary for my manly qualities, such ones as my nervous state had left to me, and after we were wed we drank from the contracting cup, which was then passed to all the guests, and the young men grabbed the bride's laces and ribbons to take home as keepsakes. They brought us up to the bedroom in the new part of the house on Wood Street, now connected to the old and overlooking the baker's congenial shop, and stood below our small, multipaned window singing. My clumsy hands could hardly remove the middle farthingale pins which held the open gown to her petticoat. The sheets had been perfumed with lavender and bay, and my young bride was too anxious to speak coherently. I took her as tenderly as I knew how.

The men sang as we consummated our marriage.

When I came down the next morning, Heminges gave me a sly look and clapped my back so hard I almost fell off the stool, seized me by the doublet neck, and we were both well in our cups at the tavern before seven in the morning and arrived for rehearsal noisily and unsteady on our feet. It was the only time I had ever seen him so. "Thou kept her warm, Nick?" he said.

"Very," I said, grinning.

"Naught's finer than wedded life!"

"Naught, master!"

After we played they excused me from further work and shoved the newly married man home, and as I ran towards the bridge I heard their bawdy shouting and loved them deeply for it. I had never loved them better than that day.

SIX

My Young Married Life

RATHER DIFFERENT IS THE STATE OF THE MARRIED MAN AMONG HIS fellows than that of the impetuous young bachelor.

After my return from the wars I had at first only been entrusted to play courtiers and soldiers and such smaller parts as were generally given to the hungry shilling-a-day actors who hung forever about the tiring-room door. Throwing my self more passionately into my craft than ever I had done, I slowly began to regain the trust of my colleagues, and with my marriage, I knew I had it at last. A married man is a stable creature.

We played at Court regularly, and though I heard all the gossip concerning the fate of Lord Essex, I kept my grief concerning it to myself. The Queen, though she pitied him, did not restore him to her favor; from the center of her adoration he fell into the obscurity of an old love grown tedious. His long, pale face grew narrow with brooding on it, the blond beard limp, and he lay bedridden with frequent periods of what I heard discussed between a few men at St. Paul's as sickness born of despondency. Our men thought it safest not to speak of it overly much, and as I was determined to keep myself from trouble, I was likewise silent. Yet I felt I had somehow betrayed him in leaving him to the disarray he had himself created and had bad dreams about it.

There is both pleasure and embarrassment for me in recalling the early days of my marriage. I wanted to make good work of it, to do it properly, and as my craft was the playing of roles, I did not think it should be beyond my skill. I was to be Husband and she to be Wife, but I came to understand quickly that if she were capable of the second, I was incapable of the first; the scattered wedding posies having faded and the loving cup returned to one of the men who had lent it, we were left to discover each other.

Then I thought, who is this stranger who not only takes her side of our bed but somehow creeps into mine, violating my thoughts? Who is this stranger? What have I done in making this holy vow?

I tried to comprehend her, as I forced an uncongenial role unwillingly into my memory, for in spite of having lived with her since first apprenticed to her father, I had made small attempt to know her. She had only intermittently captured my attention in those boyish and self-centered years; then, when the prospect of her becoming mine appeared, I began to notice her swelling breasts and the untouched virginity of her. Oh the attraction of virgins! When a boy in Canterbury I had wanted to be the first to tumble into the new-fallen snow. These small greeds continued into this more irrevocable matter.

In our early months together, under the encompassing roof of my master who was now father-in-law as well, I wished her to be all things to me. At first our lovemaking was clumsy and embarrassed: how could it not be so? In spite of my self-importance, I knew little about such things; I was a virgin in these depths. Then after we had explored each other in the tangled quilting with some attempt at silence so that no one else in the house should be able to chart our private moments, I began to pour out my curiosity for science, the world, and the purpose for which man had been created. Again the dichotomy: she loved me, but she could not understand me, and how deeply I resented her for it! She expected, perhaps, that I should be like her father; she had purported in some primitive way that all men once married would be regular, dependable, orthodox in their beliefs. This was the first way in which I disappointed her, and it hurt my pride.

We worked as we had always twelve or more hours each day in our profession, and the rest of the time I had always jealously kept for reading and studies. Pulled I was now between this need and the new one, which was to walk about the parish boundaries with her on my arm to show all who had known me in my irresponsible youth that I was walking with my wife. Sometimes I was inclined to take her down by the riverbanks and show her off to the very swans, yet at the same time I faced an increasing need to be alone. The men needed me, my master needed me, and my curiosity drove me still.

Our first quarrel came of this: she expected me directly home after our daily performance, and often I could not bring myself to do it, for I longed to stop at the Boar's Head on Old Fish Street and linger there in the back booths with friends until the long summer day had come to an end. We had not been married six weeks when one of these conversations kept me hours beyond what I had promised and I rushed home flushed with the fascination of it, exuberant with sack and stuffed with bread and fowls, as much a bachelor in my soul as I'd ever been. It was not until I sauntered into our sleeping closet (now hung with blue hangings embroidered in gold, a gift from the men and their wives) that I remembered the wedding posies and loving cup, and recalled that my life could no longer be called my own.

The horror of what I'd done in giving those vows came to me, and I chafed like a wild horse who had been caught and mounted at last. Sensing it mayhap, Susan bent her head over the embroidered border of a fine cambric shirt on which she was working. In that moment, I wanted to turn and rush down the steps, to recapture the man I had been just six weeks before, to not return. And I knew I could do no such thing.

Silently untrussing my doublet and breeches, I hung them on the wood pegs, and still she sewed, now and then wiping the corner of her eyes with the back of her plump hand. "What makes thee so silent, my girl?" I said gently, pulling a stool to sit before her. She avoided my sight, though I knew that my bare, muscular legs under the loose shirt troubled her: they gave me the advantage, for they awakened things that made it difficult for her to remain irked with me. Even in those early days the sensual pull between us tumbled over all else and made us unable to see clearly how to solve other matters.

She answered, "Thy lateness!"

"Findst fault with me, sweet?" I said. "Thine own Nick?"

And then she flung her arms about me and said, "Don't tarry on the way home, Nick! Thou'rt all my love."

We made it up the way lovers do, first with apologies, then with kisses, and then on our bed in a struggle with her petticoats and lacing, and if she did not understand or accept other things of me, in this was no quarrel between us. Yet after, my inquisitive mind would not be still, and I began to spill out the conversation I had had in the hours I was away from her: it was of the age of the earth, for though biblically it was supposed but five thousand years, I began to find reason in the antiquity of mountains and seas that it might be older still. She muttered that Scripture alone was truth for her, and then she fell asleep. The passions of sexuality lead that way, and I soon slept also.

It often troubled me that though I had begun to love her very much, it was not all-in-all to me, but only part of my existence. She was not particularly interested in the things that compelled me to push out more and more against the constraints of my world, striving and searching for I knew not what. Yet from that time I rose from the tavern booth in the middle of the most engrossing conversations and muttered, "I must be home."

Then Gus Phillips or our new clown, Robert Armin, who had recently joined us, laughed and said, "Hast worn through the wedding sheets already, thou boy! Thou shalt fare like thy master with another babe yearly, by Our Lady!"

I was careful not to let them see my impatience, for some of our fellows still suspected my steadiness, and I smarted with the remnants of my impulsive youth. John Heminges had only just informally released me from my indentures on the night before my wedding. "Thou art a man among us, Nick," he had said when he ripped up such papers as there were and presented me with a small share of the company as dowry. "No more 'prentice but a sharer."

They made a place for me in the midst of them for discussion of repertoire, profit, and expenditure, and the men would say with a smile, "But we can't begin. Nick's not come!" This I'd earned and took it with joy. A dozen actors had shares now, and we knew each other's strengths and weaknesses as if we were one man. If someone dropped a line, another caught it without thinking. My moments of greatest happiness, simple and unthinking, were found in battle scenes and dances when I could pour out my strength and exuberance. We were one together then, and I looked about me and said, we're the Lord Chamberlain's Men! And it seemed I could never want anything more.

We performed constantly, purchasing new plays, assigning parts, rehearsing new plays, and I often spent the long walk across the bridge and down the bank of Southwark getting new lines by heart. By the stage door was our sheet with lists of entrances and exits, and there I waited my cues while the stagekeeper thrust a bloody head or a lace handkerchief or some other prop into my hands before I strutted out before the audience. Then after we had played we often found ourselves at the Boar's Head or the Mermaid on Cornhill, starving as we were and parched with thirst, and sometimes a boy would come in dragging his feet shyly with a note for one of us from his mistress. We passed it around and threw it through the air.

"Who'll have her?"

" 'Thy manly grace . . .' In faith, how she doth write."

Once a note was for me and I slipped off by myself to take advantage of the kind offer, creeping home to Cripplegate Ward that night full of shame. There had been anger in the act, my repressed curiosity exploding, my independence asserted. I thought of excuses as I ran up the stairs as a boy does who fears the switch, and found her radiant. "Oh Nick," she said, "I'm with child." And then all the disquieting, unsettled moments between us seemed as nothing.

"It shall be a boy," I shouted joyfully and swung her about the room in my arms. Rebecca was also with child again: should she deliver safely of it, it would be the fifth, for she had given birth once more some months before my marriage. Gruff was I to my good master on account of it. Would he not leave her shift to herself? I muttered these things and wondered how much of them were but jealousy. Then my secret and most precious hours with Susan in our chamber, my head against her swollen stomach, feeling the mystery of life and warmth within. And yet to be a father! How to instruct the child and what to tell him of the world? My happiness mingled with my apprehension.

On a February morning but several months after, we had set up to rehearse a new tragedy in the empty Globe and were standing about the charcoal brazier discussing whether we needed another extra actor or could make the change of costume rapidly enough to employ only those presently under agreement, when Pope's boy Robert Goffe whispered to us that there were men outside who wished to speak with John Heminges on immediate business. "What business, wag?" murmured my master, but he thrust the scriptbook at me and went to meet them as he would any good customer, adjusting his doublet and thrusting back the thick, greying hair with his hand.

Puzzled he was when he returned. "Is it Gray's Inn again and *Harry Fifth*?" asked Armin, munching on egg and bread.

"Nay, *Richard Second* to play here tomorrow afternoon."

"That old history about the king's deposing!" muttered Condell. "Not a line's in my head: no one could wish to hear it. How much have they offered?"

We gathered about the brazier, rubbing our hands to warm them, as he explained. Friends of Lord Essex had come to make the request: Sir Charles Percy, Lord Mounteagle, and others, and the offer was forty shillings over our gatherings for one performance of the piece. Armin flicked the egg from his beard, cartwheeled twice (he was a limber, delightful, fresh-faced young man who had replaced the caustic Will Kempe and whose friendship I more esteemed the better we came to know him), and leapt off with some of the boys to dig for the copied parts which we prayed we still had about.

"I like it not," murmured my master when roles had been assigned. Phillips pointed out then that there could be no harm, and we all parted to walk home to learn our lines while the light still lasted. With script in front of me, I dodged the shopping crowds on Cheapside. My role was entirely new to me, for when we had performed Richard years before I had still been young enough for the Duchess of York. The story of Harry Bolingbroke, unjustly deprived of his inheritance by the willful, unstable Richard, who returns with an army, deposes the king, and takes the throne, had been fashionable some years before. The words of the dethroned monarch moved me yet again:

> I'll give my jewels for a set of beads . . .
> . . . and my large kingdom for a little grave,
> A little, little grave, an obscure grave . . .

We played it through once the next morning, scrambling into whatever costumes the stagekeeper had managed to assemble. Two of the clock came too quickly, and when the horns were blown thrice the galleries were already filled with many of the men I had seen coming and going through the gardens before the battlemented Essex House off the Strand. Some had been at war with me. It was not one of our best performances, and the stagekeeper had to whisper lines several times. Tom's apprentice skipped a whole speech, though no one faulted him for it, and we were glad enough to wash off rouge, throw the neck ruffs on a pile to be laundered, and hurry home again.

News came quickly of the Queen's anger. Too many young men were rallying around the disgraced Essex, and, becoming more nervous and fragile in her old years, she took our history of a lawful monarch's overthrow as a personal statement of our support of him. In the gardens of Whitehall it was rumored that she had wept, raged, and cried, "Know you not that I am Richard?" Never had fault been found with our company by either the Queen or the Master of the Revels: whilst plays from other companies were rigorously scanned for sedition or heresy by the Revels Office before approval, they hardly looked at ours before stamping them.

"God-a-mercy!" John Heminges said as the news came to him as he stood in our kitchen the next morning, shirt yet untrussed. "Christ's wounds that we have offended her! Long life to Her Grace!" Then he belted on his sword and buttoned his doublet to walk over with Augustine Phillips to Whitehall to settle the matter. His honesty served him: we were found innocent and the men came home. Silent we were on our fears: if the Queen had remained angry it might have meant our dissolution.

" 'Tis rumoured," Phillips muttered as we walked down Milk Street together, "that Essex hath said the Queen in her dotage now hath a mind as crooked as her body." Pursing his lips beneath the black mustache, he said no more.

After that long day, because we had come so near to danger, the men ceased to speak of Lord Essex. I was repelled by their disloyalty, and once again my old love arose. This is how I came almost to join his rebellion.

I had gone one morning to fetch the first half of a new play by Dekker, playwright, pamphleteer, gossip, and general man about the taverns, of whom it was said he knew enough about the underworld of city cutthroats and cutpurses to be worth his life. The first several months of Susan's pregnancy had safely passed, and now she was exhausted and cranky, puzzled by the peculiar drain on her emotions, and wanting more of me than I was willing to give. And I had no other thoughts in my head but my lord Essex and what his next step should be and how I could aid him. Honor still called me. I could not help but listen, for I was but one and twenty years of age.

I was always glad of a chance to go to the taverns, where I could find the university wits arguing about logic and government over herrings, yellow bread, and sack. Old Harry Head Tavern lay between Westminster and the city; there these luminous, intelligent men welcomed me. I liked the playwriter Ben Jonson best for his sardonic humour and the circle of fast-thinking young poets who were his company. He had killed in a duel and been branded on the thumb for it, a fate that had nearly been mine once or twice. So I lingered with Jonson and pale bearded Dekker some time before folding the three acts of the script together and turning with some reluctance towards Southwark. We were to clean and oil the flying mechanism that day, and I had promised John Heminges that I would be quick.

Passing Charing Cross, someone touched my sleeve. "Thou muckheap, canst not turn for a friend?" the stranger cried. "Canst not stop to greet one with whom you drank so merrily?"

It was Jack Lord, the mercer's apprentice who had sailed for Cádiz. Stuffing my script under my arm, I shouted, "Christ's wounds, fellow! What dost?"

He was his tall, swaying self, with hardly a bit of flesh over the elongated bones, though the pimples of his youth were now scars upon his chin. "Thou went for a soldier after all, Cooke! Boys we once knew said they saw ye in Ireland. A true heart's in thee after all."

"Wert there as well?"

"Ah, never to be forgotten! We were men there." Glittering eyes which did not move but watched me: his boot kicked at the base of the Eleanor Cross. Something odd was about him, as if he had been running.

We shook hands and I told him I was off to Southwark.

"On this day?" he said. "This, the best that ever this rotting carcass of a land hath seen?" Pressing me against the Cross, he put his thin mouth to my ears and whispered, "Essex takes the city today, and every true-hearted man will be with him. What had to come hath come at last."

With that my heart stopped nearly within my breast: so many emotions and purposes coursed through me I felt almost as faint. My master shaking his spring watch and waiting for me to come, my heavy-laden Susan, lethargic in her last weeks. Yet perhaps those things were unimportant; perhaps here was what I'd been meant to do. Here perhaps was the service I was meant to give: perhaps the truth lay in that I was never intended to be married and yet once again had taken a wrong path in the progression of my life. The eager face of the man, his beard uncombed, the scars of childish pox marks, attracted and repelled me. Oh the conversations we had shared of our devotion to Robert Devereux, Lord Essex. We had wanted to wear his colors, move our heads the same way, speak with the same peculiar angry lisp. We had not been ourselves but him.

"Well, I will walk with thee," I said cautiously, because I could not bring myself to refuse him utterly, to close a door which had meant all-in-all to me. "Has he men?"

"Two hundred or more."

"Means he to take the city with but two hundred?"

"The men will rise in every ward when they see him come, as thou hast come with me. The apprentices will rise: he counts upon the sheriff to call them out."

Almost running were we as we turned up the Strand, rushing through the orchards and gardens towards the battlemented mansion through whose massive iron gates one could observe the courtyard. Horses, men with swords and muskets, stewards running this way and that: two hundred men or more. I had not expected to see such a sight near the city of London. "Come with me!" shouted my friend Jack Lord. "Come with me if thou art man and stand for the sweet flower of England! He shall be king at last."

God knoweth how deep lay my struggle.

"Nick Cooke!" murmured my friend. "To complete what went awry with the bloody Irish bastards, give me thy hand! Take thy rapier and walk with me through these gates." We were buffeted by horsemen coming in, and cursed for foolish jades, and all the time I looked bewildered from the turd-trampled yard and the glitter of swords to the plumed hats of the men. His voice lowered to a growl. "Nick Cooke," he whispered.

Then I spoke. "Nay," I said, "I must return. I've my work waiting for me." And I walked rapidly past the church of St. Clement Danes towards Whitefriars by the water, my knees weak. "What, coward! Thou meal-bag," he called, but I did not turn back.

When I arrived, John Heminges had already climbed to the hut on top of the Globe to inspect the wholeness of the ropes which let down chariots and ghosts from the sky; sometimes he still descended himself in the course of some drama, that being no light burden upon the mechanism. Seeing the bent head, thickly grey-haired, and the heavy chin whose shape I knew so well, my throat swelled at what I had nearly done, and I threw off my doublet to work beside him.

"Hast seen Dekker?" He did not mention that I was late come, and I made it up by insisting on the heavier work. It was very quiet in the Globe: a few birds settled on the thatched roof to watch us, and the boats on the river moved swiftly. Morning passed peacefully, we falling into the solid and good rhythm of our work. Ever since I was a boy I had liked to work beside him, and as I grew older, I felt the need to compete and do better. Yet it was unnecessary: he had always made me know how valuable I was to him.

An overcast and chilled day it was, but our work kept us warm enough: he had been thoughtful to bring bread, cheese, and bottled ale, and after a time we stopped to eat, overlooking the river. It was so peaceful that I almost forgot what I had heard the hour before.

He wiped his mouth and said, "Look across on the bank there! Thine eyes are sharp, Nick! What do those men? Canst hear them shouting?"

It was faint enough across the water, yet it carried the way sound will on muted, grey days when the clouds seem to compress into the earth. I wanted to say, nay, I know not, master! but I felt my safety and stability were linked somehow in my trust in him and his in me. "Essex hopes to take the city."

"God's blood! How many men hath he?"

"Not above two hundred."

" 'Tis madness."

"Aye: would God had made him a wiser man."

"Hast changed in these thoughts, Nick."

I had hoped to be silent on the sadness in my heart, but it was not to be, and I spoke with the difficulty one always faces when letting go of a long-cherished ideal. "When I ran off . . . I saw him as our hope of England. The Queen hath guided us steadily. I've thought of it ofttimes since my return."

For a long time we stood close together looking from the window of the hut, which had been splattered with bird droppings: I forced it open and the cooler breeze from the window came at us. I felt life in the pure wet air and could not get enough of it. "What will the Queen do?"

He said, "He'll lose his life for this; she'll bear no more."

"Aye, it fears me."

By the time our work was finished and we walked home, our fellow Condell had come to tell us about it. The emotional band of young wellborn men had risen to follow the impetuous Essex on a march through the city to demand arms from the sheriff, to rouse the citizens. Yet no man had come forth and no arms were given: housewives snatched their washing from the lines as they passed and shopkeepers looked through their windows, and returned to their scales and cash boxes. Only one peddler of hot pies shouted out, "Long live Essex!" It had the silence of a dream. Why did no one cheer? They had cheered at Whitehall when he tilted. Yet along the streets they rushed to nowhere past the half-timbered houses that lay in winding, dirty streets all the way down to the Thames. At Ludlow Street they found soldiers had strung a stout chain across the crossing and stood with pikes to hinder them. "Nick saw them go," John Heminges said.

In the days that followed, news spread that both Essex and Southampton were sentenced to die by hanging, drawing, and quartering, but their sentences were altered to beheading in respect for their noble birth. On Southampton Her Majesty hesitated; then, as he had no male heir and she was reluctant to have his peerage die with him, she commuted the sentence to indefinite confinement in the Tower. The morning of Essex's death she appointed.

On the night preceding we played a comedy before her, and no performance had ever been more difficult for me to deliver. Though I capered and danced, my heart was dead within me, and I could only analyze again the tumultuous feelings in my breast for the brilliant old woman before me, weighted with the heaviness of her dress and jewelry and the divine right of her throne. She had signed his death warrant: he would rot in the earth in his beauty and youth whilst she would totter down her palace halls with her arm across her face against his ghost watching her from every dark corridor. And with all of this, I felt an outrage of disappointment for his poor judgment. Two hundred men, an immature and unthought action! Such behavior had long been my own, and it was with personal outrage that I shouted out in silence against him for his foolishness. And still with these thoughts I played, leaping in the final dance before her, bowing with a doffing of our velvet, feathered hats. "May it please Your Majesty, the play is done . . . we strive to please you . . . grant us your hands and say amen."

After we had collected our costumes and locked the swords in our well-worn sword box, which had traveled throughout the south of England and back many a time, we stepped into the ferry home. The wind blew under our cloaks and the immutable Tower was dark against the sky. I only thought, there he waits prepared to die. What good did I ever do him? What strengths had I to influence him, but in my idle fancy? It was only a febrile boy's desire to serve him: dreamer and poet that I was, I'd failed him.

Then I turned to Shagspere and muttered, "I can't bear this!"

He answered nothing, but grasped my hand in his, and I closed my eyes fiercely against the tears that burned them. At dawn died my lord Essex in his thirty-fourth year, protesting that he loved the Queen. It took three blows to sever his head and all was over.

Not bearing to be with anyone that day, I walked alone to the Globe and busied myself with sorting through the many boxes of playscripts kept there. The hours passed, and though my feet were icy with the cold, I was lost in my self-appraisal. In what way could I have served him better? Had the beauty of him intoxicated us and made us think him fitter to rule, and by this had we encouraged him towards his foolish end? The Queen was ancient and brittle and yet she was our Prince and ruled us well. We prospered in her stability: good things can be said of stability, such as blue hangings threaded with gold to hide the secrets of a new-married couple's long and tender nights.

Footsteps across the dry dirt outside the tiring-room door, and I did not look up but knew by the rapid, slightly congested breathing that it was our youngest apprentice, Mark Forster. Then I saw his face was shining as if it were Shrovetide when he'd go pancake-begging with the other lads throughout the parish. "Oh Nicholas, your wife's time's come early," he said. "And you have a son. Master said I was to make haste to tell you."

I seized my cloak and ran down the bank towards the bridge below the chapel where high above the roof the head of my poor lord was newly set to rot. His face was turned sorrowfully out to sea, and I thought, oh farewell, my sweet, brave Essex! Leave me thy idealism but a wiser way to use it! Farewell my lord, and all you've meant to me.

My wife was awaiting me with our son Christopher in her arms.

THE
THIRD
PART

The
Plague Year

I HAD THOUGHT THAT ANY SON OF MINE SHOULD EVEN FROM HIS BIRTH make difficulties for those about him, but he was sweet. The first time he smiled at me I was so taken with it that I bounced him too long and had to surrender him to Susan to pacify. He was my fancy, my heritage, a new extension of myself; I was a father and my former instabilities faded from me. And I made mental lists of what I should tell him of the world when he was old enough to hear it. Sometimes as he lay across my lap, early memories came to me that rose from I knew not where, and I felt that someone must have loved me greatly in the first years of my life, and taught me tenderness.

Shagspere came more often to dine, bringing coins which he told me to put aside against the baby's future. He liked to rock Christopher in his arms and sing him nursing songs. Many an evening I watched my old friend with my child, satisfied in a silent, primitive way that my married life went so well, feeling (and reluctantly admitting it) a slight sense of superiority that I achieved so easily what was for him an impossibility. And yet there was the subtle suspicion always that he had some inner gift, some spiritual knowledge, that I had not. He was always slightly removed from us; even in the best times, you felt he was standing apart, watching himself and others. Of course, we had known for some years that he was far better than ordinary as a writer, but how do you judge a colleague? A colleague is not a god: you see him half dressed, unshaven, tired (when the muscles of the belly slump, and the skin's pale and ugly from a winter's enclosure in thick clothing). You see him when he snaps because he's troubled with love or illness, or when a quarrel comes to shouting over the deletion of a scene and he yells, "Cursed fools, be damned then!" Or you hear his slightly sarcastic humor when nothing has gone right in a performance and we have all worked hard to pretend that nothing could have gone better. I loved and needed him. In my secret moments I knew that of all men he understood me the best, and I wasn't sure I liked it, for he knew my weaknesses as well as my strengths.

In March of the year 1603 our Queen lay dying in Richmond Palace and all the bells in the city fell into anticipatory silence. Dust gathered on the benches of the theater galleries; not allowed to play, we could only wait. Death brought not only her release, but freedom to the Earl of Southampton, for we saw him in the streets shortly thereafter, sobered by his two years' imprisonment in the Tower. Then James of Scotland processed through the city streets over the shouting of the crowds on his way to claim his succession to the English throne. Magnificent temporary arches large enough for his carriage to pass under were erected on major routes of the city: each of resplendent carved wood, each embellished with men and boys dressed as nymphs, satyrs, or gods, each welcoming the new King with poetry and song over the shouting of the crowd. The scantily clad actors shivered in their gossamer costumes, the instruments barely stayed in tune, and His Majesty was fretful and bored and wanted, so we understood later, only to be at home in bed.

At our supper table there was no talk but whether or not he'd patronize us, and how much it would be worth. Other companies were courting his favor: Heminges was anxious and could not sit still, but walked about from stair to door repeating reasons why we'd be favored and then again reasons why we'd be not. News came but several days later: we would be summoned to play, we would wear the King's red livery in his coronation procession, and we would be renamed to the King's Men and await his pleasure. Shagspere promised us a Scottish tragedy, and the women gave prayers of thanksgiving that we had prospered once more. Yet hardly had the ink dried on our new charter and the royal livery been hung on our pegs than the plague deaths began to rise, and the theaters closed once more.

Sometimes a half-crazed man wandered through our parish streets pulling the strands of his greasy grey hair and shouting that the pestilence to come would destroy us all for our sins. Heminges's younger children laughed at him, but my little son was afraid, and buried his face in my jerkin, clinging to my buttons. And I shouted at the old soul, "Be off, fool!"

We had plans to tour rather than stay idly at home, and I was nervous for the safety of the women and children. Some weeks before we left I found a dead black rat in the rushes of the kitchen floor and spoke to John Heminges about it. " 'Tis the warmer months that brings them out," I said. "We ought to clear this muckpile and wash the street before the door. There are fleas in the rushes, too."

"I'll send the boys to sweep these away and buy fresh ones."

"Nay, master, scrub the stones and leave them bare. Before my birth the scholar Erasmus wrote of the uncleanliness of floor rushes."

He seemed surprised but he said, "Then so be it, Nick," and so we threw away the decayed and soft-trampled rushes and scrubbed the stones of the bare floor.

By late spring, the pestilence had worsened, and all public gatherings, save church services, were still banned. We began to chew orange peel in the streets, and the price of rosemary, which warded off disease, rose to six shillings a bunch. As we rode out of town once more to begin our tour, we saw men dying beneath hedges, in the streets, at the doors of the unfinished plague house in St. Bartholomew's. I trusted the women of our house to keep themselves and the children safe: they would wash the street before the house daily, carry fresh rosemary, and allow no rushes on the floor.

Thus we turned southeast towards Canterbury and the coast, I driving one of the heavy carts laden with props and costumes, and Tom Pope beside me, his fat hands on the stretching knitted wool of his breeches. I glanced at him with some impatience: why would he not take better care of himself? Though he still taught fighting and tumbling, he had long since ceased to dance with the clowns. Walking itself had become increasingly tiresome for him, and we had gradually restaged his parts. "Thou bully wag," he said, "master of learning and family man, Nick Cooke! Whence comes this pain in my gut from time to time which rips me?"

"Hast a pain, Tom?"

"Aye, pisspot: wouldn't know it?"

"How to know it when you say naught?"

He laughed (he still had strong yellow teeth) and punched my arm until I winced. I said, "Hast consulted the physicians?"

"Nay, I like not the scurvy lot of them. There's naught can trouble me for long! I'll tour until I'm ninety."

Though we rode in silence, I noticed that he touched his large stomach once and again with a puzzled look on his face. More quietly than was his habit, he asked, "Where lieth the soul, Nick? Wat Raleigh writes it's in the heart: what think ye?"

"I know not, Tom: if it be a thing of spirit, how can it be in one physical place?"

"Go to! Thou art a clever lad! Sayst my young scholar, shall I turn to flowers when I die? I'll make a whole field of flowers! Then shall these roses and daisies arise again at the Resurrection? Eh, Nicholas? What sickens me to the gut is a serious man: dost think me honest fair?" And he laughed, digging his elbow into my side.

His questions troubled me. The spirituality of my young days had almost left me, my church attendance was perfunctory, and I had no satisfactory answer for him. One had to answer such yearning questions from the heart, not only dully quoting Scripture. For the next few days I trailed after him, coddling him in little ways, until he shouted at me, and I abandoned the bad-humored old man to his pains and prejudices.

Thus we drove our heavy two-wheeled wagons laden with oak trunks stuffed with costumes and armor along the rutted English roads towards Canterbury, the boys walking ahead whistling and whipping the high grasses by the side of the dirt road with new switches. A fine day for a boy to be a young actor, to rush into kirtle and wig, and after two hours' time to turn boy again and stable the horses and wrestle with his friends in the very innyard where we had played. A fine season to be an actor with the excitement that whispered before us as we came into town.

Art come? What news from London? What plays hast brought?

And in the innyard platforms, leaping from the balcony rail with sword drawn, the sound of hautboys, and our man on viols. We passed churches along the way, some still empty from the time of the Reformation and overgrown with weeds, with birds nested under the roof and grass between the floor stones. I passed the modest church in which I had hidden on my escape from Canterbury and had dreamt the dead were risen to condemn me. We had no time to stop, so I took some flowers from the tumbled-down gravestones and stuffed them in my breast.

We arrived at Dover on a Sunday, and Shagspere asked me if I'd walk out with him to the sea.

To be alone with him was one of my greatest pleasures, so difficult in the crowded rooms of London and with our busy lives. We climbed down the ageless chalky cliffs in the steps and paths the Romans had left when they retreated from Britain, the sea before us grey-white and flecked with foam. His high chest greedily drew in the air, his right hand stretched in mine. Ink stains were embedded on the thumb and first two fingers which never entirely faded no matter how fastidiously he washed his hands. He said, "Come, Nick! I think too much of work these days: let's leave these things behind."

"Hast bought yet more land?"

"I do then and anon. Ah Nick! In Christ's name, how mighty is the sea! Canst fancy how small our little world is? Canst fancy it? How futile that we should try to own it." We stood on the sand with the slightly chill wind blowing our hair and the spray of the sea in our lungs.

"Hast been to France, Will?"

"Aye, when I was between my marriage and my playing days. I lived by my wits and did as I pleased."

"What didst please?"

"To have my bachelorhood and my wife at home as well."

"One can't have both."

"Not satisfactorily, no, but I did it. Not all duty will turn me when my soul insists on going its own way. But Susan's a sweeter lass than the one I bedded in the woods."

"Aye," I said boastfully, gladly. "Aye, she's sweet."

We had come almost to the edge of the water and stood a time watching the gulls. "I'm glad for thee," he said suddenly. "Marriage has suited thee better than ever it suited me. Yet harken, Nick! When the time's come to leave the theater I'll go home there. I hope I'll ignore her shrewish tongue; aye, she wears the wrongs I've done her like a Cross. She saves them up till I come back to tell me how wretched I've made her."

"You won't think of leaving, Will!"

"Nay, not yet. Why, I'm still strong though past forty! Many a man's old at my age, but I'm strong yet."

I teased him. "Dost love? Thou sayst naught of thyself in these matters, though there are rumors enough! Dost any lady hold thy fancy?"

Stooping to pick up a pebble, he smiled. "I love many things and many people, and lust comes . . . God wot, it cometh still! Yet, the sweet Lord be thanked, it's not like it was once. Other things are dearer to me, smaller things: conversations, the cold air of the morning when I have slept well. The house in Stratford, New Place . . . sometimes in the morning before I rise I see it and know it's mine and go over it beam by beam in my head. Then the warmth in my stomach's like wine. Ah Nick, we don't speak enough, do we? And yet, the thoughts of thee and thy child pass by me at the oddest times."

The spray of the sea rising up to us, the gulls above, the wind in his fine, brown hair. The salt wet air filled my nose and lungs, and the grey-blue sea rolled away across the broad channel. How pale and clean the sand was, and white the cliffs, and the crying of gulls filled me. We pulled off our shoes and hose, and our feet were pale. "Pah! Shoes!" I said and taking his, hurled them up on the dryer sand. Then we picked up shells, waded into the cold water, and splashed each other. His one gold earring shone in the warm sun of this summer day and his wet, creamy trussed shirt clung to the high-boned chest under the open jerkin. There were grains of sand on his full lips because he had wiped the back of his hand against them.

"Some people say," he began, "that Nick Cooke will be as fine an actor as Burbage."

"Mayhap."

"I've not thy grace in speaking."

I shrugged. Certainly he had never been more than an adequate actor: he played all roles the same, spoken evenly and well enunciated, and from my natural theatrical versatility, I sometimes smiled to hear him. I said suddenly, "Will, canst bear my secret?"

"I'll not share it."

"Thy word!"

"Nick, canst doubt it?"

"My boy Christopher shall be no actor but a scholar: aye, to Cambridge when he's fifteen."

"My purse is his."

"Why, I'll have the money by then, Will."

"Nay, thou dreamy lad: you spend all on books."

I blushed that he knew me so well. "I'd like half a dozen children," I said. "But Susan doesn't conceive again and runs to old women for potions which sicken her. I've read her charts and they say there'll be no more."

He frowned. "Put no faith in astrology, Nick."

"The wisest men do."

"Be wiser than they."

"I'd like to believe that I've made my own fortune, and not the stars or the will of the Lord, but I know not! I serve John Heminges's profession and never planned such a thing. I suppose it was ordained long before I ever came to be."

We walked a time in silence, listening to the waves and the gulls, and dazzled by the sun on the white cliffs. Coming back at last to the place below the ancient steps, we could not find our things. "A pox on it!" he shouted. "Some urchins have come and made off with 'em. We shall go back like boys, shoeless."

The long Sunday afternoon had begun to draw to a close, and we climbed up the steps and looked back over the water before turning down the soft path. Before us we saw the inn against the darkening sky and our cart with the familiar heavily strapped trunks standing alone in the yard.

"When thy boy's a greater lad," he said, "ride down to Stratford and we'll teach him to poach even as I taught thee."

"Ah Will, how I love thee!"

"Dost love me?" he said, pleased. "Why, love's a splendid thing to have, a useful thing, a sort of cloak against the cold, so to speak. Ah, Nick! I would have made a bad master to thee, living as I did in my mind. Much time has passed. Have we gone separate ways, dear fellow?"

"I feel no separation from thee."

"Liar—at times thou hast. Now and then you've found me tedious: I think of rents rather than philosophy. Small things about my honor concern me immoderately. In coming to my old years, my life loses a certain imagination, though I praise God my writing groweth better. 'Tis been years since I drank and whored the night away, years since I wanted it. Eventually I suppose I shall whine because my landlady's not heated the ale sufficiently, and dwell on it half the day."

"Hast spoken with Tom, Will? He troubles me."

"His weight oppresses him."

"But he won't eat less."

"No he won't. No one's ever been able to tell him anything. Now he's old and worse than ever. Some things we can't change, falcon."

There was a pleasant fire at the inn, and we were hungry for supper. The men had decided to change the comedy we played, and were rehearsing in the common room with the tables pushed aside. From the kitchen came the sound of tin plates and the hot smell of roasts and pies. "Like a rebellious schoolboy," he said wryly, "I sometimes needs must assert my singularity by coming a little late."

I slapped his arm and pulling him by the sleeve, kissed both his cheeks so hard that the taste of him (slightly unshaven, seawater, tobacco) stayed with me for a long time after.

Thus the tour ended and I came home again to the pitiful city, many of its doors posted with plague warning: a half-empty parish, for many had shut up their shops and gone away, and the tailor's sign hung silently in the thick air above his boarded window. Tom Pope said gravely there was more to see, and so I went.

O God for the pity of it! Men half crazed stalked the streets proclaiming God's punishment for our sins, and women ran in tears to the houses of unlicensed physicians to sell their plate for physic against the plague which would not prevent it. Some said it was water they sold, of a distillation of flowers. I walked past the shuttered houses until night fell, and then the plague carts rumbled over the cobbles with their awful cry, "Bring out your dead!"

The weeping of the living rent me, and as they crept from their houses bearing heavy bundles on their backs and the carts, more heavily laden still, rolled once more away towards common graves, I turned back to my house.

We could not play, and I had little to do but look about me in the following days. The city was hot with the filth of ages, and nothing it seemed could escape it. Flies settled on the dungheaps, on the stagnant water mixed with horse urine on the uneven cobbled streets, on the fruit in the market. They settled on our trenchers as we ate, and though we boiled beans with wormwood and sprinkled the distilled liquid everywhere to kill them, they nestled in the very linen sheets. A stench arose from the hot city, and the executed bodies of water pirates, left exposed by custom to three tides after their hanging, reeked in the sun. All day long the bells tolled for the repose of the souls of the dead.

Of these vile things, which did I touch? Which clung invisibly, malignant under my fingernails, in the folds of my breeches? I played with my son, and the next day he began to shiver and complain of an aching back. Susan whispered, " 'Tis plague, I know it. 'Tis plague!"

"It could be no such thing."

"Aye, for the old woman who knits was taken with it."

"Christ's blood! Did you touch her, Sue?"

"Nay, I stood outside the door to bring her alms. 'Tis plague, Nick! A man in the next parish was cured of it by garlic cakes under the arm!"

" 'Tis never plague," I muttered, but when I felt his hot forehead I walked out without my hat to knock on the door of the physician between the Brewers' Hall and Gayspur Lane. Long I knocked, but there was no answer, and when I listened I heard only the sound of a cat locked inside who cried from hunger. "He's gone," someone said. "With his houseman in the cart; there's naught he could do here."

The other physician in our parish, who lived on Milk Street, was not at home, and his housekeeper could not say when he would return; when I mentioned plague she drew back and spoke to me through the cracks of the door. My heart pounded with my thinking as I walked home: it could not be plague, but some childish fever, and if I kept him warm and quiet he would certainly be well. Yet as the night came on and his fever and aches increased and the other children of the house whispered anxiously on the stair, I wrapped him in a clean sheet and carried him to the garden shed.

Dust covered my old alembics and vials. I made a small bed from a trunk and sitting beside him, opened my book of Galen's medical treatments. Too much blood sickeneth a man: this I knew. Making soft sounds, I carefully tied a band about his little arm and opened a vein, letting it bleed some drops into a cup. He whimpered but allowed me, watching me with great hot eyes, and I remembered other eyes which had trusted me in my innocent physicking, and that I had succeeded. Or had I? Had Tobias died of thirst and fever in the Irish hills? Was all my instinctive faith in myself but vanity?

I whispered, Lord, if thou lovst me, let me heal him.

After a short time Susan came scratching on the door. Leaping up, I opened but motioned her away. "If it's plague you may catch it, love."

Her beautiful violet eyes challenged me. "I care not."

"Trust me, Sue, and I'll manage it. Art fair ill thyself with sleeplessness. Go away, heart's love, for this night only."

There was a metal antimony cup in the house which had been half filled with wine so that the metallic substance might enrich it, and a few spoonfuls made an effective purge and might force the illness from his small round body. Yet he couldn't swallow it, heaving it back when I had poured it through his lips. Several times that night Susan scratched upon the door, and I begged her patience. So distracted and weak was she that I feared for her.

At the end of the second day, having tried all methods of drawing the fever from him by the heat of fire and dropping elixirs through his chafed lips, I covered my son warmly and rushed off. Quite dark it was, only my lantern showing the way. The apothecary's shop by Ironmongers' Lane was closed and boarded. He had taken his family and fled the plague, and when I banged upon the door of another physician on Cornhill Street who had once aided my master in sickness, I was told he had also gone away.

"God's wounds! Is it plague, Nick?" whispered my master from the door when I returned. Then Susan flung herself against me and shouted that she would come, and I kissed her hand and begged her to mind her health. She was to my belief in the early weeks of pregnancy, and as weepy and ill as it had made her before. The child I brought to her, and he smiled and began to chatter of some sweet she promised him: this she put into his hands against my warning, and went away only on the promise that I should call her should he worsen. Half that night I saw her standing by the window, looking down upon the garden.

We had several herbal remedies in our house locked in the Dutch cupboard by the stair as well as oils of spices and powders of metals. One thing after another I tried to persuade my son to eat mixed with barley sugar or sweet wine. On the third day the black boils appeared on his body: I had not the courage to tell them in the house. Hardly able to hold my hands steady, I lanced the boils and washed them carefully. More came. He whimpered, too ill too cry. Then I threw down the book and buried my head in my arms, rocking to and fro to his labored breathing. I knew nothing. Why had I stayed in the acting profession and not devoted every hour to healing? I was impotent against this thing and his pain, and there was nothing I could do but sit beside him the night long, stroking his silky hair and feeling the collapse of the body I loved.

Susan wept at the door: through the cracks I pleaded for one more night, that he was close to better, that she must trust me. Her father came at last in his nightshirt, and coaxed her away.

On the third evening my son Christopher began to fight for breath. Ah Jesus, that there should be so much air about us and he not able to take in any of it! My hand on his little chest, the deep, spasmodic gasps. Flinging back his head, my little son died in my arms, eyes open, mouth open still reaching for the final breath. Absolute silence, and yet still warm. Still warm he lay against me, only where there had been two heartbeats there was one alone.

I wrapped him in my shirt for a shroud and carried him quietly through the garden past the sleeping house, across Love Lane and to the graveyard of Mary Aldermanbury. The sexton had gone out with the death cart, leaving the graveyard unattended: by the light of the moon I made out that a new deathpit had been dug, and the stench of the dead rose from it mingled with the clean waxed cloth in which they had hastily been wrapped. For a long time I held the still little body against me until I heard the cart coming down Aldermanbury: then I knelt and lowered him gently into the pit as I had sometimes carried him sleeping to his bed. And I broke two twigs from a tree and tied them together with thread pulled from my jerkin to form a Cross to lay on his body.

"The Lord love thee as I've done, Christopher," I whispered and fled through the churchyard and across the parish. I should have gone home at once, but I could not. I could not allow it for the possible infection I carried and I could not allow it for my grief. I could never go home and tell her that Nick Cooke who fancied himself a physician had allowed her son to die.

Half the night I wandered about the silent city, losing myself among the streets, along the dark river, and around and about St. Paul's, where the booksellers' stalls were shuttered. Up Paternoster Row I went, walking the length of the wall from Ludgate to Moorgate and then to the fields of East Smithfield behind the Tower where Essex had spent his last night. The King's Men were scheduled to tour again within the week: even as I had nursed my little son in the shed, my master had continued alone to clean, pack, and sort. I could not go with them: I was beyond acting. No kings, lovers, and rebels could come from me. Thus I stood outside our house in the grey summer dawn, knowing that when the morning came my sleeping wife would descend the stairs with her hair not yet braided and rush to the garden door to find us, a small bowl of sugared fruit in her hands.

I wrote her with the pen, sand, and paper I had left in the shed to chronicle my son's illness and I slipped it under our door.

My own love, I had not the wit to save him.

Then without looking back I walked away.

Thus began my first day in the city of the dying. The streets were empty, and once I came across a poor soul who I thought was sleeping against a boarded house, and found him dead. Night fell again and with it came the rumbling of the carts over the cobblestones, the heavy wheels bumping into the ruts, the awful cry that I had first heard as a boy: "Bring out your dead." Still I walked on in the streets of almost perfect darkness, feeling my way with my hand on the houses and tethering posts, hearing the sounds of sobbing here and there, and then a quarrel and a child whimpering. I bought a torch from one of the taverns that had not been boarded and deserted, and walking down the winding streets to the river and back again, saw the awful Cross scrawled on many a door and the pitiful sign: "God have mercy on us."

When I could walk no longer I rested on some barrels in a street without Ludgate, faint from hunger, though my stomach rebelled at the thought of food. Only one dim lantern burned above the doors of that street, and after a time I noticed a small, black-gowned man emerge from within. I knew from his black garb and walking stick that he was a physician. "Master, what is o'clock?"

"Past eleven, good fellow," he answered wearily.

"Are they stricken in that dwelling?"

"Aye: the father has died and the wife too ill to help him. The children huddle in corners: each time I return I dread how I will find them. What dost here, man? Art seeking my help?"

I fought my sudden urge to weep, shaking my head and unable to answer him. He said softly, "Thy wife? Thy child? Ah, Christ have mercy. Hast any sign of fever or nausea? Give me thy wrist. The air about here is foul. Walk with me if you will. I have lost a little one as well." He put his hand under my elbow to steady me, and we began to walk through the empty city towards the river; and it seemed that every fourth house was boarded and locked. It did not matter where he led me.

Stopping beneath the sign of a basketweaver on Fleet Street, he examined me more closely. "Why, my man, you can but stand! Hast eaten this night? Shalt dine with me? I'm alone, for I've sent my wife and the rest of my children to the country."

"Why did you not follow? Most doctors have fled."

"Conscience prevents it, though what I do here's little more than nothing. Come with me and we shall learn each other's names."

The gates to Blackfriars were unlocked: no sentry questioned our entry, and the street down which we walked was as silent as ever I remember it. His house was as empty and dim, and even when the lanterns had been lit, there remained a hot, unhealthy, musty smell about the room. No hangings covered the wall, the whitewash of which was paler where pictures had hung. It seemed as if no one lived here longer, and no one would ever return. "I sent much of the furnishings with my family," he said, "and the rest hath gone; someone came in to rob when I was out and took what plate I have. There's cold pie: shalt share it with me? And wine, which makes me sleep. Tell me thy name."

"Nicholas Cooke, actor."

"Of the Globe? My children are rare fond upon the comedies. An excellent one of Mr. Jonson's I recall, and you among the players! Forgive my rude and hasty introduction. I am James Fitzwater, trained to medicine at Cambridge and Padua, where I took my degree fifteen years since." He gave me his hand as formally as if we had been introduced under more propitious circumstances and in not quite so dour a place. " 'Tis a rare city, Padua, more fine booksellers of anatomy and map volumes than I could afford in my student days, and since then I have not had the time to return. I remember standing in the theater of dissection, hardly able to see for insufficient candlelight. I did so much have enjoyment in those days. But my talk mayhap is tedious to you. Hast a fondness to medicine, my friend?"

"Aye, some," was my dull response.

"Hast tried a hand to it?"

"Then and anon."

We sat on either side of the uncarpeted table, and he could find no napkins. I took a slab of pie with my knife, but put it down almost at once, unable to bring it to my mouth. He said in a fatherly way, "Thou must not remain fasting," and divided the portion into smaller bits with his own knife, some of which I managed to swallow. He sugared my wine, and the warmed, sweet drink comforted me.

Dr. James Fitzwater was a small, finely built man with a pockmarked face: I judged him to be fifty and was surprised to learn him some years younger. His conversation was animated, interesting, and eager. A large head he had, and hands enormous for such a delicate body, and his fingers could span far on the organ keyboard if he had been a musician. But he'd not been bred to music: he knew nothing but the body. The top of his head, when he bent it over his plate, was balding. I dared not take my eyes from him, for I fancied that he and I were the only ones alive in the city, and that if I lost sight of him, I alone would remain. He broke more bread for me (it was hard, and the crumbs fell in the cracks of the table and to the drying floor rushes, which had lain there many a month) and said, "My dear young friend, tell me of your loss."

"Ah, could I have healed him!" And then I began to explain to him how I had read Galen's medical books beside my son as he labored to breathe, and found nothing to help me. I explained imploringly, hoping he would tell me something.

But he said, "Nay, there was little more you could do. So you have read Galen and, you tell me, the field surgery books of Ambroise Paré? It's Fracastorius of Verona's book on contagious diseases that's most valuable. Hast read it?"

I shook my head.

"He hath isolated several putrid sicknesses, hath writ these are spread by small matter which increases in the sick body. Should this pestilential matter be in the pus of a boil of a victim and it should enter thy body, then the spirits within thee should increase it."

"Galen said pus was a healing thing."

"Paracelsus had the wit to throw Galen's books into the fire."

"He discovered little more. Mercury harms more than it cures."

"What else canst suggest?"

"Naught," I said and was surprised that I laughed. We fetched another bottle of wine and found a hard cheese moldering in the heat of the cupboard which we ate without thinking. "Then in thy reading, doctor, thou hast studied a great deal."

"Aye! Much good is coming from the University of Padua! I've read what I might in any language I could understand, saving the Arab doctors, whose meaning escapes me. I am licensed under the College of Physicians and by their laws may not cut a man to heal him but may purge him until his very bowels be spilled into the bowl."

"Concerning Fracastorius."

"Concerning him."

"I'm drawn much to his work: I've read something of it as well. How should this pestilential matter pass, say, from thy body to mine?"

"Mayhap through the skin, mayhap the air."

After he had left me to sleep, I took down the Fracastorius from the shelf and began to read by lantern; then I pushed away the book and walked up and down the silent parlour. Fracastorius had been a poet and alchemist as well, although he also consulted the stars; his theory of contagion, however, fascinated me above anything. Did this small putrid matter which passed unseen into the body and multiplied there cause the high fevers of many diseases? In multiplying, did they heat? I slept only towards the coming of the dawn, and when I woke I fell to thinking on it again.

We broke the rest of the hard bread together. "It's passing strange thou art an actor by trade when all thy mind's set to physicking," he said. "We have much we can discuss with pleasure: would our meetings had been in better times!"

Staring at the floor, I said suddenly, "When these plagues pass, I would 'prentice to you! I should throw over everything else to learn what you know!"

He shook his head. "Much would I like to have thee! Yet consider the laws of this profession: thou art a married man and cannot study to qualify in the universities here or in Padua unless a bachelor! And if you 'prenticed for thy learning, why you must serve seven years before you are allowed to wear the black gown. In that time how wouldst maintain thy wife?"

"Then there is no way for me?"

"None that I can see, my friend, but who can tell? Who can say in which ways life will lead thee? Ah, you have brought to mind some pleasant memories. I have thought this very moment of a small bookshop near Trinity College in Cambridge, hardly big enough to fit a cot within, and a man most foully dressed and friendly of spirit who sold secondhand medical books. All could be found there, even things not yet written! Books piled on the floor, to the ceiling, thousands it seemed, Latin, Greek, Arabic, my friend, the great healers of Persia. Hebrew, dear fellow. Books we spoke of, books we exchanged, he never removing his pipe from his mouth. When you go to Cambridge, turn away to the right down where the washerwomen live, and there you'll find him. His name is Samuel: tell him James Fitzwater who had but one pair of breeches and now hath three sends his fond regards."

Many more memories he was pleased to share with me, of his heatless room overlooking the quadrangle where the washing water froze each night, of rising at five to eat bread in the dining hall before entering the library to study by the palest of morning lights. Then we walked out to the hot street, the flies settling everywhere, the rats dead in corners, and a young woman holding a dead baby against her, lying against a shop where they had sold copper lace and other trimmings for dresses. He muttered, "Christ save us, save us! We can't purge this plague away, and leeches won't draw it from the blood. I have packed my trunk to leave and join my family, but I do not leave. But thou, my young friend! Shall we not part ways here, thou towards Cripplegate and I to my work?"

I shook my head.

"Then come thou with me," he said, drawing my arm through his. "Carry this small bag and we shall speak of dissections in Padua. One teacher could never get enough corpses and would steal them from the gallows, an arm or a leg at a time. He couldn't get more under his cloak and pass the city gates with it . . . had to pretend he was carrying a sick dog. We were ill from the smell, but when he'd come we'd shout, 'What do you have, master?' 'The torso whole of a cursed damn soul that killed his kind mother and father!' he would shout and hurl it, stinking and dried, among us. One young lad from Rome fainted dead away. Christ's wounds, I remember him! Wash thy hands, young pigs, he told us. We had a good time then."

"And Cambridge?"

"There I first studied lungs, and watched the girls bathing and learned to give strong enemas. Thou smilest: thinkst thou this work's so fine? Wait till thou hast done it, my friend, and come and tell another tale. I see Cambridge hath some sentiment for thee: your eyes shine. What is the name of thy wife?"

"Susan."

"Hast she word of thee?"

I hung my head, and he squeezed my arm. "You must have courage to go to her! The fault was not thine, dear friend. My wife is Elizabeth, and I love her so it is difficult to be from her company. Come! Let's see what can be done to end this cursed plague and have us to our homes again."

Later I learned that eleven thousand died that year: nay, more. They died calling on the Lord, barricaded with their terrified families behind marked doors, or on the church steps or crawled outside the city gates and dropped beneath the laundry lines of Moorfields. We pressed leeches and purged, and brought in live fowls which we forced gasping to the suppurating sores until the bird died. At each house I threw out the vermin-crawling floor rushes and washed the floors with fresh water and opened the windows. There were but half a dozen doctors in London and Westminster who had not fled. You saw the faces of surgeons and mid-wives and once a physician and then he went away and later we heard he had died. Then my friend said, "Christ's wounds, Nicholas! We were at Padua together, he and I." And I saw the fear of death pass his face, stronger than any compassion, and he struggled with it and crossed himself.

"Hath God forsaken us, my friend?"

"Dr. James, I know not."

Death covered me: the sweat of the sick soaked my shirt, the smell of their clothing was in my unwashed breeches. And once we were so wearied that we slept amidst a family of four stricken, unable to rise from where we had fallen.

As I rested there, a great silence came to me. It is the silence that one hears in a cathedral when it is almost empty, a healing silence, more reverent than the sound of the waves against the shore. I shivered in its loveliness: my aching body softened. I thought I heard the sound of singing: one pure boy's voice at the end of a great cathedral choir, uplifted to the apse. Then it ceased and all was silence once more. At last, from the very center of my body, I felt something stirring and a voice inside of me said softly, "Nicholas."

It was very distinct in the pronunciation of my name, of an unheard clarity, and shocking the way it is when you are cold and someone else brings her warm body suddenly next to yours. In this clear, sweet, low way the voice repeated, "Nicholas."

The warmth increased, filling me until my body was suffused with it; it mingled with the silence, and yet I did not dare move, for fear it would leave me. Contented I was, as if I were a small child again and in my father's arms. After a time I heard the boy singing once again, and imagined that I walked towards the sound down the long nave of Canterbury up the stone steps which mounted to the choir. And as I came through the dark wood choir screen, drawn towards this child as I had never been drawn to anything in my life, he turned and smiled at me.

I fell into a dreamless sleep, and when I rose the sun was very bright through the opened windows. The streets below wound down to the river, and I heard in the alley below the voices of children throwing a torn leather ball to each other. That evening James Fitzwater sickened, and I lanced his boils but it did little good. In his last hours he was yet lucid. "Go back to thy playing of roles, my friend," he said. "We know nothing more than Aristotle, and he was a pisspot fool. Tell my Liz should you see her how sorry I be."

"Paracelsus, James!"

"A pox on him. Go to Cambridge, Nick, to the shop by the washerwomen near Trinity, and give my regards to Samuel who sells books. I owe him four pennies: for a kindness give it him. I have not so much about me at present to give thee."

I ran down to the cistern for fresh water, and when I came back he was lying with his eyes open staring at the ceiling. A cry of grief broke from me. He could have taught me; I could have learned from him. Angry I was that he had abandoned me and at the same time ashamed of my irrationality. Then repentant, hardly able to speak the words, I knelt beside his body and, in a hoarse voice I hardly knew to be mine, began to utter the prayers for the dead from the Book of Common Prayer.

"I am the resurrection and the life, sayth the Lord; he that believeth in me, yea though he were dead, yet shall he live. And whosoever liveth and believeth in me shall not die for ever. We brought nothing into this world, neither may we carry anything out of this world . . ."

With the tears running down my face I spoke the words as if they could bring him back again.

"The Lord giveth and the Lord taketh away, Even as it pleaseth the Lord so cometh things to pass: blessed be the name of the Lord."

Hearing the carts coming over the cobbles, I wrapped his compact body in a sheet and carried him to the street. As I stood beside the grave, the light of my lantern showing the cheap tin Crosses on the bodies of many strangers which lay about him, I wondered if Our Lord had truly turned his face from us, and we drowned in our ignorance.

I could not go home.

There was no hospital for the victims of the plague, and they died where they were stricken. They died on filthy sheets, on straw-filled pallets laid on cracking wood floors, their faces parched and uncomprehending. Sometimes I poured water into their lips, which spilled out again as if the throat had closed. Death was quick. It took only three days, sometimes less. They were thrown into common plague pits, and others came to take their places. Oft I looked down at one face and thought it was another. Oft I thought it was my son who lay in my arms, and wept for him more than the person who actually grasped my hand imploringly, his soul pushing out against his putrid body, as if I had some power to hold him back from death. The scientist in me could not turn away: horrified, compulsively drawn to the wretchedness I saw. And I thought, but this last one . . . if I do not release her hand she will not be taken. And even as I grasped the fingers of the dying, they left me and were no more.

I walked about the city streets and saw the fetid water in lead drains, the open dungheaps, the cesspools and dank cellars full of rats and fleas. In all the herbal gardens of the city I knew not of one plant which could cure what had descended upon us. The physicians and surgeons purged and bled and the people died.

When I returned to the empty house of James Fitzwater in Blackfriars on the twenty-second day from home, my back had already begun to ache; I attributed it at first to weariness, but it did not pass. Fever and vomiting followed. I rolled to my side and vomited until I thought my stomach would burst through my throat. And then the shaking and vomiting again, and I cried, Christ help me! After that everything became unclear. The black swelling pushed from under my testicles and armpits, hot and painful and unrelieved. My lungs burned; I vomited blood. I screamed in the pain of it and knew someone's hands. Who lanced the boils? Someone had to hold me down. In my screams I tore my throat. Then they were gone, and when I awoke the beautiful sun was coming through the small windows of the doctor's house in Blackfriars. Two dead men lay by my side.

Too weak to move, yet I lived, and when the cart came to take us away, I muttered my name and they left me. There was no one to nurse me anymore, and after a time I was able to crawl about until I found a bottle of sweet wine which we had not finished and some hard bread. I lay half in a dream, not in this world and not in the next. My lanced wounds stank, there was no one to wash me, and on and off I heard the faint singing of one boy's voice in a Psalm.

I dreamt the vision of Ezekiel and that I awoke to a desert full of white, dry bones and that a great wind blew and there was no living soul there but myself. Then I was parched with thirst and unable to stand, I crawled about, turning over this bone and that and weeping, calling the name of my son Christopher. And I said, "Shall these bones live?" as the prophet had done, but there was no answer.

I knelt in the sand, withered with thirst. Then I tasted water, felt it spill down my throat, cool and sweet. Who had given me drink in my illness? I never knew.

The dark winding streets, and the overburdened wheels of the death cart, and the joking, sodden men accompanying it, and somewhere a woman shrieking. Before me extending from the sheeted dead in the cart was a man's hand, and though I thought I knew it, I could not remember. Only when they had dumped them into the common graves I understood it was Will Shagspere. I climbed down into the grave, roughly turning the bodies and looking into their faces, which shone pale and grey in the torchlight. The faces of those who had died under my care, grey-lipped, disintegrated in my arms, and Shagspere was gone.

And I cried, can these bones live?

Why do you cry out, Nick? I heard him say. All men are mortal and I not less than these. Don't concern thyself with things thou canst not change.

Don't go . . . you must help me!

How can I help thee, my falcon?

To understand myself.

I felt his warmth, and we became one. After that he gave me his fine hand as he had when we descended to the Dover beach, and said, let us look for our sons, thou and I!

He had become an archangel and lifted me in his powerful arms, weak and fainting as I was, and we flew together past the burnt spire of St.

Paul's and into the immutable firmament, into a world where the sky was the purest blue and the floor of clouds, and though the day was bright there were many stars even brighter, and the sun and moon hung together. Have we reached heaven yet, friend, I said.

Nay, it is further still.

Oh it tires me, Will!

Nay, do not be tired, Nicholas! It is further still.

Yet even as he spoke, I felt his strength lagging, and that mine was quite gone, and even as we flew we began to slip back to the earth, and we tumbled down, and down and then down, falling over each other, and I cried out, "Before it is too late, tell me . . ."

I woke to the little room which overlooked the streets to the river, the straw pallets on the floor, the chipped pitcher which held water, and the pisspot with its thick yellow remnants of those who had died, and the Cross of sticks that someone had stuck onto the windowpane. Jesus help us. Who had been here?

Too ill to rise from the floor and too distracted to know what I had dreamt and what could be true, I lay there and heard the bells toll for the dead, and after hours drank the water, which was dirty, and listened to the silence of the house. I wondered if the children with the leather ball might ever come again or if the plague had taken them too.

When I awoke once more it was morning. It astounded me: but why should I live, Lord, when these others must die? The sun had risen and women went for clean water and all went on just as before. Only I had changed, should never be the same again. Oh give me compassion to return to my home, to forget what I have seen, to serve John Heminges and the men and grow old in my relative stupidity, asking no more what cannot be answered. We are created helpless in our mortality, and there could be no remedy for it.

Holding on to the wall of the stair, I passed out into the brilliant street and down to a deserted part of the river, where I made a little fire and then burned my clothing. There was a house which had been abandoned and ravaged by thieves: there I found breeches and a shirt to fit me, and in these strange clothes I went home, using a stick to lean on and wincing with the pain of my clean but unhealed sores.

Susan was in the kitchen rolling out crusts for pie, and I stood by the door with my heart too full to speak. Then she looked up and cried out. "They said you'd been seen but I could not believe that you would live . . . and not come to me."

"I have come."

"I've said the prayers for the dead for thee."

"Then unsay them," I answered, and fainted on the floor.

When I awoke I found I had been put into a bed with clean sheets; the door was shut, and Shagspere sat beside me. He told many things of the brief tour without me.

After a time, I said, "Were all the men spared?"

"None was touched, but in the Lord Admiral's Company two were stricken."

"And in the parish?"

"Forty gone."

I lay against him like a weak child, and he let his arm rest across my back: I remember the sun was coming through the small panes of the window. Then he covered my legs and left me to mend.

The love of others comforts us. I slept.

TWO

Syon House

NO PLAGUE COULD KILL HONEST TOM POPE, YET HE DIED THE FOLLOWING year of a growth in his belly which had long troubled him. I spent all my free hours by his bed making up mendacious tales of women I'd had to please him, while his children (some grown and some yet small) and apprentice lads went to and from the room with frightened eyes. "Give me food: I starve," he muttered. "A fart on thee, pigs! Give me bread." They brought him a hot posset and he poured it into his mouth, the egg dripping in his beard. Nauseated, he vomited. "Take away the pillows, Christ's wounds, take them away." Grasping my hands with a look of terror, he said, "Shall I turn to flowers and yet rise again, eh Nicholas?"

"Thou shalt sit at the feet of God."

"I would rather in my own kitchen. Bring me food."

"Nay."

"Dost not hear me, boy?"

"By Our Lady's mercy, Tom!"

"Nay, take it away. I leave thee my love, Nick. Wilt thou do well, wag? Bring pen and paper to write my wishes. I shan't fit in the parish coffin. John Heminges is a good man! Pray for me each All Soul's Day! Ah, the children, the children! Never mind . . . take it away, it matters not anymore."

The bullying, the giant voice and thick tread, the common tradesman sweat of him and the oversized shirts (aye, I could have wound about my hips six times the trussing for his jerkin!) were gone. I'd have known him a mile off, tromping through the thick grass of Southwark, his arm about his orphan girls. His opinion of rival companies was succulent: a fart on the whoreson pigs, they're not worth to kiss a tinker's arse, Nick!

These things were lost to me.

After we buried him, we closed up his house in the parish of St. Mary Overy. He had died owning the crest of a gentleman and left mourning rings for us all and his small brood of children to the loving care of my master and mistress, who never minded a child more. He'd been a man of some riches, for he'd bought property in Southwark, and we found a heavy box of coins and women's jewelry under a loose plank in the floor of his bedroom, and though he left most of his shares to his own apprentices, he remembered me with a small portion as well. These I locked in the chest under my bed where I had thrown the many medical books which the wife of my late physician friend, James Fitzwater, had sent over to me when she returned to London to close up the empty house in Blackfriars. They included Dr. Caius's great treatise on the sweating sickness, a book on herbs and the influence of the stars upon them, and Thomas Wright's *The Passions of the Mind*, concerning the interplay of mind and disease. He had accumulated as well many loose pages in his own writing on the makings of oils from sweet marjoram or rosemary flowers or mustard seeds, salts of cloves, nutmeg, and wormwood. No approval had he for the more dangerous metallic treatments. I thought to compile his work into a book but couldn't bear to begin.

I no longer believed in my power to hold back death: the thought of my past audacity brought shame. I fled from these memories and from myself, forcing myself into my actor's life, invaluable to John Heminges and my troupe, in the double house on Wood Street. Heminges was ill himself that year (some say affected by the death of his old friend, and God wot I give credence to such things), and much fell upon me. Many a night I sat up trying to reconcile the week's spendings and takings, or to cajole the apprentices to their new roles. How difficult those days were! Only with Rebecca Heminges did I find some peace. Her small hands shaped and restored the sweet ordinariness of life: jars of preserves neatly marked, children sent to school with hot cakes in their hands, tables scrubbed, wicks of lanterns trimmed. Sometimes, sitting in the coffer chair of an evening reluctant to mount to bed for my weariness, I would have liked to throw off my life and crawl into her arms. There was no lust in this, just a man's weariness. "The hour's late, Nick!" she would murmur, and reluctantly I would bid her good night.

There was a further reason I delayed the ascent to the small chamber hung with blue brocade. I wanted no more children, for the thought of such brought an agonized sense of betrayal towards my dead son. I longed for the cool, unmoving waters of celibacy; it was not allowed me. Susan had not been with child as we supposed months back, and now wanted desperately to conceive; she wept most bitterly when one of her married friends on Addle Lane walked down the street with swollen belly. Her body told her she could have many children. This for her mediated the loss of Christopher, but my loss did not heal. The futility of our short lives plunged me to despair. She could not reach me, neither could I reach myself. The plague year had taken from me any jubilation I had ever possessed. Nothing stirred in me but my useless grief. At night I tried to read, turning my back on her quiet crying. Why had I married her or come back to her again? I was not a man like my master, experiencing death as merely a passage to the joys of Heaven and quietly accepting the will of Our Lord; my restlessness, my need to rearrange the world to my idiosyncratic liking, lacerated both myself and those close to me. Susan was a good and loving person, parsimonious with candle ends and excellent at knitting new heels into worn hose, in every manner as orthodox as the childish hymns she sang to her small siblings, in every manner as predictable. Of such fabric are wholesome parishes and sturdy nations made! Alone with me in our chambers, she was richness and golden; she was as sensual as a warm summer day. I recall her standing barefoot in her white shift, legs innocently apart like a boy, pushing back her tangled hair and weeping until her full mouth seemed bruised and swollen, having jumped from the bed because I would have naught of her.

And then she struck me, sobbing, and I tried to make her understand, and we held each other in our grief. She was like her father in some ways, as concentrated and devoted: nay, she was not the placid maiden she had bred herself up to be, modeled mayhap on stage heroines and ballads and treatises on the modesty of women. She was pure concentration, and her concentration was on me. What could I do with such, unable to respond, unable to move?

The plague left naught but wretched memories in the city. The nameless mounds in churchyards over which the autumn leaves fell, new neighbors come to scrub and occupy houses in the parish where whole families have died. Once I found the little man of wood and string which Shagspere had given to my son: it had been caught behind the heavy feet of our curtained bed, and I began sobbing so hard that Rebecca ran up the steps to me, and rocked me in her arms. Then, unable to bear our memories, I retreated once more to my books. Susan, standing with trembling mouth and her round face all wet with tears, and the boyish feet under the plain white nightshirt, clenching her hands, whispered, "Nick, canst love me anymore?" But I couldn't tell her: I didn't know. The division between the stultifying grief inside myself and my theatrics left me more hollow and aching than ever before. I played insolent French kings, poetic lovers, brave captains, and though there was no heart in anything I did, my popularity rose. One of the men said it was because I seemed to be beyond sorrow: tall, strong, and defying mortality. This is what they saw in me. And whatever I played, the unthinking fools paid their pennies to see it.

Desire returned, but without tenderness. Not bearing to bring it home with all the emotions involved (her tears, my own, the empty cradle we could not bear to carry to the attic), I began a brief alliance with a Frenchwoman. I was cold to her; she complained of it, and it ended. Another involvement followed shortly: what shall I say of these things except that they meant nothing to me? One beautiful young woman told me I was heartless: I had never been called that before and it shocked me, yet I supposed it must be true. Thus passed the first winter after the plague left us: going about our ways with the hearts half dead within us, the engravers busy with memorial plaques for church walls, we tried to remember how we had lived before.

In the spring of that year the mathematician and astronomer Thomas Hariot returned to my life. Perhaps he saved it as well, for I had little inclination to live and no courage to die.

People who have touched lightly on one's life at an early stage, having done some act of kindness or recognition, appear often deeper and more complex when we come upon them again in our maturity. I had seen Hariot occasionally around the halls and courtyards where we played. Many of the nobles for whom we worked thought us uncouth, quaint, somewhat savage, mayhap unwashed. Like the older men in the troupe, I was gracious to them, thanked them profusely for their occasional gifts of gold and patronage, and was glad enough to shake off their company. Hariot stood apart in his plain linen and brown doublet, somewhat occupied with his own internal world, cordial and reserved. I sensed that he understood things I had not yet the wisdom to question. He had been navigator and explorer. A mutual friend told me he had voyaged to Virginia almost twenty years before as chronicler and historian and written a book about the habits of the savages there; upon return, he had become a member of the loosely formed club of inquisitive minds which hung about Walter Raleigh, Kit Morley, and the Earl of Northumberland and which some called "the school of night." I sensed he was a deeper man than he would let most know.

Mathematics drew me: in the stupor of my exhaustion, I found a kind of peace in the clarity of trigonometry. I could not bear to think of medicine; my mind stagnated and turned once more to my childhood love of the heavens. I wanted to study the positions of the stars and to measure the wanderings of the planets: to measure things exactly, oh Christ! To measure anything absolutely, undeniably! I craved the precision of angles and the satisfaction of geometric proofs. The vagaries of the human body which eventually must sicken and fall from shining life into a corpse past response, past wanting, nauseated me: my previous determination to physick and its shameful failures repelled as well. Angles, altitudes, and equations were absolutes: if I could understand them, I could count on them and they shouldn't let me down. And so after a performance at the Earl of Northumberland's London home, I sent one of our boys with a note for Mr. Hariot, asking if he might speak with me.

The reply, sent next morning to Wood Street, was that he would see me with pleasure and would be at Syon House that night, should the trip not inconvenience me. I was all eagerness to go and hastened through the gardens of the Northumberland estate half an hour before the time. A cheerful footman escorted me to a few small rooms at the top of the house, and there Tom Hariot awaited me.

It had been many a year since I had come as a boy to these rooms, and I glanced about once more with pleasure at the speculative glasses and quadrants, and the crucible and furnaces, for, as I had suspected, he plunged regularly into alchemy as well. Laboratory papers in his individualistic cipher, his drawings of the planets, the moon, and the sun and another which I later learned was a chart of sunspots were neatly stacked on the table. A most slender, grey-haired man he was, though not past his fiftieth year.

We sat down to wine and cakes, and playing with the crumbs, he smiled at me slightly and said, "I had thought one day you should return here, Master Cooke."

Surprised, I answered, "You have remembered me."

"Quite well: a boy with long dark hair in his face, a ruddy mouth resentfully set, eager to understand everything, grateful for any kindness. Deep curiosity is rare, my friend! Most men have no patience for education."

"On that I've come," I answered. "I wish to study with you."

"That would give me great pleasure."

We spoke for some time on my work and his, for he divided his time between research and the tutoring of his lordship's children. I had begun to walk about and after a time opened the window to look at the stars. "Master Hariot," I said, "let me put the first question to you. Is what we look upon infinite? Or hath it an end?"

"My friend, what do you ask me? Can finite comprehend infinite? But surely you've read the works of Giordano Bruno, the Dominican monk who held there to be innumerable worlds in this dark and fiery sphere. The Roman Church burned him alive for his views."

"In your opinion, are there innumerable worlds?"

"My dear Cooke, I only know what I see: Bruno understood much instinctually with a pure and higher vision. I am a natural philosopher and not a visionary. Read his books and then search your own mind for some of the things you seek to know. So you wish to study with me! Understand I have no patience for mediocrity: there is no time for such. Your friend Morley was much of the same mind. I think mayhap it ended him, for he could be fair insolent. I've been waiting for you to come back, for I've something to give you." Searching in the small drawers of his cabinets, he brought forward a brass pocket nocturnal notched for the hours and marked for the pointer stars of the Great Bear. "The night before he was killed I supped with him, and he spoke most fondly of you."

"He had no interest in me," was my dry reply.

"You are mistaken!" he said sharply. "He thought you remarkable, and said it more than once." He studied me closely, and then looking tactfully away, added, "He knew too much mayhap, was too clever, spoke too loosely at times. Impulsive as he was brilliant. Keep this, if you will, in memory of him. May his soul rest in Our Lord."

"He would frown to hear you say it, sworn atheist as he was!"

"Untrue! He comprehended an infinite spirit. Do you remember the passage from *Tamburlaine:*

> . . . that he that sits on high and never sleeps
> Not in one place is circumsciptible,
> But everywhere fills every continent
> With strange infusion of his sacred vigour . . ."

Then he concluded, "He left us much."

I nodded. Holding the nocturnal in my hand, I understood Morley's uncomfortable bequest to me, received mayhap as he held me against him so many years ago, and that was his restlessness, his need to express and to understand. It was a gift I was not sure I wanted, yet there was no way to rid myself of it but by suppression, and that I seemed unable to do with any lasting success. I wondered wryly if I ought thank him and if even now, wherever he was, he knew my thoughts.

Hariot had poured more wine and beckoned me. "I've heard talk of thee, Cooke!" he said. "They say you served as physician in the pestilence which has passed, though you've no certificate for it."

"I stayed but I failed. We've no knowledge against this thing. It must be caused by something small, infinitely small. What think you! Could we invert the speculative glasses used for telescopic sighting to see what small matter harms us?"

"I fear the smaller elements can't be seen, for the glass has too many imperfections. I try it no longer, neither does Galileo in his work, but in the Netherlands I understand they attempt it still. But look! The night's clear and I've some far finer speculative glasses than before: The magnification's greater and the distortion not quite as bad. The moon's full as well. We shall see the craters and mountains distinctly."

It was an evening cool with the river breeze, and Syon House lay in shadows behind us. We walked over the paths between the empty flower beds, he carrying the tripods and lenses wrapped in soft cloth. When he had fastened the leather-covered tube to the wood stand, he said, "There lieth great Copernicus's mountains of the moon."

Enlarged was the left side of the full moon, its mountains and craters, pregnant with light. Shifting the perspective glass to the north, I brought the Pole Star and the stars of the Great and Little Bear into view; they quivered in their refraction through the imperfect glass. "Can you measure the moon's distance?" I asked.

"I have some calculations."

"And the planets and stars as well?"

"Nay, they lie too far beyond our sphere. I'll show you the equations and you may try it yourself if it please you. God knows how far they be, though my friend Kepler is working on the distance of planets by calculating their orbits. What are you seeking, my friend?"

I could not quite answer, so I was silent. We watched for an hour more before he bid me good night and I rode reflectively back to London under the stars.

Though I thought much of beginning to grind a microscopic lens and spoke to Hariot's man Torporley for preliminary advice, I had not the time, and for the many months that followed my visits to Syon House ceased. The talk in our kitchen was wary, for with the Guy Fawkes conspiracy to blow up Parliament and the King that November, Henry Percy, Lord Northumberland, was suspected for his protection of Catholic rights and sent to the Tower. "Speak not thy mind on this overly much, Nicholas," John Heminges said. He knew me well, and for the protection of our livelihood, I bit my tongue.

We men of the theater lived on the munificence of the lords and landed men about the King, and apart from them. We served them, we entertained, danced, and made our bows, and went home like dull merchants, carefully shaking the dust of any partiality or involvement from our boots. If the Sovereign found displeasure with a lord and imprisoned him, we discreetly sought engagements elsewhere. Now politics had seized me fiercely once more. Henry Percy had fought for Catholic rights, but anarchy was not in his character. He was a man of science. I knew of him and understood him well, for it was my business to understand character. Thomas Hariot was also taken for having privately cast the King's horoscope, a forbidden and seditious thing. He was judged innocent of intended harm and shortly released, but not until St. Paul's Churchyard was again rechristened with traitors' blood from the execution of the men involved with Guy Fawkes's conspiracy. The goriness of it appalled me, but I could not keep from it, though it was a time before I could taste food again.

THREE

Wood Street

S CIENCE POSSESSED ME ONCE MORE.

Yet I was not free to follow it as I would. I had a demanding profession, and resumed studies distracted me somewhat from my work. I was teased rather than criticized for this: some of the men thought it was a love affair. How could they begin to know? They had become burghers, merchants, vestrymen. They were among the rising class of craftsmen in London, delighting in their stability and fortune. I was in the very youth of my imagination. A boy of fourteen just gone up to Cambridge could not have lusted more with the desire to follow the curvaceous paths of knowledge to wheresoever they led him. This adolescent creature hid beneath my exterior man: the outer self and inner self parted pitifully, and I knew not how to bring them together. And how it hurt me to live divided as I did, and have no idea how to put my worlds as one.

More uncontainable yet and most peculiar since I had once again begun to chart the skies was the renewed physical closeness of God: I felt Him in the mist in my face, in an apple I held in my hands, and sometimes walking through the narrow streets of Cripplegate ward, I knew He watched me. My first and most holy commitment had been to Him. These thoughts came with the science, and I did not know how to pull them apart. I would have spoken of them with Hariot, but there was a shyness of personal speech between us: this alone I lacked of him.

And one day while ferrying back from Syon House, I realized that it was not simply an hour here and an hour there that I needed. I wanted a whole new life which would express the parts of me long dormant, and whatever that life might be, I needed to break away from Aldermanbury to find it. The outcry of the spiritual, the outcry of the natural philosopher and intellectual pulled at me, yet all day long I was the actor, sometimes fourteen hours a day six days a week or more, entertaining, playing out great kings and foolish lovers. Every ounce of my energy, as vast as it was, was needed for something or other, and John Heminges, always seeing a way to improve the theater, suggested new tasks to fill the spare minutes I might have. When these were done Susan was waiting for me: "Stay with me, Nick!" she pleaded, and she'd pull down her white smock, and twist her long hair about her. I gave in to her sometimes; it was not lust and I am hesitant to call it duty. In her womb was mortality: babies were born but to die again. How I loved her and how I ran from her! She could not begin to understand these things.

Then we quarreled and I shouted and she wept, and my master mounted the stairs and stood anxiously outside our room. "Nick, what ails thee?" he said to me as we walked across the bridge to the theater, and like the boy of old that I'd been I looked down at the stones and muttered, "Naught." We had two theaters: the exquisite candlelit, renovated Blackfriars, the bulky and open-to-the-winds Globe, and I wondered when he'd suggest finding a third. I wanted to shout out in my protestation against everything that pressed against me: bed hangings, silver plate,

King's livery, reputation, my much-talked-about profile and muscular legs and the other divided parts of me which were so stupidly idealized wherever we toured.

There were no more women. In one of the most embarrassing moments of my adult life, I had been confronted by John Heminges on the subject. Rumor had become too great. There was both a delicacy and a firmness in his confrontation of me, and once more it brought me to mind the positions in which we stood to each other. He treated me respectfully; he'd hardly ever treated me as less, even when I came but to his shoulder and he had to haul me by the arm from pummeling some other apprentice over a trifling matter. Still, he had trained me from a child and given me his daughter. I promised him that there would be no more of it, and the conversation left me faintly sick that it had to be said at all. Once more I felt that he was a better man than I, less swayed by imagination, impulses, darker moments. Therein came my competition. His illnesses were done with and he had resumed all his parts and was managing both theaters excellently. He would have shown me reasonably that I should curtail my mind, I fancy, if he could have, but that was beyond his talents. How could he do it when I couldn't do it myself?

Yet he knew me and my work: he knew me well. And the Lord be with me and guide me, for he loved me as his son. This was the worst of all. Even in the fight scenes when I fell badly once, he raised me and I felt that old burdening kindness and it stifled me to know it.

Thus went my life in the years 1606 and 1607. I was nervous, haughty, quarrelsome with friends and strangers, torn between science, which was both my escape and fruition, and my life at home, wherein lay my duty. In the winter of 1607, Thomas Hariot and I saw the great comet which men still speak of, tearing open the dark night sky with its light as it came. Many astrologers called it a presager of disaster or great fortune, depending on how one interpreted it. Hariot remained silent, his fingers gingerly to his ulcerous lip. The papers in his chest grew in quantity, the desks scattered with silver drawing tools, compasses, and a quill pen with ink dried dark and full of memories laid across the wood surface. Fog formed repeatedly on the lenses with the bitter cold as we tried to draw what we saw, and calculate whence it had come and whither it might go. I ferried down the river after performance on my rare free evenings, ripped by the wind and unable to stay away. He had some letters from the astronomer Johannes Kepler in Denmark to whom he had sent comparative notes, and was calculating the comet's path as seen from London to send him.

Kepler's work both disturbed and fascinated me; according to his letters his computations increasingly suggested that the five planets moved in elliptical and not circular orbits around the sun. I was drawn to the uneven course of Mars, experiencing it as an extension of my own orbit in the world. I fought my own mixed dedications: the ordinary versus what can never be fully contained or expressed. Our first months of mathematics and astronomy taught me the perfect dimensions of heavenly things, perfect equations, perfect shapes. As we progressed, the perfection splintered into as many possibilities as the light through the prisms which so fascinated us. There was no charted or predestined path meant for all, for the smallest planet had its individual one. This is what it spoke to me, and true to my emotional and poetic makeup (quite different from Hariot's path of proof by equations and experimentation), it both drew and repelled me.

One asked a question and got many more: irascibly, I sought final answers. I intimated, but could not prove, an illimitable universe. This made the geographic location of Heaven a question, not to mention the doubts it raised as to the veracity of certain biblical passages preached to me from my earliest years. Ecclesiastical wisdom insisted it was five thousand years since the seven days of Creation. Hariot shook his head in silent disagreement. Thus I allowed myself to be slipped slowly into the deeper inquiries where absolutes blur. I would have pushed away all the world if I could.

Late afternoon on a windless February day, a happiness so great as I could never have expected came to my life, for my friend Tobias from the wars returned to me.

We had played at the Globe, and had just finished the last dance of a Ben Jonson comedy, when Augustine shouted for me from the watering trough by the tiring-room door to hurry into my boots, for someone waited for me. Throwing my cloak over my arm, I walked out supposing it was a lady and wondering how I should best send her off. There waited my friend, leaning against a tethering post near the Falcon with his arms across his chest, smiling at me forgivingly as if I were late.

With a great cry that might have frightened the rebels from the bogs, he had me in his arms, crushing his face against mine own. Sweet musician of the camps, he had been. And here he was in most ordinary workaday Southwark the very same fellow, with his wheat-blond, wayward hair, short beard, and enormous soft hands. Pushing me off, holding me by the arms so he could gaze at me, he demanded, "Art my Nick?"

"The same blasphemous fellow!" I shouted. "Pisspot, where hast been?"

"Here and there."

"Didst not write, scurvy dog!"

"I feared thee dead!" he said simply, and then with his eyes misting added, "Any fool who had stayed must have died."

"I thought thee the same."

Behind us over the boardwalks came the last of the playgoers, and through them, hands shaken and praised, some of our men: Augustine Phillips with his nearly grown son, a lanky lad and not a bad actor, and small neat Robert Armin, his bag of juggling clubs over his left shoulder. "Come with me to the Nag's Head!" I exclaimed hastily. "How came thee hither? But nay . . . not here."

I flung my arm around him, and despite Phillips's call that I was to meet him within the hour, I did not turn about until we had rushed through the door of the tavern. The drawer, whom I had tipped now and then, warmly greeted us, asking after the performance, and showed us to an enclosed booth in the back. "Shall more candles be brought?" he inquired, opening the door and wiping his hands on his apron. "Wilt have dice, masters, or cards? I bid thee welcome."

"Candles, and in time send the lad."

"Anon, sir."

Three fat candles came with a brass holder thick with old wax. Doors shut behind us once more, yellow-gold candlelight on my friend's pale beard and flushed, happy face, I hurled down my cloak and throwing myself across the table, took him by the ears and kissed his mouth and cheeks until I was breathless. He had not changed but for some small crevices near his eyes. "Didst not write!" I blurted. "I should trounce thee for it. Eight years, pisspot."

"I meant to come myself before."

"Wherefore didst not?"

"Trouble with the farm, and she was jealous and held the purse strings with what crooked farthings they contained. I am a fair hand with cattle now, Nick! Ah, Christ's wounds, eight years since I've seen thee. Did I not say I'd come to London and find thee an I lived? Ah, she was a flaccid and aged one, my Margaret Collins of Wicklow! She nursed me, thou must know, when I stumbled into her yard. Nursed me into her bed . . . seventy years old an she were a day, Nick, but kindly, most kindly. Taught me to nurse cattle as well and to clip a sheep clean. A strange and poxy conclusion to the war."

"What happened to the girl then?"

"Oh the little one! Went back on my troth! Found the cottage empty. I have seen thy name listed with the players on bills posted by the gates when I came through the city this morn. Thy master took thee on once more?"

The shy, freckled boy from the bar having knocked, I ordered beef, mutton, chicken, bread and beer and sugar, which came promptly. "Aye," I answered when I had closed us in again, "he took me back and I've done well. How couldst remember things so idly spoken!"

"Nick, art my brother: 'tis sworn. I owe my life to thee."

"Nay! Thy wound was slight."

"Men died of lesser." The hands which felt mine were calloused, the nails rough and broken. He wore neither ruffs nor pins, and some hurried needle had stitched the plain cuffs to his jacket. Ireland returned as I touched his fingers: the disgust, the fallacy, the feel of the cold iron tips of our pikes. I shuddered.

"Friend," he said. And then we began to burst out with everything that had happened in the eight years since, from the inconsequential to the momentous. Sheepshearing, the loss of his shy virginity to an eager, elderly bride, his proficiency in Gaelic, his loneliness without me, his apprehension that I'd be sentenced with the men who rebelled with Essex, his despair that he lacked the courage to find out. On my part I spoke of my work, my master's house, the news of the city under the King. He'd begin a thought and the same exactly would come to me at that moment, and we shouted with laughter. Some writers I knew knocked upon the door, hearing my voice, and the freckled thin boy came with cheeses and a chalkboard to note what we had consumed. Tobias had eaten much: the table was littered with chicken bones, and I recalled he was always hungry in the war. "How long since hast dined, boy?" I demanded.

"Money's short: after my Margaret died her sons from her first husband came and threw me out most nicely. Across the channel I went, serving as ship's mate, and then begged and sang my way to York. My mother being too occupied to have much to do with me, I turned my way here. But thou hast lived and prospered, Nicholas Cooke. A man would not need ale, friend, to be drunk with joy for thee." Once more he kissed me and then looking away, murmured, "I can't believe me Essex's gone. I never thought the old lass would put him to death. It must have grieved thee painfully."

Throwing myself moodily back on my bench, I played with the rind of cheese. "Nay, I'd lost faith in him."

"And yet it grieved thee still."

"Damn thy soul, Toby! Must know my looks even?"

"Thy looks? I hardly know thy face, man, but for thy eyes. Responsibility sits on thee like an alderman! Where's the soldier who thought roughness next honor? That doublet's worth a king's ransom, sweet my friend!"

"Position once scratched for begins to own a man," I said wryly.

"Thou hast mistook! Dost think it irks me to see thee fine? Nothing could please me greater! Tell about the theater: next to music, I love it on my soul! I've writ comedies for a boys' school in Dublin to keep from starvation. Mayhap they'll fetch a price to my good."

"Read them to our men: they'll buy them if they love me!" We fell to the cheese and sugared sack. The boy knocked again with a message from our apprentices, who had thought to find me here, and I impatiently thrust it in my breast, this time bolting the door.

"Hast married, Nicholas?" he asked.

"Yes, I'm bound in holy wedlock, and she's far better than I deserve. These matters are more complicated than we ever could suppose when we lay in our tents, lusty and youthful as we were, and whispered of them!"

"Aye, far more complicated, Nick! I've been a married man as much as thee: 'twas done honestly, calling of the banns. Her sons twice my age did not take it kindly, as I have related. I must begin again. Can you make a playwriter of me? There's naught else I can do."

"On my soul!" I cried, rising at once. "Come home with me. For thou shalt suffer at my hand shouldst go from me again."

"Where dost live?"

"Why, Wood Street within Cripplegate! . . . as you said you'd find me there, for I still live at my master's house, who's now father-in-law as well and a good old man."

"Thou cans't not yet be bound 'prentice!"

I shook my head. "Nay, only bound in respect to him, in obligations which are far more irrevocable ways to bind a boy, and not so easily grown from." We opened the door, blew out the candle; I threw money to the bar and, striding into the cold, windless liberty of Southwark, pulled him towards the river. He was as astonished by the city as those who have come from France to see it, and for a time we leaned out over the small opening between the chapel and the tinshop on the bridge, and I pointed out to him Whitehall and Westminster, and the earls' houses whose private wharfs jutted to the water. Women coming from the shops with packages turned to smile at us, he flushing and jabbing my side, and stumbling to look after them as they went. I pulled him up Gracious Street and left to Lombard where the jewelers and goldsmiths work, and past the icy, white water which fell steadily from the Cheapside conduit and past the lines of shivering water carriers. A thousand questions he asked me, for, as in the old days, he was curious about everything. In his clumsy stride he ran to catch up with me, thrusting his arm through mine once more: the flat nose, broken in a childhood fight, sniffed the market air. All in all he was like the good-hearted lover in our plays who wins the lovely girl by the fifth act and the audience walks back to their ferries laughing and saying, "The blond fellow . . . he was a merry man, I liked him well! Much joy to his bed." I wondered if he could see me as well as I could see him, and rather hoped not. And in that moment my disappointment in myself rose like an ache in my chest.

What had happened to the boy who'd gone to war and fought the barber-surgeon to rashly treat a wounded friend? I had been an emotional, irresponsible fellow then. I had been so many different kinds of men in my life, and it seemed that I yet searched for the proper one to represent me. Should I be that Nicholas once more with him? I drew him to me, my arm in his, and told him rapidly, as if there would not be enough time, of the past eight years, the plague and the loss of my son. On the corner of Milk Street before a buttery stall, he took me by the arms and stroked my cheek with his knuckles.

"Ah Nick!" he murmured. "My dearest wish for thee is that sorrow shouldst nevermore come thy way! All that I can promise is that never,

never shall it come through me. God knoweth I have thought of all we spoke, and remembered thy words. Canst love thyself at last, my friend? Thou ought, for art come a splendid fellow."

"My thanks!" was my reluctant reply.

"I bear the scar yet of my wound, Nick. Thou saved my life I fancy, and cared for me like no one's cared before but the old Irish widow, and her I had to bed. What were the vile things you made me swallow? I sometimes thought you had become a great healer."

I stopped by the almshouse. "Nay: I try it no more."

"Why, my brother?"

"Death wins all in the end. 'Tis only a matter of time."

"I felt a great force of spirit in your hands."

We moved close to the doors to allow a coach to pass us, spewing up dirt from the large wheels. "This spirit is the Lord's," I said dryly, "and He does not share it with me. 'Tisn't His will, as my master Heminges says."

"He may say it, Nick, but you drew out my fever. Now 'tis said thou art one of the finest acting men. When I came to London and noted thy name posted I all but shouted and said to one of the water carriers, 'Who's this Nick Cooke?' and he said, 'Why any fool knoweth he's the best actor with the King's Men next to Dick Burbage, who's going on for forty and growing old.' 'Is Cooke a great tall fellow, handy with a sword?' 'Aye, he's a fine-looking man.' 'Didst know he'd been a soldier?' I said. 'Nay, indeed!' 'Aye,' I said, 'he was a soldier and we served under brave Essex . . . Essex's last farewell.' "

We walked towards Cripplegate, and as we came closer to Love Lane he dropped his voice and murmured, "Thy other fancy besides physicking I remember . . . you would have been a priest! I knew I'd come safely from the army camps if I had thy prayers. Art not ordained?"

"Another fancy."

"I thought it more. I had thy prayers!"

"Leave off, boy!" I cried impatiently. "Fools can pray, and many do.

I'm always wanting to be this thing or that thing, and it's my passionate humours that make it so. They could bleed me for it, but I might be bled to death before they'd all be gone. I'm a married man and a shareholder in the finest acting company in England now: those other fancies have passed. Do me a kindness and not mention them further, as thou lovst me."

He seemed surprised, but he said, "As I love thee, Nick!" He kissed me and I punched his shoulder and shook him a little, and then we went inside.

He was very soon part of us. Sent to sleep upstairs with the apprentices, he wrestled with them and told them fancy stories of the war which I knew were never true. The men liked him very much and agreed to buy one of his comedies. He wrote light and charming plays, not the melancholy poems of rejected love which he had left to me and which he was astonished that I'd published. John Heminges received him warmly. He made friends of the children, but then he made friends of everyone; he would sit on the stones of the kitchen floor and fold a paper so that it became boats and hats and kites and secret messages. Away from the wars, he spilled gentleness and good nature whenever he went, and he loved women. Even little girls enchanted him and climbed over him, pulling his pale-blond mustaches and trying to find the sweets and apples he hid in his sleeves. Yet girls ripe for marriage awed him into stupidity or speechlessness, though he told me, after some months of planning to court one of Robert Armin's daughters, that he felt himself not good enough for any of them. "It will never come to be between a young woman and me," he said.

Sometimes in the evening John Heminges would get out his instruments. Tobias was reacquainted with his viol, which I'd kept in its case under my bed, but he was greatly disappointed that he played badly, being out of practice and his hands roughened from farming. His singing voice, though, remained a sweet tenor, still pure, and he read music perfectly. Some of our players and their wives came over of an evening and we would sit about the trestle table singing and playing. Heminges was an excellent instrumentalist and put aside his accounting books to join us, and we passed about the parts of madrigals and read them with pleasure, Susan and Tom Pope's girls, whom she called her sisters, on the treble line.

In Toby's simple affection for me, I felt myself the better man; I hated to part from him, for it was like parting from an undefinable part of me that I could no longer craft alone. I thought of him on the ferry rides to Hariot and took him with me once, where he followed little of our conversation. Then he began to throw his commendable energies into writing comedies for us, reworking old Italian plots, and our men hired him at a shilling a day to act, for he was an excellent comedian. His comic servants and bumbling, pompous young lovers made everyone laugh, and I taught him some of the tricks of tumbling and falling that Tom Pope had once demonstrated to me.

I could never be entirely withdrawn with him. At night when I went upstairs I often remained a long time by my door, watching the shape of Susan's small shoulders in the shadow of our bed. In what manner was I conducting my life? No prayers eased my passage into sleep: my old dreams and anxieties forced me into the deep marital bed until they suffocated me, and always by my side was her unfolded hopeful hand, which said, do come, Nick!

I found solace in a peculiar way: as I slept, and gently in my dreams, I always brought to mind the voice of a single chorister singing alone in the great choir of Canterbury. Yet when I walked the length of the nave to find him, picking up my step, he had gone.

Like warmhearted children, Tobias and my wife began to play together, sometimes chasing each other about the knot garden and around the baby-minder of our kitchen. When I came through the door she stopped, and her full breasts under the bodice lacing rose passionately up and down in her interrupted play, her cheeks rosy the way little girls' are when discovered in private, uninhibited moments. Another friend was to be married and all the girls were forever hemming things in corners, and giggling, fleeing if any of the men came in the room, leaving linen scraps and a silver thimble on the floor behind them. Bulky and loving Tobias was alone allowed to be with them. He sang them ballads to his viol or danced one of the smaller children on his knee. And coming in the door I felt he was easily entering a world from which I had excluded myself.

It was in the spring, on the day Will Shagspere told me of his retirement, that I found my little church again.

We were returning from the tour which had taken us to the Dover coast and were riding side by side behind our company and the wagons towards the end of a long afternoon. "Art grieved at my parting?" he said as an afterthought. And he reached out and took my hand, chafing the back of it a little as he'd first done so many years before when we walked back from Southampton's house in the darkness, privy to each other's sadness.

"Why should you go?" I answered. "Thou art some years from fifty."

" 'Tis old enough."

"A piss on that! John Heminges hath ten years more than thee." I glanced at the high forehead, the sensual and restrained mouth. No one in years to come ever captured in paint or stone the passion of him, only the merchant and dreamer.

"Heminges will never leave the theater while he has breath to speak. Didst mark him as we played in the innyard today? Standing behind the curtain, ready to supply the missing line. His whole life's in this. 'Tis best so. If we both left, the original men but for Condell would be all gone, and Condell's swelling in the legs more each year. Kempe, dost miss him at times? Never a kinder colleague! Christ's wounds, Nick! John hath the spirit of genius in his craft: only in this he taught thee. My play of shipwreck and magic shall be done far before Christmastide. Then nothing else shall keep me here . . . shares sold, property transferred. No speeches, prithee! I want to go quietly, gradually, without passing the loving cup or tears. When others cry I tend to do the same."

"What, to dull little Stratford over the bridge?"

"Aye, to the place I ran from."

"I never thought thou wouldst do it."

"The years pass: one desires a circle of continuity, perhaps."

"Thou knave, thou shall not long for us."

"Aye, I will. What I'll long for most is not the playing, for my body's had quite enough of that. It's my fellows I grieve to leave behind me, Nick! John and I have known each other almost twenty years; he pulled me from some wild nights, and we often talked until the sun came up."

"I remember."

"Nay: we kept these things from thee. Thou wert but a child." He slapped my shoulder lightly and said, "I've pulled thee from scrapes thyself, my friend."

"Aye, God wot!"

"And thou helped me alway. Dost remember when I was sick of the mercury cure?"

"I sat with thee all night."

"Thy will to heal. Ah, Nick! I'm tired in a peculiar way that makes me want to make a little garden and watch my granddaughter grow. We're rather alike, you and I, in that we don't quite fit into molds. I knew it the first time I saw you. I'm a petty man sometimes, more small-natured than I'd like to be. Yet we've shared much, have we not?"

We spoke of many things as we rode along that spring afternoon, as if he wanted to tell me everything he'd kept from me. A life revealed more complicated than I supposed and of a tenderness I had not imagined, divided between loves and angers, disgusted by lust and time and again possessed by it. What surprised me was how well he knew the men. Some of them who had played with us for a shilling a day had slipped my memory, but he knew their children's names. We talked about love: he knew all the shoddy romances that had hurt and embarrassed the men of our troupe now and then. I asked him casually if Heminges had ever been untrue to his wife, and he threw back his head in laughter. "Why, he's in love with Rebecca and it's never ceased in the twenty years of their marriage! It's she who . . . but, that's a private matter, falcon, and let it remain so. A bit of a wild lass she was, but you would not have guessed it."

After a while he turned the subject to something of which we all knew and on which he had for the past three months maintained resentful silence: the publication without his consent of the sonnets he had written years ago to the young Earl of Southampton. "They were only meant for his eyes," he said. "Of all things that ever I writ these were most private! Our printing laws are whoremongers. I could bring suit against a man for stealing my pen but not publishing my poems. God's wounds, Nick! I thought he threw them out years ago . . . used them to wrap pies or start fires, or something suitable."

"You've told me little of the matter."

"Embarrassment prevented it. He was just come eighteen when first we met and I some ten years older. I was in his mother's hire to write him sonnets to persuade him to marry, and as I knew him better, the things that came from my pen astonished me. I adored him to my cost, for he was all that I could never be. Then we proceeded to love the same woman. To sacrifice my principal interest came naturally, ready as I was to give over everything to serve him. Do not heed rumor: no physical love was exchanged between us. Inhibition forbade me to consider it seriously, and he would not have stooped to raise me. I was a playing man who wrote a little to better my pocket."

"Then you loved him very much."

"I would have died for him, but that passes too, you know. Passions for all worldly things, be they women or crafts, leave us. Grandchildren and gardens perhaps remain, and friends. Aye, Nick, friends remain!"

I was silent. I wanted to ask him what sort of love it could have been, each love being different from another in some way, none quite the same. Had he loved him more tenderly than ever he had me? Yet I couldn't ask, and it hurt me enough to bring a swelling of the throat, old friends as we were, man as I was. Another question came: had I loved this man myself? And how? Would I have had him as lover if he'd wished it? It embarrassed me to think of it: since my adolescence I had been clear that men were for friendship and women for lovers. Yet there had never been a way to truly discharge the emotions between us, his hesitant yet passionate caring of me, my unwilling and yet humble need of him.

He was not one thing to me: he was all. There is a part of me that awakens and breathes with one friend and a part with another: this man was all parts. Then to lose him! Would it be a handclasp and then good-bye? I had always wanted him to tell me what no one could tell another, to define my purpose, to sanctify my choices. He said simply, "When you came as Heminges's boy, thou knowst, I was sick with loneliness for my son. After a time, the lad dying . . ."

I said, "I know."

"Dost truly, falcon?"

"Aye, friend."

On the dusty road bound from Canterbury to London City we traveled. I remember that the ravishing sun was slipping beneath the trees, and we, in our conversation and the equally potent silences between it, had fallen even farther behind the other men. It was then that we passed the little church in which I had spent the night so many years before. I had passed this way several times, yet never mounted the path again. Suddenly I said, "It fancies me to see this place! Take but the quarter hour and come with me."

Dismounting, we tied our horses to a tree and walked up the path through the toppled tombstones and cracking grave slabs towards the door, shading our eyes from the sun. The shabby miller touched his cap, and I had the amused notion that he thought me a gentleman. "Hast been here before, Nick?" said my friend.

"Oh aye: in this county I was born."

"I thought you from Sussex."

"I never was."

"What have you not told me, false fellow?" he said, slipping his arm about my shoulder. We began to walk about, the tangled high grasses catching at our boots and embracing the grave slabs, some of which were as old as the fourteenth century, tumbled and grown with moss. I moved my hand along the solid old stones of the wall; the roof, which had been of wood, had been broken through, yet inside I could still see the shadows of the pews, and smell the scent of wet stone, old wood, wild things hiding.

Standing there, I began to tell him what no living man knew: of my father hanging motionless at rope's end, of the strangers in my mother's bed, and all which followed of my life here. The twilight and the memories, were too much for me, and I had to stop a few times to control myself. He exclaimed, "In all these years to keep this from me, I who have watched for thee! What a burden of fear thou hast carried! Show me the place where the boy slept that I may know thee better." In that way I reentered my church for the first time in thirteen years, his arm in mine.

Cold it was with the chill of many winters. There was neither Rood nor Communion table, memorial plaque nor colored windows. The stone baptismal font had been knocked on its side, and neither lectern nor pulpit remained. As desecrated it was as if the Devil himself had come in a wind, and carried the congregation away.

The last sun of the day came through the broken window above the altar. "Hast never been back before?" he whispered.

"Nay, not since that day."

"Didst never feel the want of it?"

"Nay," I said. "Nay."

He looked at me then as deeply as he ever had. "I remember the sign concerning which you asked me when you were but a boy," he said. "Dost remember? I think thy sign has come this very hour, Nick Cooke." Too moved to speak, I only nodded. I let him throw his arm around me once more, and we walked outside to mount. The sun left us; the day chilled. We rode into almost darkness before we came to the inn.

The tour ended, and when I came home I found Susan with her hair neatly braided in ribbons as she knew pleased me well. I buried my face in that hair and in her sweetness. Yet I did not know how to find the words to begin to tell her that something had happened on the Dover Road which changed me irrevocably, and that I wanted to begin my life again.

FOUR

Parting

From the time I returned to Aldermanbury, I knew I was going to leave the theater and all I had known and walk up that steep winding path to the stone church amid the tombstones. I dreamt of it so often that I hardly knew what streets I walked, only my mounting upwards, the weariness in my legs, the wanting to be enclosed there by something in a protective way as I'd longed to be enclosed since my earliest childhood days. And I spent all the time I could manage by myself, away from Syon House and away from Wood Street.

Yet though this troubled longing never left me, I remained an excellent man of the theater. I was an actor to my bones, for a man may grow towards something new, yet retain the basic structure of all he had been. For fifteen years upon rising each day my thoughts had always been of the part I was to play and intuitively I rehearsed in my mind the particular dancing or fighting, the emotions, the interactions it would require. My few moments of sloppiness had shaken me back to my inbred discipline. I was naught if not reliable, a solid colleague, and I could no more let down our men in any way than have turned on my fellow soldiers in the wars. As after the plague year, the greater my inner turbulence, the better became my work. I responded to the fear of my growing desire for change by knitting myself more irrevocably into the ordinary world which had for so many years sustained me.

One morning I chose to leave early, pretending the need to pay some money on books I'd ordered, so that I could be alone with my thoughts and walk in solitude across the bridge, seeing our bulky, weather-stained theater rising against the sky, feeling the mixture of pride and bondage that it always brought to me. For almost every day of the past fifteen years I had walked briskly into this tiring room or another more humble one, taken my first costume from the stagekeeper, and consulted the sheet which was tacked to the wall for my entrances and exits and what props I needed to have each time. Rapidly I laced my doublet to trunk hose, joking with this fellow or that. Then as I walked from the tiring-room door into the sunlight pouring down on the stage, I was instinctual life and energy. Craft and passion held me and my voice rang out against the galleries, powerful and deep. If it was a part I had done often, I sometimes thought of other things—astrolabes or measuring the height of stars—while I spoke, yet only once or twice had the stagekeeper to shout a line at me, and that was when I had a shivering ague and the actor who covered my roles was sick as well. I was born to the trade, Armin had once said to me. Nick, thou'rt born to play in this wooden O! Aye, thou't be heroes and knaves forever at two o'clock each day by the grace of God!

Spoken so fondly, and yet so encapsulating of me: such fondness from others hath its imprisonment. What did they mindlessly praise? I did nothing of my own. Never in my life had I tried to be an actor. From the first time they laced me into a farthingale at the King's School, I instinctively knew that I had to breathe deeply, speak more clearly, and let every man in the farthest seat know my thoughts from the turn of my shoulder and the look on my face. From before Heminges took me I had grace, yet today as I began to truss the points of my hose, a hundred unwanted recollections of my early years with him gathered into my mind. He had taught me, defended me, loved me perhaps. I didn't like to admit it, for I planned our parting. How was it to be done without ripping, bleeding? Ah, we were somehow one together. He had made this creature which was us craftily, with his easy-speaking manager's way of melding diverse substances, this great and cunning alchemist, this man with the sore back and the ofttimes rushing heart and a mind for every penny the company ever spent! I was in his crucible.

I cringed, I shouted. Well, was it not true?

As I trussed my doublet to my breeches, I muttered quarrels with him, revised them, mentally ripped and threw them away. He was the greater man, aye.

Not as I lived would he be! Yet what madness I spoke! I saw nothing properly. Aye, he was a good man. How well he cared for the boys: shy young fellows who looked enviously at me, for I was the best swordsman in the company and the most athletic of the actors. I coddled them and tousled them and threw them over my shoulders at times until our shouting woke the babies. These things passed my mind as I stood with my hand on the curtain of the tiring room, knowing how many lines were left before my entrance, my body gathering its concentration, my mind panting from its silent feud. Naught to shout at but my own audacity. Jacob wrestled with God: I wrestled with a sense of injustice that I knew was more phantom than angel.

It was a court scene, and most of the actors were onstage. I should never care for any group of men as I cared for these fellows: Burbage, Condell, good-natured Armin, philosophical Augustine once the philanderer! Like sack and late hours and the chimes as we guiltily came home past midnight, how sweet were these common things: the smell of wood, sweat, and burning coal of the tiring room, the sound of our boots on the platform. Walk center, turn, speak. It may rain; then there shall be the patter of it on the thatched roof which protected our stage and on the faces of the crowds about our feet. Rain or fair weather, we shall finish our play and end with the volta, the men dancing and the krumhorns playing from the gallery. The lutanist would pack his instrument and we'd begin the walk home past St. Mary Overy and across the bridge, arguing over what had gone well and what must be altered. Then after supper John Heminges would pry open the double knots on the cracked leather purse, stuffed with the day's takings; it would be emptied on the trestle table to count, that very table where oft I looked across at his face, awed with my mixture of admiration and dislike. The judging boy I was: he never minded it! The coins often fell through the cracks to the floor, and the smaller children scrambled to retrieve them. It was the face of our sovereign James that was now engraved in the money.

Marry! said our men. Other companies break apart, but there's no sign of it with the King's Men! The Lord hath looked after us well! Why, none of us had silver plate or wall hangings in the old days; it was a penny here and a penny there to pay the rent, and everyone said only a fool's an actor. Nay, by Our Lady! Why, but thirty years ago the only actors were the guildmen dressed up in Advent to play the kings bearing gifts, or the piping boys with their tedious Latin tragedies. No one was an actor thirty years ago, and look how we've come! If it had been fool's work old Heminges wouldn't have left the grocer's business, for he knew where the pennies were, and none slipped through his hands.

I agreed with them always: by Our Lady, it's truth! No pennies slipped, no child fell away in vast disobedience. Why should they be so wanton and rash? No man as sturdy, as simple and open-natured, as crafty and consoling as he who'd taught me. Two or three times a week after supper, the men filled our kitchen, and the talk was much the same. Lord knoweth, there are so many writers come to London six theaters cannot use all their plays. What sayst thou, Henry! What rent hast thou for the Southwark houses? My girl has a fair dowry to her, and I'll not give her to any tailor or chandler, mark it. Mark it!

Give thy daughters well, said John Heminges. Eh, Nicholas?

Aye, Master John!

And so it went. Hot warmed ale, bread broken and the loaf passed among us. A clay pipe: the women hated tobacco, but it was good for physicking. And always some new young and shy boy as apprentice to be teased and taught and allowed in the midst of this genial, unforgettable company. I had never fought for it: it had been given me by a woman's instinct for my needs and talents and a man's determination that I should not fail. Else I had become a vagrant and a thief in the streets, perhaps else I had died.

Then why could I not stay? Perhaps I was not meant to grow comfortably fat on heavy meats, count my lands and rents, doff my hat to the gentry who might pay me better for doing so, say, "Wife, wife, where's my stuffed gown?" I was no vestryman. These things protected me, bound me, imprisoned me. For one moment I understood: I must go away and come to an understanding of myself, and I must go alone. The impossibility of it filled me with shame. I pushed it violently from my mind, as violently as I had pushed the wheelwright from me to protect my life.

Then it was my turn to enter the stage: I heard the spatter of clapping which always greeted my entrances, no matter which role I played.

Yet I could not speak the words to begin breaking this bond, and the more silent I remained the larger it grew, a lump which would allow nothing else spoken. Our actor Robert Goffe was to be married, and I thought, at the wedding I'll tell them. Yet tell them what? That I wanted to leave them for a mildewed church on the Dover Road? That after all these years of striving for stability, I craved a harder, more original life? What was the righteousness in such things? One didn't leave a profession to wander in indecision.

The wedding came and all its festivities, and I could not speak. The sackbutts and recorders played, the loving cup was passed, the bride's ribbons snatched from her gown and her hair to be distributed among the young men. I followed John Heminges into the inn kitchen where he had gone about the fowls, and caught him with a platter in his hand. And I said, "Master John, should I tell you that I wished to leave this profession and go to live on the Dover Road, what would you say?"

"What that thou art in thy cups, boy!" he answered.

The day faded, the children quarreled, the dogs fought for the bones in the inn's floor rushes, the bride leaned wearily against her young husband, hardly caring for the games anymore, looking as if she were about to weep. Our men packed up their instruments and the sun began to set down the west part of the river and catch the spires of the churches with its gold. I didn't go to sing the wedding couple to bed but walked down to the river with Susan to watch the last of the sun. Back and forth we walked, she lifting her blue gown carefully to avoid the muck of the docks. The gulls sailed above us.

I was drunk enough to tell her: I thanked God for it.

"It was a fair wedding," she said.

"Oh aye!" I said.

"Dost remember our own?"

I could remember nothing of it at the moment but I lied and nodded my head. Then it burst from me untidily. "Sue, I must go away for a long time perhaps. I'm going to a church on the Dover Road near Canterbury."

"To live?"

"Aye."

"Oh no, Nicholas!" she said at once. "Oh no, indeed we couldn't. 'Tis very far off and I shouldn't like it there at all."

I had no intention of taking her; I hadn't even thought of it. The prospect had not entered into reality, but in my most private and unspeakable dreams. She knew my thoughts and cried, "Shalt go without me!" Then she wept, clinging to me and sobbing.

To leave was against all code of possibility: to leave alone was past that. I wanted to hurl her from me, to shout: leave me alone, I don't want thee! I want only myself! Yet so dreadful it seemed that the shame of it canceled the thought. There on the wood dock beside the river which moved unrestrainedly to the sea, I allowed my heart to open to my wife. I thought, ah, what a fool I've been! What a fool I've been! I have her love and she'll go with me wherever I want to go, the only person in all the world who so foolishly believes in me!

Fantasy turned to reality: they intermingled and I knew not one from the other. I had been an actor all my life and slipped from myself to that I played with such ease that there seemed no difference, and in moments of near panic I knew not what was feigned and what was true. I whispered, "Aye, Sue! Come with me if thou wilt. God forgive me that I've ever kept myself from thee." And I told her what was in my heart and what I planned to do. This bond that so easily came to other men, had never come to me . . . this marital bond. I had pretended it, acted it, done a fairly good job of it. Away from the protective custody of my wife's father I might find it, for it was all I needed to make me whole. I said, "Dost love me, Sue? Dost love me, not thy father's 'prentice who wedded thee, but the man that I am?"

She whispered, "Oh aye, thee as thou art!" We talked there until it was quite dark and then we went home hand in hand towards Cripplegate Ward to tell John Heminges about the chapel.

At first he laughed at me, and then he said as he had earlier in the evening, "Thou art drunk in thy cups! To bed, to bed, boy! Daughter, take him to bed and give him aught to make him sleep." His bawdy comments which ofttimes delighted me in their wholesome lack of shame suddenly offended. Still I knew he was not quite sober from the wedding, even though as a heavily built man he could drink a great deal and not show it. Then he scolded me, falling into our oldest roles together. "Nay, I like not these games, Nicholas," he said. "We have a new play to read at seven tomorrow morning: get thee to rest."

"Nay."

"Sayst thou, dear boy?"

"Aye, that I do."

"Ah," he said charmingly, playfully, "ah, Nick!" The big man in happy and propitious possession of all about him: money boxes, wife, daughters, sons, good food and drink, wall hangings, me. Towards no man in my life have I felt so many different things, and now to reach out for something (I knew not what) that I felt I must have, that I could no longer bear to do without, and have him suggest that bed's play could make me forget it!

"List to me," I said. "I speak from my heart. Aye, list to me, Master John! I've seen a chapel on the Dover Road and I want to buy it."

"Buy it and be hanged, merry boy," he said joyfully.

"Nay, and to restore it and take Susan there to live."

Then he ceased to smile: he listened. His energy was poised as before a comic moment on the stage, judging the anticipation of the audience, knowing them and his body well. He hesitated and was sober and the business manager once more. "What means this, Nick?"

"As I've said it."

"Which chapel?"

"One we passed as we rode towards London."

"I remember it now," he said. "Thou art drunk for certain; 'tis not fit for anything at all."

"It's fit to be a house of prayer once again, Master Heminges. I'll restore it and obtain the Bishop's blessing for service to be read there. And then please God, I'll take first deacon's vows and then the vows of priest as I was always meant to do." If the words were unexpected to him, they were much more unexpected to myself. I was trembling so hard that I had to hold on to the table's edge: I felt almost as if I would faint. In obstinacy, with tears suddenly pushing against my throat, I reached back into my life and took what I had once wanted more than anything in the world. It was all I wanted now.

He was silent for a moment. "Dost jest with me, Nick?"

"Nay."

I could see that he was puzzling how to manage me, to cajole me from behind the table up the stairs and into bed so that in the morning all would be just the same as before, and we'd go off together to the Revels Office or meet some new playwriter at the Mitre for beer and pie. It was beyond his comprehension that the morning, and all the mornings following it, would not bring this. It was almost beyond my own.

"Thou sayst shalt leave our company and be with us no more."

"I am."

"If you struck me, Nicholas, I'd take it better." He threw down the keys he still held and took my face in both his hands the way he'd done when he'd first tried to know from whence I had run so many years before. Tears stung my eyes; they were more from the shock of my sudden declaration than from his answer to me. I felt he'd misinterpret them, yet I could not turn my head away from him without shoving him off, and that I was unwilling to do. In his thick hands was my first experience of constant and genuine affection: he poured it simply, gratuitously, into everyone who touched his life and work. I wanted it and couldn't bear that I wanted it. The bulk and solidity of him had all the memories of my earliest years: sharing his bed on tour, waking from nightmares of my first master and finding the comfortable predictable warmth of him, and being so grateful for it.

He would not let me turn my face, and I lowered my eyes not to meet his. He stood slightly smaller than myself, yet I knew with a shudder in that moment who was the stronger man between us. "Canst do this, Nick?" he said. "Of all boys I've taught it's you I've given all I know, all I could gather to tell thee! Ofttimes and again forgiving you more than what was due thee, Nick . . . cherishing thee, God only knows the reason, ofttimes past my own sons!"

I couldn't bear it, and turned away to control myself.

"Ah, Nick!" he muttered, and he would have gone on but he began to stutter. One critic of our theater who did not like him wrote scathingly about this occasional fault, and nothing could have hurt him more. As a young actor he preferred the acrobatics and then proceeded to play pompous, silly old men because of it. Yet he had confided to me once on our long walks that he had always fancied himself to play the hero, and if it had pleased God, he would have been made like me, which embarrassed me, for I'd done nothing to earn my looks or my height: I had used them, they had entrapped me and entrapped others. Perhaps they had also entrapped him in thinking me a better man than ever my faults had made me.

In his stutter he knew he weakened, was fallible, tempted to plead with me. We sensed at the same time Susan's presence, for though she'd been standing all this time by the foot of the stairs, wiping the tears from her cheeks, looking from him to me and then back again, we had forgotten her. He said sharply, "Leave us, girl, leave us! To bed!" Her sister Mary came down the steps, wrapped in her shawl, and coaxed her away. I was sorry to lose her mediating presence; I was sorry to be alone with John Heminges.

He said kindly, "Sit down."

"Nay."

"Nicholas."

"Nay, 'tis best said standing . . . master."

What could I tell him? He had given me all freedoms, all considerations. There was but one unspoken stipulation. He had formed me to serve the theater and that I must continue to do. Standing in his kitchen, I tried without speaking to ask him to release me for the love he bore me, and in equal silence his eyes told me that for the love he bore me he would not. Then I felt my anger rush through my body: in such angers I had leapt, stabbed, killed, and nothing frightened me more. Yet though he knew my angers, he did not back down: he trusted he could win me to my better, more complaisant self. And I would offer my submissive prayers of gratitude, pushing away my thwarted independence, that once more he'd not allowed me to plunge into the abyss of my own wanderings and vagrant desires, and as I'd done that time long ago when he'd so rightfully punished me, kiss his hand.

I wanted to vomit with the thought of it.

Then he said patiently, "Speak to me of thy plans, Nick. Wilt shut me away from thee? At least let me give thee counsel."

I wanted to explain it thoroughly, from the beginning, and yet it came out badly. "I never came to this profession of my choosing."

" 'Tis true: you were given to me by fortune."

"Then why do you oppose me?" I cried.

"Nay, I oppose thee not."

"Do you not, master! Other men have left the theater for the church. It's God's will for me: I know it."

He said, "Again, let me counsel thee. Sit down." He offered me the great chair and this time I did not refuse, for I felt shaken with anxiety. What reasons would he give me? I did not want to listen to them, for in his reasoning, as the whole troupe knew, he was so often right. He leaned across from the bench and put his hand on mine and I dared not for any respect I'd ever had for him pull it away. He said, "Nicholas, since the death of thy son thou hast fought against the very ways of nature God ordained. How can you serve Him if you will not abide by His ways? Dear fellow, the will of God is often confused with a petulant self-will. You were born to be an actor, sent to me from I know not where for this purpose. There spake His will for thee."

"It seemeth of another way to me."

"Knowst thou this truly, Nick?"

"Aye, truly . . . truly, master!"

He shook his head. "Your intentions are honorable, Nick, and your heart's good, and I saw it from the first! Yet your nature is still turbulent. How can you extend to others God's peace, that passeth all understanding, when thou hast so very little in thyself?"

I pulled away my hand and nursed it moodily, as if he'd slapped it. I could have risen and gone upstairs and he would be gracious enough not to follow me, and yet I couldn't leave him. Like the voice of practicality, the merchant's voice, his held me. "As for this little church," he said, seeking my shoulder to touch since I now withheld my hand, "as for this fancy of thine. Why Nick, I know it, walked about it myself. Aye, it does draw one in a ghostly way, Christ save us, but the holy presence is there no longer. It's half falling down and there's no benefice or living attached to it. How will the money come to restore it?"

"I shall do the work myself."

"And Susan? How will you maintain her?"

"Do you think I'd leave her to want?"

"I do not think nor judge, dear Nicholas. But we all hear her weep at night when you've not come home, and long is the time we've waited for her belly to swell again."

I leapt up and walked across the room to the door; for a moment I wanted to rush out, and stood there fighting my fury, my back to him. "Ask not these questions, John Heminges, as if I were still boy to you!" I said when I found my voice. "Or do you think she's more daughter to you than wife to me? Dost think it?"

His face, when I turned, showed that he was sorry he'd gone so far. "I've never thought it, Nick. I've always wished you joy of her and she of thee and I still do."

"So be it then!" I shouted. "Let's have no more of this conversation! Find men to fill my roles and to do the work I've done and send me the income from my theater shares and it will maintain me until I'm made priest. I've earned the shares: they're mine."

He opened and closed his hand for a few seconds as he had once when someone had asked for a loan. Then he closed his fist and the man who stuttered was quite gone. "Nay, Nicholas," he said. "Thou knowst the rules. If you leave you must sell your shares to a working actor in the company. The rule is the same for thee as for any man that's left us, as for Condell's widowed daughter who sued me over the same. No man not working with us may own shares, and the same is for thee."

Then I struck the table with my fist and shouted, "Does nothing matter to you more than the Globe, Master Heminges? Do you love it more than your flesh and blood?"

"Yes," he cried unthinkingly. "Yes, more than my life . . . more than my life, this company, this theater! Dost thou know what it is to love something so much that every morning you wake to think of it and every evening make sure it's safe from harm? 'Tis a life in itself, this thing we all made, that you have helped to make, Nicholas! What dost make me say? 'Tis not all I've loved but 'tis intertwined with all the rest. Dost not know! Very dear are my wife and my children, and God knoweth, God knoweth, Nicholas Cooke, most dear art thou to me! I would not turn thee off when thou crossed me as a boy because I wouldn't give thee back to Morley and I would not see thee hanged for a thief. I kept thee and brought thee to this trade . . ."

I knew nothing but that I had to stop his pain, to console, to heal, but he pushed away my hand, shouting, "Wilt go, Nicholas? Art mindful of aught but thine inconsistent way of fancying this and that thing until you tire of it? Dost fancy to wear a cassock now, Nick? And shall it hurt Our Savior when you weary of His service as you've wearied of mine, when you leave Him as you now leave me and this company we've made?"

Pounding my clenched fists on the table, I cried out in rage. "It's unjust, John Heminges! You remember what you want to remember, and it's only half the truth. Have you forgot how I've served you?" I could sense by his strained breathing how hard his heart beat, and my naive and untrained physician's instinct stopped my other feelings. Had I not feared for him I might have struck him for my humiliation, but the need to heal was stronger than anything else I knew. I knew his mortal limits, though he seldom recognized them himself: he was a heavy man who had drunk too much and danced too much, and he was fifty-four years old. Many stronger men never reached that age.

Running to the cupboard, I poured him a cup of hellebore water, holding it insistently to his lips. He took it clumsily, for his large hand trembled so, but he would not drink for his life while it was still in my grasp. After a time he wiped his mouth and said, "I'll buy thy shares: no one who's not a player may own them. I'll give the worth they'll be two years from now as best I can calculate, and if I've done unfairly, I'll send the balance on to thee. Twice you've left and twice I've forgiven it you. But if thou goest this third time, Nick, thou shan't return anymore. Would you'd stayed and passed on what I've taught thee, what Tom Pope, rest his soul, taught thee!"

"Would that it were, John Heminges," I whispered.

"But as thou wilt, always as thou wilt. Thou art my daughter's husband

and I pray thee care for her. May Jesus guide you." And then he turned and went up the stairs.

I managed somehow to control my agitation, but if I had expected pure jubilation at my new freedom, it did not come. As a boy I'd plotted it, exasperated by his careful ways, wary of his love for me. Now I'd broken the bond and was set free much as a ship in the midst of the seas, with neither backstaff nor sea quadrant to guide me. I had seldom felt so utterly alone.

Susan lay curled into herself, having wept to sleep. Lighting a rush-wick, I began to list what I would need to do, what I should sell and what I should keep. My life should be made unaided, with my own hands: with my own hands I would restore this church. There should be money from the sale of shares to maintain us for two years, during which time surely I should become a priest and receive a benefice. In spite of Heminges's good example, I had saved no money but spent my coins on books, astrolabes and compendiums, crucibles and furnaces, drawing sets in engraved silver boxes and mathematical tools. My collection of beautiful things was badly crammed into our small bedroom, and I fancied a pretty country parsonage adjoining the church, whose little rooms would be fitted with polished cupboards for my collections. I would have a sundial in the garden. And each week the words, the beautiful, undefinable words of the Holy Communion service on my lips: this thing too holy to consider rationally should come through me every day. What foolishness not to have done it before! My vacillating images of God, my unpredictable relationship with Him, to be solidified at last. No longer would there be painful unanswered questions. In the Hands of the only One who could contain me, I would be safe.

Too much thinking on the undefinable frightens; too much of the other world appalls. I sought the warm crevices of my wife's body for consolation. "Dost love me, Sue?" I whispered, and in answer she turned and embraced me. There we made love, muffled and agitated, I embracing the one human certainty of my life, this young woman who had never once ceased to love me. We lay still together after it was done, listening to the sounds of the house and the night: John Heminges's angry voice, which rose and died away, the placating whispers of Tobias, who had gone to him, and a deep church bell from far off. I slept at last and dreamt once more that I entered Canterbury Cathedral and heard the voice of one boy singing alone in the great choir. And then I walked the length of the nave and up the steps and saw the boy who sang there and knew it was myself.

Four weeks later we found that Susan was pregnant again.

I had become far too enmeshed in the company to leave quickly. My duties were so entangled in the managing, the acting, and the training of the apprentices, that it would have been a hardship indeed. Spring came and we toured once again; then when Susan entered her third and fourth month of bearing, she was pettish and sick, and I remembered the first pregnancy with Christopher and brewed flower teas for her. In weariness, or when the silent disapproval of John Heminges was too hard to bear, I closed my eyes and imagined myself walking up that steep path to the church through the high grass, and hearing the birds singing in the drooping trees.

By the early fall Susan was swollen and stunned with the immense burden of her stomach, my duties had been divided among the men, and Tobias had been released for two weeks from his roles to accompany me to Canterbury. The great trunks used for our touring were lent us and packed with cooking pots and linens. Rebecca could not wrap enough things for me the morning we left, and kept running back for more, jostling the boys who were dragging the trunks to the cart with great fuss and strapping them in with greatest care because they were mine. Our older boy said, "Shall I leap and fight like thee one day? How can I without thee to watch?"

"Watch thy master."

He turned, disgruntled. "He plays naught but old men: thou knowst it, Nick."

It had to be done. I went back to the garden where I knew I would find him, carefully clipping his vines and tying them to the brick wall as he always did when troubled, and there I knelt and bowed my head for that last time. "Your blessing, sir," I said.

And his hands trembled as he laid them on my hair, and he said, "May Jesus and all the saints bless and watch over you, Nicholas Cooke. And may the Holy Ghost be thy comforter and give thee wisdom and endurance for aye." Then I seized his hand and kissed it and wiped my wet eyes against it, and went away.

As I mounted the driving board, Armin came forward shyly and pressed a leather purse into my hand, saying it was from all of them. Later when I poured it out onto a cloth on the church floor, I was speechless at their goodness. It lasted a long time and some of the smaller coins went for food, when we were reduced to needing them. But that was to come.

THE
FOURTH
PART

ONE

The
Church

WE TRAVELED OUT TOWARDS THE CHURCH, MY POOR WIFE SHIVERING in the constant misty rain of early fall and jolted by the wretched muddy roads. At the inn where we stopped to rest we could get no room to ourselves but were forced to share one with a merchant and his wife, who snored loudly through the whole night. When we reached our destination towards evening of the second day, Susan was in tears from exhaustion.

We thought to make a bed for her in the little rectory, but when we ran up the path and through the gravestones to look through the window we realized that the floor was thoroughly piled with old wood, broken bricks, and scrap iron. Tobias and I unloaded the trunks from the wagon, laid the straw mattress which we'd brought from Wood Street upon it, and made her a temporary resting place at the foot of the hill, protected from the mist by a cracked painted canvas which had once been hung over the back area of our stage to represent a raging sea. "Why, this is like the Irish gypsies," he said enthusiastically. "Nick, we're back in our soldiering days! Thus we lived, dost recollect it?"

"Aye, friend! Light the lantern and come see where our services shall be."

It had been the end of a warm spring day when I last saw my church and I had ceased to remember it as it was but only how it should be. Now smelling the musty, decaying roof beams, I wondered for a moment if we were in the right place. For a moment I was sorry I'd had Tobias come inside. But he only walked down to the chancel and shone the lantern on the broken glass window above where the altar had been. "This was a fine church! Ah, there must have been some wonderful singing of Psalms in these walls!"

I was relieved he thought so. "Thousands like this are yet empty. My father told me about the churches back in the 1530s before the King made his soldiers tear them apart and send the priests away homeless."

"Was he old enough to remember it?"

"Nay: his father had told him."

"What did happen to thy dad, Nick?"

"Why, he lived to be a hearty old fellow and died a man of property. Jesus's wounds, Toby! They've kept pigs in the sacristy, or worse! This is a job for me, and one I'm longing to do!"

"Twill be a great deal of work, I fancy me."

"Feel my strength."

He came at me, roughly feeling my arms and back. "Aye, thou hast it!" he said. "They'll miss thee on the stage."

"That's play: what I intend to do is real."

With something between a hug and a tussle, he released me, and we walked about for some time more. Behind where the altar had been was much rubble; there he knelt to pick up a lovely carved wood angel, about ten inches high, whose wings had broken away. "How fair it is!" he said with awe.

"Likely this lass stood by the Rood many a year. And when it's rebuilt I'll fashion her wings and mount her up again." In the musty chancel I stood, scenting rotting wood, old canvas, weeds, and stone, and listening to the happiness within me. How blessed I felt at that moment, how fortunate, how directed by a greater will than my own, feeling it about me as one feels the sun while lying on the hill. O Lord uplift me, hold me, never let me go. How long have I been in returning to Thee!

I looked down at Tobias's profile, the rough-cut pale beard, thick innocent mouth, and strong chin. Soft and stubborn-bodied was my friend, and how grateful I was to have him there! He sensed my glance and said, "Darkness is on us: what shall we do with Sue?"

"She's as warm and dry as two soldiers know how to make her: leave her to sleep."

He jumped up, placing the angel on a barrel, careless in dusting his knees, the moist dirt on his wide hands. "The whole of the rectory's as bad as this?"

"Both rooms."

"How wretched she'll be to see it, Nick! There's never been a bit of dust in Heminges's house, nor a sheet not neatly folded in lavender leaves!"

"That's one place: this is another."

"Wisely spoken."

"Still, best we begin to tidy it."

"Aye," he said, "I'm with thee."

We ran through the high grass amidst the tombstones, leaping over them and chasing each other. "You'll wake the dead," he said. The rectory door was swollen shut, and when we forced it with a hammer and crowbar (creaking and rotten and crumbling to our touch), the smell of mildew met us. "Aye, 'tis a far way off from Wood Street," Tobias said. " 'Tis haunted here, friend."

"Nay, fool!" Yet in the chill silence, scented with wet earth and rotting wood, we stood in the dark little rectory, and such ghosts watched us from every corner that a shiver went from my neck to my feet. I stood again in this moment transformed: I was once more a boy in my mother's house, and almost saw in the corner her low bed, her russet hair now mingled with earth, and the soft sound of her singing.

Lighting our lantern, I flashed it round.

"Where's the other room?"

"Oh, it's hardly more than a closet around the back, but it will be mine. I'll have a proper bachelor's library and laboratory here, mark ye! See an I shan't do it, Toby!"

"I believe thee in all."

"In all?"

"In all thou sayst thou shalt do, and thou wilt, Nick."

We began to heave aside wood and scrap iron to clear a space before the fireplace. The lantern blew out, I cursed it and made a spark with flint and steel to light the wood. Damp it was, smoking and stinging my eyes so that I had to stop my work to wipe them with the back of my sleeve. If the dead lay in resentful silence in the weedy churchyard, they had to endure our bawdy songs of "The Trooper and the Lady." One of those moments of perfect contentment came to me as we began to throw out rubble from the doors. My affection for him rose like wine in my blood.

"Ah Toby!"

"Nick," he said.

"Thou pretty whoremaster."

"Aye, that I am."

We worked for a long time whilst Susan slept, and the crescent moon shone down upon the rectory and in its vague light the whitish stones of the bell tower (there was no more bell, and its emptiness was poignant to me) seemed an earthly evidence of the greater Heaven to come. We had ale in a bottle and meat in pastry, and hated to stop for the rhythm of the affection between us. He playfully seized my arm and we wrestled and laughed together. Then we walked out among the graves to smoke: under the moon and empty tower he lit his pipe and offered it to me, and we sat crosslegged on a mossy stone. He said, "What, cony! Wilt keep this heap of rubble and stone? You could sell it back for what the stone's worth, you know!"

"Nay, on my life! It likes me well here!"

"Nick."

"Friend."

"Who'll bring forth the babe?"

"Marry, myself."

"Knowst thou of such things?"

"Very well, to my cost."

Before we slept we descended to the wagon, and I carried my wife to the soft blankets lain upon the floor before the still-smoking fire. Then Tobias and I rolled ourselves in our cloaks and wished each other good night. He fell into the good rest of the man who does not think too much: I edged into the uneasy sleep of a man who cannot cease thinking. The presence of my sleeping wife and the unborn child within her stayed in the center of my mind. I had taken her away from everything she'd known, and it was a new responsibility that, like sour wine, I winced slightly as I tasted. She had lost her own mother young and been not to her father's knees when he'd moved to Wood Street in Aldermanbury to marry the widow Rebecca; since then she had known nothing else but the gregarious household of boys, siblings, theater men, servants, peddlers, actor's wives. She had awakened by the bells from all over Cripplegate Ward and said her nightly prayers by them. The silence of a deserted church and rectory was beyond her experience. If only we had a bell, but it had been melted down for the iron years before. Still I felt she could well do without the lot of them: I would be all things to her. And I nursed my resentment that Heminges had doubted me.

With the first light, I went to look at my church once more: humble in my hope, I knew I must go alone. There it was, worse than my dreams and far less poetic in its reality, knee deep in rotting hay and the remains of a pigsty in the sacristy. No assembled parish life was reflected here: neither altar cloth nor candles nor Cross. No glass remained in the windows, the woodwork was decayed and rotten, and the floors were littered with rubbish. In the little chantry I stood and prayed silently for the dead I had lost. And when I went outside and climbed to the top of the hill through the thick wild grass my heart lifted, for I could see the bell tower of Canterbury five miles off in the grey early light, and hear the ringing for matins.

The farmer had walked over bringing a large round dark bread and half a pail of milk. After we had prayed over the bread and asked a blessing on our new house, Toby and I threw ourselves into further clearing the rubble from the rectory's floor while Susan stood apart, weighed down by her swollen body and bewildered how to begin in such catastrophe. She looked rather as she had once when left out of her friend's game of cup and ball and watched us, her full upper lip lifted a little hopeful and a little appalled, as we pulled out broken wheels, tools, ploughs, chairs, crockery from the rectory and piled them before the door. In our turning the trunks upside down to find the tools we needed, the clean baby linen fell in the mud. Her lips trembled. "Why, it will wash, mouse!" I said.

Tobias whispered to me, " 'Tis because she's with child!" and he teased her by pretending to scrub the linen on an imaginary stone, bent over like an old washerwoman, and she laughed until the tears came to her eyes. We could not find the soap nor needle and thread, we couldn't find my hammers, but we managed to fetch stream water and wash and hang the baby linen by a rope strung over the gravestones. One could not dry by the chimney, for it was foul with bird droppings and ancient soot and covered us with small specks of greasy black dirt which might have been left from the time it was a regular little popish parsonage, and the priest baking his own housling bread with each piece stamped with the Lord's sign. I thought, shall I bake housling bread and stamp it? Shall I bless it and transform it into the Presence? The thought brought a rush of darkness, almost a pain behind my eyes. And then I was quite myself standing there again in the cool early fall, competent and composed.

Neither hook for the pot nor bake oven for the bread was there, so we walked over to Canterbury for our dinner, leading Susan on the back of the drayhorse and stopping at the Cathedral for Evensong. The singing of the boys brought its tender renewal of strength: I hung upon the sweet sounds which rose and died away against the great apse, mulling on the many diverse ways a man can go before finding his true course. On the way home I began to talk about my schooling: I had seldom spoken of it and Susan had not known it at all.

"I could never make a priest," Tobias said. He told us of his failures on the Irish farm, his longing for good music and taverns, books and friends. "Naught's better than good fellowship and honest love between man and wife!"

Susan said, "Aye, naught's better!"

It had a thoughtful tone to it; I remember we were almost home, and I said gently (very much enjoying being her protector, my strength against this unlit road), "What thinkst thou, mouse?"

"It's this . . ." Her voice trailed off and she began to say inconsequential things, and I knew that whatever thought she had begun she didn't intend to finish. It irked me that she had a secret from me, but when I teased her I saw that she was close to tears once more. Women near their time are emotional.

The little rectory, as plain as it was, was comforting; it was comforting to shut the door against the graves. We sat about cracking nuts and talking and passing about the wooden mug, which we heated in the ashes. Rather like children on their own for the first time were we: no schedule directed us, no watch cried the midnight hour, no peddlers came to announce the dawn. She fell asleep beside us on the swept stones of the parsonage floor. I put my ear carefully to her belly under the loose gown, for she had long since put aside her stays.

"Tobias, there's two heartbeats besides hers!"

"Nay, not two."

"Fellow, I hear it! Put down thy head here."

"I hear but one."

"She waxes too great for one."

He murmured, "Ah, thou devil! Thou hast all good fortune!"

"Thy time will come, boy."

"The woman's not been born will have me."

"Likst children well, dost?"

"Aye, and thee?"

"Aye! Mark it, Toby! They'll be many babes running down the hill in little smocks."

I lifted Susan tenderly into our new sleeping place; we had brought in the straw mattress from the wagon and constructed a rough bed that day, and it seemed a fairer bed than we'd had in Wood Street, for this house was mine alone. Yet as I stripped to my shirt and sat upon the edge to pull off my hose, I felt a sudden peculiar loneliness. It seemed an ocean of separateness between myself and Tobias: the darkness which lay in the few feet between us was thick and unwholesome. He would return to London shortly and I'd have him no more.

"The floor lacks comfort!" I whispered. "Come here with us where it's soft to lie."

He laughed. "With thee and her! Nick, art in thy cups!"

"Whoremaster, what thinkst I mean by it! Nay, come, if thou lovst me. I shall miss thy ugly face when thou'rt gone."

With a shrug he climbed good-naturedly beside me, and I slid my arm about him and in the darkness remembered much of our friendship and how I had trusted him during the wars when I was too hurt to trust another soul. "Speak soft, thou'lt wake her," he said.

"Toby . . ."

"Aye, friend."

"Have I done right?"

"What, in coming away? Why Nick, it's perfect right and good! No matter what the others say, I see the priest in thee, and 'twas thy prayers which got me safely from the camp."

"Sayst thou!"

"Aye. All shall be well! Nick, I know this in my heart, I've always known it for thee. Mark this. When thou art ordained deacon I'll come to see it."

"I'll write thee."

"When shall it be?"

"When the church is restored."

"Marry, that will be long!"

"Nay, I think it not."

"She loves you more than she'll ever say."

"Who told thee such?"

"Why, her little sister."

"Then it's true. They were very close."

"Good night, friend."

"And to you, Toby."

We slept in the closeness of friendship and woke to the sun through the glassless windows of the little rectory, the birds in the low dark trees. No ghosts lingered in rectory or graveyard.

The two weeks passed; we had managed to purchase a few chairs and a table, and he had showed me how to cut glass for the windows, one of the many things he knew how to do in his cheerful, sometimes sloppy way. "It will do; it will serve," he said happily time and again. Then he had to return on foot, for we were to keep the horse and wagon; many hugs and playful punches were exchanged to lighten the tenderness we felt. And many messages I sent through him for all the men, their wives and children, their boys. "Thou shalt watch over John Heminges," I added at the end. "He works more than he ought."

"Aye, Nick, all these things!"

"God be with thee, friend."

"And thou the same. Where'er thou art, there lieth my better self."

We stood on the hill and waved to him as he went. The days grew colder, and I had just managed the two windowpanes and had the chimney swept and patched the worst spots on the roof when winter arrived and my wife gave birth. It was twins, and I delivered them and cut the cords, holding them in my arms, remembering much. The cold and long hours and little sleep affected me. Susanna and Matthew, as we had baptized them in Canterbury, cried a great deal. Sometimes to have some uninterrupted rest, I slept in the church, where I had begun to read the Psalms amidst the rubble morning and night. I fell ill myself, and we had a bad time for some weeks. It was the first of my long illnesses since the ones I had had as a boy. Susan ran between making possets for me and cradling the children. My strength returned erratically and very slowly, and I longed for Tobias and his good-natured humor and patching of things. I brooded upon the loss of his companionship, and once when I opened a box of my books I remembered how long it had been since I'd read anything.

Advent came, but we were too troubled with weakness and sickly babies to ride into Canterbury for services. I said the Christmas prayers myself and we wished each other the joy of Christ's birth.

The coming of the twins brought the first of our complicated, uncharted tumbling into vague troubles which we could not quite define and had no idea how to solve. I had never known babes to cry as much and as loudly as did these two of ours, protesting perhaps the drafty house and Susan's fumbling. Dinner was never served on time, and we often ate it each holding a wailing child. The house required a great deal of work, and I'd done little more than clear the nave of the chapel in the several months we had been there. Sometimes I'd stop and listen to the astounding quiet. Only the dried leaves blew against the cracking tombstones, and sometimes the iron gate creaked. Then I found the sounds of London coming into my mind: the cries of pie vendors, the whistling of children, and the monstrous clatter of iron wagon wheels on the cobbled streets. It faded, and there was only the wind or the far off bells of Canterbury, singing me once more from my vague sense of discomfort. The illness had not left me quite as strong, and it puzzled me, for I had hardly ever in my life been ill.

I had not yet presented myself to the assisting bishop of the diocese of Canterbury to be interviewed for holy orders. One morning having walked over to do it I found myself drawn to the places I had known as a boy. The same gargoyles from house and bridge stared coldly at me as I walked towards the West Gate. Our house had fallen to pieces years before, and across it was strung washlines. I felt my mother's presence. The wheelwright whom I had so unwillingly served had been taken by the plague and his house shut up. There in the marketplace was the bull stake.

My beloved undermaster was long gone, and the headmaster a stranger who nodded briefly to me as I crossed the schoolyard. Of the Cathedral canons, those I recognized were grown old. None noticed me. I had much changed in my years away from the city. Still, I left Canterbury disturbed in a way I could not understand, hurrying home to my small house and church. Months passed. I studied Scripture, meditated on it, felt the soft ecstasy of it in the breeze across the grass of our little world: the ecstasy and impossibility in the creaking of our floorboards, in the fall of burning logs, Susan's lips, slightly chapped from the damp of our rectory, against mine. I felt it in my children.

These babes, how clear they return in my memory, pulling and chafing against my rough shirt, dragging me happily from my sense of purpose, opening my love once more. In those days was I also happy as one is when in the process of becoming something. My soul, bewildered by the romance of my vocation, stood openhanded to receive benediction as a child, knowing it's been good and hoping it will be loved, stands to receive sweets. And I was greatly loved by my wife, in a way in which I had never been loved before. We shared an eternal returning to one another, one bed, one life. Alone with her I felt cleansed.

Yet I experienced an increasing difficulty in answering my letters. On the day our Susanna and Matthew were three months old I received one from Shagspere and another from Tobias, protesting my silence. I didn't quite understand it myself but that I had expected more of my first half year on the Dover Road and in retrospect felt I'd done very little and was ashamed of it. I had spent the day in Canterbury pricing glass for the chapel windows and found it much more expensive than I anticipated, and then I watched the priests walking towards services. They were pure and young, and I had seen and done so much of which I could never tell. It had been with some forced boldness that I dared walk the Canterbury streets at all, fearing someone would recognize me. One old canon indeed stopped and stared at me as I walked across the little bridge. In addition, I had a burden which these dedicated men had not. I was a father and a married man.

I came to bed after washing the supper dishes, and knew as one does by the bearing of a shoulder or thigh in an intimate beloved that something troubled her. Something so obvious came to me at once: in a very real and potent way, Susan was a different person from me. I felt the distance between us, as one feels along a wall in an unlit house, and wondered how long it had been coming about, and the vague sense of loneliness which had touched me the night Tobias lay in our bed returned.

I thought, what do I fear? No one will come to harm us, for I'm faster and stronger than any stranger. Yet this thing I fear is coming from a more personal darkness, and that is deep within myself.

"Well, mouse!" I said.

She answered nothing.

"Mouse, what troubles thee?"

"I miss my sisters!"

It came with such force of passion, like something long withheld which bursts forth. I think I understood it long before, perhaps before she herself knew it, and yet her sadness must become mine, as intertwined as we were. "What else? Why dost cry? Susan, tell it to me."

"I love thee better than you can love me."

It resounded inside me and fell away like a stone falling into a deep chasm, echoing on the walls until you don't know if you still hear it or only think you do. And the echo left me shuddering and silent and I was fierce to drive off its last vibrations. "Nay, sweet mouse! I love thee always, absolutely . . . thy sweet face, thy little ears. How canst say it? How canst!"

"Tell me how you love me."

"With all that I am."

"Didst not love me always."

"I was a fool, a cursed fool." I could not bear the suggestion of division from her, for we were all that we had. "But what sayst thou, mouse? It's you who pushes me away. I felt it tonight, yea every night I come to thee. Dost not want me any longer? Thy Nick? Dost not care for me?"

"I'm weary!"

"You must sleep a little in the day."

"I cannot! They . . ."

"Nay, turn to me."

I wanted to kiss her but the babies had begun to fret and we both rose and each took one, walking up and down the almost perfectly dark room. Moonlight shone on the frosted window; it was very beautiful, and her hair was long, dark, and swinging. When the babies slept we returned to bed, and I twined her hair about my fingers and began insistently to stroke her breasts to bring, in the reawakening of desire, our relationship into something defined and comfortable for me once more. "Now my rose and my lily," I said. "What wouldn't thou say that night when Toby was with us?"

She grew very still.

"Sayst it, Susan!"

"Nay."

"Come, my own!"

"It was too silly."

"Then . . ."

"Then . . . I had thee by magic."

I was astonished. "By magic, Sue! What can you mean?"

She whispered, "I had thee by a potion. The old woman on Addle Lane who sold rags gave it to me and said I must put it on thy meat. It was before you went away to the wars."

"In Jesus's name, what was in it?"

"Some sort of matter."

"What sort of matter?"

"Nay, I know not."

Whispering, "Oh my love, my love! No potions were ever needed for thee and me." I pulled her into my arms then, kissing her hair until she sighed and opened herself to me. Just before she slept she lay her head on my shoulder and whispered, "Wilt write to my father for me and say all's well?"

"Aye, my mouse."

"And tell my sisters that we see the Cathedral from our hill."

"It shall be done."

"Shall we go to London to visit them one day?"

"Aye."

"But when shall it be, Nick?"

"When I'm ordained priest."

"Must it be then? That's far off, mayhap."

I said quietly, "When I ride back to your father's house I'll be ordained priest and this church full of a singing congregation once more. He'll not say that I failed; he'll not say it." Then I gathered her to me, and we slept until the babies woke us shortly before the dawn.

We were to walk the next day to Canterbury to hear Evensong at three.

The heavier blankets to wrap the twins were still damp from the washing, and I drove the fire high, smoking the room, making them weep and howl. She had a hole in her boot, and I found leather to patch it, and by the time we set off it was past the noon hour; they howled to nurse and we had to stop again. The wagon had broken the week before, but I said a winter's walk was a good thing, and she agreed, only the road was full of muddy ruts from a faint snow, and our feet were cold by the time we saw the walls of Canterbury. It was not half an hour to Evensong and there was not time to dine.

By the time the Psalms had been sung and the Magnificat begun the babies were weeping once more, thrusting their stubborn bodies into her shoulder, kicking at the blankets. She cast me a desperate look and left quickly, bundling them against her, and I felt bad to let her go alone, and gathered up our things to follow. She said, "Nicholas! Go back and hear the service sung and I'll wait thee here."

"Ah, love! Had we remembered the sugar rag, it would have quieted them."

Pulling the blankets to cover our children carefully, she said quietly, "At home, my stepmother knew just how to make such rags, and the babes hardly wept. Come, darkness will be on us within these three hours, Nicholas! We'll dine at home." And we walked from the engrossing town, past the taverns and cook shops fragrant with cooked food and the conversation of learned men. I closed my ears to it.

We were happy in spite of such small difficulties. Sometimes we were happy as children alone in our secret place, often disorderly, unscheduled, and wildly sensual, and then we left the dinner to cook, the beer to brew, and the wash in heaps by the door. Sometimes we lay long in bed together, hearing the rustling of mice in the storage room which was to be mine. Snow fell and we rose as little as possible. Then I was ill again and then she as well, and gradually the spring began to come. Though I had done little more than clear the rubble from the church, our little house was neater: I had built her a brick bake oven, and many a day it took me and no help would I have. In the early chill April days we walked about the tombstones, some half fallen, and broken Crosses, and read the inscriptions. These signs of death contrasted with our exquisite aliveness. For lunch we had bread and cheese, and many birds flocked to find our crumbs along the path. At night I showed her how to read the time with my nocturnal, aligning the two great stars of the Bear with the Pole Star. Before bed I knelt in the church and said the evening Psalms, often hearing the wail of one twin or the other from the house beyond. There on my knees, memory took me.

I heard the sound of the men's footsteps as they carried the black-shrouded body of my hanged father to his grave. One hand has escaped from the wrapping, and trailed on the dirt. Then the endless sobbing of my mother, and I hid my head and tried to sleep. I had to go to the infant school for my lessons the next day; I had to go or they would have beaten me. The sense of childish impotence returned with such pain that Psalms and collects vanished, and I knew not how long I knelt there.

When I returned my wife said, "I've baked new bread for thee."

The intensity of the memory hung about me like the cold, yet by and by its exact shape disappeared, disintegrated, and present reality took its place.

So we somehow got through the first winter, and in the rainy days of late April she came to tell me to my astonishment that she was pregnant once more. I was not happy with the news. Here in one and a half little rooms two babies seemed quite enough. I wanted to read, to think, and to write. The memory of the well-heated and comfortable rooms at Syon House, with its excellent chairs and servants to bring me wine and meat, returned to me with poignant longing. There had I first read Giordano Bruno and other great theologians and philosophers. These thoughts I pushed away and prayed to God to let me be content. The wind which blew across my hose and the smell of blossoms were but air and flowers. Since that one evening's awful memory, He was within them less often for me.

Her religion was practical: mine various, mystical. I could not tell her these things which plunged me into sudden silence in our most intimate moments, and left me immobile with sudden grief with my hand on her soft body.

In May the men came by on tour, and several stopped to see us. They generously admired my bake oven and handmade cradle and teased me for my roughened hands and simple clothes, remembering that I had always been a dandy and couldn't bear anything but the cleanest lace and linen. They patted Susan's belly, already slightly rounded, and said I was become a good husbandman and would henceforth gather from my own little garden the plentiful fruits of my labor.

John Heminges took Susan away to speak with her, and Tobias and I walked over to Canterbury and back again, talking of his hopes and mine. "What, not deacon yet!" he said.

"Nay, we've had too much to do."

"Why, I've looked forward to calling thee parson!"

"I needs must study more. I'm memorizing the Gospels."

"In truth!"

"Toby, it seems a priest should be a finer man than I."

"Thou art all that's needed."

"Dost think so?"

"Aye, on my faith. Nick, write me more often."

"You've my hand on it."

I was once more sorry to see him go.

TWO

The
Husband

I N THE DAYS OF HARD LABOR THAT SPRING, WHEN I FIRST SHOVELED AND
swept the church floor and decided that the roof would have to be
replaced altogether, it came to me that marriage between two people
is quite a different matter when the circumstances in which it is played
out are changed. And I speculated whether her individual strengths and
mine were not diluted by this union.

Yet the visit of the men and the long talk with Tobias had enriched me
and heartened me to my purpose. Summer came, and each day I rushed to
my work: a regular pattern reevolved, engrossing for me but lonely for
her. I was an independent man (more independent than I knew even
then), delighting in losing myself in reading and thinking or in hard labor,
delighting in the full steady breathing that accompanied my work, by my
strength and by my youth. My mind was filled with Greek philosophy
and the Psalms, architecture, music, medicines, alchemy, the phases of the

moon, and the Gospels, which I could say almost perfectly in both Latin and English.

At first Susan had scrupulously avoided speaking of Wood Street, but now each dinner it seemed as if any subject led back to that one, until it became such a reproof that I could hardly taste my meat and often took it out with me to eat as I worked. No social company but laborers lay about us, and there was no public cistern to which she could go to draw water and speak with other women; she needed the society of her sisters, the winter afternoons of sewing by rushlight and summer evenings of preserving fruits and each morning at six the joyful social marketing, kisses interchanged on street corners, laughter ringing down the lane. To console her I brought home yards of blue cloth for curtains and seat cushions, the identical material which we had left behind in Wood Street: costly it was and too much work to hem and hang alone, and she soon abandoned the project in the exhaustion of the babies and the new pregnancy. In our most ordinary house, really little better than a farmer's, it would have appeared strange.

I remember her clearly from those months: plump, sometimes sullen and retreating into herself, sitting for hours at a time with her sewing in her lap and her foot on the cradle. I recalled once when she had been not such a little girl, and angry at someone for something, how I'd found her hiding up on my bed, biting her knuckles furiously and whispering to the whitewashed walls of the injustice done her. It was one of the few times I'd noticed her. I'd tickled her to bring her from it, and she'd jumped up and spat at me and ran away. The spitting had left me curiously agitated, pulse heightened, sexually excited I suppose. Now I tried my previous unsuccessful remedy of tickling and overpowering her; she bit my hand lightly and ran off up the hill, and I had to climb after her and apologize before she would return. Her unhappiness embarrassed her; she felt if she were truly good she would be happy, for she loved me. She struggled with it and went about for days washing, singing, running to me with memories and ideas for the house. Then she fell into the curious, silent withdrawal once more.

"Why beloved, the problem's this!" I said. "I'm neither layman nor deacon, but in my heart somewhere between. When this thing's done, happiness will simply come to us." I digressed further into studies and craftsmanship. I was learning from the Cathedral workers how to make stained-glass windows, and carve angel's heads into the armrests of pews. I wanted only to create and learn: it was the first steps towards becoming the student once more that I had always longed to be. My passion for deciphering the mysteries of how man is put together returned yet again.

Flinging myself from chapel to churchyard, I had dug a bit about the back of the rectory in the late summer months to see if I could set some spinach in the beds. She was five months gone with child and sick with it, and I was glad enough to be left alone to work. More, I was delighted to uncover some very old bones and a skull encrusted with wet, wormy earth, and I thought excitedly perhaps I should have a skeleton of my own which I could study. I had never been able to study such a thing but from drawings and prints. And in this my medical passions returned.

I shouted, "Sue, come and look!"

She came out with her arms wet from the washing. "What's that?"

"A whole skeleton, I think. Here's the thighbone."

"Nay, Nicholas, don't uncover it. We'll be cursed."

"Why, in what way could we be cursed?"

"It must stay buried there until the Resurrection comes."

"The Resurrection shall not come before supper: then what's the harm in digging it now?"

I gathered the bones in a cloth and brought them into the little storage room which had become my library, my Syon House and re-creation of all I loved best, and I forgot everything in excitedly wiping the wormy earth away and assembling them with the help of my anatomy book. She came to the door to tell me that the oven wouldn't heat hot enough to bake, and I said, "Never mind. I am missing two ribs, but here's most of the fellow. Lazarus I shall call him: look at his teeth, how he grins, Sue! He liked a good bit of mutton, I warrant!"

"Wilt keep it here?"

"Yes, mouse. Look how the knee's constructed: to this is attached sinews and muscle. Didst ever wonder how easily the knee bends, whilst with older people sometimes a swelling comes?"

"But here in the house, Nick?"

"Where else?" was my happy reply.

"An thou wilt," she muttered, but that night she lay rigid and silent next to me, and when I coaxed and teased her, she began to cry. "I can't sleep as long as it's there," she said. "And my milk's almost dry because of it."

"Thy milk's dry because thou art with child."

"My mother's milk stayed!"

"Mouse, there's no logic in it."

She burst out, "Had I a charm or some other thing!"

"What, to sprinkle on thy breasts as thou didst on my meat? In faith, sweet girl!"

"Bury it, Nick," she sobbed. "Bury it, bury it, bury it."

I jumped from the bed and angrily went in to gather up my bones, and walking to the graveyard in only my white shirt, hurled them back into the earth. When I returned she was huddled under the quilting with the babes, who were both sucking unsuccessfully at once. "You see, it won't come back now!" she said. "Did you bury them properly and pray over them? Did you, Nicholas?" After arguing with her some time I returned and shoveled dirt over my skeleton and prayed the Lord's Prayer. And as I brushed the dust from my bare knees, I was torn between the ridiculousness of it and my disappointment. The bones were buried, but the milk stopped completely shortly thereafter and we had to give the babies ale. Sometimes when I came in from work I found her asleep, huddled as best as she could with her swollen stomach. And I whispered, "Oh mouse, do trust me! Truly I shall make thee happy again."

The loss of the skeleton awakened my earliest fears that I should grow old and die without ever understanding the things I so desperately yearned to comprehend, that I was somehow not meant to have them. I didn't realize how angry it made me, but when I thought of it or passed the shallow grave where the bones lay unavailable to me once more, my stomach trembled with resentment at my wife. I began to spend money recklessly on books, and every one I coveted I bought, writing to Hariot and Tobias to send others. In a moment of weakness I bought a beautiful Italian quadrant in Canterbury, meaning to set up an observatory in my little room, the place where I had begun to hide every evening from dark through bed. It had no window but I knew where I would cut one, and how I would make the frame to open outward and show the sky. Alone with Susan in the country, I began to build a life away from her inside myself. How hungry I was and how wretched I felt! And how much I was unwilling to look at her round, averted face.

It was the early fall when I walked at last into Canterbury to the Cathedral to request my ordination as deacon from the assisting bishop of the diocese of Canterbury, the Right Reverend Edward Peter Leeks. A man of middle years, he was new to the city, and as I was the first young man to approach him for ordination, he was delighted as well. Most enchanted he was that I had left the acting profession to reconstruct a desecrated chapel and dedicate my life to God. Gladly, he said, he would ordain me within the month in the absence of the Archbishop, whom pressing business kept in London. In this way went our conference and my confession; I accepted his blessing, and after I'd left the Cathedral close, leaned against the wall with my heart beating as if the parish watch were after me for the crime of long ago.

I had left so much from my confession. I omitted the stabbing, my love for Rebecca, my thievery and brawling, and the one totally satisfactory killing of another man during the wars. I omitted my infidelities, my unconfessed sins, my true birthplace and surname. I acted as well as I had ever been trained to do. Kneeling, I had spoken of my love for God. That was the truth. I loved God, as one adores someone far off where there is no possibility of uniting. The bishop approved of me with no further questions.

I had bought a book that day in Canterbury to teach myself Greek. In the following weeks I labored all day and in the evening studied, pushing away the sound of Susan's plaintive walking to and fro on the floor in the main room of the rectory, while I studied in damp solitude in the adjoining room, which was really not much bigger than a shed for storing logs or hanging meats. Indeed, the old hooks in the ceiling made me wonder if the old rector had illegally taken deer, cut them, and dried the venison there. On and on I studied, hunched over the makeshift table with my hands over my ears, half to keep them warm and half to shut out the sound of her weary walking. She walked until it became a stumble, then fell into bed until the babies cried.

"Nicholas."

"I'll come anon, my pet."

Then after a time, softer, "Nick."

"Shortly, cony!" The worse I felt about my studies, the more I tried to make it up to her. Hence I reconstructed the bake oven, because I had made it too small, bought a cow for her to milk and make us cheeses, constructed swinging cradles, yet in all this, her vague apathy, her afternoon headaches, and her crying spells did not cease. Then I burst out, "How can we prosper an thou art this way!"

She stood trembling, wide-legged, with a face so passionate under the unironed white cap that it startled me, and took the jug of milk she was bringing to the table and flung it across the room. "Because!" And in that instance I realized how much like myself was this young wife of mine: idealistic, disillusioned, furious, repentant. I looked at her and saw my own reflection, and how it startled me.

And her ringing voice: "My father would never have brought me to such a place!"

"Then pray why didn't you marry a man like him?" I muttered. "There were merchants aplenty and grocers in Cripplegate!"

She cried the words out as if they were torn from her as a babe comes, ofttimes tearing the body which gives it life. "Because ... I ... loved thee!"

"Ah Sue, leave me be, leave me be!" I would have retreated to the church, but she caught my arms and covered my face with wet kisses. Her tears burned me: my love for her flowed like the milk from the smashed pitcher, uncontrolled, filling cracks of me that fain would have remained closed.

At night I began to dream that I had returned to my boyhood and had been granted my Cambridge scholarship and was a scholar there at last, waking at four for prayers and study, attending lectures all morning, walking with my black-gowned fellows to Kings College Chapel for Evensong. In this dream I had no wife but only my fellows, and I woke with such a sense of unhappiness that I was guilty towards the lovely girl who lay sleeping at my side. Mournfully, slowly I kissed her face, asking her pardon.

In October our new baby, Cynthia, was born, two months before her time. I have never seen so small a child, so perfectly formed and so delicate. We did not expect her to live, and kept her by us all the time for warmth. By the time we knew her life was safe, Advent had come. The damp and cold settled in the chapel and I was ill once more, needing nurturing and comfort, weak as a child myself. I had counted our money and found there was not so very much left, for I'd bought many expensive things. Like my poor mother before me, I did not know where the coins went once they were in my hands.

Susan, being exhausted from the nursing babe, myself, and the twins, who were not yet one year old, knew nothing of these matters.

THREE

The
Deacon

IT WAS THAT ADVENT (THESE COME UPON US SLOWLY AND HAVE OVERTAKEN us before we know they are there) that I recognized my low spirits, and henceforth they never utterly left me, like a limp or a bad knee that plagues one from time to time. I thought, "I lose my mind, and what will she do?"

Nothing terrified me like that.

We were coming to the end of our money: I had not been careful and had not spent enough time in searching for a benefice to keep us in the little church. Some wealthy man, for the good of his soul, might endow my church for the cost of its minister. Often a bishop had the funds to grant, sometimes a private landowner. Pennies put into the collection plate could not keep Susan and me in food, even if pennies came. We were a church without a congregation. I needed to find someone to give a benefice so that when ordained priest I might buy our cheese and bread from this money, not worrying for other work but devoting myself to the Lord's. In the meantime, I began to write, hoping to sell my scripts.

After Lent, the men came touring once more, and Tobias visited me alone for my ordination to the holy order of deacon. As I washed my hands and face before leaving for the Cathedral, he stood by with his arms folded, saying, " 'Tis high time, Nick! You can't put it off and forever like a bashful lad who won't give over his virginity." He told me cheerfully of the theater news. He was much applauded for his playing of unwanted suitors and good-hearted fools and still sang in a sweet, pure-pitched voice. Wood Street suited him: he respected John Heminges with all his heart, unconsciously emulating him. After years of wandering and those of marriage to an elderly Irish wife, he had come to a life which suited him well, and he upheld it with respectful platitudes: we always do thus, thus and such is never done. Nay, Nick, 'tis not fitting.

Susan had dressed the children, but at the last moment felt too unwell to proceed. I was by this irritated that we should be late and almost came to words with her about it, while Tobias compressed his lips and looked as uncomfortable as when he had tried to learn bits of Gaelic. This settled, we went without her, she standing at the door to watch us go.

Tobias took my arm. As we walked through the gates of Canterbury to the Cathedral with my white alb over my arm so the walk shouldn't muddy it, I became conscious that of the two of us he was now the stronger. With it I felt a weakness, a faintness so unaccustomed except in times of illness that I had to stop.

"Why, what ails thee, Nick!"

"Naught."

We walked in silence, so rare between us, as we entered the great doors and turned down the nave as I had so often done in my dreams. Throughout the service I would not raise my eyes, but kept my glance on the marble inlaid floor as I'd often done as a boy during the reading of the collect. In the formal words of the ordination, Bishop and presenter questioned my learning and godly conversion and read the litany. Then they said to me, "Do you trust that you are inwardly moved by the Holy Ghost, to take upon you this office and ministry to serve God for the promoting of His glory and the edifying of His people?"

And I said, "I trust so."

Many other questions followed, to which I answered, "I do believe," or "I will do so, the Lord being my helper."

The Right Reverend Edward Peter Leeks laid his hands on my head, saying, "Take thou the authority to execute the Office of Deacon in the church of God committed unto thee: in the name of the Father, the Son, and the Holy Ghost." I hardly heard him, for the memory of coming home on my father's shoulders on marketing day had returned to me; I could recall the sweat and thick burlap of his ugly coat. They had laid him to rest in a common grave and given into my little arms the coat, and I'd stood stunned, not knowing whether to hurl it from me or hold it tightly and never let it go.

The ceremony ended. I was blessed and told that I might now read and preach the Gospel in churches, and that if I conducted myself well in the diocese of Canterbury to which I was appointed, I could in one year's time be ordained to the priesthood and say the service of Holy Communion. We began to walk home in the cool autumn air, my prayer book under my arm, my alb rolled into a bundle. Just outside the city walls, I began to walk rapidly ahead of him. He, being stout and shorter of wind, called after me, but I did not slacken my stride. At last I stopped and he came up to me huffing and said, "Why, the Devil, Nick! Why, look at thy face, as if thou hadst seen the world open before thy feet and Hell yawn. Why, dear fellow!"

He wanted to touch my arm, and I could not bear it.

He said, "Why Nick, dear fellow! What dost?"

How he loved me and yet how little he could understand these things! Three times he tried to pull me against him and three times I shrugged him off, stumbling forward, feeling tears come and dry up unshed, seeing trees past me that I would have pounded with my fists to silence the voice inside me.

At last he cornered me against the wall of a small stone granary, roughly and tenderly pushed my hair from my face, and said, "Wilt not speak?"

"I am unworthy of what I've been made today."

"The Devil says it! Why, what foolishness! What man could deserve it more? Nick, dear fellow! Whence doth this come?"

" 'Twas acting, Toby! How well I played my part, and they believed me as when I've played out Prince Hal. I've told them naught but lies to be made deacon. Neither this time nor before have I told man or priest the truth of all the man I've been . . . to Will most, yet even then leaving much unsaid. Marry, if thou knew it, thou wouldst not keep me company here! And for these lies I can never be forgiven."

"Nick, dear fellow," he murmured, stroking my hair still in that idiotic way as if he'd been mother to me, the ordinary way he comforted apprentices with bloodied knees or gave a thick arm to old men who needed it to walk down Wood Street.

After a time I came more to my senses. I felt quite cold, as if somehow I had slipped from life itself and no one knew it, no one at all, least of all this fond and foolish fellow who would not let me go. "Leave off," I murmured a little roughly, and then took him by the shoulders and put him from me. "I need no wet nurse, neither do I want dancing on the knee. 'Twas a moment's weakness, no more. Say no word to her, upon thy troth! Ah, thou comforting spirit! God's blood, thou hast stood by me in everything, Toby!"

"In what have I stood by thee?" he said innocently. "All's been on your side. I am but a simple fellow, Nick, without a soul besides thee and thy sweet wife to love me."

"Nay, all the world loves thee," I murmured, pushing him from me still further with a cuff to his arm. "Here we stand on the Dover Road, grieving for what? I'm happy enough, only troubled for the pennies of the matter. I must find a benefice soon, Toby. I've little money left."

"Here's my purse."

"No, fool, that's thine! Why, coxcomb, what thinkst thou! I'll manage it: fear not, fear not."

He stayed two days with us, helping me with the roof and the floors, throwing himself into it as if he himself were to be priest there. We were extraordinarily happy, walking arm in arm, and he was willing to talk for hours to Susan about the life of the house on Wood Street, the many people coming and going and the ringing of the bells of Cripplegate all the day long. When he departed she retired to cry and I fell back into despair.

It came hard and black this time, and unremitting. Each day I rose from my bed with difficulty. My lack of money I had tried to hide from her, and only when we began to discuss the buying of fabric for baby linen and I hesitated, and she persisted, did it come out. Then she pressed her hands together as if I'd told her the best news in the world. "Then let's go home!" she cried. "Oh Nick! Let's go at once."

"Susan," I said, "know one thing. I'll not leave here until I've gotten what I've come for, and I will never let your father know how badly I've done. Not if I die for it."

"Ah!" she cried. She began to weep.

I had no defense against her tears. "What can I do?" I muttered. "Shall I send you back? Would you like that, mouse?"

"What, to leave thee, Nick!"

"It seemeth best."

"Nay," she said, "I want to return to Aldermanbury. 'Tis my fancy in all my waking hours how we'll return, what they will say to us, how we shall walk down the street across the square to the church with your arm in mine as when we were first married. But I must return with thee, Nicholas! I can only return with thee."

"Don't ask it of me."

" 'Tis thy pride that speaks."

"Would you have me without it?"

"I would have us home again."

"Don't speak of it!" I shouted. "I cannot, I cannot!" And before I knew it I slapped her. She stood looking at me in total astonishment, her cheek slowly flushing, and then she raised her fingers delicately to it as if she did not know quite where she was. Tears ran down her face.

A most peculiar thing had happened: where my young wife stood I saw another woman weeping, and I the child of her body who could do nothing to help her. Someone had struck her, a stranger who had come through to have his way with her. I could do nothing, and now the stranger was myself.

All my little ones had begun to cry. I rushed out into the night, threw myself on a grave slab, and held on to it as if the Devil might come and take me. Wanting to die, I pulled my bodkin from its sheath, and slid it under my body, its point pressed towards my heart. How fascinating a game it was: to be so near and yet have my will, my stubborn and self-preserving life's will, prevent it. To die, to sleep, perchance to dream. Well, I knew those lines. And I whispered, oh Will! Didst ever feel near to as bad as this? He must have, to have writ those lines. His boy had died, Essex had died, and he wrote them. And I thought that before I died I'd like to read them again, and others that had meant so much to me. Thus, I thought of my books lying there and my plans and fancies rather than her. In creative and philosophical patterns I thought of the blood which pulsed in my heart just beneath where the knife point lay, my own vanity and games, my deception, self-love, my vanity . . . again that. The vanity of the church! Both the masters in my old school and the man who had raised and protected me knew me well: I was fit for no such vocation.

I had not God, only vanity. And for this I'd thrown over my whole good life and brought her to misery.

Do it, thou fool.

And yet I could not: not others, not myself. Each man is created to walk this earth for one ordained purpose and cannot pass this way again. Yet mine was . . . what? And then she came to the door: I could see her shadow in the moonlight. "Nicholas?" she whispered, and her voice was hoarse from weeping.

She didn't like the graveyard at night and I did not think she would come past the door, but come she did, holding out her hand so that only the tips of her fingers should touch the stones. She came forward slowly, for she knew not where I sat. Then I threw my bodkin down and embraced her, my head on her soft breasts. She cried out, for I had frightened her. I didn't know for a moment if I wanted to end my life or both of our lives. These thoughts passed as madness: I pulled her down with my kisses, and we made love on the stone under the moon in the shadow of the church that was ours.

I said, "Shall I always bring hurt to others? Shall I never succeed? And the one thing I have wanted in my life vanity, vanity and nothing but that?" I wept.

She replied with the gracious charity that came to her at those moments, in the solemn, absolving voice: "Thou'rt all my life."

Shortly thereafter we discovered that she was with child once more.

I had not meant her to conceive. Privily one of our men had sent to me the waxed linen sheath to slip on in the critical moment, but our need of each other had been more critical still, and we had not run to fetch it. Astounded, I feared for her body and that the womb might tear. I feared her exhaustion and blamed myself, and yet I lusted for her greedily and seldom left her to sleep. I wanted her to escape from myself, and in this was the only true way I wanted her.

Not bearing to be alone in the little house, I would go walking whenever I could, and forgetting, not come home for hours. Sometimes I returned and found her asleep in bed with all three babies close to her. "Oh Sue, I'm sorry," I whispered and went out to sleep in the chapel, my cloak as my only covering. This place I had loved with all my fancy was fast becoming my prison and tomb.

I thought, we must return to London.

Then I pushed the thought away.

On Ladyday I walked into Canterbury and began to look for work. People shook their heads: what was my trade? Where 'prenticed and to whom? When they heard that I was a poet, actor, and singer, they smiled to themselves. I offered myself to learn any trade, yet why should they hire me? They could have a boy for free to work under them, and I was a married man and needed wages for myself and family. I walked until my feet hurt from the sharp cobbles and then I walked slowly home. There was no smoke from the chimney, for I had not gathered wood, and I suddenly said, I am going to die here. This is the end of all my life, and I alone have done it.

FOUR

The Wife

I RETREATED TO MY STUDIES AND WRITING. THE CHURCH, ONLY PARTIALLY completed, also reminded me of my ineffectuality, and sometimes I gave the excuse of being too tired to say the morning and evening prayers. My discouragement entered my body: for the first time in my life I felt as if I were growing old, and wondered if my life would be short. I could see nowhere to turn.

Yet every person of wealth I had ever known or played for received my urgent request to allow me a stipend to serve as priest in this church, from some lords who had hired me to declaim poetry at a wedding to another whose wife I had secretly fancied. I hesitated to write to Hariot's patron, Henry Percy, Lord Northumberland; he still stifled in imprisonment, and as we had never met I did not wish to intrude upon his troubles with my own.

There were dozens of churches in the diocese of Canterbury: one more was unwanted. Should I obtain a living of any sort, I was likely to preach to the birds and the ghosts and my ever growing family of children. In the midst of this dim realization, I managed to write three comedies and sell them under Tobias's name. The Globe bought one and played it several times. As I understood, John Heminges was not listed among the comedians, for he'd retired as an actor the year before, though he still managed the company and was financial adviser to every other troupe in central England. He had done excellently, and I, having left his company, had done nothing at all. We began to use the last of the small coins that our men had given us when we had gone so hopefully away.

The fall had come again. We had been two years there.

I cannot remember when my children began to slip from my mind. So preoccupied was I with my anxious thoughts, so depleted with the sense of failing them, that I seldom took them in my lap, or rode them on my shoulders down the hill anymore. And one afternoon as I walked from the church through the tombstones towards our little house and saw my two-year-old twins playing in the dirt before the door, I stood under the old tree and thought, do I not love them? Or have I no heart to care? And what manner of man doth it make me?

They held out their stones and leaves to me, but I could not come nearer and fled in shame to the church, closing the door and flinging myself on my knees. Something beyond my power had seized me and was drawing me towards it; my strength was weakened and I could only pray with dry, stiff lips. And even in this horror I could hear the cheerful voice of my little daughter calling to me to come and see what she had made.

Whistling brought me down the hill: a passing soldier had brought a letter from Tobias, and I had to rummage about my things to find a small coin for his trouble. Rapidly, greedily, I read through the warm, scrawled writing and then rushed half ill up to the house. "He's coming this day or on the morrow," I said, and I looked about me. Everything was unfinished, unpolished, half sewn: the infant in the cradle, the two dirty children on the floor, and my wife with her swollen belly lying indifferently on the bed. I began to hurl things about and ran to the stream to bring water to wash.

"Cony, sweet mouse!" I entreated. "Do get up and help me."

"Nick, I can't."

I laid my face against hers, my hands seeking some of the softness and givingness that she'd always had for me. "I'll do it all, never mind; 'tis my fault," I muttered. "Only love me, love me always, Sue! Without it, I die."

"Yes, always, Nicholas, always!"

The reconciliation, and then the slow cracking away again, like a bowl badly mended, though each time I said it wouldn't be. She pleaded, "When he comes, tell him I'm ill."

"Nay, he'll want to see thee."

"Nicholas! He'll tell my sisters how I look, and I can't bear it!"

I've done this, of course, was my silent response. The fault's mine and no one else's but mine . . . but no, she doesn't try. She doesn't try at all! Then the fault's with her as well, and between us we sink deeper and deeper away from the possibility of either of our dreams.

Towards the middle of the afternoon we heard the sound of my friend's horse, followed by his enthusiastic bellow at the gate. Unwillingly emerging from the house, I met him as he climbed the path, his arms spread wide, clumsily and with great affection, to hug me within them. Did he not see that I must hold myself apart from him? We had come too far from the two young men who sang madrigals together in Wood Street, with the buttery loaded with good foods, chests of clean linen, and baby clothes.

He was all over me, pummeling and embracing; it reminded me of Tom Pope's tender mauling, like a great bear to the young. "Shan't I be invited inside the rectory?" he said. "Marry, I'm thirsty for a drink of any sort. I've spurred the poor horse on to reach thee and go back again. We must play in Court three days from now and they couldn't let me off longer."

"All's well, but Sue's sick and can't see thee."

"What troubles her?"

"I was loathe to write it: she's with child once more."

"Ah, thou very Devil. Canst not leave her alone, eh! One could fain be jealous at the potency of thee, friend! Show me her."

"Nay."

He fell away from me, rubbing his neck. I left him there and came back with a mug of ale and some of the morning's bread. He took it but did not touch it and after a time he said quietly, "We've had no letters from thee nor news of her. I'm sick with worry. Thou lookst as if the Devil had taken thee to Hell and back, Nick! What ails thee?"

"Naught."

"Thou liar."

"Leave off, Tobias."

"Hast a benefice?"

"No: I've given over trying."

"And the priesthood?"

I was silent.

"Nick," he said, "what madness! What madness to have come here to do this thing, and then not to do it, and be reduced to I don't know what. Nay, look at me!" He took me by the elbow, and I flinched at his touch and for the way in which he knew me and for the lies he wouldn't believe. "Thou art the best of me, thou art myself!" he said. "We've mingled our blood. I cannot believe thy wife's ill! How comes this? I've never seen thee half so wretched."

I broke from him. "Why must you make me say what I don't want to? She's so miserable with me it breaks my heart! How unfit I am to make anyone else's life, when I cannot successfully make my own."

He cried cheerfully, "Come, Nick! Close up the church, pack thy wagon and thy family, and return with us to London! Play the prodigal son and John Heminges will have thee again, by my troth."

I could not answer him.

He muttered, "Ah, this is a great sorrow! Thou hast all a man could wish for, and cannot progress forward. How can I serve thee, Nick? What good doth my friendship?"

Then I grasped his hands. "An thou lovst me! Take her and the babes back to Aldermanbury and leave me alone awhile. Do this one thing for me."

"As thou has said it," he muttered, "but Nick, I like it not."

I shall not forget telling her the news. She tried to gather things to her, dropped them, sobbing in little gasps like a child. And frantically I kissed her and swore my love to her and that I should come anon, anon dear heart! As they drove down the rutted road in the cart we'd come away in, she looked back with her face distorted with weeping, and I felt my heart would break.

What madness had possessed me to send them off! I had bound her life to mine and the lives of the children and felt myself half a man without them. There was surely something I could do to keep us together, but the only thing which came to me was to return to my actor's life. Bitter to consider it, yet I could see no other way. I had sold my shares and would never return to my father-in-law. I must work for a shilling a day as an extra actor, but my popularity with the London audiences would serve me and eventually some other company would take me on. There would be the long sweet hours in taverns, after the audiences had gone home and we had wiped the paint from our faces: we would talk of poetry, metaphysics, the elliptical orbit of the planets. How hungry I was for such talk! My separateness alleviated by sack and fowls, our conversation protected by the enclosed tavern booths, we would speak of magnetism and the new world. And men would stop by and say, "Thou art home again, good Nick!"

I would walk back between sobriety and inebriation, walk the path towards Cripplegate which I could meander drunk, blinded, or in my sleep and behold the faint flickering light in the horn lantern which meant home. "Thou art home, good Nick." In my fancies I went back to the days before I had quarreled with John Heminges, and Susan and her sisters fussed over me, pulling off my wet shoes and drying my feet and heating ale to warm my stomach.

Somehow I would re-create the world I had lost.

Thou art home, good Nick!

The fancies mingled with others: the old one, the prevalent dream of walking down the Canterbury nave to the sound of singing. Only the nave was crowded with Will Shagspere, Condell, Armin, our men! And one of the boys would say, "Thank the dear Lord thou'rt come! Wilt teach me how you turn about with the broadsword and leap from the gallery? Wilt teach me, Nick?" And I would answer, "Yes . . . yes, wag! Only give me leave to rest awhile, for I'm very weary."

I spent the months that followed in the solitary company of God, and even as I dragged myself from my bed each morning to my studies I could feel the weight of His displeasure. These days were dreamy and sickening; I know not what I ate or drank. I thought, tomorrow I shall go back to London and begin again. And yet I did not. I was utterly alone: not even my sordid ghosts returned to vex me.

Letters came with passing soldiers and merchants: the old sweet letters of Aldermanbury, stockings mended and dyed, children ill and cured. Sometimes I opened them and sometimes forgot about them for days. Nor did I answer: what could I say? I had not progressed at all.

One I left for a week under an unwashed plate, and when making to scribble some figures on the outside, turned it with the vaguest curiosity to make out the words under the butter stains. Slowly as I read it I sank into a chair which rocked on the splintering, uneven floorboards.

My dear Nicholas,

Three months have passed since my daughter returned to Aldermanbury with her children and still we have no news of you. Some days ago she came to me and begged me to write once more to question the state of your mind. Do you wish to be her husband? She loves you very much and will stay by your side forever if you truly want her. This is a serious matter and she must have an answer from you.

Heminges

A crow called from the roof. From the path came the sound of cattle driven to pasture farther outside the city walls. I sank farther back, gazing at the piles of my remaining books on the floor, the bed which we had never draped, my doublet slung across the trestle table, and by the brick oven a little carved wagon which I had made for the children and whose cracked shaft I had sworn these past six months to mend. I walked into Canterbury and drank myself sick. The gargoyles watched me as I stumbled home. One young canon of the Cathedral who had been at my ordination called out pleasantly, "A good eve to thee, Deacon Cooke!"

The letter, crumpled and butter-stained, lay beside the empty lamp. How many times I began to answer it in the weeks which followed, and in indecision and self-condemnation threw the drafts away! It opened a question I was unwilling to consider: did I wish to be married? Was there possibility of anything else? I fell away from the sweet routine of my religion, and said neither morning nor evening prayers. Having no more money, I worked for a time for a day here and there, losing myself in my reading and drinking enough so that I should sleep. The thought of losing her, the thought of keeping her, both drove me to unbearable pain and conflict. I made no steps towards London: I thought, tomorrow I shall go, and then again, tomorrow will be the very day.

More letters came, begging my response. They fell behind the bed or were stuck, forgotten, in the leaves of Virgil's *Aeneid,* which I had begun to reread. The last letter from my former master was most succinctly writ. It informed me that Susan, for my silence and abandonment, had made up her mind to appeal to the ecclesiastical courts for a writ of annulment of our marriage and that he reluctantly agreed to stand behind her. He added that she sent her love and prayers for me. He said further that she wished to marry Tobias, now of the company, who would take good care of her all his life, that they begged my understanding and felt it all for the best.

I flung the letter across the floor. Marry *Tobias*! Leave me and marry *Tobias*? Surely it was a jest and nothing more. He could not find any maid to marry him, let alone John Heminges's daughter, who in every way adored me. They had gone from their senses, the lot of them.

Scrambling for the letter on my knees, I smoothed and read once more. Christ's wounds, it was truly writ: "to marry Tobias of our company." How dare this former master of mine approve of this obscene manner? And how could my wife suppose my friend was a better man than I? Leaping up, I threw a heap of laundry and papers to the floor in search of my mirror. Was I not myself, whose very look could melt her?

I looked in the glass, but I did not know the face. Then I remembered. I had seen such a face before. The face behind my face was that of my old master the Bull, of a man discontent with the world who wants to strike out at others because he cannot bear to be with himself. How far from myself had I come that I could be turning into such a man? And why had God so thoroughly abandoned me? Or could He not come near me, so fiercely was I barricaded against everything, so terrified of the prediction of my old headmaster Dr. Judd that I should end like my father? And did it matter anymore?

Canst not love thyself, Nick? the friend of my heart had asked while we were at war and hanging my head, I had murmured in the green dampness of the night, no.

I owed a great deal of money in the neighborhood, and to pay it I sold back the church and rectory to the miller for a storehouse once more. Then I put the best and more valuable of my things in a pack, which I lifted to my shoulders, and I set off to walk to London to reclaim the wife I was not sure I wanted, leaving the church and all it represented behind. The miller was even then moving back his bags: he touched his cap cheerfully to me and wished me a good day.

THE

FIFTH

PART

ONE

Cambridge

On early Sunday morning two days later I walked down Wood Street and into the Heminges' kitchen. Breakfast was done, and the family upstairs dressing for church, but Rebecca had come down looking for a child's missing shoe, and she ran up to take my hands. "Ah, we've feared for thee!"

"Where's my wife?"

"Walking in the garden. Don't fright her, Nick, an thou lovst her. She lost the babe she carried and still weeps for it."

My heart swelled with pity as I went into the garden. There she stood, on the other side of the herb beds, thinner than I remembered and smaller, and I knew only that I needed her to forgive me and love me once more.

"How is it with thee, Sue?"

"I've not been well, Nick."

"It pains me to hear it, love."

I would have gone to her, but she pulled away. "You must stay away, for you frighten me," she whispered.

"Canst love me no longer, Sue?" I was ashamed of how weak I felt, wanting to weep, wanting to make love with her and push away all the bad things that had been. We began to walk about the brick beds of the knotted herb garden, she on one side and I on the other, the scents of marjoram and rosemary filling the silence between us. I had intended to be scornful, and all that came out was a hoarse whisper and her name. How abandoned I felt! And how peculiar, how light-headed to see her look at me without falling into my arms, pouring open her heart . . . she and I who had been married so long, made love so poetically!

"So you want to marry again," I murmured. "Not four months gone from me and you want to marry again. To my friend whose life I saved. It passes decency."

She explained it as simply as I had once explained the letters of the alphabet to her. "Thou art not the man for marriage: aye, you've chafed in it, and for the longest time I thought the fault was mine. How I wept for that! Oh how I have wept for it, dear heart."

"Dost love me no more?"

"Nay," she said, "I love thee, Nick."

That encouraged me. Then we could go back as before, she and I. What else could I want than to be sweetly, ordinarily married, she walking one babe and I another the whole night long. I would have leapt across the garden bed, I would have promised.

She said, "I love thee, Nick, and I'll love thee all my life, but I'll be thy wife no more. For you have never wanted to be married, and it's made me most unhappy. Let me go to make another life and wish thee well, aye, with all my heart. Let me go, dear Nicholas."

I cried, "Sayst it, cony! What hath Tobias but his good nature to recommend him? Shall he sit of an evening in the very chair where once I sat, this man for whom I'd have given my life? Sayst it, cony! Canst remember all the sweetness betweenst us, thee and me?"

"Nicholas, grant me a writ of annulment and let me go. I was bred to be an actor's wife and want nothing more: in this I shall live and die. Thou needst quiet and science: I, company and family life. We differ. Ah, Nick! Let me go."

"Dost wish it?"

"Aye," she said.

Then I burst out, " 'Twas surely your father who hath put such thoughts in thy mind, he the warden of the parish where it is forbidden to put asunder man and wife!"

"The thoughts are mine."

"The help is his."

We had stopped under the apple tree. "Nay, Nicholas!" she said. "Tell me that we'll live together in a manner where I do not cry myself to sleep in loneliness and you not chafe in this marital bond, and on my life I'll stay with thee forever. On my life."

I was silent: no words came. At last I said, "Canst want this parting?"

"Yes, truly."

"Then 'tis granted. Ah, Sue . . . *no longer mine!*"

She began to cry. Then we were in each other's arms, and the leaving of her or she of me seemed impossible to think of. She whispered, "Let me go, Nicholas. God bless thee! God keep thee always in His hand!" She ran inside weeping, and left me alone under the apple tree.

Thus began proceedings for a divorce. Church laws permitted only separation *mensa et toro,* from board and bed, which had to be granted by the Archbishop's court; a marriage could be terminated only by being declared null and void by reasons of consanguinity—were I first cousin to her, were she niece to me. Such were the laws, and clever men knew how to get about them. I had very little to do with it, only that we were called before several churchmen and I confessed just learning that my marriage to Susan was forbidden because of our related blood. My father had been Heminges's brother William, a mercer out of Kent, and I being a bastard had not known this until these very months. From Kent came the very William Edward Heminges, a bewildered elderly man, to swear as much. The lies stunned me, but I obeyed: I did not obey John Heminges, nor my conscience, nor my will, but a genuine need to serve the woman whom I could no longer call my wife, because I felt I had failed her in all other ways. Though I wanted to shout out, "But what of our sweet nights of love? The bake oven I made her? How I tried to teach her to read, though she cared little for it?" I said nothing but what I had agreed to say. So my actor's training sustained me, though I was already beginning an undefined and lengthy illness, which manifested itself with such dizziness that I had to hold on to the table to keep from falling.

Physical debility born of grief: for years I had read what scant literature there was on this subject, shaking my head over its improbability, being a strong, youthful, haughty man. What God had joined together was put asunder with legal documents, tears, consoling hands on my shoulder. The men knew, of course: we had no secrets from one another. Yet the friends who could console me most were beyond me: Shagspere away in Stratford with his daughter's marriage, Heminges unforgiving, Tobias torn from my heart. We were granted an annulment, I consented that my wife keep the children, and thus my marriage ended. All the past years were as if they had never been. I saw Tobias, but never alone; across the room I saw him with much bitterness. And when it was over I walked to him and said I despised him too much to hit him. His eyes filled with tears and he stumbled from the chamber with the woman who was mine no longer at his side.

Why was it so difficult to bear to have what one wanted?

Robert Goffe brought me back to Armin's house, where I was put to bed at once. That afternoon, between vindictiveness and sorrow, I wrote to John Heminges and poured out much of what I'd never told him. I wrote of the stabbing of my first master, my boyish theft of his coins, my disinclination to be married. I never truly loved her. Those words flowed from my pen, whose quill I pressed so violently that I had to call Goffe's boy to trim the nib once more. Know ye, Master Heminges, that I took her for the theater shares she brought me. Know ye my vocation was naught but vanity, which Our Lord had the wisdom to so correctly perceive. Know then, master, as soon as I am well enough to walk from Aldermanbury, you shall not see me again.

Exaggerations, falsehoods, wanting to scratch out with the scrivener's stone whatever respect and friendship there was between us. The most hurtful thing I could have told him, to my scant credit, I did not. He would never know for his sweet wife's sake that the child she bore so patiently and lost so long before her time might have been mine. Yet I wrote violently, wanting to close the door between us that had never been entirely closed before—this man with whom my life had been so long intertwined. I sent it by the boy, and mayhap he lost it and mayhap delivered it into the hands of my father-in-law. I know not, for I heard naught but a silence as still as the fields before the great winds and rains come. And then I was too weak to think of it further.

I slipped into grave illness.

That I prevailed through those days is more in thanks to the strength given to me when I was first created than to my own efforts. There can surely be no worse patient than one who has no particular desire to live. How much blood they took from me I can't say, only remembering that once in my feverish delusions I attempted to knock down the doctor who took it and he swore never to come again to me. Then drained from purging, bleeding, and the enema bag, I was propped up in bed as I had been in this parish long ago and allowed to have my books once more. Rebecca Heminges had kept the stack of medical volumes left to me by my physician friend after the plague, and these I skimmed through, not having the strength to read.

I sent word to Tobias that he should care for my children, call them his own, and be a better father to them than ever I could be. I knew they had moved to a little house in the parish of St. Leonard's. Armin told me, shaking his head, that though Susan cared for her new husband well enough, she would never love him as she loved me. This was some consolation. And I sent through him the little brass nocturnal which had been Morley's with instructions that when my children were old enough they should have it and be taught to read the time by the stars.

Armin hugged me before he left on his errand, and after he'd gone I found myself bruised by his comfort: the shock of being close once more to a loved one, the memory of Susan's body enclosing mine. I did not dare risk being touched again. For months no one could come near, and if a man brushed by me in the street I shuddered as if he had burned me. Lying in my clean bed, overlooking an apothecary shop, I slowly began to plan my future. There was but one thing left for me, and that was to become a physician and begin to obtain a greater understanding of the body and the interplay of body and mind. In this work I should forget myself and all I'd done and all I'd lost.

And I knew that I must go to Cambridge to study healing.

I had nothing left besides my medical books, with which I would not part, and a few other treasured volumes and my Italian brass astrolabe, which my mistress had saved for me when I was away. These last I sold, which gave me enough to sustain myself for a few months, and with very little in my pack, I set off to walk to Cambridge. Armin and John Rice made up a gift for me as well, to which gold coins were added which I suspect came from sweet Rebecca. Though many would have helped me, I wanted no more: it was enough that my children would be cared for and some of the men still loved me. I cared not if the division between myself and Heminges ever healed: bitterly, I had no wish to see his face.

I was thirty-one years old and once more I began again.

As with most things in my life, I found Cambridge to be rather different than I had imagined it, though because it had remained an ideal so long in my heart, I would not give this up in the face of more prosaic realities. Ever and forever all my life, the warm beige stones of chapel and bell tower have stayed as I first saw them that Michaelmas term when I came up to university as a matriculated student at last. No sensation is clearer, neither of love nor of subsequent achievement, than the first buttoning of the black scholar's gown which I put from me only to sleep in the three years to come.

I signed the Admission Book, which noted my residence at Corpus Christi College, as well as the Grace Book, kept by the University Registrar. An upper room on the south side of the quadrangle was given to me, which I shared with a sharp-voiced clergyman from Dorset who was matriculating as an adult, and a poor theological student, sixteen years of age, who confided to me he would rather be at sea. We shared a desk. Dress was of the plainest, ruffs forbidden, Latin our language of ordinary conversation.

At five in the morning we were assembled by the bell to chapel for service. Breakfast followed in the long, chill hall: the chatter of youthful voices over warm ale, the deeper, more somber ones of older men such as the fellows and masters, such as myself. Some sons of earls had come with their private tutors and ate apart. For four hours in the morning we attended lectures: the public ones in the Old Schools or private ones in dining hall, chapel, or tutor's room. Afternoons we studied, and I began to learn, not in fragmented ways of a skeleton dug from a Canterbury graveyard, or a text read to save the life of a child, but in a methodical and disciplined way, the ancient study of medicine.

We learned by lectures, by disputation with the masters, and by the art of declamation, in which we expostulated upon a chosen subject in a set speech which would display our rhetorical ability and our knowledge of the classical writers. Passionate disputation, with words running like blood, once upon "Whether celestial bodies can be the cause of human actions" (I taking the negative) and then again upon the Platonic thesis "That men are nothing else than their souls," continued to the great hour of nine at night while the snow fell upon the bridges over the river Cam.

I was a pensioner, having money of my own to spend upon my education, being therefore below the fellow-commoners and above the poor sizars. Still, no heat comforted our rooms. Some of us ran up and down the courtyard before bed, gowns flapping in the dark, to warm our feet before we slept. Shortly after I had come I walked out across from Trinity, where I found the street of washerwomen and on the second floor, the cramped, narrow bookshop of Samuel, of whom my doctor friend had told me. He was a little scraggly fellow who spoke six languages, including Arabic. Friends we became, and many a book did he lend me. From his stock came what knowledge I possessed of obstetrics.

Sixteen colleges filled the crowded walled city of Cambridge, each with hall and library. Enriched I was with the profusion of books. In the library of King's College I found a magnificent psalter brought home from the Cádiz expedition by the Earl of Essex, who in his days as Chancellor of the University had often sent up philosophy questions for disputation writ in his own hand. Masters, fellows, and professors ambled down streets in their gowns, talking of sedition, foreign policy, stingy stipends, and mathematics, and nodded at us when we doffed our hats to them. In back streets were taverns, booksellers, whorehouses, tailors, shoemakers.

At Christmastide the clergyman fled home and the young student transferred to other rooms. A second man of nearly fifty years came to share with me who, in his poverty, borrowed my hose until I had none of my own. He having left, others came whom I cannot remember. There was little space for us, and none but senior fellows had a room to themselves. One, a fellow of Greek literature, took a liking to me and showed me the three gates of Gonville and Caius College. The first, a simple doorway, was called the Gate of Humility, the second, with its classic design, the Gate of Virtue, and the third, with four Ionic columns, the Gate of Honour. Through these, the praelector said with a wink, I should pass to wisdom. He took me to dine at the Eagle, where he told me much of his life and I confided little of mine.

I studied mathematics, which included cosmology, geometry, and astronomy, and attended lectures on theology and the Code of the Ecclesiastical Law of our realm. Most of my studies, however, were in anatomy, comparative anatomy, dissection, embryology, something of physiology, and a great deal of herbology and the study of pharmacopoeia. The textbooks I had already in my possession: Galen and Hippocrates and the Vesalius *De humani corporis fabrica* or *The Fabric of the Human Body.* The third, written perhaps sixty years before, disagreed fiercely with the others.

Students who had come from brown-walled Padua, with its arcades and bridges over the river, told me of the dark semicircular dissection theater where the ghost of Vesalius was master still. Linacre had studied there, as had Harvey, now one of the most famous physicians in London, and Dr. Caius himself. Here lay the discrepancies. Galen had said that every man possessed an intermaxillary bone. Not finding it, I asked my teacher where it might be, whereupon he angrily answered, "Man had this bone when Galen lived! If he has it no longer, it is because sensuality and luxury have deprived him of it!" Galen believed there to be no marrow in the bones of the hand; he believed that during parturition there is a separation of the bones of the pubic symphysis; he believed our thighbones to be curved. Still we studied Galen, some professors correcting the errors, others insisting no error could be possible.

In Paris they studied years without ever seeing a living or dead body. For a fee some students and I were given an aged, disintegrating corpse to dissect, and between gagging in corners and burning herbs against the smell, I first pulled from the thorax and abdomen the long intestines, stomach, liver, kidneys, lungs. A complexity of muscle and vein greeted me: I did not ever expect to comprehend them. I would have wept or put my fist into the wall in my frustration. Yet that day I understood Fabricius's observation that the venal valves are always directed towards the heart. Of Ambroise Paré and the black magic artist Paracelsus we were taught nothing.

Paré had carried a preserved corpse with him for twenty-seven years, the muscles removed from the right side so that he might refresh his memory of heart, lung, and diaphragm before surgery. We took our corpses to church when we were done, and buried them with due ceremony. A few of my fellows towards the end of the second year departed for Padua, saying the teaching was finer and they wanted to mount Galileo's platform and touch the dissection table where Vesalius had worked. I stayed, for the dream of Cambridge would not let me go.

Thus passed my first two years at university. Wainscoted halls glimmering by torchlight, architecture both ancient and contemporary, cloistered gardens and chapels, the river Cam, which ran sweetly behind the colleges under heavy willow trees, and in which, come spring, the students illegally swam. On the riverbank, which we called the Backs, one could watch the swans. The libraries, where we went at dawn and left at dusk, feeling our way down the dim stairs, for no candles were permitted, were serene. The rattle of chained volumes: the leather bindings of well-used volumes; the books of Trinity, of St. John's, and of King's. The bitter cold of winter, in which we hacked and coughed through lectures and dissections; the spring, in which corpses were left to be buried and we studied fevers and herbs. The three terms of the university year and my loneliness, rushing down the stone steps from my room at the sound of the ringing bell which bespoke mail had come by the carrier, and hoping it was for me.

In the third year of my studies my money came to an end.

I had existed for some time in increasing poverty, eating very little, struggling with the lessening physical strength which did not allow me to endure these things well over time. Though not as endurant, I was as stubborn. I daresay my colleagues found me dull: oft my lecturers were irritated with me, for I questioned everything. Yet early in my third year the long hours and lack of food told upon me. I sold my cloak and wool vest, and my seven-volume Vesalius. And when there was no more I tried to make a bit of bread last through the day, then falling so ill that the college fellows thought they should have to send me away. In the worst of my fever, a stranger rode into the quadrangle with a package for me. Inside was Shagspere's two-volume set of the Holinshed Chronicles, rather the worse for wear, and tucked under the cover, wrapped in an old accounting sheet, was more money than I had seen for the last two years. "For Nick my falcon," read the inscription, "who as a boy left these very books on his windowsill in the rain. Come to Stratford when thou art made doctor and we shall have merry times."

Once more, if not for him, I would have died. I sent for beef and salads and tarts, redeemed my Vesalius from my bookseller friend above the washerwomen's street, and within two days was well enough to attend a lecture on the blood, such as they knew of it. For I always understood that we were but at the beginnings of these things, and my worst fault was my impatience with others, with myself, my argumentativeness.

I formed my principles in those solitary days, and quite unlike were they to any then put forth by the College of Physicians or the worthy lecturers at Caius College, many of whom had studied in Padua; some of the older men had known Vesalius. There was much talk of the brilliant Harvey, who had begun to study the circulation of the blood in London and came to lecture. I longed to speak with him, but my lack of position forbade it. By trade I was an acrobat and performer. By desire and inner directive a physician and healer. I craved my credentials as a man craves food: nay, more. Yet my beliefs, which I did speak of now and then, were often laughed at.

I no longer believed in any way that astrology could affect human sickness or well-being. Furthermore, I propagated that excess bleeding and purging weakened a man. I would have thrown out half the remedies in the apothecary stock if I could. Deep was my belief that many illnesses arose from uncleanliness and many arose from unhappiness, the sort that so grates a man that it becomes a cancer or a blockage or a failure of the heart.

I had worked with the grinding and polishing of glass only a few times in my life under the instructions of Torporley, Hariot's man, to make an effective microscope. Now, grinding as fine as I could and struggling against the impurities which marred it, I began to make a perspective glass which would enlarge small things. I examined with curiosity the hideous body of the common flea, and a strand of my own hair. A candle lighting this display from below, the heat against my cheeks, I began to see what had not been seen before. Yet instinctively I knew there were smaller worlds not yet touched and one substance of which all was made. Since my alchemic days I had sought it, and now I could not longer bear not to know it.

My appearance, about which I had always been rather vain, became unprepossessing. The first few grey hairs appeared about my ears, though only the visit of our men on tour brought it to my attention. I would have liked to see Shagspere more than ever, but my pride forbade it. My clothes were shabby, and I did not like to make such a figure before him. I did, however, send him a copy of a treatise I wrote on the variety and causes of plagues, and he returned a letter of several pages, thanking me for my kindness and saying that he believed I would become a quite remarkable doctor. "But you know, Nicholas, I've always thought it," he said. He mentioned his garden prospered and his daughters were fair, good-natured girls. That seemed to please him most.

I fought vanity. The other men of our troupe who were my age had families and houses, property and silver plate and wall hangings. They did not sit by a single rushlight in an unheated room. Yet I never turned back again. I rose before dawn to be at my studies as soon as it was light enough to see the page. The body of man which the Lord created began to reveal its subtle secrets to me. No passion had ever taken me like this one.

In those days three things sustained me: my desire for knowledge, my wish to make a credible contribution to the world before it was my turn to tumble into the dust, and my comfort in music. It was the singing of the boys and men in the church services at King's College Chapel or St. John's which gave me the courage to continue when I felt I could not go on.

At night sometimes I wandered down to the Backs by the water and looked up at the stars. Calmness came to me then, and the potent words of Morley's play *Tamburlaine* returned:

> Nature that framed us of four elements
> Warring within our breasts for regiment
> Doth teach us all to have aspiring minds
> Our souls whose faculties can comprehend
> The wondrous architecture of the world

> And measure every wandering planet's course
> Still climbing after knowledge infinite . . .

The writer had caught me as I tumbled through my universe long ago, and showed me with his words how man can push apart the structures of the world with the desire for knowledge: worse, can drive away those who love him in the pursuit of it. I had been born with a need to comprehend, yet frailties had entangled my feet, led me down unknown paths, turned me about like a child in a game until I no longer remembered where I was going. God knoweth I had never wished harm to any man. Yet was this truth? I have known angers, the Lord wot, which have shaken me so that all about me threaten to crumple should they escape me. What God wanted from me I could not tell, for He had never made anything easy or clear. The only thing I understood, as a stubborn man finally acknowledges something after being repeatedly knocked about by it, is though I had longed all my life to serve Him, it seemed He had no particular use for me but perhaps as a healer.

I was at Cambridge three years, including some months of assistantship to a local doctor, before I earned my doctorate and licentiate, following which I intended to return to London to practice medicine and spend my life discovering what unseen things tore us untimely from this earth. I wanted a mastery over death: by the time plague came upon us once more, I wanted to be ready.

TWO

The Physician

UPON RETURNING BY FOOT TO LONDON, I WALKED AT FIRST TO THE parish of St. Leonard's and stood awhile in the street, watching the children at play. I was not certain which were mine until I saw Susan come from the house and clap her hands to call them. Her belly had swelled once more, and I thought, not bad work, my brother! Thou hast done as well as I! (This wry comment born of my pride, I suppose. Thou hast done as well as I!)

They would not have known me either.

Then I went away and found lodgings on Old Fish Street Hill by the waterfront. All this part of the city was crossed by narrow filthy streets that descended to the river: this one was dangerously steep in bad weather. Near east to us was the bridge, Billingsgate, and a schoolhouse to teach young boys to cut purses. Shortly thereafter I presented my degree licensing me to practice physicking to the College of Physicians, and began to serve as doctor in the City of London.

I had but one room above the fishmonger family of honest George Thompson, and this was crammed with apothecary jars, my medical books, and my tools for grinding microscope lenses. I dined and slept alone, for I wanted no man's company and still could barely tolerate any friendly touch. Only with my hands on another's sickened body did my loneliness find comfort and my life purpose. Occasionally the actors I'd worked with sought me out, and one told me that Tobias sent word he'd kept my wishes, and my children were well. "Shall I say how you do?" one asked.

"Tell them I shall yet get on," I muttered.

"And nothing more?"

"Nay, that must suffice."

He looked at me with compassion and went off, nor did he seek me out again. In my solitary method, I began to continue my studies by observation and speaking with the other men who healed. It seemed an abomination to me that surgery and physicking were so divided, but risking the loss of my credentials, I dared not go against the laws: as a physician I could prescribe bloodletting, but must call in the barber-surgeon to perform it, though this particular rule we now and then ignored. Pulling my medical books from the trunk, I began to reread what I had read so often before. Paracelsus had said that nature had provided a cure for every disease: had she not created orchids in the shape of testicles and thus indicated that their juice will restore lewdness to a man? Butter left in the sun several days cured the body of colds in winter, and black hellebore gathered under a full moon gave a man a strong heart. I had grown up with John Heminges's remedies culled from the garden.

A small apothecary shop lay down the steep path to the river, and I liked to sit there at the end of a day, enjoying the quiet company of the owner and the smell of cinnamon and bay. It was neatly and closely packed with scales, weights, pestles and mortars, and speckled green-glazed drug pots. Dried herbs, leaves, barks, and woods were stored in wooden casks and boxes hung from the ceiling; there was also oil of cloves, which spoke of other parts of the world, and rosemary tea, which evoked English gardens. He sometimes offered me a piece of candied ginger, and I would read by the last light through the mullioned glass window, hearing the iron hoofs of horses on the cobbles of the sloping street, and the games of children at the cup and ball.

"Is this real mummy powder, my man?"

"Nay, sir doctor! Thou knowst the price of genuine Egyptian mummy has tripled since the old Queen's death. We must make do with a cat or dog when we can get it."

"What lieth here?"

"Marry, those are poisons."

"How much is needed to end the life of a man?"

"Why should you ask such a thing, sir! 'Tis not to be thought of."

"Say how much."

"A small spoon in a glass of wine."

"Only that?"

It was the closing of the day when we had this conversation, and as it made him nervous, he began to speak defensively about his trade, crossing himself now and then, promoting the virtues of herbs. I helped him put up the shutters; it was in those first months of my new profession the closest interaction with another human (save my physicking, which was another matter) that I allowed myself.

"Myself I believe in purges," he said, "and nothing is better than a little metal in wine. Why, there was a lad of this parish suffered from thick worms of the stomach, three inches or more in length, that came near to kill him. We brought him to vomit and vomit and he's never been troubled since! May I be buried if this isn't the truth, master!"

He invited me to his house for supper; at the end of the evening said, "I believe you're a good doctor, my friend, for you know Galen through Paracelsus well: I've not met a man who knoweth their works better. So I speak to you as a friend might: there's hardly a Christian soul in Fish Street dare speak with you, for you scowl at everyone as you rush down the street. Should you smile more, you would not live in such poverty."

"Good friend, my heart's troubled and my face does not conceal it," I said. Yet when I had enough of being alone I sat an hour in his shop, and he was tactful and silent company.

To create friendship was almost impossible for me. I couldn't bear to smile at others and lived so poorly that sometimes I could hardly afford my dinner, much less the hired woman who grumbled over my shabby clothes. She expected more from one of my profession, and I heard her say to someone that I was probably a necromancer and distilled evil potions after dark; I caught her muttering prayers when she accidentally broke one of my precious vials while gathering my dirty hose.

I thought her a fool, but then I thought most people were fools in those months, and I walked out about the city to avoid her muttering company. London was the center of medical knowledge in the country, and I wanted to understand it all. I wanted, in those long days, nothing more. Besides the apothecaries' guild we had the guild of barber-surgeons, with their fascinating autopsies of executed felons four times each year. The art of cutting had fascinated me since the wars, though I would never trust my own hands to do it, and I made friends with the barber-surgeon who served our area. He let me go with him one evening to bleed a man and cut another for the stone, and after we had seen the patient put to bed, we walked through the dangerous area of Cold Harbour Stairs towards the water. "Herbality is nonsense," he advised me as we parted. "Open bleeding relieves a man's suffering; too much blood is the cause of all trouble. Open a vein and the diseased spirits will pour into your bowl."

"Aye, thou sayst! And thus we bleed to rid the blood of bad spirits, and purge to rid them from the stomach, and give enemas of tobacco smoke and sack to rid them from the bowels. It healeth, but not always! My friend, we know almost nothing."

The sign of a pawnbroker clanked in the wind above our heads. From the water came the sound of boats creaking against their ropes. "Thou art hard on thyself and worse on the rest of us."

"I can't be otherwise."

"A child must crawl ere he can walk. The development of medical knowledge takes time."

"We have crawled since the Greeks! And there is no more time."

We quarreled over trifling matters, and I kept his company no more. Sometimes I spent a few hours at the College of Physicians, where we would argue principles. "My masters, I think there's more to the body than the four humors and four elements," I said. "Mayhap four hundred, nay, more! We say that when a man's melancholy, he creates an overabundance of black bile, and to rid oneself of the bile rids the melancholy. 'Tis reductionalism, 'tis fool's simplicity, my masters!"

"Hast never seen a man vomit it?"

"Aye, I've seen it, but the good humor which follows comes from the relief of pressure on the stomach and not from a relief of melancholy."

We came to shouting about the matter of bloodletting. I heard one of them refer to me as "Master Dr. Cooke, who asketh questions no sane man can answer nor any crazed man, of which foremost is himself." And I had to control my temper once more. Most fascinating of that year were the lectures given by William Harvey at the Royal College of Physicians on the circulation of the blood. "It is plain from the structure of the heart," he told us, "that the blood is passed continuously through the lungs to the aorta as by the two clacks of a water bellows to raise water. . . . Whence it follows that the movement of the blood is constantly in a circle, and is brought about by the beat of the heart. When I first gave my mind to vivisections . . . I found the task so truly arduous, so full of difficulties, that I was almost tempted to think, with Fracastorius, that the motion of the heart was only to be comprehended by God."

Sometimes when faced with pains and swelling of the abdomen in a patient which would not be treated or the fevered body of a small child on the edge of death, I walked down by Dowgate Wharf to think: wiser men than I had walked there many a year, for my city was well over a thousand years old, and I fancied I felt their presence still. I knew little more than the other physicians, and sometimes I did better, and sometimes not as well, and my failures threw me into unreasonable despair, for in all that I failed I blamed myself alone. In the two years in which I lived on Fish Street, I kept a small portion of poison in a little jar on my top shelf, and sometimes I almost felt it watched me. When I couldn't sleep at night, it watched, and once I got up and opened it. This was followed by hours spent on my knees, sobbing. My desire for God had never left me, though I felt He had washed His hands of me. He demanded an impossible perfection. Anger intermingled with my prayers. Then, bending my head to the floor, I asked for forgiveness.

Was it yet another sin to think upon these things? Had I not sins enough in all my life, the seduction of the small jar on the shelf, my abandonment of the companionship of man? "Love one another as I have loved you." This was an impossibility for me: I could do much, but not this. I could understand any medical book, yea even a little of those writ in Arabic and thoroughly those writ in Greek. I saw the travels of the blood and the crafty valves of the veins in my dreams, like a poem, like a mystery. Yet to love one another . . . that I could no longer do.

Thus, much of my small fees was spent in fines in my parish church, for I seldom attended. How could I go? I was not fit to sit among good men and women in their Sabbath hats, singing ordinary prayers. My love of God and my fury at Him were both violent and did not fit into the ordinary and neat hymns. In all this was a constant disappointment in myself to encompass true knowledge and understand all wisdom. I didn't open the little jar of poison again, though, as I said, it watched me every night of those two years.

I was, in spite of this, a healthy man, curious in my desire for life and knowledge, physically strong, and gathering once more a power that came from I know not where. Time healed me. Mayhap it did better than herbals and metals. Eventually I found that I had less anger and a subtle, deep sadness took its place. I understood that I knew in part, through a glass darkly. I put away childish things and allowed myself to live in my stumbling, human way. One elderly woman I healed told me I had compassion: mayhap. I was born with some, I think, and the rest life had taught me. I began to allow myself to love, but could not permit anyone to love me.

Without seeking it or understanding why, my reputation began to grow. Mayhap for that I was a mystery, for people like such things. However, I remained in my simple room above the fishmonger, and if I had extra money, I put it aside for my children. I knew Tobias would not be a wealthy man, and I'd a fancy that when my son was fourteen he should go up to Cambridge as a scholar. I fancied settling in some healthy business the future husbands of my girls. I imagined these deeds done secretly, yet, that somehow they would know that it was myself who'd done it. That somehow they should one day understand my faults and yet know in spite of this how much I adored them.

Among my patients was an elderly Bishop of the diocese of Winchester who, because of some rumored disfavor or scandal, was now living quietly in a private house near the old monastery grounds of Covent Gardens to endure most bitterly his pain from gout. When first I was called to him I found him with his swollen foot upon a stool, cursing the nervous young priest who was his secretary. His bad temper amused me, and I didn't mind lingering, for his sitting room was beautiful, rather the sort of room I had first imagined for myself when I was a boy, thickly draped in red, the shelves heavy with more books than one could read in many a year, including Kepler and Copernicus.

I examined the color of his urine, hoping that he would speak to me. I liked everything about him, his veined hands, which grasped the carved arms of his coffer chair, the brilliant thin face with its emotional, shrunken mouth, waiting my opinion, knowing beforehand that he wouldn't trust it. His pain touched me because he was so offended by it. No man himself expects to grow old; in each it seems like a mistake, like a misdelivered letter. Yet I felt for him: I saw myself in him, and I touched his foot respectfully, sending for a basin of hot water to dip a cloth in and hold gently against the swollen foot. He winced, and his body stiffened. Then he said, "You have the hands of a healer, my fellow."

"My lord is kind." Yet he had no inclination to speak with me further, a doctor without a single court client and no fur on his robe, a doctor without a silver-topped walking cane or any of the other perquisites of my trade; and after he had sent his boy to the apothecary with my prescriptions, he motioned me away to his secretary to be paid. Why of all the prosperous doctors in the City of London he had fetched me from just west of Billingsgate I did not understand, though weeks after I would learn it was on recommendation from a curate whom I had cured of stomach worms and who swore to my wisdom. My Bishop did not lack for comfort nor pulpit, for I was told he preached now and then at St. Paul's. His name was William Sydenham and his age near to five and seventy years.

I had planned to spend the next morning by myself and was irritated when the boy came knocking at my door with orders to come at once. I walked quickly over (I could not afford a horse in those days) thinking something had gone wrong, and found him much better. I was irked that he had called me away from an interesting morning of polishing a new convex lens. He sensed my irritation and said, "I've need of thee! Did I not pay thee enough? Draw a stool near and apply the hot wet cloths as thou didst yesterday . . . nay, gently! Thou thinkst of other matters! What can compel thee more than thy patient, eh, fellow?"

I thought to myself, much! But you couldn't know it. Letting my mind drift away to my lenses and the titles of his books, I stroked the still-swollen foot, feeling his eyes upon me yet. He muttered, "Methinks I know thee and yet it can't be. Where were ye schooled?"

I told him that I had come late to my profession, and when he asked me what I had done before I hesitated and said, "My lord, it matters not."

"It would satisfy my curiosity."

"That you've not paid me to do."

"Hasn't thy trade taught thee to placate the powerful, my man?"

"No, my lord. That's a skill I've never learned."

"Ye are a fool, but not as bad as most. Come sup with me and let me know you."

I had never supped with a bishop, and was somewhat askance as to what to wear. My part-time housekeeper had refused to return when she found I had bought a human skull to keep on my desk, and the cassock in which I dressed myself was not particularly clean. Catching sight of my reflection in my landlady's glass, I thought wryly, thou supst with bishops now, thou, Nick! And yet a shabby fellow thou art!

It made me smile, and I felt in a good humor by the time I reached his white stone house. He had set a table glistening with good things and Italian glass, yet small enough so there would be little separation between us. I would have preferred a larger table. I didn't like my muscular leg next to his shrunken one. How much I feared mortality! All my work was but a bitter battle against it. How I fought, and each elderly body seemed the reproof which told me how foolish was the battle.

I thought of the sophisticated rules civilized men develop to be with each other, so unlike the hotheaded relationships of boys, and I wondered whimsically if we were schoolfellows of equal age what our conversation would be. That made me smile. "What thinkst thou?" he said.

"I thought of your youth, my lord."

"Why thou peculiar man!" He laughed and showed his small, blackened teeth, and thrusting aside the voluminous sleeve of his brocaded gown, he lifted the glass. "To thee, Sir Doctor, and my better health."

We spoke of literature and medicine and joked together in Latin, and after he had refilled my glass with wine several times I felt better and no longer wondered what he really wanted of me and what I would allow myself to have of him. We had set the boundaries of a bantering and wary relationship, the only sort I was willing to have. "My lord, a simple diet is best for the gout," I said.

"A piss on thy opinions! Thou art my guest and not my doctor tonight, and caution goes but poorly with rich meat. Tomorrow thou shalt come as doctor and we will curse the dinner guest together that led me to this excess."

"What, shall I curse myself, my lord?"

"With enthusiasm, and then deny the cursor."

"That would make me a man of many parts."

"As I suspect thou art," he said. "I like thee, Sir Doctor! I can see from the way you looked at my books that you've studied much. What hast read? Look there, and tell me."

I needed no further invitation to look through his shelves, and there I found very fine editions of several of Bruno's works. I thought, so that's it. He is drawn to the thing I have most fled from in myself, my insistent questioning of the infinite.

"Tell me what pleases you," said my Bishop. "But speak honest and fair, in God's name."

Thus began our relationship, the most peculiar yet in my life and the only one I could at that time tolerate. I knew at first that he cared about me because he could be totally himself in my presence, and yet he trusted men no more than I and tested me to trip me. And I resented his caring, though I needed it, and we thrust between us as both bridge and barrier readings from the eminent philosophers and mental explorations of that wondrous and unbounded realm which some called science.

He cursed me when he felt I answered foolishly. To counteract my hurt, I learned to parry with him much as Tom Pope had taught me, to leap away from where his sword fell and to thrust with my own. He was a more able man than I, not only because he was better read and traveled (far, far better) but because he would not linger in the contemplation of his imperfections. And he was a more protected man because he trusted that God would never let him go. In the hours with him, fortified by sack and roast fowl, he began to know things of me: that which I would (my scorn and disappointment) and what I would not (my hopes, my childish need of affection).

"What keepest thee at thy lodgings that thou comest so reluctantly away?" he asked once.

"I seek to find the lens combination for speculative glass which will allow us to magnify microcosmic matter."

"Fool, it can't be done."

Then I had to bring him my glass, and he cursed his poor eyes and had to come so close that the candle nearly scorched his hair. I showed him a flea, and he was astonished and excited. I showed him my finger under the glass as well, and he said, "In Christ's name, to build such a thing! You've intelligence and determination, my friend, and nothing's worth more than those together."

Tears filled my eyes. It shocked us both, for ours was not a relationship where we laid down our weapons, but where we kept them close to our sides. Another physician I knew threw up his hands when he heard who had become my patient. The gouty foot healed, and I continued to dine with him several times a week at eleven, except when he had a service to intone. "Why do you not come?" he said. "Art an infidel, my man?"

"I don't come because I don't wish it."

"A bishop asks thee."

"My answer's the same."

"A friend asks thee."

"Then, my lord, I will."

I kept my promise, but the service haunted me. Something happened to him when he approached the altar and bent to kiss it that tore apart my self-restraint, and I stood by the pillars of the church, bowing my head against what I felt. Another presence walked beside him in those services so strongly that I ceased to see the old man at all, but felt something much higher. Where had I seen my Bishop before? And I puzzled to know my previous connection with him.

It came: he had intoned the Holy Communion Service in Canterbury once when I was eight or ten years old. He was a much younger man, of course, as he strode across the chancel: bone-thin and very hard, strong wrists. From those hands I had taken the bread and wine, and it was then that I had sensed the immensity of the presence of something far beyond the rigid limitations of my life. I had an urge to speak with him so much, but we were ordered back to class, and after school was dismissed someone told me he had gone away from the town.

Aye, I knew him. And so much awoke for me again that I would never have awakened again, God knoweth, and I could not make it sleep once more. Then I came sometimes to hear him preach. In his infrequent sermons (which rambled at times), the spirit of the infinite burned so hot in my breast I couldn't bear it and once left before he finished. He asked me next day if he'd offended me, and I shook my head, unable to answer without breaking the code of parrying intellectual banter between us which we so agreeably had constructed in our hours together.

"What's thy secret, Sir Doctor?" he said gruffly.

"I'm not paid to satisfy thy curiosity, my lord."

"Then may I be buried if I see thee more!" he shouted. I took up my cloak and left him, wishing I could throw away my pride and turn back. The next morning as I was composing letters to him to explain myself without revealing myself, a pale young priest was at my door, pleading for my services. My lord had spent the night feverish and in agony, and when I sent for the hot water and began to tend him, stroking and chiding, I humbly wanted to let him know (I was too proud to say it) that I was sorry any displeasure with me had brought him to such pain. All that morning I sat with him.

I said, "Your servants could lay these cloths as well as I."

And he withdrew his foot, his thin mouth trembling with a kind of rage. "I find our conversing unsatisfactory," he said. "Never have I spent so many hours with a man and known nothing of him. Yet I like thee well."

"And I you."

"Tell me of thyself."

"Nay, my lord."

"In confession if thou wilt."

"Nay, my lord!"

He muttered, "Then I'll ask no more. Only stay for dinner, wilt thou not? I like the comfort of thy companionship, thou miserly, stingy fellow! I'd bully thee if I could but thou won't have it. Leave off! I've bullied enough men. Be silent an thou wilt, pisspot fool. But know this, thou proud madman: I have in my way a need of thee that goes beyond the laying of cloths. But you have a need of me that you cannot even know."

My hands trembled as I replaced the books we had been searching. "What need can I have of you, say that?"

"The words, boy, are yours to speak."

What can he know? I muttered silently. By Our Lord's Body, what can he know? Yet it was a while before I could turn and present a face to him that satisfied me.

Our conversations which encompassed all else began again. We spoke of Mr. Harvey's experiments in the circulation of the blood. We spoke of the gestation of the fetus in the womb. Each day I planned what I would not reveal, and each day I revealed more and checked myself for it. He had begun to know me truly, not only that I could not abide sugared wines and heavy meats made me sleepy but where my pulse lay. Yet once when we quarreled and he did not send for me, I came to him. We didn't make it up with words of honest affection as had always been between the theater men; the Bishop and I used gruff words and somehow all was forgotten by the evening's end. He asked if I liked women, and which ones I liked. On this I was silent. He said he had had a wife who'd died young, and then a young girl for years, but now was past those things and then wondered why I had left his sermon weeks before.

What had he said? A forgiveness mentioned that I no longer believed in, perhaps. It had burned me too hard, and brought the tears too close. In all this we were still doctor and patient, yet something more. I hardly dared call him friend, for his ecclesiastical position divided us. He had what I had wanted so badly: he walked in Christ's shadow as priest and acolyte, and I walked forever where that shadow had ceased to fall. My unspoken failures stood between us and made me push him from me. Because I had come to need him perhaps more than he needed me I could not let him know it. I put his illness and rank between us.

He waited to know me, sitting back, watching me massage his foot, judging the foolishness of my reticence. He said, "I warrant you have more friends than you know what to do with, and more women, a handsome fellow like thee!"

And without raising my head and without checking my words, I muttered, "I don't want women, and as for friends, I have none: thou art the only one who bears my company."

"How can that be?"

"It is exactly so."

"You burst with withheld compassion, my man. Hast ever considered taking holy orders? Hast ever thought to be a priest?"

The blood rushed to my face, and I turned my head away so that he would not see it. He said, "Nay, look at me, fellow! It's often passed my mind in the past months, and this morning it comes on me again. Hath never felt the call to God's service?"

I was silent: I could not answer.

"Damn it, speak! Pisspot fool, in respect for my age if not my office, answer and do not sit like a boy about to be whipped."

"I am astonished at your question, my lord."

"There's something in the manner of thee! I sensed it from the first."

"I salute your perception. At one time I took deacon's orders."

"Why didn't tell this to me?"

"I prefer to forget my ordination."

"Why, goodman fool?"

The story of the little church and my wife began to pour from me and once allowed to begin, would not stop. His small, rather shrunken mouth moved thoughtfully as he listened, and I myself fell silent at last. How could I have put myself in his hands? I did not see him as a kindly confidant. Had he probed at my sexuality perhaps for prurient interest, resenting the encroachment of age and greedily desiring to drink mine? Was he probing at my disappointed vocation for the same unclean reasons? I hated him for that I had told him.

He said, "The children are thine no longer?"

"No, my lord, I wished it so."

"Didst love her?"

I made myself look at him steadily: well, know me, then! Know me, old man, and then tell me to return no more! "Aye, my lord. But these things are never simple, never pure with me as they are with other men. All feelings are complicated past my own comprehension . . . mayhap God understands them. I do not. And how can I hope to discover what infinitesimally small substance composes everything if I cannot discover myself?"

"Wouldst still be a priest?"

I put his foot carefully on the stool and went to the window before answering. I remember the sun was just falling beneath the majestic houses over the river, and the light shining on the water of the Thames. "Why did you ever call for me to heal you?" I asked. "Should I go home, you would have your acolytes at my door until I had no peace! Today you've pulled all my other secrets from me against my will, painfully."

"Untruth: you wished to say them."

"I know not what I've wished or wanted! Yes, my lord, the priesthood is what I longed for since first I could remember, but everyone thought me ill suited for it. In nothing in my life have I come through with honor without hurting someone who loved me." And I told him about the fight with my first master, my days of thievery, the betraying of my young wife and the adultery with Rebecca Heminges, and last my stubbornness in the two years in the little church, "which was self-will, and had nothing to do with vocation, my lord!" Before I was finished I was fighting the old faintness, and I thought, dear Christ! Don't let me faint before him and he'll know the weakness of this man he befriended and despise me.

"Say the rest," he said.

"I don't wish it."

"You lie once more."

I turned to him; tears filled my eyes. "What would you hear next?" I shouted. "My private, my secret blasphemies? My ingratitudes and failures? Shall I tell you that I am as I am, and then rid myself of your messengers which will not leave me to myself? Then know me, my lord. I have in my heart a desire to serve, yet I've withdrawn again and again from all I love, cringing at my limitations. My body fears encapsulation: I fear the love of others. And still pathetically I plod along. I have not yet ground a lens so fine as to see any germ clearly, nor have I found a lens so powerful as to reach God. And yet I feel that He has put . . . cures, remedies . . . and locked them therewithin as clearly as His image is in me, locked. My unseeingness stops me. I have never once seen God, and yet I feel Him more intensely than I feel you. I feel, unscientifically, without proof or hope of ability to prove but my own compulsion. It burns inside me so fiercely that it should kill me, yet here I stand to say these things. God and the power of understanding are all that I have ever craved. Next this, nothing is worth having."

He said, "By Our Lady! I had not thought to hear so much. Turn thy face to me. It's come to me at last. Could I be such a whoreson fool not to have known where first I saw thee? Once or twice I went years back to hear the King's Men play, and you among them. I oft wondered what became of thee! They are farts and dullards who now have your roles."

That made me smile, if anything (God knows) could make me smile. He said, "Because you were angry at injustices done to you and those you love and could not march in perfect rows with your young fellows, wert discarded? Hast discarded thyself? That is indeed sin, to discard oneself."

"My master's wife, sir . . ."

"Hast repented it? Do you believe you can repent and be unforgiven? Is then all of Our Lord's promises naught but lies to thee? Take this my gift to you. A priest you shall be."

"Impossible."

"Nay: look at me! You must have a house and living, and one that doth not take all thy time, for I need thee here and you need thy quiet hours to study. Take wine, take wine, fool boy, before thou faint on the floor and we shall have to call in yet another physician more fallible than thee. Take wine, thou young fool! Give me thy hand."

He had extended his hands to me. I had told all there was to tell of me, and still he gave me his hands. "Wilt allow me the pleasure of this gift? Wilt allow thyself to take it from me?"

And I said, "Aye, my lord."

"There's in my giving a parish that might suit thee, which right of presentation my family hath owned these hundred years. 'Tis a small one not a few miles from here whose priest hath recently died. It shall be thine."

"What parish is that, my lord?"

"St. Mary Aldermanbury."

"Indeed."

"Dost know it, my fellow?"

"A passing acquaintance."

"Will you take it upon thee?"

"Aye, my lord, with all my heart."

It was a spring morning the day before I was to be ordained that I walked back through the streets of Cripplegate Ward and sat for a long time on the stone wall, looking at the church of St. Mary Aldermanbury. I knew every floor stone, every memorial. I knew the sound of the pews creaking against their pegs, the icy draft through the windows in winter. I sat looking for a long time before I heard the footsteps of the man for whom I had come this day.

John Heminges turned down Aldermanbury, his broad-brimmed wool hat low over his grey hair, his thick shoulders under the brown cloak. "I cannot believe what's been told me!" he said breathlessly, stopping at a distance from me. "Art not fit to tend the graves about thee, much less serve as priest!"

God knows what I expected his reaction would be. Vaguely I remembered my angry letter to him, vaguely the years of silence between us. Yet my heart was full of my happiness, and I reached for his hand.

He pulled it sharply against his chest.

"John Heminges," I cried, "nay, do not turn from me! Only give me your blessing and I'll serve well while I've breath to say my prayers. Trust me to do this thing. Only trust me this once more."

"Speakst thou of trust? Will you remind me of how I trusted the little thief I sheltered? Aye, Nicholas, I know thee by thy own confessing! Where was my good mind and judgment one early winter day long since past when I pitied thee and bred thee up to acting? Time and again forgiving thee this, forgiving that. You've stolen from me, betrayed your fellows, married my daughter without love and brought the indecency of annulment upon her, taken upon thee a deacon's vows and abandoned that too. Now you come bravely into the parish I have worked for all my life and say to me, 'Kneel before the altar and take the Body and Blood of Christ from these anointed hands.' But I leave these matters to thy conscience. I resign as warden to this parish. Never will I set foot in the church of St. Mary Aldermanbury again."

And with this he left me.

THREE

The
Priest

AFTER HE LEFT I WALKED INTO THE CHURCH AND FELL TO MY KNEES ON the chancel stones, the verses of the Fifty-fifth Psalm sounding in my head: "For it is not an open enemy that hath done me this dishonor for then I could have born it . . . but it was even thou, my companion, my guide and mine own familiar friend. We took sweet counsel together, and walked in the house of God as friends."

The sharpness of his words had stunned me. I regretted that I had not let him feel the sting of my own anger, the slap of my tongue, for it was not only I who'd offended him. Had he not refused to stand behind me in my vocation as deacon in the little church? Had he not reprimanded me when I had been called to heal during the plague? He had been compassionate for the loss of my son, but still he had reprimanded. Could he never see that I might indeed be suited for a life other than the one for which he'd raised me?

Yet how could he have known the vocations I sought were the deepest call of my soul, those which it tore me utterly to have refused? He could not judge me other than he had in our first days when I was but the boy. And it broke upon me that we would never more take sweet counsel together, oh my guide! My throat swelled with remorse, and for a long time I tried to put together the years of my life with him, to rearrange them differently so that he would have blessed me.

In trying to push him from my life in years before, I had lied to him, for I'd loved his daughter with all my heart. Mayhap not at first, when I knew little of loving but my own petulant desires, but later, born of our thousand moments, the joys and disappointments. I grieved for my fallibility, for my imperfections and the hurt I had given, for the things I had done which might never be undone. I grieved for my children, who would never know me, for those I had lost to disreputable death, for the men who had believed in me and fought for me and now might never greet me warmly again. And I prayed for the courage to go forth even with these griefs and begin again. Kneeling on those familiar stones, something older than all the earth cleansed me. My years of turning my face from God had ended; He had extended His Hand to me once more, and in the open palm was all that was worth having. God had never turned from me: I had turned from Him.

And I heard His low, humorous voice saying, Nicholas.

O cast me not away from Thy presence: lift up Thy countenance before me and give me peace.

What sort of priest should I have been had I gone my original ways and been sent to Cambridge as I wished at the age of fourteen? A bookish man, thinking that my superior knowledge of Testament made me closer to God! I would have perhaps been able to keep a promise to my poor mother, and perhaps not. I was but a child then; I could do no more. Sitting on my heels in the tiny church, I smiled slightly. There would be a secret covenant between God and myself which I would renew each time I took the holy Bread and Wine. And that covenant should be only between us. It was this: that I would trust Him to guide me, and do my best at His work, and that He would never abandon me. Yet with all this sweetness I needed more: I needed human confirmation and a human arm on my own. (I have always needed that, you see, which perhaps is where my troubles began and ended.) And I went with full heart, the tears of a boy pressing against my throat, to my ordination and to this blessed fool of an old man who believed in me.

My Bishop, William Sydenham of Winchester, was at the church before I came. Impatient as always, he stood up when I entered the vestry. Then he said, "I see from your face that you think on your imperfections. My young friend, we are all imperfect. Only God is perfect, and we poor folk do the best we can to struggle towards it. Expect thou otherwise? That what occurs today will turn thee into a sleepy, unruffled sort of fellow, placid as mother's milk, dull of mind and wit? Hast expected this all thy life? You must go on expecting it in vain. Only Our Lord could work such a change, and 'tis my belief He'd find it wasteful to do it. For the promise and commitment is all that is needed: else you come as a compendium of what you have been and continue to be, from your irrational search for the smallest particle of matter to the tears I see in your eyes."

I fell to my knees to kiss his hand, but he withdrew it gently and laid it on my head instead. "It's done, it's done. Thine offenses are forgiven. Wilt forget them now and do what thou hast always been meant to do?" And his kiss on my cheeks, the bristles of an old man who has not bothered to shave too closely, his surprisingly soft and careful lips. Once more against all resolution affection had prodded me from my shell: how grateful I am for such prodding! Without it I would never have come to many friendships and loves. I would never have come to this.

Then we were before the altar and Communion was given. There, under the curious stone eyes of dead saints and lauded laymen, I closed my eyes and renewed my promise with God, and He renewed His with me. My Bishop whispered, "Thou smilest. Another jest? Peculiar fellow!"

Of all things this is the one I would not tell him. I thought, the gift of ordination hath now been laid upon me, to use, to serve, to never betray. I am ready for it now.

"Go in peace to love and serve the Lord."

And I whispered, "Thanks be to God."

Thus I came home to Mary Aldermanbury once more: the slope of every stone step leading to narrow shops, the tavern and tailor signs, the worn places in the city wall, my private streets of humiliation and joy, of commitment and abandonment. Over this was the grey stone church, neither wealthy nor elegant; surrounding it the graveyard and a processional walk which wound under the trees. The priest's house had been cleaned by the good housekeeper, who had known me since a boy, and she had polished and scrubbed so well that I hardly had the heart to tell her that the new-laid floor rushes, sweetened with flowers, would have to be taken away. She needed time to acclimate herself to my peculiar ideas of cleanliness, and I was prudent enough to broach the subject carefully. It was a splendidly cozy house with a sitting room, kitchen, and four small sleeping chambers.

The vestryman gave me my keys and pressed my hands. I thought everyone would know me in the parish, but they did not: many new families had come and built and some older ones moved away. It had been seven years since I had lived in Cripplegate Ward. Of the personal details of the dissolution of my marriage, little was known. Heminges was a silent man when troubled and not inclined to gossip. That I had been an actor was remembered, but more than one actor in those years became priest. That Susan had been mine was discreetly discussed, but it was assumed that our belatedly discovered ties of blood had necessitated an honest annulment. She did not come to the church of Mary Aldermanbury, that I knew. So I was free to create my own reputation according to my abilities. God possessed me. In the weeks before my induction as vicar of the parish, I liked to go into the church quite late and sit there in the darkness, hearing His breath and mine. And absolute peace came to me for the first time in my life.

One of the first letters I wrote at the desk by the window overlooking my church was to Thomas Hariot. I had not seen him in seven years, and heard from a fellow physician that the cancer which grew in his mouth and nose had worsened. In my wanderings and exile (for so it now seemed to me), I had scarcely borne any man's company. Now at my own desk, a shelf of books at my right hand (for I had of course spent the first of my priestly stipend on books), I dared to ask for his friendship once more.

It was a long letter, for I told him the truth of what had happened. I begged that though I knew his physician to be excellent, he allow me see him and think over his problem. I told him I had neither speculative glasses nor astrolabes anymore, as everything had gone in my days of poverty, and it would mean very much to me if I could visit him at Syon House to look at the skies. I wrote with grief of my knowledge of the continued imprisonment of both his patron, the intelligent Northumberland, and of Sir Walter Raleigh, whose mind as revealed in his many writings (though he had never known freedom in all these years) inspired me. I wrote lastly of my small work in developing a microscope. And I signed it, "In devotion, thy Nick."

Thus letters passed between us. A religious man, he believed absolutely in the power of God, even though he told me once that some of the Old Testament had probably been miscopied by early monks, for the world was by his reckoning at least twenty thousand years old. "Do not let my illness trouble you overly much, my friend," he said. "I believe in God Almighty; I believe that medicine was ordained by Him; I trust the Physician as his minister. My faith is sure, my hope firm. I wait however with patience for everything in its own time according to His Providence. We must act earnestly, fight boldly, but in His name and we shall conquer. *Sic transit gloria mundi, omnia transibunt, nos ibimus, ibitis, ibunt* . . . so passeth away the glory of this world, all things will pass away, we shall pass away, you will pass away, they will pass away . . ."

These letters, mingling the infinite and the practical, were my treasures: I could make an inquiry of him and he always answered it intelligently. This was his greatest gift: he was unafraid of the power of his understanding, and with him I was free to be unafraid of mine.

I was inducted as priest into the church of St. Mary Aldermanbury with prayers and singing. It was a rainy spring day, but the skies had just begun to clear as we began our walk down the processional path through the graveyard, the four boys carrying the willow wands they used to beat the boundaries of the parish to mark it each year at Rogationtide, the clerk carrying the Bible and several vestry members with the Communion plate and incense, seldom burned since the Reformation but pleasing to me. I liked archaic customs and I still do. Then we went inside for the ceremony and Communion service.

There, crowded against the back wall of my small ancient church, were the King's Men, almost all of my good colleagues, grinning at me with folded arms as they had from time to time from the tiring room, when I had a difficult and lengthy speech to make, and they felt very glad it was not theirs. Some of their wives and children had come as well. There were Condell, Armin, young Nat Field, and Robert Goffe, who had been so fascinated with my soldiering days; and George Bryan, John Lowine, and Sam Gilburne, who had joined us just before I first went away. Hardly had the consecration of the wine and bread begun when the door creaked and Shagspere also slipped in, his wet hat in his hand. He told me later that his horse had thrown a shoe, and he had ridden with difficulty to make up lost time in the spring rain.

He was tired after his ride, though he insisted he was not, but I was proud to be able to ask my housekeeper to air the sheets in the extra sleeping closet and perfume them with dried flowers. In all the years of our relationship, he had never been my guest before, and I gave him far too big a supper, very little of which he could eat. "My appetite's not splendid, Nick," he said. "Age excuses it."

The old hesitancy of speaking much of himself irked me: I had always wanted more of him. I said, "Ben Jonson's long since gathered his plays together into a folio: wilt thou?"

"Nay, I've other matters which interest me."

"Such as?"

"Tending my garden and walking about my property. You smile."

"It's not what I expect of you."

"What you expect, dear Nick, is that I shall stay always the same, which I shall not. I'm quite lazy, and it suits me well."

I showed him my own garden, which had not been tended since the last priest died, and he gave me advice about spinach and parsley; then we walked about the parish to a woman whose swollen stomach hurt her unceasingly. He watched me with folded arms, and when we had left, said, "My son-in-law's a physician and it taketh all his hours. How will you manage the duties of priest and doctor?"

"I take fewer patients: my studies compel me. We shall be holding live fowls to plague sores again one day if we don't come by something better."

"And of physician and priest, which is dearer to thee?"

"They intermingle. Sometimes I can't tell them apart."

"Ah, Nick! Nothing brings more satisfaction than to share this day with you! Thy collar suits thee, sweet boy, more than a soldier's jerkin, aye, more than the roles you played. It gives me peace to see thee like this, Nicholas. Thy rest brings mine own."

We were up late that night talking of old times. I reminded him of the poaching songs he had sent to me and asked if he recalled the verses to write them down again, but he smiled and shook his head and said they were long gone from memory and he was surprised that I wanted them.

"I warrant people will read thy poems many a year," I said, but he shook his head and answered, "Mayhap. Yet still in passages Kit Morley is finer."

He wanted to be off early the next morning, so before prayers I took him to his horse, giving him some herbal remedies I believed in against his pallor and the headaches of which he complained. As we stood before the church door, I took him gently by the sleeves of his leather jerkin as if there were something sacred in the bone within. "Thou art my soul's love," I said, "and always have been and always shall be. My friend, my fellow, my beloved . . . aye, more. I'm no poet to say it."

He seemed pleased. "I've always held thee the same, my own dear wag," he answered. "As much as one man can for another . . . and as thou sayst, more." Then he squeezed my hand for only a moment, and I stood by the church door to watch him ride away towards Aldersgate.

I never saw him again.

FOUR

St. Mary Aldermanbury

M Y HOME FOR ALL MY LIFE WOULD NOW BE IN LONDON AT THE LITTLE church of St. Mary Aldermanbury, which held so many memories for me.

This was my world. One hundred and nine parish churches rising up against a grey sky over the river, beggars thick with stench stopping my stride with their outstretched hands. On the hem of my cassock the dirt of every street. A lad singing to his viol in the back room of an inn: "Shall I come, sweet love, to thee . . ." In this little corner of Cripplegate shall I do my best to bring us closer to the wholeness of body and heart which we must find in this world before we can achieve it in the next. I wake in the mornings older, a little older. I have come to an understanding with myself at last.

As a priest I cannot run away from God but confront Him, allow Him to suffuse me each hour of my life. My collar speaks of it. The wine fills me and I have beaten my breast three times: Lord, I am unworthy! And often I lie in longing for Him and know my loneliness again. Often I must wait. Then He returns sweet, bittersweet. Christ my master and beloved.

My usual way of loving people (when I do love them) is absolute, jealous, nothing withheld, childish, demanding. Of these dubious qualities my cantankerous Bishop became the beneficiary, for after my confessions and emotional ordination, it was useless to lie to him anymore about what kind of man I was. He appreciated it, for he had lost to death many of the friends he trusted and I took their place. It was burdensome at times: he called me when I would rather not have come and dropped in to see me at the least convenient moments. Nothing was terribly convenient: I had always twenty-six hours of work in every twenty-four, which left me sometimes sleepy and irritable. And my need to be with others vacillated with my need to be alone.

When I failed to visit him in his splendid rooms, he came to my more squalid ones, where bandages and star charts covered all surfaces, and he found himself sneezing in the presence of my cat. Still he came, and with his sensitive foot on a footstool, we soon poured out to each other our disgust with shortcomings (our own and other people's), our delight in the new work in gravity and optics, and our curiosity for the new world. "What meaneth this Kepler, fart of a fool! I cannot understand what the man says. Must he write in mathematics whilst sensible men are content with honest Latin? Squares of periods of revolutions of planets in proportion to what? Once more, make it plain an thou canst." Astronomy held us past hours, and once when I showed him his own skin under the microscope he winced and said, "Marry! I'm an uglier fellow than even I thought!"

"What sayst thou, Cooke!" he said one night in his unceremonious way. "Meanst to stay a bachelor?"

In yet another subject he had caught me unaware. God knows, had I not loved him so I would never have opened my door to him again, for there was nothing in my personal life that he did not storm into and knock about. "Aye, my lord, it suiteth me well."

"The loss of thy marriage troubles thee yet."

"Then and anon."

"Put it aside in thy thoughts."

"It returns unawares."

"Dost see thy children?"

"Sometimes I walk towards Moorfields and watch them play."

"Dost not speak?"

"No, my lord."

He was silent for a moment and then announced abruptly, "Dost intend to stay a pisspot celibate, Cooke? Thou, a strapping fellow with a man's blood in thy veins? 'Tis pity that I have only the desire myself left and not the performance."

I said wryly, "I would give thee my performance, if I could. I want it not."

"Art made in the ordinary way, fellow?"

"My lord, I am most ordinarily made."

"Then how canst bear the heat in thy blood?"

"My mind hath other matters."

"Go to!" he said with satisfaction as he left. "Scurvy pisspot priest, I'll marry thee yet and sing at thy window whilst thou makest the good deed! Thy health I'll drink to thee, Cooke."

Marriage, as my old friend Tom Pope used to say, is a serious matter. Constant, inescapable intimacy suffocates me, and I am more wary of it than I have ever been rationally able to express. As husband I failed. The intimacy of touch which the healer or priest experiences does not frighten me: I am the giver. They healed me as I healed them, and my reputation among the one hundred and twenty families of the parish began to grow. Perhaps only someone who has suffered very much can give compassion, and in compassion there is healing. This is not herbal or metallurgic in its remedy, but something more. On my good (and not impatient) days I felt it coming through me, and of medical and spiritual wounds I saw small difference.

There was one lie I told the Bishop. From time to time I wrote to my children, and sometimes I threw the letters away and sometimes saved them. Never did I send them. Sometimes I wept. It is no matter, and I'm content with my decision regarding them. They have found a better father than I.

I am alone. No woman waits for me, and occasionally the silence of my house appalls me and I curse my choice. Oh, I am not averse to kisses, and often in my solitary bed I long for them. I am not averse to sexuality, but I fear it: I fear its disruptive power. And yet a wife! I think on it, and the young women, looking shyly at me as I walk towards the river, have their own thoughts on this matter. It may come but it shall not yet.

I was priest and physician in St. Mary Aldermanbury but six months and hurrying down the round stair of my house to dress for matins when I found John Heminges standing in my kitchen with his hat in his hand. I had thought myself past hurt that he had not come to my induction, and yet it returned to me as I saw him. He said, "May not an old man of this parish come to the priest's house, Mr. Cooke?"

"I have service to sing. Sit here if you will, and I'll send the house-keeper to you." And I walked away towards the church, my heart pounding under my cassock. How I got through Matins that day I remember not, though it scarcely mattered, for few people came to the seven-o'clock morning service, the women being at market and the men at work. Secretly I hoped he would come; he did not. Yet he was waiting for me when I returned, seated before the fire with his thick hands on his knees. I brought up a stool to sit beside him.

"I had not expected you, sir."

"I'd not expected to come."

"What has brought you here?"

"Needst ask? Ah Nick, is it not time?"

Then I murmured, "Aye, it's time. But master, I should have come to you first."

He said at last, "How to begin this? I've planned it so often. In the theater one memorizes and speaks. You did it well, and so did I! Life's not like that. The throat catches, the tongue stumbles. Personally I stutter. I've always hated that I stuttered."

"It cometh only when you're troubled."

"Knowst that of me?"

"Aye."

"Nick," he said, "I was young when you came to us! Will had just begun to write. We hadn't a farthing, had we? At times I sit in my kitchen late at night and expect to hear his step. Condell and I sometimes think to collect the plays in folio. So many never were published, the others badly. Some manuscripts lost, others burnt. Many lines have slipped me. Christ's wounds, my memory's grown old as well."

"Ask them of me."

"How canst remember?"

"Master, how can I forget?"

He put his hand on my arm. "Nicholas," he said.

It stunned me into silence; I bit my lip and turned my face so that he should not see it. "Nicholas," he said painfully, "of my daughter . . . it's over, it's done, God only knoweth who had what part in the doing of it. Annulment . . . it seemed almost a sin, yet they're happy enough together, and thy children grow well. Dost wish to know these things? I think mayhap you do."

"I lied to thee in my letter: I cherished her."

"It gladdens my heart to know it."

I said then, "There's one confession I have held from you."

There was absolute silence between us. Then his hand returned to my shoulder. "Ah, Nick," he said, "that thing which sent thee to the wars. Do you think I didn't know it?"

"Who . . . told it thee?"

"She did herself in her illness. She lost the child she carried and told me that night."

"Then why . . . didst . . . take me on again?"

"Because I knew you regretted it, because the fault was not all of thine own doing. And because I could never by all my will put thee entirely from my heart. You were sent to me, Nick Cooke; you were sent to me to keep you from yourself, to guide as best I could. And that trust I tried to keep, though it rankled me many an hour, many an hour!"

I covered my face with both my hands for shame.

He did not speak for some time. Then he said, "Make me no saint in thy thinking. My anger's fermented in me these years. I live without grace. Christ bade us forgive and yet I can't entirely do it. I come to thee today saying that I wish it, and I cannot, and yet who is to forgive what? Was I overly strict with thee? I cherished thee always against all my judgment! Did I try to make thee aught that thou wast never meant to be?"

I could not speak, not for my life.

"And doth it matter now? 'Tis over. God wot you've suffered, by thy own deeds, by mine. And my heart's heavy these years in pushing you from it. Mayhap for your troubles you'll serve God the better. Wilt look at me, dear boy?"

I uncovered my face at last and looked at him. "Many men speak of thee," he said. "They say you're a good physician and a good priest. Not a man about here but who does not praise thee."

Then he said, "It's said you have no senior warden here."

I took the keys from my belt and loosened the one to the parish chest and laid it on the table between us. I could not risk giving it to him directly lest he refuse it. He sat there with his hands on the table's edge, and the love I had for him filled my eyes with tears. How could I tell him? How could he ever understand that it had never, never for one moment in all my angers and resentments, left me, and that it never should until I died?

"We've come," he said slowly, "almost strangers, and I don't rest well for it. Our Lord bade us forgive."

"Aye, master, those words I repeat every day of my life."

"And yet the man that I am is unwilling."

"The man that I am can't fault thee for that."

He hesitated and held out his hand. "I was thy master too long for me to ask thy priest's blessing, though one day I may come to do it, God cure my pride! And thou wert my reluctant boy too many years for me to offer thee mine . . . yet, Nick, there must be more than hands in this. Then let me say as I used to do: well done, Nick, well done! And have it be right between us once again."

He took his hat and went away, and I went to the window to see him go. When I turned back to the room, I saw the key to the parish chest was gone. I have known many moments of happiness, but none I think greater than this.

Never is there anything finer than on a day in early spring to walk to the gardens of Whitehall and see the flowers: in these moments all things are possible. Then home again where the coming of twilight brings its predictable melancholy. Is it mere wanting of my supper, or the primitive loss of light, or the vague exhaustion of a body which had supposed itself quite young once more?

I am not the man I would like to be. Impatient, impulsive, given to tempers and resentments, I have brought my restlessness into the very house of the Lord. We have a pleasant, sometimes ordinary relationship and sometimes an ecstatic burning one, very much the relationship with a person with whom you share a small house and board. I am cantankerous, one day grateful and the next stubborn, accusatory.

Does one find peace irrevocably in this dirty, sweet, tattered world, this mystical and yet unholy place in which we have woken? Aye, for sweet moments. I have found it for whole days and then must go looking anxiously, irritably, for it again like an old fellow who has mislaid his slippers. And yet in a living world of perfect beauty and peace, would not we grow quarrelsome and bored? In a heaven laid out before us for our delection, would we not quarrel like children with nothing particular to do? Then is not this world of inconsistency and inconsistent peace the only sort that we imperfect souls could abide? In spite of my deep faith, nay my passion, for Jesus Christ my Master, these questions nag me and have a way of hurling me rudely from the center of my peace.

Sometimes friends visit and we talk for many hours. Other nights I go to my rooms, play my viol, take down the books I have loved so much, and read myself into sleepiness. Sometimes I turn my telescope to the stars. Before I sleep I pray. I lift my heart unto the Lord, who has taught me to know myself and shown me my path. He has lifted His countenance upon me, He has been gracious unto me. And He will bide with me always in the spirit of truth, even to the end of time.

LONDON, 1617

Historical
Notes

The novel closely follows the actual development of the King's Men and the political/scientific climate of the age, with some minor transference of dates for dramatic enhancement. Of the historical characters depicted here, some words should be said on the following:

John Heminges, first a grocer and then an actor/theater manager, lived most of his life in the parish of St. Mary Aldermanbury, which lies a few minutes' walk from St. Paul's Cathedral in London and where presently stands a memorial acknowledging his production of the First Folio of Shakespeare's plays. A respected churchwarden and, in the first part of the seventeenth century, the much-loved dean of the London stage, Heminges fathered thirteen children by his wife, *Rebecca,* and died in 1630. Shakespeare left a mourning ring to him.

Thomas Pope, clown and comic actor of the troupe, lived for most of his professional life in Southwark with a housekeeper and many children whose father could only be guessed at; he died of unknown causes in 1603. He is traditionally believed to have been the first Falstaff.

Will Shagspere (I have used an alternative Elizabethan spelling to allow his depiction as a person and not a literary deity) left his wife and children in Stratford to become a London actor. "Honest [a generous spirit] and of an open and free nature," his colleagues called him. Though he left no autobiography, his works clearly reveal his character as complicated, proud, loving, private. He died in 1616, not having concerned himself with the publication of his plays.

Kit Morley (the alternative spelling of Christopher Marlowe), the enigmatic poet, blazed into the London theater in his early twenties with his bloody, haunting, gorgeously written plays. Kit numbered among his friends members of the nobility, scientists, poets, and cutthroats; he was arrested several times for fighting and left a mixed reputation as both a violent heretic and, as one poet called him, "Morley, darling of the Muses" or "kind Kit." Apparent in his writing is his sexual preference for boys or men. He died in a tavern brawl in 1593 at the age of twenty-nine; his three killers were acquitted of his murder.

Thomas Hariot, one of the most private and brilliant minds of the early seventeenth century, left only one published book at his death in 1623; his mathematical works were compiled by a clergyman friend. Hariot never published his astronomical findings, fearing accusation of heresy, though he corresponded as an equal with Kepler and Galileo and sighted the moons of Jupiter at the same period as did the Italian astronomer. He was part of what Shakespeare called "the School of Night," an informal group dedicated to scientific truth but suspected by many of sorcery.

Will Kempe, Henry Condell, Robert Armin, and *Augustine Phillips* and the apprentices *John Rice* and *Robert Goffe* were well known on the Elizabethan/Jacobean stage. The music of *Byrd* and *Tallis* can be heard in most Anglican churches today; the plays of *Dekker* and *Jonson* are found in most libraries.

Of the aging *Elizabeth* and her willful young love Robert Devereux, *Lord Essex,* nothing need be added to the many dramatizations of their explosive relationship. *Lord Percy* remained imprisoned until 1623; *Walter Raleigh* was executed in 1618. The young patron of the arts, the *Earl of Southampton*, grew into a sober citizen of the realm and became one of the first patrons of the state of Virginia. My *Bishop of Winchester,* William Sydenham, has a nature and name entirely of my invention.

Nicholas Cooke is a fictional character. He is derived, however, from several notable men of the period: the great sensual mystic and churchman John Donne, the brilliant young actor Nat Fields, the astronomer Thomas Hariot, Dr. Caius of London and Dr. Hall of Stratford (Shakespeare's son-in-law), and the playwright Ben Jonson, also known to be a bit of a brawler. Innumerable letters and private diaries of other seekers, visionaries, and family men under the reigns of Elizabeth and James, among them actors who became doctors, priests who went to war, and boys who struggled from terrible privation to become great men, also inspired me.

Of the theater companies and their traditions:

There were two categories of theater companies in Elizabethan London: the children's companies (boys only) and the adult (men and boys). Women did not come upon the London stage until 1630, and then but briefly until the Restoration. Cathedrals and schools would use their singing boys for profitable playgiving; I have combined for dramatic purposes the St. Paul's Boys with the Blackfriars Theater Company. According to many scholarly books on the Elizabethan theater, some boys continued to play women until their early twenties. With Nicholas's rapid growth and highly masculine nature, he would have by necessity graduated earlier to portraying his own sex.

Of the language used in the novel:

Elizabethan speech was slangy and difficult to capture, both flowery and casual, irreverent and respectful. These were men and women in a hurry to get on with life, lingering for very little except love. Rendering a modern interpretation of everyday sixteenth-century speech requires a certain amount of compromise and imagination. I've freely mingled "thou" and "you" as the casual Elizabethan would have done. The speech between men was that of passionate friendship.

Of the world Nicholas knew:

Four hundred years have brought many changes to England, though surprisingly much remains of the Elizabethan world. Still standing are the ruins of the church of St. Mary Aldermanbury and, a short walk away, renovated Aldermanbury Square with its lion's-head spout. The overhanging houses, crowded taverns, and mews are gone from Wood Street, whose original winding lanes are now lined with office buildings. Old St. Paul's was destroyed in the Great Fire of 1666, when the melting lead from the roof ran down the street; choirboys still sing in the new cathedral but are far better behaved than Nick's fellows, for they no longer rush into the congregation to demand money from the worshipers during service. Though only a plaque reminds us where the Globe and Bear Garden stood, the church of St. Mary Overy (now known as Southwark Cathedral) is still a busy parish. In Canterbury, of course, much is preserved, including the original, haunting cloistered walk. The King's School, which expelled Nick for brawling, regularly sends its boys to Cambridge and Oxford.

Walking through these streets, I stood between times, as the novelist is privileged to do. It is only a breath from 1617 to the present. Nicholas's civilization—passionate, materialistic, spiritual, and exploratory—was very much like our own, only a little smaller. We share our frustrated stand on the edge of scientific discovery and new conceptions of the infinite.

Acknowledgments

Research for *Nicholas Cooke* was conducted in London (Science Museum, Museum of London, Globe Museum, Greenwich Observatory, Wellcome Museum of Medicine, Westminster Abbey, Southwark Cathedral, Syon House), Oxford (Museum of Science), Canterbury (Cathedral, King's School, town precincts), Cambridge, and Stratford-on-Avon; and in New York (New York Academy of Medicine Rare Book Room, General Episcopal Seminary St. Mark's Library, Union Seminary Library, Midtown Research Library and Rare Book Room Arents Collection, Mercantile Library and Lincoln Center Library of the Performing Arts, and the delightful, cozy library of the English-Speaking Union).

In particular, I would like to thank Elizabethan scholar Dr. A. L. Rowse for his encouragement and research materials, Madeleine L'Engle for her constant support and advice, the English-Speaking Union—New York Branch for sending me to Oxford, Dr. Robert Nagel for his scientific coaching, my late "stepfather," the medieval scholar Dr. Henry Pachter, for his work and library on sixteenth-century "physicking," and the many great historians who have ferreted out the customs and living world of the Elizabethans and whose work I have loved since a child.

I should also like to give acknowledgment for the generous help and support of many people: my writing group (Elsa Rael, Katherine Kirkpatrick, Ruth Henderson, Casey Kelly, Shellen Lubin-West, and Judith Lindbergh); Dr. Saul J. Farber, Rhoda Croft, Bruce Bawer, Ellen Beschler, Gwyn Gilliss, Scott McNulty, Maria Menna Perper, Edna Johnson, Judith Ackerman, Renée Barrick, Patt Pontevolpe, Sally, Timothy and Josiah McGaughey, Vernon Trapp, Linda Lanza, Stephanie Low, and Karen Lee Bowers; the Reverend Dr. John Andrew, whose words have so inspired me; the Reverend Stuart Kenworthy, the Reverend Ivan Weiser, the Reverend Dr. Duane Arnold, the Reverend Dr. Frederick Shriver, and the Reverend Dr. J. Robert Wright; my parents, my sisters Jennie and Gabrielle, and my sons; friends, clergy, and musicians at St. Thomas Church and the lovely sisters of the Community of the Holy Spirit; my editor, Mary Cunnane, her assistant, Caroline Crawford, and the Norton staff; and most specially Ruth Black, Gertrude Dewey, and Jack Rizzitello.

About the Author

STEPHANIE COWELL, a native New Yorker, has been studying the world of Elizabethans her whole life. She published several stories in her late teens and early twenties, subsequently became a classical singer and international balladeer, and wrote lectures on English social history for colleges, schools, and museums. She co-founded a chamber opera company and produced several Renaissance festivals. *Nicholas Cooke* is her first novel.